THE GREYHOUND GOD

WESTERN LITERATURE SERIES

THE GREYHOUND GOD

KEITH LEE MORRIS

UNIVERSITY OF NEVADA PRESS / RENO, LAS VEGAS

Western Literature Series

University of Nevada Press, Reno, Nevada 89557 USA

Copyright © 2003 by Keith Lee Morris

Manufactured in the United States of America

Design by Carrie House

Library of Congress Cataloging-in-Publication Data

Morris, Keith Lee, 1963–

The greyhound god / Keith Lee Morris.

p. cm. — (Western literature series)

ISBN 0-87417-555-0 (hardcover : alk. paper)

1. Greyhound racing—Fiction. 2. Travelers—Fiction. 3. Idaho—Fiction.

I. Title. II. Series.

PS3613.07735 G73 2003

813'.6—dc21   2003006538

The paper used in this book meets the requirements of American

National Standard for Information Sciences—Permanence of Paper

for Printed Library Materials, ANSI Z39.48-1984. Binding materials

were selected for strength and durability.

First Printing

12 11 10 09 08 07 06 05 04 03

5 4 3 2 1

FOR MY PARENTS, WILLENE AND FRED MORRIS;

MY SISTER, KRISHELE; MY WIFE, ANGELA, AND

MY CHILDREN, LONDON AND NATHAN.

I LOVE YOU ALL IMMEASURABLY.

WE SHALL NOT CEASE FROM EXPLORATION

AND THE END OF ALL OUR EXPLORING

WILL BE TO ARRIVE WHERE WE STARTED

AND KNOW THE PLACE FOR THE FIRST TIME.

T. S. ELIOT, "LITTLE GIDDING"

ACKNOWLEDGMENTS

The following list is much too short to include all those who have helped this book come to life. But, in addition to those folks to whom the book is dedicated, I feel especially indebted to these people (listed more or less in the order in which I came to know them) for their friendship, support, and advice: all of my extended family (particularly Mr. John Butler Morris and Mrs. Juanita Viola Laura Buckley Lee), Jay B. Lewis, Bryan Czarapata, Pat Roark, Chase Sanborn, Doug Leckner, Bob Halstead, Lou and Nancy Siebenlist, Laura Rains, Denise Morris, Lois Leibowitz, Cynthia Cruver, Tim Bable, Howell Colbert,

Joseph Race, Rodney Bickham, Ron McFarland, Alan Solan, Peter and Daisy Massey, Charley Packard, Ethan Hauser, Steve Almond, John Metzger, Victor Cruz, Chip Greer, Jim Clark, Fred Chappell, Michael Parker, Lee Zacharias, Frank Day, Mark Charney, Brock Clarke, Wayne Chapman, Martin Jacobi, Susanna Ashton, Lisa Golden, Rebecca Kurson, Jodee Rubins, and Zach and Beth Corontzes. I would also like to thank the English departments of The University of Idaho and Clemson University, the MFA program at The University of North Carolina-Greensboro, and all the students I've taught at these schools (so many of whom have impressed me and made me proud). I greatly appreciate the assistance of The South Carolina Arts Commission, which supported this novel through a research grant, and I offer a hearty thanks to all the nice people in Wisconsin who made my research trip there both pleasant and worthwhile. Joanne O'Hare, my editor at The University of Nevada Press, is wonderful. And I would like to thank the entire town of Sandpoint, Idaho, just for being what it is, and what it was to me at the time.

LUKE

JUNE 10

I'm Luke Rivers. I come from Idaho. Sometimes during all my travels, and working in various places in different towns and states pretty much all over America, I've come across people that are I don't know exactly what you'd call them, more sophisticated maybe, and they're usually dressed nice, and usually a couple, like a man and wife, and I've kind of struck up conversations with them because I'm just like that—curious about people and where they're from—and they'll at some point get around to asking about me, the guy's wife mostly. She'll say something like, "And where are *you* from?" just trying to be polite, and I'll say, "Idaho," and then both at the same time they'll kind of nod real slow and not say anything. As if they were thinking to each other, *That* explains it. But I'm not sure it does.

This morning my wife Jenny took our five-year-old son Jake and the old Honda Civic, which is hers anyway, and left, and I can't say I exactly blame her. The hardest part is she didn't even wake me up to say good-bye. She could at least have let me say good-bye to Jake and told me where she planned on going.

They must have made plenty of noise. Jake's pretty much a wild man, especially in the morning when the ball's just started rolling. He was probably even jumping up and down on the bed like he does in every motel room we ever go to. In motels, he loves the beds and the Cartoon Network and the elevators the most, that is if the motel we're staying in has an elevator, which it usually doesn't. We stay in a lot of places called stuff like the El Sol and The Pines and The Bar S Ranch that are just laid out flat next to the highway. Which is fine with me, but it is nice to get a place with a pool at least for Jake if it doesn't cost too much. Especially since the last place we were at down in Council Bluffs he actually swam a couple of strokes all by himself. I waded from the shallow end and held my arms out to him, and he pushed off the side, and I stepped back trying to be real casual so he wouldn't notice, even though it made my stomach drop when he was in the water and out of my reach, but he kicked and paddled to get to me.

I'm sure of one thing: Jake didn't know Jenny was taking him away from me. He'd have never done it. I doubt she outright lied to him, but I bet he just thought they were driving to Burger King to get a Croissanwich and were packing up some things so we could get an early start. Sometimes they have to do that, the two of them, because like today I'm not exactly what you'd call a morning person.

The other surprising thing is Jenny left all the money from the track last night. Well, she took a hundred bucks. I don't know how much she had in her purse that she never told me about, but I hope overall it's enough to get her where she's going. I'd have to be an asshole to hope she ran out of gas money on the way to Mendenhall, Mississippi, where her parents live, because I'm guessing that's where she's headed, and had to beg money from somebody along the road.

Let me say right now that what I do for a living is bet on dogs. Jenny would say I'm a bartender and she was a waitress and we were a regular family that lived in whichever place that we've called home at one time or another. But bartending is what I do to help keep us afloat while Jenny has her way and we act like a regular family that just wants to settle down and live like normal Americans. What I have a *talent* for is picking dogs at the greyhound races. I've got a whole system and everything.

Here's how it works. It's different from horse racing. A horse has got a jockey and a dog doesn't. A dog's just on his own. In a horse race, if two horses bump into each other, it's somebody's fault. There's a disqualification. So in horse racing, because there's *rules,* the best horse wins most of the time. Not so in dog racing. Too many things can go wrong. A dog goes off at 1:2 odds and gets knocked down in the first turn. Tough luck. It happens all the time. So at the dog races, if you just keep betting the long shots, you'll win eventually, and win big. And here I mean *intelligently* bet the long shots.

So we were at the track last night in Rapid City, and we were pretty much down to our last dime because I hadn't had much betting luck since we left the last town we lived in, which was Heron Lake, Minnesota. Heron Lake was a pretty nice town if you like things peaceful and quiet like Jenny does.

I was about at the point where I knew I'd really screwed up again. One of the ways I can tell I've screwed up is if we don't have money for a motel room and have to sleep in the car by the highway. Not that my bets were bad. Another part of my system that's foolproof is that the amount of money you can possibly lose is controlled by the small amount you bet. It's usually a twelve-race program. I bet six dollars on the 1st race because of the daily double, then four dollars every race after that, a win bet and a quinella—which means you have to pick the first two dogs and they can come in in either order—so I can't possibly lose more than fifty dollars in a single night. And that's if I lose every bet. Not that it's much comfort to Jenny, having a system like that. Not if me and her and Jake are sleeping by the side of the road.

Which looked like it might happen. By the time we got done paying admission at the track, we had sixty-two dollars, fifty of which was rolled and stuffed into the left rear pocket of my Levi's, where I keep the betting money, and twelve of which was stashed in my wallet in my right rear pocket, where I keep money for me and Jenny's beers and my cigarettes and Jake's hot dogs and Cokes. Also it was bad this time because we had just totally up and left the apartment in Heron Lake. Usually when I go out on the road to play dogs, we'll do it right after we've paid a month's rent somewhere, so if I screw up and lose everything we'll at least have the apartment to go back to, and can just get new bartending and waitressing jobs and start all over again.

Before the 1st race I bought me and Jenny a beer and Jake a hot dog and Coke, which left just five dollars in that pocket. I watched the odds till one minute to post then laid down a two-dollar daily double, a two-dollar quinella, and a two-dollar win bet. Forty-four dollars left in that pocket.

It sounds like peanuts—two dollars here, two dollars there. But it's a fact about me that I'm what I think you'd call a prudent bettor. I don't play high stakes, and I never even raise the stakes at all unless I'm already ahead. Like I say, long odds is the key.

So the first race I take my seat between Jake and Jenny right before the bell goes off, and I tell Jake we've got the 3-6, because he likes to know. I light a cigarette and take a drink of beer and say my prayer to the Greyhound God, like I always do.

The 3 dog breaks so far ahead that by the first turn I know my only worry is if he turns out to be a groupie, which is my name for a dog that actually doesn't like to run alone and will let the other dogs catch him on purpose just to have some company. But I already knew that wasn't the case from what I saw in the program. This dog either won or got whipped bad, and mostly got whipped bad, which is why the odds were so good on him. With a dog like that, it mostly depends on if he breaks good. He did, so he won.

Then we had the 2 dog in the 2nd. Usually in a case like this, when we don't have much money and Jenny's watching me like a hawk, I'll let the 2nd race ride. Sit there and talk to Jenny and Jake like whether the second half of the daily double comes in makes no difference in the world, like whether or not we've got a place to sleep is the farthest thing from my mind.

I had a good feeling about the 2 dog in the 2nd race, though. He was actually a longer shot than the 3 in the 1st—a dog that had won only once, enough to get him out of Maiden class into D, where he hadn't done shit. In five of the last six races, the program said he "broke and faded." That's not good. But I saw a little glimmer of hope in his last race. He "gave ground" and finished fifth. But he finished just two lengths out. In other words, he faded at the very end. Sometimes that's a sign that a dog's decided to run, that he's gotten tired of following the other dogs' tails and is ready to take a lead and hold it. The odds stayed high till the very last, and even though I knew it would piss Jenny off, I couldn't resist running up and laying down another four dollars to win. I was breaking my own rules, but I had a feeling.

I sit down, light a smoke, take a drink, and pray. Jake's yelling for the dog before they even come out of the gate. And what do you know but our number 2 dog breaks on top, running like he's bound for A class. By the time they hit the top of the stretch, he's about four or five lengths out front, and Jenny's by now jumping up and down, clinging to my shirtsleeve. But I was waiting for the fade, for the old engine to sputter down. This number 2 dog was not a finisher, I knew from the program. And he ran true to form. The other dogs came on, the number 7 especially, I think, and it ended in a photo. Jake was saying, "We won, Papa, didn't we?

Didn't we win the double?" and people were looking at him the way they do, and Jenny had her head in her hands. I could hear her saying softly, "Fuck, fuck, fuck," which is something she learned to say from me and not her daddy in Mississippi. Then they flashed the results, and there was the big gold number 2 right square on top of the board. We all shouted and hugged each other. I kissed Jenny on the lips, which is something we don't do much anymore.

I went up right away to collect. That's something else I always do—get my money right away, so I can put it in my pocket and feel it there and think about it while I'm deciding on the next race. With the win ticket and the daily double, we made five hundred and eighty bucks. I put $380 in Jenny's purse, which is like our version of a savings account, and $200 in my back left pocket. After that, I felt comfortable raising the stakes a little, and the rest of the night went like some kind of dream version of dog racing, like what I imagine when it's late and Jake and Jenny are asleep and I'm all alone, watching infomercials on TV maybe and not paying any attention, and I can just see winners rolling out one by one like I knew they would, like my vision of what should happen happening.

Time after time our dogs were coming in, Jake jumping up and down on the bench and Jenny and me laughing. It was warm out, and you could hear grasshoppers off in the fields, and the bugs buzzed round and round the track lights. We ended the night with six more win tickets and four quinellas. We walked out with close to $2,000. And when we pulled the old Honda into the parking lot of the Black Hills Motel, I said my silent Thank You to the Greyhound God, who I've never said anything about to Jenny because, like she says herself, she never even believed in Santa Claus, not really.

Jake was asleep by the time we got him in the room. I carried him in with his arms and legs dangling down, his face looking up at me. He's gotten so big you can't keep all of him held up at once. We put him to bed, and everything was great at first. We were riding a high. I went to a convenience store and picked up some beer, and when I got back to the motel even the wind blowing up dust in the parking lot and the semis roaring by on the overpass looked beautiful to me.

Jenny made a toast to all the dogs at Rapid City Greyhound Park who'd made us what we were today. We took all the money, mostly twenties and fifties, and threw it in the air over the bed. Jake was covered with loot. Jenny grabbed the Kodak and snapped a picture, which she hardly ever does. We're not that big on pictures for some reason.

After a couple of beers, Jenny got tired. She took her travel bag and went into the bathroom to get ready for bed, and I gathered up all the money and counted it again and found the bills that had fallen on the floor. Then I sat on the bed and watched TV. There was racing on, some triathlon. All these crazy skinny fuckers that think they're in great shape because they've worked their bodies practically to death. I was an athlete in my day, and I don't see anything athletic in these triathletes. They've just taught themselves to suffer better than most everyone else. You sort of get into watching it in a sick way after a while, though, and I was kind of interested in the story of this woman who was the two-time defending champion and was like two miles ahead in the marathon part with only two miles to go but was having stomach cramps now and having to stop and throw up a lot.

So when Jenny came out of the bathroom, I kind of didn't notice at first. But then she sat down on the bed next to me and asked what was I watching. I started to tell her the story about this crazy woman on TV, but when I looked over at Jenny she was wearing this very skimpy see-through nightshirt that I'd always told her was sexy, so I knew what was up and I stopped talking.

When Jenny and I first met, sex was definitely the most important thing in our relationship. Or I don't know, maybe beer and baseball ranked in there somewhere. We spent a lot of time driving over to the next county that wasn't dry in the Chrysler Le Baron convertible her father bought her for graduating high school to get beer and drive around listening to the Atlanta Braves on the radio. But sex was definitely up there. You wouldn't know it, but I'm actually the kind of guy that people are often attracted to. Nothing is unusual about me except maybe my hair, which I keep about shoulder length, and it's wavy and kind of halfway between blond and brown, but people always tells me that I have a nice face—a nice face or an honest face, depending on who's talking. And I think that was what made Jenny attracted to me, got the ball rolling sex-wise right from the start. We did it in my little shack, we did it in her house when her parents were gone to Wednesday night church service, we did it in the back seat, we did it in the woods outside Mendenhall, Mississippi, with the mosquitoes chewing our legs off. To her the sex was a naughty little secret, but to me sex with her was mostly sweet. She always wore perfume and took the time to look pretty, so that when we got right down to it, it was like unwrapping a piece of candy.

I figure it's been two or three months now since we had sex, though, and so I guess that's what surprised me last night. But it seemed like a good idea. The problem is, though, that the way Jenny gets in the mood now is talking. And what she wanted to talk about last night is all the money we'd won.

I knew where that was going. "Where do you want to move to?" she asked me.

"What do you mean?" I asked, like I didn't know.

"It should be someplace you really like," she said. "Someplace you wouldn't mind staying. Where do you want to stay?"

Already the sex idea was gone. I could see things turning ugly. "Shit," I said, and lay back on the bed. I looked over at Jake, who was kind of sprawled up against the wall, where we'd pushed the bed up against to keep him from rolling off the way kids do. Looking at kids when they're sleeping breaks your heart. You better hope you're ready for it.

"Oh, please, Luke," Jenny said, looking up at the ceiling. "Don't even tell me."

I went over to the dresser and grabbed another beer and sat back down with it on the bed. "Do we have to have the same old conversation?" I said.

She shook her head and pulled her hair back from her eyes. Her hair is long and straight and brown now. When we met it was dyed blonde and she had a perm and used to put it up with one of those little clip things. "You're ruining everything," she said. I didn't say anything. "I thought we could be together tonight for a change. Look at me," she said, and showed off how she'd dressed up sexy for bed.

"I guess not," I said.

That was all the talking. I don't think either one of us had the energy. I can tell you what she meant, though, and what my answer was. She was saying Let's quit this, let's take what money we made tonight and rent a decent place to live in a decent little town, maybe Sandpoint, Idaho, so you could be close to your mother, maybe that would help, and we can get jobs and be patient and get better jobs eventually and Jake can go to school and we can still be poor, it doesn't matter, but decent poor, not trash like we are now. I'm not sure why my answer is always no.

Like I say, when I woke up they were gone. Right now they're passing through Iowa, I bet, or Missouri, and Jake is in the back seat starting to miss me, the same way I miss him. I can see the truck lights flashing by. I've been on that highway at night a thousand times.

JUNE 11

I met a guy in New Orleans once, this is when I was bartending at this hotel in the French Quarter just before I moved to Mississippi and met Jenny, coming up on nine years ago, who told me this story about how his wife and kids died in a fire when their house burned down. It was an eerie story even back then before I'd had Jake, because my brother Mark got killed in strange circumstances when I was younger, and it made me remember him in a way I didn't want to. But it was also strange in the way the guy told it. It was late, 2:00 A.M. maybe, and there was only one other couple in the bar sitting at a table, and this guy was on a barstool. I was cleaning up, dumping the ice chests and just half listening, and he very casually started into this story about how he was driving home from out of town one winter day with the radio on. The news announcer started talking about a house fire in Lafayette. A woman and two children had been burned to death after a fire started from unknown causes. The guy started thinking while he was driving that if something like that happened to his wife and kids while he was gone, he wouldn't know it. Then they had the fire chief on the radio, and he said that a lot of old homes like this one had old gas furnaces that hadn't been checked in a long time, and that an explosion like that could have been the cause, and this guy started thinking how his house was old and they had a gas furnace that he needed to have checked for safety. He said he got sleepy thinking about it, the voice on the radio going on and on and him thinking about his old house and his wife and kids and the need to have things checked out, maybe there was lead in the water pipes, too.

The way he was telling the story, so casual and sort of sleepy, I kept thinking it can't be his house and his kids, and I remember I'd stopped right in the middle of stocking the beers in the reach-in and was just kind of frozen there listening with a beer in my hand and my back turned to him. He got all the way home, he said, and even when the cop cars and fire engines were outside his house and his house wasn't even there anymore, just burned down to noth-ing, he still said to himself for just a split second, *What happened?*

The guy went on to say what surprised him most was how the people on the radio and the house on the radio weren't his family and his house, how he'd never thought even though the descrip-tion on the radio matched his own house and family exactly that it was actually them, that the whole time it had been someone else's house and family they were talking about. He said that sometimes he still forgot to believe in it, that when he thought about the day his family got killed in a house fire he remembered that there had been another man whose family got killed in a house fire that sounded exactly like his, and that he had heard about it on the radio while he was driving home. He said sometimes he felt sorry for this other man, and wished he could call him up and tell him how he'd gone through the very same thing.

I feel a little bit like that guy, I think—in a much less drastic way, of course—but I think I understand the basic feeling. It's like this thing hasn't happened with me and Jake and Jenny, but some other people who live like us and act like us and are having all the same problems. Any minute now, it seems like the door might just open and Jake and Jenny walk right back in. All I've done so far today is hang around the motel waiting for her to call.

The room's not very interesting, although they do have pictures of what I guess you'd call local color on the walls, so you can learn stuff by looking at them. These pictures also help you remember where you are when you wake up in the morning. For instance, this morning I woke up out of a totally dead sleep, like I hadn't even dreamed anything at all during the night there by myself and had just shut everything off like a faucet, and when I woke up it was like trying to start over from nothing, I was all alone and I didn't know why or where. Then I saw a big picture of Mt. Rushmore over to the side of the bed and I immediately knew everything.

There's a picture of Deadwood back in the gold rush days, a muddy street with stores and saloons and the street just crammed with people and wagons and horses, everybody there trying to strike it rich. Also one of Wall Drug, back in the old days when it was just a regular store where you might stop to buy medicine or get something to drink, and there weren't half a billion signs along the interstate for five hundred miles in every direction telling you how great it was and all the shit they had. I looked at these pictures off and on for a long while this morning, and I thought about them as much as I could come up with anything to think. But I couldn't escape the fact that I was really just here in the motel room for one reason, and that was hoping that Jenny would call. And that kept not happening all day.

For a long time in my life I didn't want to do anything but be by myself, or at least keep moving from person to person so the faces changed fast enough that you never really felt like you were with anyone in particular, but maybe you wouldn't feel so alone either. It seemed to me that the only way I could be myself was if I didn't have to let anyone else know me, not really—like their knowing me would take something away, like the piece of a puzzle, and that that piece of me would have to belong to them. And then once I got hooked up with Jenny, and it started to be something that I knew would last a while, I guess you start to forget what it means to try to hold onto an idea of what you are that's separate from that other person. You kind of lose track of being yourself, your own self, and just blend into this new thing which is two people together, and then three when Jake came along, and that just kind of naturally takes the place of the you you were before.

And so after a while here in the motel room, after I'd got done looking at all the pictures, and then watching The Weather Channel for long enough to know what the weather was like pretty much all over America, I started feeling like I didn't have anything to do and nowhere to go, and it was like even my hands and feet knew this, and I started walking back and forth across the room and raising my arms up and down for no reason. I wanted to quit doing that, so I lay down on the bed and stared at the ceiling, and the whiteness of the ceiling seemed to get bigger and bigger, like an ocean, and I recognized that I was starting to have my same old trouble of being able to find myself and know who I was and hang onto it, and I was surprised that in such a short period of time— like two days—my mind could change back so far as to have this old kind of worry, where it seemed like I was actually sinking into the ceiling and getting lost.

What was interesting about this point, though, that made it a lot different from when I was really in bad shape a long time ago and had to go to the loony bin in Orofino, Idaho, and take it easy for a while as they say, is that I was completely well aware of how my thoughts were getting kind of strange and dangerous. It was like while I lay there on the bed watching and kind of sinking into the ceiling, I was also in some part of my mind floating up around the ceiling and looking down at myself. And that, once I thought about it, got to be reassuring, because when I was really bad I couldn't see myself that way, I couldn't understand that what I was thinking or doing was a way of going off the deep end. Being crazy means not only not being aware of yourself, but not being aware that you're not aware of yourself.

It's a confusing thing. I sometimes am very sorry I'm not smarter. It seems to me that really smart people, like my psychologist from back in Orofino, Dr. Blumenthal, for instance, can take a certain thing that a person does or thinks, or even what they think about themselves, and kind of peel it apart layer by layer. Like if you took a flower, say, and you started taking off the petals, and there were always more petals inside even the ones you saw at first, but you weren't surprised by this at all and were able to just keep pulling them away, until finally you had gotten all the way down to a bare green stem. To some people this stem is ugly, but to the really smart people it's a beautiful thing, a thing that's real for only a few people like them who can get to it beneath the petals, which are all that the other people, the ones who aren't so smart, think are pretty.

And so lying there on the bed, I started thinking about Dr. Blumenthal and the old method he taught me of refocusing. The way to refocus, this is according to what Dr. Blumenthal taught me and what I used to try to do every day for years until Jenny came along and I didn't think I needed to so much anymore, is to try to stop and think and listen to your own mind *in that very moment* and understand what the bad thing is that you're feeling, and then try to figure out one thing that you can actually *do* at that moment which will make you feel better, even just a little better, about what's going on. From there you just take it moment by moment until you've managed to refocus your mental energy in what you'd call a productive way. After a while you will begin to formulate patterns. You will identify certain things you do and ways you think which cause you to feel anxious and lost and distressed, and you will find other things that you do and think which help you to think and feel better, and you will naturally drift toward these better ways of thinking and doing and away from the more harmful ones. This is what Dr. Blumenthal said, and it worked for me, when I was nineteen and got put in Orofino for thinking and doing harmful things.

There were a lot of reasons. My family—at least my grandmother from the time I was little and later my dad, as I came to see—was very religious. That to me is the biggest thing. Dr. Blumenthal always wanted to relate everything back to my brother Mark's death, like that was the thing at the very bottom that I had never really thoroughly dealt with, and that my breakdown when I went to college at the University of Idaho was like this event from my past that I'd always tried to turn my back on, but which had finally bitten me in the ass. And I didn't really try to argue with him, but to my way of thinking it's like the *reason* I had such a hard time with Mark's death and refused to truly understand how it had affected me had to do with how I was brought up, the way I was taught by my grandmother. And I know exactly when my breakdown started, and it wasn't with Mark but with the system of thinking I had used and I guess you'd say applied to Mark.

I was in my philosophy class. The teacher, Professor Wykowski, was a very smart guy, smarter even than Dr. Blumenthal, I think, because his intelligence was the kind that he could keep getting to the heart of a subject from just about any angle you could think of, whereas Dr. Blumenthal would always relate things back to what I guess he learned from his teachers in psychology class.

I didn't make it too far past Plato and Aristotle in my philosophy class, but I would have liked to if I hadn't flipped out. It was all very interesting to me. I was always arguing the Christian point of view I learned from my grandmother, which I'm sure must have been very annoying to Professor Wykowski, but he never said so and always took what I said seriously.

One day he started talking about what he called the Problem of Evil: If God loves everyone, like the Bible says, and God is all-powerful and he can do anything, like the Bible says, and God knows everything that there is in the world at all times and all places and all people, like the Bible says he does, then why is there evil in the world? Why do any bad things happen?

As soon as he said it, I started having that feeling I had this morning, that floating feeling, as if I wasn't connected to my body anymore, and I think that was the very first time. Professor Wykowski was still talking, and one or another of the students would say something back every once in a while, but I didn't hear any of it like actual words, more like bees buzzing in a jelly jar like when I used to catch them in the backyard when I was a kid, like I couldn't understand human language anymore or what it meant. The subject of class discussion was already something else, but I didn't know what it was, and I couldn't find a way in to what they were saying because it didn't make any sense, so I finally just blurted out, "Because God gives you a choice. You get a choice between good and evil."

There were a few people in the class that kind of laughed like I was stupid, and then it turned out they'd already been talking about this very thing and I was maybe five minutes behind. But it was like I was only talking to Professor Wykowski anyway, and he was only talking to me because he could see I was the only one there who it mattered to, and even though I felt kind of sick and empty I was still very thankful for him and the way he took me seriously.

He went ahead and explained it again for my benefit, how couldn't God if he was all-powerful and all-loving arrange it so that everyone did have free choice and everyone did recognize the nature of both good and evil and they could choose whichever one they wanted, but because God loved them all and it was in his power to do this, he would make it so that all people always freely chose good.

In this kind of desperate state I was getting to, I suddenly started coming up with new ideas that we hadn't even talked about, and even the class started paying attention. I asked Professor Wykowski, But then wouldn't that just make it impossible to really understand evil, like could you actually understand something that didn't even exist in the real world, and he said that was a good point, but would it be necessary to have an understanding of evil in a world where it didn't exist, was there any reason that we would *need* that kind of understanding when evil posed no threat because everyone freely chose good? He said for example take the concept of infinity. Could we as humans actually *understand* infinity, did we have an actual example that we could really *see* as being infinite, and why would we need such an example when we lived in a world where all individual life was finite?

And right away I said, But the reason there's evil in the world and bad things happen is so that God can teach us lessons, so that we can kind of understand that our lives *aren't* infinite and prepare for death and the next world, and he said what would be the importance of teaching us that lesson when our lives would contain nothing but good and then we would all die and go straight to heaven, since all of us would have freely chosen to accept God's Grace? I said, But there's still pain, like physical pain that you have to go through when you die, and wouldn't you want to have some kind of lesson in that, and he said that was a good point to discuss also. Why was there pain? Why did our bodies have to hurt? Why did we have to deteriorate and experience pain and die? Didn't that seem like the ultimate insult? Was there any possibility that an all-loving God would have created physical pain? And as far as the other part went, what about impersonal evil? What was the lesson one learned by being drowned in a flood? What lesson did being struck dead by lightning teach?

When he said that I quit talking. It was like the blades of a giant pair of scissors going around me and squeezing shut and cutting me in two. On one side it was like a blade in my mind that made me suddenly realize that I wasn't so much arguing with Professor

Wykowski, but that Professor Wykowski was actually like a stand-in, a human stand-in for Common Sense, or as Dr. Blumenthal called it later when I told him the story Reason, and that I was a stand-in for what I'd always believed in, Faith, and that all the people like my grandmother and my parents only had faith because they'd either never thought of the Problem of Evil, like my father, who used to go around asking God "Why? Why? Why?" all the time after my brother Mark died, or because they actually refused to think about it, like my grandmother, who refused to think about anything that the Bible didn't tell her to. The only ways to have faith were to be ignorant or stubborn.

And as I could feel that blade sort of cutting into me, I recognized what it meant, and the other blade went straight into my heart. When he said that about struck by lightning and floods, I could see my brother Mark's face very clear, how he was when he was six years old before he died. Mark didn't die from impersonal evil but it happened just as fast, someone shot him in the head with a shotgun while he sat in my father's patrol car where they were parked at the grocery store, and I had always comforted myself by thinking that Mark was doing just fine now because he was with God and Jesus in heaven. I used to ride my bike to this place called Chuck's Slough outside my hometown in Idaho and sit there under the birch trees by the water thinking about how good it was that Mark was in heaven. And now I couldn't think that, and I knew Mark was just dead under the ground where we buried him, because there was no Christian God and no such place.

JUNE 12

What I did today was buy myself some clothes. This morning I sat around waiting again for Jenny to call, and again she never did, and again I started to feel bad about myself and about my life. So I said to myself, "Luke, buddy, what you need is a little refocusing." It almost gets to be like a game or a puzzle, where you start trying to figure out what thing it is you can do to get feeling better, and all your choices start to occur to you and then you have to choose which is the right one. Last night I chose to go to the races, and that was the right choice because I won a lot of money again. Then at first today I decided to watch the news on TV, that I needed to catch up on my current events so that I wouldn't seem stupid about things if I happened to run into an intelligent person anytime soon. I don't think at all that watching the news or reading the newspaper makes you smarter, but it's funny how people, even smart people I've noticed, *think* you're smarter if you know some of what's going on in the world.

But it was like I lost points in the game or chose the wrong puzzle piece, because watching the news made me worse. The news was all about disasters today. It was like the news people were giant ants with these gigantic antennae that spread all out across the country and felt around for the horrible things that had happened to people during the night. And they were just the kinds of things that helped ruin my life for a long time, like forest fires in California and tornadoes in Texas and floods in Tennessee. Lots of impersonal evil.

So I realized that I had made the wrong choice and turned off the TV. But I wasn't what you would call significantly more depressed, even though I made the wrong decision. Back before I met Jenny when I was traveling all around, I would go through my refocusing routine, and if I turned out to make the wrong choice, I would be very angry about this and everything in the world would seem terrible and dark. And when I had kind of gotten all the way to the very bottom of my hopelessness, I would start to think that no matter what choice I made it was always the wrong one, and that I was better off being crazy like I was before when I wasn't making any decisions at all, and things seemed just to happen to me one thing at a time in random order. There were even a couple of times that I almost decided to just leave wherever I was and walk all the way to the loony bin in Orofino, Idaho, and knock on the door and ask for Dr. Blumenthal and see if he would take me in for free. I would imagine what an incredible relief it would be to just stay in the hospital and let someone take care of me. The only reason I didn't actually ever do it was that I was always about a thousand miles from home.

A lot of the wrong choices I made were more a result of what I had to choose from. Usually these bad times would come when I was in a new town and no one knew my name yet and I had maybe just started a new job or hadn't even gotten one yet, and I would have something like seven dollars and fifty cents. My choices would be something like have lunch or drink beer at a bar. If I ate lunch, I would come home to my dingy little apartment and I would be sleepy and bored, and I would want to go out and talk to people and have a few drinks and I couldn't. Or if I chose the other and drank beer at a bar, I would come home when my money was gone and then I would get hungry and there would be only crackers and peanut butter maybe and a plastic cup of water from the sink. Either way I would get angrier and angrier until I would usually end up punching the wall. If the wall was something hard like wood or concrete I would smash my hand and not be able to use it very well for a couple of days, and if it was soft like drywall or paneling I would knock holes in it which I would get in trouble for later on. For a while I even thought about this when I tried to find a new place to live—which was better I mean, soft walls or hard ones, considering the consequences. Later on, I got better at living with these what you'd call limited options, and learned not to punch the wall. I became the person I was when I later met Jenny at the age of twenty-three.

So after I gave up on TV and was taking a shower and at the same time thinking about what was different now from all those times long ago, I suddenly started laughing, even though I was alone, because I realized what a nice thing it was to be in a motel room shower and maybe fifteen feet away inside my gym bag was a huge pile of cash, mostly twenties. Right then and there I decided I would do a little shopping, which hadn't even occurred to me.

I called a cab and told the driver to take me to the nearest mall. I ended up buying three new shirts, a pair of Birkenstocks which I never owned before in my life, some Levi's, and—get this—a tie. I have the receipts right here, and adding it all together this cost me $236 and change, which is the most I've ever spent on clothes in my entire life.

The three shirts I bought at The Gap. I like The Gap because all the clothes are pretty basic. If there's one thing I truly hate, it's people who try to substitute clothes for a personality. I think this happens mostly down South, but maybe I'm a little biased against Southerners from working at Beamon's for awhile, which was Jenny's dad's clothing store in Mississippi. Beamon is Jenny's maiden name. Jenny Beamon. Jenny Rivers.

At Beamon's you got all the First Baptist Church people, the important ones who were like Jenny's dad and owned businesses and things, and whose major concern in life was to make sure that no one could mistake them for rednecks. They did this partly by how they acted and the things they talked about and who they associated with, but mostly they did it with their clothes and their hair. But there are certain ways of acting and dressing out here, too. This area, for instance, eastern Montana and Wyoming and North and South Dakota, is big into western wear. Jenny calls it The Land of the Wide Belt Buckles. You can't go wrong around here with a cowboy hat and cowboy boots and a tight-fitting pair of Lee or Wrangler jeans.

I don't care for western wear, though, so I ended up in The Gap. The salesgirls were all about sixteen and didn't pay any attention to me. They took turns waiting on the customers and the one that wasn't busy was always on the phone talking to their boyfriend. They all looked like they couldn't wait to get the hell out of South Dakota. I bought my Birkenstocks and Levi's in this store called Black Hills Adventures where all the salespeople were guys who kept talking about backpacking and rock climbing and didn't pay much more attention to me than the girls at the other store. What ever happened to those old guys who used to be very friendly and helpful and called you "young man" even if you were maybe seven years old and sat down and put your shoe on with a shoehorn?

The place where I got my tie was much better. It was some chain clothing store I don't remember the name of. I was just in there kind of wandering around—browsing you might say, although my mind was beginning to get preoccupied with the idea that I was buying all these clothes in a way that I had never done before, and how Jenny would have been so happy for a chance to buy a new dress and some clothes for Jake. Maybe we could have taken Jake to the toy store, too.

But I was standing there in front of these ties, looking at them and touching them kind of without meaning to, and this attractive lady who looked about my age came over and asked could she help me. She had blonde hair that was dyed, I guess, because it looked like Jenny's used to, with the roots grown out a little darker, and she was very tiny, I mean about five foot two, but with a nice figure, not built like a stick in other words. She was dressed what I'd call very professionally looking and she had a real simple wedding band on her ring finger that I thought was white gold like mine and Jenny's except it turned out to be Dakota Silver when I asked her. Who knows what's the difference. But there was something nice about her eyes—maybe that they were kind of like Jenny's, a sort of soft, light brown or what you call hazel. She looked like someone you could talk to.

So I just started in shooting the breeze. The first thing I noticed was her ring, so I asked her about that, and I think it kind of put her off for a minute. But after she answered, I changed the subject and started talking about ties like I was supposed to. I said, I don't know why, "I'm looking for a tie to match my suit."

"Oh, good," she said, and livened up a bit. "What color is your suit?" she said.

"White," I told her. I realized right away what a dumb answer that was, even before she kind of couldn't help smiling. "It's just one suit I have that's white," I told her then because I could see I'd given her the impression I only had one suit, and it was white. Of course the number of suits I actually own is zero. "I'm in a wedding," I said.

"Oh, that's nice," she said. "I'm sorry I smiled, but I couldn't help thinking what you'd look like in a white suit." She glanced up at my hair and my scruffy-looking face and smiled again.

"I guess I should cut my hair," I said.

"Oh, don't do that," she said. "It's nice." Then she kind of looked down real quick, and I felt like we were standing too close together. "Who's getting married?" she asked.

"My sister," I said, even though my sister got married to a real estate salesman named Roger about fifteen or so years ago, who always bored the hell out of me but my sister seemed to like him all right.

"How nice," she said. "I hope she'll be very happy." I thought that was an interesting thing for her to say. Not "I'm sure she'll be happy," but "I *hope* she'll be happy," as if she really did hope this but knew it didn't always turn out that way. It made me wonder a little about her marriage. Mine also, like could she maybe see something in my expression that told her what was going on in my life.

"I hope so, too," I said.

"Well," she said, "this one won't do." She reached out, and right when she did I saw I'd been standing there the whole time with this brown tie kind of draped across the palm of my hand. She put her hand right above mine on the tie very gently, and I let go.

"That's what I was thinking," I said, and she smiled again.

"A white suit," she said. "I'm not used to picking out ties for a white suit. What other colors are in the wedding party?" She was very into the subject of tie selection suddenly.

"I'm not exactly sure," I told her after I thought it over for as long as I could.

"Are you sure you're not supposed to be choosing a bow tie?" she asked me.

"I don't think so," I told her. "They never said that."

"Well what color is your shirt? The shirt you're wearing underneath?" She could see I was really struggling.

"White," I said. This seemed like the only safe thing.

"Don't you know any of the other colors? What color is the bride's bouquet?" I shrugged. "What color are your shoes?"

"Black," I said.

She seemed to think this over, then there were a lot more questions like did I have a black vest and so on, and she ended up telling me that she was sure what I needed was a black vest and black bow tie and I should check in the department store for formal wear. After that I got out of it by saying that maybe I should just get a tie for one of my other suits, like my gray one. Then it got easier, and she helped me pick out a nice tie in what she called a gray and crimson blend.

Here's the thing about me and ties. I never owned one in my life, and I never wanted to. I've worn a bow tie twice, to my senior prom and my wedding. I wore a neck tie twice also, and neither time could I figure out how to put the damn thing on. The first time was at Mark's funeral, and my dad put it on for me. It was one of my dad's ties. The second time was at my dad's funeral, and Jenny put it on. That was one of my dad's ties also. After the funeral, before me and Jenny and Jake took off again—this was right at the end of the time when we were still living in Spokane, Washington, for three years, and Jake was still a baby—my mother tried to give me my dad's ties and I said no, and my mother cried. I'm sure I'd have worn a tie to my grandmother's funeral also, but we were "on the road" at the time as they say and didn't find out about it for a few weeks.

I never liked ties. In fact I think I have an unknown phobia. So I plan on never wearing this tie I bought today, and later I'll probably throw it out. But right now it reminds me of the friendly conversation I had when I bought it, and how I felt good leaving the store.

In the taxi on the way home I felt good also, and I started to see things pretty clear and make decisions. I started seeing how I'd bought these things for myself as a kind of subconscious omen. Even though naturally I felt bad that Jenny and Jake weren't here with me and we could have turned it into a family outing, it was like I had accepted the fact that Jenny wasn't going to call until she got tired of her parents and was ready to talk and work things out.

I guess it's unfair, really. I mean I'm not counting on Jenny getting back together with me because she thinks our life together is so great or anything, only easier. I guess that's the way the whole thing's set up. You have a kid, and then you both love that kid, and with how crazy the world is it takes both of you to keep that kid you love happy and safe. And even two people that love him more than anything in the world isn't enough—horrible things can still happen that I don't even want to think about, not with him so far away.

Every morning of his life since he came home from the hospital, I woke up in the same bed he did. We never had enough money to afford two-bedroom apartments, or even two beds, and when he was little and in his crib and he'd start to cry, Jenny would take him out and breastfeed him in the bed with her and then she'd fall asleep. Jake was born in December, and we lived in downtown Spokane in a kind of seedy area. I'd walk home from the bar where I worked in the freezing cold, and into our little apartment where the air was warm and there was the Christmas tree dark and quiet in the corner. I'd stand in the doorway to the bedroom and watch them in the light shining from the kitchen. I'd get in bed and stay as far to the edge as I could because I was afraid I'd roll over and smother him. There were times when he looked so little it didn't seem possible he could live through the night. There he'd be every morning, though, curled up in Jenny's arms. After a while I got used to it, and I'd find myself rolled over next to them in the morning.

When he was about a week old he got jaundiced, and they sent us home from the hospital with these things called bilirubin lights that we were supposed to put him under. You had to stick him in his crib buck-naked except for his diaper, with his belly button still not totally healed, and put a blindfold over his eyes and leave him there for hours. When we put the blindfold on him he screamed, and Jenny said she couldn't do it and took him out of the crib and held him close and cried with him. I thought this meant he might die, because we didn't leave him under the lights long enough, and I went in the bathroom and locked the door and cried all by myself.

I won $1,118.70 at the track last night. One thousand, one hundred eighteen dollars and seventy fucking cents, and Jenny and Jake aren't here to enjoy it.

The night started off horrible. Even though I sat down alone and smoked my cigarette and took my drink of beer and said my prayer to the Greyhound God, every one of my dogs finished dead last. By the 5th race I'd just about decided that the whole thing didn't work without Jake and Jenny. I chose then to go to the last resort, the 7-8 quinella and the 8 to win. For some reason this is the only part of my betting system that Jenny ever gets really into. The idea is, if all else seems to be failing, you bet on the lanes. After I'd been going to the races for a couple of years I noticed that the 8 dog seemed to win the most races and the 7 dog the second most, which made the 7-8 quinella the best bet as far as I could see. I started keeping a chart for a long time. I had sheets and sheets of notebook paper filled with results from tracks all across the country we'd been to and sure enough, when I added things up, the 8 dog won something like four more times out of a hundred races and the 7-8 quinella came in about three more times than the rest. That's a pretty small difference, but it's a difference. It's helped us win some much-needed cash the last couple of years.

Right when I bought the ticket, I had one of those deja vu experiences where things seem weird and different like an earlier moment in your life. I couldn't wait to go tell Jenny was the thing. I absolutely forgot she wasn't there. Like I say, Jenny loves the 7-8 quinella, I'm not sure why. I guess it's because I actually sat down with her one night on the motel bed and explained it to her. It was something definite I could show her that made sense, rather than just why I had picked a certain dog out of the program in this one certain race, which I think Jenny always believes is just luck. But she gets real worked up when I bet the 7-8. It's a great thing about Jenny that, when it comes to the 7-8, she only seems to remember the times we win. I wish she was like that about other things.

But after I turned around from the ticket window I knew she wasn't there, and I was aware suddenly of being alone in this kind of high-up silence that seemed to spread out from me in all directions, like I was looking for somebody or something over everybody's heads. I walked down outside to my place along the rail and they were loading the dogs, and I could hear them barking and then the bell and the metal whine of the rabbit starting up and the track announcer's voice saying, "Here she comes!" and then right at that moment off in the distance a train whistle, like it was talking to me about some other place. I took a drag on my smoke and felt the taste in my mouth, and then the tangy taste of beer, and I said "Please let me win" very softly in my head to the Greyhound God, this time actually believing for that second, like I hadn't in a while, that there actually was such a thing.

Right then the chutes opened, and my 7 and 8 jumped out clean and fast. The reason I think for why the 7-8 works out best is two things actually. For one, the start is slightly staggered, meaning the outside lanes get to start just a tiny bit ahead, the reason being, of course, that they have to go wider around the 1st curve. But that doesn't always happen. For instance if the 8, or less likely the 7, breaks very well, he can sometimes manage to get a full body length ahead of the other dogs *before* the first turn, meaning he can cut across and take the turn on the inside. In that case it turns out, I mean it stands to reason, that the stagger was actually more like a gift. They give him that little extra space to take the turn wide, but then he runs it inside. The other thing is the dogs are usually packed tight into the first turn, and lots of times there's a collision and dogs will go tumbling all over. This is how a lot of the favorites get knocked out. I've only once in all this time seen a dog actually get knocked completely down and then get back up and win. And since the 7 and 8 dog are outside and have the chance to go wider than the other dogs, they're less likely to get caught up in a collision.

So what happened in this race is both dogs broke great, but at the curve the 8 dog had actually got clear of all the other dogs *except* the 7, and he cut right smack in front of my 7 dog, and the 7 pulled up just for a split second. In a dog race, one little moment of hesitation like that can mean you're beat.

My 8 dog was running like a cheetah, like he was a whole different breed of animal altogether. He was so far ahead on the backstretch you could have parallel parked a truck between him and the other dogs. But since he was the favorite in the race, going off at maybe 8:5, I think, I naturally had my win ticket on the 7, who was the long shot at 30:1. And let me say right now that, judging from the program, there was absolutely *no reason* to believe this particular 7 dog was capable of finishing close *at all*. I was picking lanes in this race, not dogs. If I'd been picking dogs, I never would have chosen the 7. He had horrible times and he'd never finished in the money on the recent races listed in the program, and there was no glimmer of hope like I talked about before.

What usually happens when a dog gets behind like that is he just follows the other dogs along to the finish, and that's exactly what the 7 was doing this time. But then on the far turn a strange thing happened. All the dogs behind the 8 were sort of bunched together pretty close, and the one nearest the rail all of a sudden started to drift wide for no reason whatsoever. He cut over in front of a couple other dogs, and they all kind of had to slow down, but there was no collision. But right there next to the rail it was like the parting of the Red Sea my grandmother used to read to me about, and right there in this parted sea was my 7 dog moving up, just flowing right in to fill up the space, like water. When they hit the stretch he was in 4th, but the 2nd and 3rd place dogs were running a little wide so there was plenty of room, and for no logical reason that awful 7 dog outran them. They didn't even need a photo for place.

I collected my money and started looking at the odds and dogs for Race 6 on the TV screen up by the betting window. It was about five minutes to post when I noticed something very strange concerning the quinella. When the odds maker sets the odds for the program, at least at the old-fashioned tracks like Rapid City where they don't have this new computer rating index thing, it always goes like this. The favorite is listed 5:2, then they go 7:2, 9:2, 6:1, 8:1, 8:1, 10:1, 10:1. This will usually get somewhat out of whack in the actual betting because of the outrageous hunches people somehow choose to follow at the track which I can't even imagine. I trust the program, and only the program. I don't even mess with tip sheets.

On the quinella board, like I say, at five minutes to post the 6:1 dog and one of the 8:1 dogs were paired at 999:1. That's as high as the board goes. It could mean actually 999:1, it could mean 10,000:1 for all I know. I didn't get excited yet because stuff like that usually changes real quick. There's a lot of old-timers and gambling addicts at the track who pay close attention like I do.

But at one minute to post, it was still 999:1. At that point I started getting nervous, not because I was afraid I might lose, but because if I won and the odds were still anywhere near that high I would get into a situation where I'd have to deal with the IRS, and I've never been quite sure how that works—whether they might start checking me out about taxes, where my record is not exactly what you'd call squeaky clean.

I went ahead and bet two dollars on the quinella anyway. I went back and looked at the screen right at post time and it flashed 250:1, which made me feel better since I knew that was under the tax limit. I got down to my spot on the rail just in time to do my routine. By the time they got to the stretch, my two dogs were already in the clear. It was that easy.

I kept winning after that, too, but nothing spectacular. Two more quinellas and a couple of win bets. But I'd raised my stakes so they paid a little better than normal. I walked out with my betting pocket jammed full again, and all the other ones, too. I'd lost track, but I counted it out when I got home to the motel. Like I say, $1,118.70.

It's enough to make you wonder. I know there's not really a Greyhound God. It was just something I made up on my own to pass the time, but after two nights like that it certainly can begin to make a person wonder.

JUNE 13

I'm leaving Rapid City. I'll get a bus ticket or a train ticket or even a plane ticket tomorrow. I can afford it. Hell, I could hire a taxi to take me out of town. I've got a gym bag full of dough.

It happened again last night—all the money—and that's what made me decide to leave. This time it started from the very first race. I hit the quinella and had the right dog for the double and the other half of the double came in in the 2nd race *and* I had the win bet *and* the quinella in that one, too. After two races I'd won something like $480. I was excited about this, but it gets very tough, too, not having anyone there to share it with. I kept wandering around between races, going up and down the steps, walking back and forth along the rail. It was warm and breezy outside with a big moon, and I started feeling like I didn't even care if I won. I'd upped my stakes for the 3rd race, and I sat and watched very quietly while my dog took over in the stretch and earned me another hundred bucks on a win bet. Three races, and I was up around $600 again. Then I started getting kind of paranoid. Always when I go to the races I make sure to change ticket windows as much as I can, because I heard from a guy once that they definitely notice if somebody's winning a lot, and eventually might start asking questions about taxes and things. But the problem is that here I've been winning so much money that practically *any* ticket taker might start wondering, and I was suddenly very conscious of this and nervous about going to collect.

I'd also been drinking a lot more than usual for some reason, and I hadn't had anything much to eat, and it was making my thoughts kind of hazy. So when I went up to collect I was definitely considering how I was in what you'd call a precarious situation because of all the money, but I was also not in the best shape to make good decisions. Out of all the ticket takers, there was this one girl that I'd come to think was kind of pretty. She had brown hair tied back in a ponytail and a nice-looking face, a little round and soft. And I somehow got this idea in my head that she was the one ticket person who I could trust not to rat on me. She was actually the most dangerous one, though, because I guess I'd been having a tendency every night to go to her window more than the rest, and she would know more about how much I'd been winning. Here's what she said when I cashed my ticket—"Wow, you're really on a roll. Don't forget to get something nice for your wife."

That was a strange thing to say, and it put me in kind of an odd spot. On the one hand I didn't want to admit how much money I was winning, but on the other I didn't want to seem like a jerk who never got anything for Jenny. "Yeah, I bought her three dresses yesterday," I said.

And right away then, while I was walking away and trying to stuff my dough into my already stuffed pocket, I knew I was leaving Rapid City.

It made me sort of reckless to know that, and I kept drinking a lot and smoking too much and betting a little bit careless. I kept winning anyway—not every race, but plenty.

I haven't taken the Greyhound God seriously for quite a while. I think the more I got comfortable with Jake and Jenny the less I thought I needed to consider him. But Jenny left me, and now there's so much money, and I've started to think about the Greyhound God again.

You could trace it all the way back to when I was still in the hospital in Orofino. Dr. Blumenthal and the other people there including some of the patients actually and also just the course of time I'm sure had helped me to straighten out my mind and get to the point where I felt like I was in control of my thoughts again instead of the other way around. Which sounds like a good thing, I suppose, but I wasn't so pleased about it at the time.

The nice thing about being crazy, at least this is how it was for me, is that you don't worry about anything or feel depressed. Of course this is the result of not being what you'd call rational, but it's still kind of a pleasant way to get through the day. For instance, for a while all I did with my time was to explain to my parents and other people including my grandmother who came to visit me, this is after I got taken home from college but before they put me in the hospital and for a while after that, that I was not really who I seemed to be and that my parents were not my real parents and that I was actually born from a ball of fire. And it wasn't like I was upset by this. I mean I didn't worry about it whatsoever. All I did was explain to people all the time very calmly and with all sorts of detailed reasons how I knew I was born from a ball of fire. Once when my parents thought it was safe to leave me alone at home and go to church in the car, I took my old bike from back when Mark died and which was way too small for me by that time out of the garage and rode it down to the City Beach by the lake and stood there in the sand telling all these people in bathing suits and what-ever how I was born from a ball of fire. And this one single thing ruined my reputation in my hometown to this day. The only way most people remember me is Luke Rivers the guy who went nuts and yelled out at the City Beach that he was born from a ball of fire. Even my sister reminds me of this practically every time I talk to her on the phone, which is part of the reason I only call her or my mother about twice a year.

When I think back about this whole time in my life, which basi-cally started in that philosophy class and ended probably about three or four years later—it was about a year before I met Jenny that I started feeling like a whole different person from the one in the hospital in Orofino—I can remember it all pretty clearly, what I said and did in other words. But it's not like *I* did them, not the Luke that's here in the motel room. It's that *other Luke* that did those things. And even the Luke before that doesn't seem like me. The one that listened to his grandmother tell him about God and Jesus and believed her and went around thinking how Mark was in heaven and he would be too someday. It's like the me *now,* the Luke Rivers *now,* wasn't born from a ball of fire but was born after the idea of being born from a ball of fire had disappeared.

But it also seems to me that I was never really crazy. I never hurt anyone or did anything bad or wrong. Like I said, I wasn't even depressed or angry or confused. In fact I remember feeling kind of peaceful and happy most of the time. What happened actually was that I made other people depressed and confused and unhappy.

My grandmother for instance was the reason I finally got sent to the hospital. After I'd been kind of taken home from college unwill-ingly and was living in my old bedroom upstairs at home and would practically never leave the room—my room was actually over the garage and you had to climb this ladder on hooks to get up to it, and it was like an attic with the ceiling slanting down both ways and a window that looked out on the street—and would just pull the lad-der up behind me and not let it down for anyone to come up and see me, my grandmother would come over and try to talk to me.

One day I had actually come down to the kitchen to talk to her which I usually didn't do, and she started to get very upset with me. I was explaining to her like I constantly did about the ball of fire, and about how there was no God and no Jesus and no one taking care of us, and pretty soon I could see her start to look at me like she didn't know me anymore at all and she was tired of trying to talk to me and wanted to leave. I loved my grandmother very much. After Mark died and my father just kind of quit when it came to raising his kids, I was thirteen and my sister Mary was sixteen, my grandmother sort of even took his place for me. She was like the strong person in my life whereas my mother was affectionate but weak and my father wasn't even there where you could reach him.

So when I saw my grandmother looking at me like I was a total stranger I started to get very loud and kind of aggravated while I kept trying to explain myself to her, and then I could see she started getting scared. She got up and excused herself from the table and said she had to leave, and her face was very white and she suddenly looked for the first time like an old stooped gray-haired woman kind of struggling as fast as she could to get out the door. I kept talking to her and following her to her car, and she never said anything back and got in and shut the door fast and started up the engine, and I grabbed this big stick that was lying in the yard and started whacking it on the roof of her car while she tried to drive away. That I admit was a little crazy. After that my grandmother never really knew me again. She never got to know the new Luke Rivers that came out of all of that before she died. And I think that's sad. I think it would have been very interesting.

Maybe I need to rethink the whole thing again about Professor Wykowski being smarter than Dr. Blumenthal. It was Dr. Blumenthal who actually figured out how to help me. Professor Wykowski even wrote me a letter when I was in the hospital that kind of disappointed me, I remember, and maybe a little bit even today. He told me in this letter that he had heard about the problems I was having and that he felt very bad about it and sort of personally responsible. He said he should have understood what the trouble was when I quit showing up for his class, but that he was guilty like many teachers, he realized now, of being too busy to recognize what was going on in the life of his students. He apologized for this. He said that he didn't think too much about it at the time except to be sorry that I wasn't in class anymore because I was a fine student. He said he only put two and two together all this time afterward when my roommate called him and told him what had happened and how I hadn't been doing so hot and also how much I had said I admired him—Professor Wykowski, I mean—and would he please write me or call me because that might be a little help. So he was doing this, for whatever it was worth. He also said that it was another measure of my strong character that I had a roommate who obviously cared so much about me.

My roommate was actually my best friend from all the way back in grade school, Jeff Lundy, who was a normal Idaho kid with a dad who was a logger and a mom who was a secretary. He was in no way prepared to handle my situation which got worse nearly every day but still he tried very hard, and did a lot of things for me even after I was gone, like calling Professor Wykowski. And I never thanked him, and I never spoke with him again from the time I got sent home. He quit college, and last I heard he was driving a milk truck in Sandpoint.

But Professor Wykowski went on to say in his letter that he suspected my troubles began that day in his philosophy class when I had looked and sounded so upset. He told me that the best advice he could give me concerning my troubles was not to try to forget the ideas I had to confront that day in class, but to turn my very weakness in the face of those ideas into my strength. He was sure I would get through this hard time because I had what he called intellectual and moral courage. I was not afraid to face up to the powerful truth sometimes contained in ideas. Ultimately this would see me through. Other people, great philosophers in fact, had experienced the same thing I had, and he quoted one of them, this German guy named Nietzsche who I tried to read some of on my own later and couldn't make heads or tails of. The quote was, "That which doesn't kill me makes me stronger." Yeah right, but what about all the stuff that *does* kill you? Even as goofy and screwed up as I was at the time, I could see the problem with *that*.

But it was a very nice and helpful letter, all in all. That part where he told about me being a fine student even made me cry. But like I said before, I wasn't really aware at the time of how not aware I was of what was happening to my life. I actually felt pretty good there in the hospital with the doctors and other patients, who to me seemed just like I was, a little bit different but not insane. The ward I was in didn't have any of the really bad patients like catatonic schizophrenics and such. It was pretty peaceful, really. Lots of people seemed very interested or at least polite about my ball of fire theory, and we played chess a lot, which I just learned from an older depressed guy right then and still play whenever I can.

The disappointing thing about Professor Wykowski's letter, though, was that in my mind I was already *doing* all the things he suggested, and he, the guy who taught them to me, couldn't even recognize it. The way I saw it, if Christianity was a totally false and bogus idea and you couldn't count on God or Jesus to look out for you or award you by taking you to heaven, then there wasn't any reason to go around being good and doing what you were supposed to and following all the rules. You could just drop dead anytime and your life didn't mean anything at all. My brother Mark was six years old, and he was good and he was happy, and in the summer he played out in our yard sometimes from morning until night, and he learned to say grace at our table and he knew how to tie his own shoes and then he died, and it seemed like I was the only one around who even remembered what a good, caring boy he was. It was never the dying part that bothered me so much, but the horrible idea that your living hadn't meant anything. So to me it made a lot more sense to do absolutely nothing, except maybe alert other people to reality. So it's like that's what I was doing by going around telling everybody about being born from a ball of fire. Of course it's the ball of fire part that shows I wasn't exactly thinking clearly, and also the fact that I was sort of so idiotically pleased with myself most of the time. Later on, when I was much, much better and just about ready to leave the hospital, Dr. Blumenthal kind of admitted the same thing to me. He said he knew I really hadn't actually *believed* about the ball of fire, but that out of my somewhat disturbed condition I had created it as a *metaphor*.

The idea that what I should do was just quit made a lot of sense to me, though, at the time, and still does in a way. I even had an example to follow. My dad had been doing it ever since Mark died, I realized, except only halfway. He just quit in terms of like his thinking and his emotions, but he kept doing stuff like paint the house and go to work every day. In fact he went to work all the time. They couldn't keep him out of the goddamn cop shop. About the only place I ever saw him was driving around in his patrol car.

And I suppose I had expected Professor Wykowski to be proud of me in a way, and I felt like I'd been betrayed. That was a hard thing for me, because I thought a lot of Professor Wykowski. When I was still at school and started doing things that I thought was like acting out my new philosophy, I always imagined telling him about them. "I didn't eat anything again today. I just said hell with the idea of eating. I drank a half case of beer instead, and took a whiz in the fountain outside the classroom center at midnight when no one could see." And I imagined we'd have a good laugh over these things. Obviously, I didn't waste much time in getting self-destructive.

But in the beginning I did things according to a plan, and some of them were good things. For instance, I walked a lot. After I started skipping all my classes, I used to just walk all day. Moscow, Idaho, is a pretty town. It's not real mountainous with a beautiful lake like Sandpoint and other north Idaho places. Instead it has rolling wheat fields all around, called the Palouse, which there's only one place exactly like it in the whole world I learned in my geography class before I quit going, and that's somewhere in China.

What I would do is walk right out of town and down a dirt

road, any dirt road, all day. And when it got dark, I would look for some little stream with cottonwood trees nearby like there's quite a few of around there, and I would put on my coat and lie in the grass under the trees, usually on some farmer's private property, and go to sleep seeing the stars move through the branches very slowly and knowing the whole world was whirling through space. It was late September and early October and I would wake up in the morning shivering, sometimes with the roar of some tractor and a farmer asking me what the hell I was doing. A couple of them were quite concerned about me. I remember one morning best. There was an early frost that day. When I woke up I was bone cold and probably even frostbit a little. I was almost delirious, I think, and frightened about where was I at and what was I doing. Then I looked down and there was this perfect curled-up outline of me where I'd slept there in the grass, surrounded by frost. It made me very calm for some reason, and sleepy, and I looked around at the gold trees and the last of the stars and the sun rising over the bare fields where the wheat had been cut, and I took a deep breath that seemed like it lasted forever in my chattering teeth, and I started walking home. I'm glad I did that. At least once in my life, I mean.

But I guess what happens to you is that even if you're not behaving truly crazy, doing these kind of experiments like walking all day and night and not eating and never sleeping starts to make you deteriorate and lose track of real things. Even though you plan out how to do these things ahead of time, you can't honestly say why you're doing them, I mean in a way that shows they *mean* something. That was exactly the point, though. Nothing meant anything and at least these were things I could do with my body and my mind that seemed like honest work somehow. Why not walk all day?

Also combined with this was the fact that I started drinking too much and I wasn't used to it. In high school I was mostly a jock— I played split end on the football team—and because of my religion and everything I was pretty conservative, and I almost never drank. But I started to drink all the time in those days when I wasn't doing something specific like walking. In between walking I drank. And then pretty soon there wasn't any walking and I *just* drank—that and played solitaire all day. *All day,* with a beer or a bottle of booze or whatever right there beside me.

After that stage I really don't remember. It was only a matter of days I think before the ball of fire thing started up, and I drank and drank and drank, and I guess what happened was Jeff Lundy finally called my parents or the health center or the police, I really couldn't say. He was a good friend, and I'm sure he felt guilty about narcing on me.

But Dr. Blumenthal was the one who helped me get over the ball of fire theory. What he did that was so ingenious was something no one else had tried, which was just to totally ignore me on the subject. This was like a typical conversation we would have. I would say, "You don't understand. None of this matters because I'm not really who you think I am. I was born from a ball of fire." And Dr. Blumenthal would say, "I *do* understand. Hmm. That's interesting. Now *what* were you thinking at your brother's funeral? You haven't finished telling me." I mean that's just kind of a fake example, but pretty close to how it really happened. After a while of him doing that I just lost interest.

There were a lot of other things I lost. Like I said already, I lost my Faith. I lost the idea of my brother being still alive in spirit somewhere where I would be with him again someday and tell him how much I loved him and how much being his older brother had meant to me. I lost the idea that my mind and my body would always take care of me. I knew for the rest of my life that my body and my mind could turn on me without any warning and make me go in the opposite direction, and that this was the same for everybody, and it would happen sooner or later no matter how you felt about life. Like Professor Wykowski put it, deteriorate and experience pain and die.

There was this older guy in the hospital—I say older but I mean older to me then, he was actually about the same age I am now I think, thirty-two. I still walked a lot then, even after I was getting better, and I used to see this guy walking a lot too, around this big lawn they had with lots of benches and fountains and plastic sunflowers, and we started striking up conversations now and then. It must have been late in the spring. I left the hospital in the summer, but I started getting better in the spring, like my mind thawed out with the weather.

One day me and this guy ended up sitting on a bench and talking for an hour, or mostly he talked and I listened. After more than a year of talking about the ball of fire I was pretty tired of saying anything.

It turned out after he told me about himself that this guy was a hiker. That's why he walked so much. He had a wife and three kids and was a foreman at this sawmill in Priest River, which is only two little towns over from Sandpoint, but his what he called passion was for hiking. He used to go by himself nearly every weekend way up into the mountains on old forest service roads and trails that were all overgrown now he said and nobody even remembered them.

On one particular day he had been hiking up a very steep incline to get to this mountain ridge, he told me, and there was no trail and it was more like rock climbing. He said he was enjoying himself very much, there were wildflowers growing out of the rock outcroppings and the sun was shining and there was a nice, steady breeze. After a while he noticed a ledge over to his left a little ways, where this one huge rock kind of pointed out like a finger over everything. He said he thought it would be the perfect place to sit and take off his backpack and get out the sandwich and chips and sun tea his wife had put in his backpack for him to eat. He skirted along this ledge until he got there, and he walked out and stood on the rock. At first he felt wonderful, he told me, and he actually struggled for a long time sitting there on the bench to get this one word he was looking for. He said, Just a second, let me think, and sat there with his eyes shut tight and his head down and I was quiet while he was thinking. Actually it must have been pretty late in the spring by that time or maybe even summer, because I remember now there was this dandelion that had grown so high it stuck through the slats of the bench, and while he was talking he had started to kind of play with this yellow dandelion, just stroking it very gently with his fingers, like he was a blind man trying to identify what the flower was instead of find a word in his head. Finally he lifted his head up real quick and opened his eyes and said, "Ecstatic," like he was talking to himself. "Ecstatic, that's what I mean. I was all alone in the sky, and there wasn't any ground beneath me." Then he got real quiet and forgot about playing with the dandelion and sat real straight on the bench and started swaying back and forth, like he was a totally rigid object that someone had pushed and set him teetering.

I hoped he'd snap out of it but he didn't. He told me the rest, but you could tell he was very scared. He said that he'd been standing on the rock with his eyes closed and his head tilted back, and then it was like in a dream and he felt himself stumble. Right away he opened his eyes and caught himself, and suddenly he was looking straight down and there was nothing below, only open air for him to fall into. He said he knew he was okay, he was standing there very still and had his balance, but in his head and in the bottom of his stomach he had felt himself fall, he had felt all that open space go past him.

Then he was fine, he told me. It was only for a second. He even sat and ate his lunch the way he planned to. But afterward on the way down the mountain he would all of a sudden come to a dead stop and have that awful feeling again, like he was on the edge of the cliff with his eyes closed and then suddenly falling through space. He kept going slower and slower and kind of sticking his feet out in front of him very carefully and feeling for the ground, even in places where the trail was flat. He finally made it to his truck, but when he got home it was way after dark and he couldn't eat and he couldn't talk to his wife, who was the only one still awake, and he went straight to bed. But in the middle of the night he felt himself falling off the cliff again, and he woke up and it was pitch dark and he swung his feet over the edge of the bed and put them down on the floor and then sat there like that for hours while his wife went on sleeping.

On Monday he went back to work, and after a few days he forgot all about it. But then as it got closer to Saturday, his hiking day, he started feeling very nervous and frightened without knowing the reason, and then on Friday afternoon he suddenly froze right up in the middle of showing this new guy how to feed the saw, and he said the mill and all the people disappeared and he was just falling through space with the air rushing through his body like the sound of flames. One of his friends had to drive him home, and after that he couldn't leave. He would just sit in this chair with his feet on the floor and he was afraid to even get up and walk to the bathroom. Then about three times a day all of a sudden he would feel himself falling, and he would shut his eyes tight and grab the edges of the chair. Sometimes he would yell for help.

He ended up in Orofino pretty quick after that. His wife and kids were still at home in Priest River, he said, but he didn't know if he could ever go back there.

He said he'd gotten a lot better. He said he hadn't fallen—that's exactly how he said it, like it was the real thing—for over six months, but he still felt like he was always about to. He was still standing on the rock with nothing below. He could see it in his head, even while he was asleep.

I was really afraid by that time he was going to have one of his falls right there with me on the bench, and I started looking around for the closest attendant. But he did all right, he wasn't exactly looking any better but no worse either. He got interested in the yellow stuff on his thumb from rubbing the dandelion and kept looking at that for a while, but I don't think he knew he was even doing it. Finally I told him I was sorry I asked, but he said no, it was okay, his doctor said he had to learn to talk about it, and I seemed like a good person to tell, although he didn't say why. When you think about it, I was just a kid.

After he was done I told him how I could definitely understand, how it wasn't quite the same thing that had happened to me but I knew the basic feeling. I wish I had already had that conversation with Dr. Blumenthal by then, and I could have told him about metaphors because I think he had one too. I mean I don't doubt he really felt like he was falling off a cliff, but I'm sure it must have been from something else that was fucked up in his life. All the problems you have are nearly always something else.

Anyway I even went ahead and told him about the Problem of Evil, and it was strange because it didn't seem to interest him at all, but he right away came up with an answer that made things a whole lot better for me. This guy said, real casual, looking at his thumb no less, "Well, I see what you're saying, but that doesn't mean there's not *any* God, just that the *real* God's no more perfect than you or me."

We stopped talking right after that, but I remember telling him thank you, that that was a big help, and I hoped he got better with his falling problem soon.

And it *was* a big help. After that conversation my whole frame of mind drastically improved, and it wasn't too much longer before I was ready to leave Orofino. What I made of what the guy said was this. Just because God couldn't make the world and the people in it exactly how he wanted to didn't mean he hadn't made the world at all. It still meant that the Christian idea of God I'd been brought up on was wrong, but there were lots of other ideas you could have. For instance you could still think God was basically good, but he just wasn't all-powerful enough to get everything done the way he would have liked to. Or maybe he was all-powerful and good, but just not all-knowing and couldn't keep track of things all the time so that bad stuff slipped through the cracks. Or he was all-knowing and all-powerful but he had a bit of a mean streak. Any of these versions of God was better than no God at all.

Of course I'm not trying to say that my life after that was a piece of cake, which obviously it still isn't. There were good days and bad days, and good places and bad places, and lots of refocusing. But I got through it little by little, and I got through it all by myself, further and further away from home. Meeting Jenny in some ways helped me get over the idea that I was always supposed to be looking for something, but I was pretty much okay even before that. I'd kind of learned to just sit back and look at the world and wait. But with Jenny it was like I had been saving up things inside me ever since I left Orofino and decided not to live in my hometown, and I finally found someone I could set all these things down in front of and say, "Here I am. Look at me."

So to tell the story of my troubles and how I eventually got better you go from that day in philosophy class to the day when I talked to the guy who always felt like he was falling off a cliff. What that guy told me at Orofino about maybe there was still a God was like the last sentence, the very last word. But you could call how I found the Greyhound God the period at the end of that sentence.

One night when we were still in Spokane I'd had a pretty rough day. Jake was sick, which he wasn't supposed to be at that age because of Jenny breast-feeding and something about immunities, and I was nervous at first and called in to work sick. But it turned out he was okay, and Jenny said I might as well get out of the house and take a break and enjoy my night off, which was nice of her. Some customer at work had told me about the dog races and I figured I'd go see what that was like.

That night was the only chance I'd ever had to be alone at all since Jake was born, except for the five minutes it took me to walk back and forth to work every night. And when I was out at the track it was like my thoughts started to take over, like all the things I'd wanted to think about since Jake was born but couldn't find room for were coming out in a long, slow breath.

It must have been about April, three or four months since Jake was born. It was a very cold, drizzly night, and I remember being disappointed at that, which means it was the time of year when you hoped for a little better weather but didn't always get it. The Spokane track was depressing when you had to stay inside. It wasn't like an outdoor grandstand which you have at a lot of the tracks, the older places mostly, but you sat inside behind a long row of

Plexiglas windows that separated you from the fresh air and the noise of the dogs barking and the clack of the rabbit along the rail. Instead it was all just massive concrete, like being inside a cement cave.

So even though it was very cold on that first night, I decided to go outside. It must have been about the 3rd race, and I was outside sitting on the wet metal bleacher seats watching the dogs walk by with the lead-outs, who were wearing long-sleeve shirts under their bright orange jumpsuits, and bright orange hats with flaps that pulled down over their ears. You could see the dogs' breath all frosty in the air around them, and every once in a while one of them would shiver all over, starting through their legs and working all the way through their tails and a shake of their heads. It wasn't till I saw the dogs' breath that I noticed my own fogging out in front of me, and I was wet and starting to shiver, and I dug my hands deep in my coat pockets and hunched myself up.

Everything was quiet and peaceful. You could hear a few cars off to the east on the road that ran near the track, but other than that there was only the clink of the dogs' chains when they walked, and every once in a while the sound of one of the lead-outs' voices saying something to a dog, and occasionally a woof or chuff from the dog itself.

I was the only person outside, except for the lead-outs. I looked around at the rows and rows of metal bleachers, all empty with water dripping from them to the cement. It was like a ghost town, like you could almost hear all the people who had sat in these seats on summer nights. And in a strange way I had a little glimpse of being warm and comfortable inside somewhere, and it made me think of Jake and Jenny at home in the apartment, Jake breast-feeding probably while Jenny sat in our old beat-up rocking chair watching TV before yawning and going to bed. The apartment seemed like a warm, happy place then, not like it did sometimes when I was home and I would feel nervous and tense for some reason, like I couldn't ever just relax and breathe. Was Jake breast-feeding okay today, why was he spitting up so much of the milk, why had he pooped so many times and why was it that strange color, why was he crying, why was he quiet, should he be sitting in the sunlight from that window so long, had he got big enough by now to roll off the bed?

And sitting there in the cold I thought if there would ever be a time when I wouldn't have to worry anymore, and I knew there wasn't, and that that was the thing for all those months right before and after Jake was born that kept smothering me. And I guess I started feeling kind of sorry for myself. Maybe wondering why I had to be a bartender forever and ever, like why was that the only thing I'd ever been able to learn how to do, and why was I not one of the people who had money and lunch hours and nice cars that shined in the streetlights outside the bar at night and could come in and laugh and joke and not care about anything. I laughed and joked with them all the time, the ones that wanted to talk to me, but it wasn't real laughing and joking, just a part of the day when I pretended to be like them.

I started to feel days and days loosen out of me, kind of rolling out of my gut like thread and stretching out and out till they unraveled me. Then I was startled by the dogs running past, going by me in a flash and spooling out and away like the thread I had imagined in front of me. I felt the dogs tugging me toward the turn.

I had forgotten about the race and I hadn't placed any bets or even heard the dogs being loaded in or the bell or the voice of the track announcer. I was watching the dogs race without having any money on them, and I could just sort of *see* them run. They looked beautiful, just a blur of legs and bodies in a full-out stretch. And I felt like I was running with these dogs, like I was right in the middle of their pack being pulled and pulled along with the mud slipping beneath me. And then, as they were all crossing the finish line and the rabbit was slowing down and they all started gathering around it like they always do, barking and their tails wagging like mad, the Greyhound God came to me.

It had to be some kind of God, I felt like, that had let those dogs do that, let them run like that beautiful and powerful in the rain. I had a strong sense of something whole and complete. And yet I realized even then that this wasn't the normal God people think of, perfect and graceful and caring I guess you'd say, but that there was something cruel in him, too. The dogs ran and ran, it was like they put their hearts and their lives into their feet for that single half a minute, and they did it over and over in their lives with the same kind of hope and even desperateness again and again, and it always ended the same—with that sad and at the same time hopeful meeting around the rabbit, which they had wanted to find a living, breathing thing, even if it was just so they could tear it apart, so it would at least have some purpose after all the chasing.

And it started seeming to me that this had all been arranged long beforehand, that there was someone who wanted the running and the hope and the disappointment, and that they were watching. That's all I could take in at the time, kind of, that we were all— me and the other people there and the dogs and the race around the track and the cold and the rain falling from above and the whole wide space that faded back and back like a movie camera moving away until it took in the whole world—we were all being watched like that, from someplace. The idea just seeped right into me like the rain and made me calm and slow in my thoughts, and I turned my attention very easy and slow back to the program and the tote board and the next race, and my mind started figuring the odds, numbers turning around and around in my head, concentrating on what I would bet in a frosty clear way that matched the air.

After I'd made my bet and bought a beer, I sat back down outside all by myself on the wet metal seat, and I lit a smoke and took a drink, and right when the dogs came out of the gate I said a prayer. At that time I don't know even what I was praying for. I don't even remember if I won that race. But I said my prayer to the Greyhound God, that's what I called him in my head.

It wasn't until later that I started playing around with more ideas about the Greyhound God, and always quiet and secret from Jenny. I started going back to the idea of God not being able to get the world right, how he'd screwed it up a little bit just like you or I would, like that guy said to me in Orofino. Somehow evil had gotten in where he didn't want it, and this had caused all kinds of trouble in the world, mostly in people's heads.

So he sent Jesus to try and fix things. And Jesus did a pretty good job overall, he at least gave people a good example of how they could treat each other if they tried, and put the idea in people's heads that there might be some meaning to the whole thing and somebody looking after them, and he got to sit on the right hand of God forever after.

But of course the world still went on like it did before with lots of violence and anger and unhappiness. So God finally gave up. He said I just can't do any more. But what I'll do, he went on saying, just to make things a little better, is I'll give all the people without faith, all the people who still feel lost and confused and troubled in the world, a God of their own. This God will sit on the left hand of me, and he'll be the God of all the things that go wrong—not like Jesus who was perfect, but the God of imperfection. It will be his job to look after the sinners and the losers just the way they are, and not try to turn them into saints. He will offer them comfort when they are down, and make it possible for them to rise to their feet again and run the race one more time.

And I, Luke I mean, gave this God his name, the Greyhound God, remembering about Dr. Blumenthal's idea of metaphors. I replaced the Ball of Fire with the Greyhound God.

Now, there's an obvious problem, which is the fact that I just made the entire thing up. But who made Jesus up? Was it God, or someone like me? Did God sit in the sky or wherever he is and say, Okay, I'm going to create a son for myself and call him Jesus and send him down to Earth to spread a message of love and faith for me, or was it some poor son of a bitch like me who said to himself Okay, what the world needs is a savior, so I'm going to use this guy, Jesus, and make up this story about him that says he came from God down to Earth and did and said all these things? Did God make Jesus because people needed him, or did people make Jesus because they needed God?

It's dark outside now and there's the same big moon above the freeway. I'll leave tomorrow. Bright and early I'll make a decision how. I'll wake up in the morning and take a shower and leave here fresh and clean. Good-bye, Rapid City, and no more chance that Jenny might call, unless she calls tonight while I'm here sleeping, or maybe not asleep.

JUNE 14

This morning I checked out and paid for the last day and gave the old lady that runs the Black Hills Motel a little extra too. She was very nice the whole time I stayed there and never asked any questions about what happened to the woman and the little boy I came with.

I had planned on leaving my bag in the lobby while I took a walk and did some thinking, but then it suddenly seemed like leaving the bag there would give me an excuse to just tell myself Jenny might still call. So I took the bag with me.

I was going along through this little residential neighborhood off of the interstate, and the bag was getting heavier and heavier and I was thinking more about that than whatever it was I was going to do, and then I saw this truck with a "For Sale" sign in the window. It was a regular big old Chevy one-ton truck, which turned out to be a 1979 but still in good condition. That's what the old farmer who owned it told me and I believe him. He said he didn't want to sell it, but his wife said now they were moved to town they didn't need an old truck anymore. I didn't even look under the hood, just drove it around the block a couple of times and left my bag right there with him. Not that I know much about engines anyway. But the alignment seemed good, and I revved it up a couple of times and there wasn't any knock or miss, and the gears didn't slip, and the brakes squeaked a tiny bit but not too bad.

I asked the old guy how much and he said how much did I think and I asked him seven hundred bucks maybe? And he said that sounded fair. I looked in my bag and fished out $700, and he didn't even bat an eye.

First vehicle I ever bought with my own money in my life. I mean I was the one who picked out the Honda, but we bought it by trading Jenny's convertible her dad had given her. And like the old guy said, the truck's running great. The alignment's kind of screwed up after all, to where the steering pulls hard off to the right if you let the wheel go and the whole truck starts to shudder a bit if you get up over sixty, but that should be fixable unless the old guy rammed the truck into a fence or a cow or something and bent the frame.

I'm heading through the Badlands. If you've never been here, it's just a desert-like area, with rounded hills that rise off in the distance in white and pink and red and orange bands. The shadows on the hills blend with the different colors and stuff and all the nooks and crannies where it's eroded, and it's different from anyplace else I've ever seen.

I've been here a million times, but I remember one time in particular when we passed through on I-90 right at the tail end of last summer. We were headed from the dog track in Rapid City back home to Minnesota where we'd just moved to recently, and we'd lost all our money to the point where like I say we couldn't afford a motel and had to pull off to the side of the road when I got tired because it was too far to the next rest area and Jenny was already asleep.

I woke up just after daybreak, hunched up in the driver's seat with Jake and Jenny cuddled under a blanket on the passenger side and the seat tilted back as far as it would go and a pillow under Jenny's head. It was hard to tell what time it was because there were deep, gray clouds hanging low in the sky just above the peaks of the Badlands out my window. It made it look more like nighttime than I knew it was actually.

I had to take a leak, so I waited till this big semi flew on by and the wind from it got done shaking the Honda, and I stepped out and closed the door real quietly. I was going to just step off the road and let her rip, but there were cars that kept coming and I'm pretty modest about that sort of thing. So what I did was headed off south toward the hills. And when I'd gotten down the embankment, I suddenly started running as fast as I could off into the Badlands.

My first thought I guess was that I would race all the way to the foot of the hills, but then they kept not getting much closer and I was getting winded and I could barely see the Honda back behind me anymore. So I stopped way out there and took a leak. I looked off to where you could tell the sun must have been behind the clouds. There was a little town up ahead, and you could see tiny lights against the dark sky. The town looked very delicate, I guess you'd say, very frail out there in this wide open space beneath the storm clouds. Then the sky got really light around me for a second, and almost instantly there was a loud crack and then thunder boomed through the air. So I started running back.

When I was running, it started to seem like a movie. There was the Honda way up ahead, getting just a tiny bit bigger every second, bouncing up and down in my sight while I ran, and it was like I was the hero in an action film. Jake and Jenny were in trouble somehow, and I was running to save them. Someone was ready to kidnap them, or a tornado was racing toward them and I had to get there in time. It wasn't like I really believed it, but more of an imaginary game I was playing by myself.

Finally I ran out of gas and had to start walking, and right then it started pouring down rain, big hard drops sweeping across my face so I had to turn my head. By the time I got to the car, only a minute, I was soaked and freezing. But then right when I got ready to open the door, I stopped. There was this beautiful woman, and this perfect little boy, both inside there fast asleep. The woman had long blondish hair, a few strands hanging across her cheek, and she wasn't wearing much make-up but she still looked pretty and natural sleeping there. She had graceful fingers, I noticed, long and thin, and one hand was in the boy's curly hair. The boy's mouth was open and he was flailed out across the woman's lap with one leg out of the blanket hanging over the emergency brake.

It was like they were somebody else's family, or a make-believe family, like they'd been cast by some movie director as the perfect ones to play those parts. And I'd just wandered into this movie set accidentally from out of the desert. I wasn't really the hero of the film like I'd thought before.

But I knew all the time they were really mine, and I stood there in the rain looking at them for a few seconds, and I was thinking to myself that I had everything I'd ever need right there in front of me.

JUNE 15

I'm in Wisconsin Dells, staying at a place near the racetrack. It's a real pretty place, for a change. When I first drove in, it somehow made me depressed just looking at all the people and the traffic. So I drove right out of town until I found a dirt road, and the next thing you know I came across this place I'm staying at out of nowhere between the Dells and this little town called Lyndon Station. Outside my window there's a huge oak tree. You don't start picking up oak trees till eastern Minnesota, and that's when the air starts turning a little humid too. I used to notice these changes every time we drove over from Heron Lake. We used to make the trip over about once every week or two, and even though not always to the Dells track this place is familiar enough to me. But before we used to stay at a cheap run-down motel out close to the track. The Dells is kind of a touristy place, and even the fleabag motels are expensive. It reminds me of Sandpoint that way, a small town that lots of people want to come to, except that The Dells has only got a river where Sandpoint has a huge lake.

In Sandpoint, you can start out any direction and run into water. If you go south, you hit the Long Bridge that crosses the lake to the homes on the opposite shore and Highway 95 that runs a couple hours on down to Moscow and then all the way through the state and into Nevada and California. Southeast you hit City Beach. Go east and you end up at Hope, taking the highway around the lake. Over on that side you can watch the sun set across the water. North, you hit Sand Creek. West is Pend Oreille River, which is big and wide just like the lake only they call it the river because it used to be much narrower before they built Albeni Falls Dam about twenty miles downstream.

The last summer before Mark died, when he got good enough at riding his bike to where you could actually take him someplace, we used to ride down Division Street to the highway and then take this dirt trail about three-quarters of a mile to this inlet off the river called Chuck's Slough which is by the train tracks and had a little railroad bridge. Mark and I would take a fishing rod and tackle box and a backpack with sandwiches my mother made and a book. We would sit in the long grass by the railroad bridge and fish a little bit, but not much. Every once in a while we'd catch a trout, but usually not. The point was more to just sit there.

I used to sit and read books to him. We read *If I Ran the Zoo* and *Fox in Socks* and *The Children's Book of Bible Stories* and one whole long book even, which was *The Cricket in Times Square* that took about three different trips to Chuck's Slough to read. We spent quite a few days there that last summer before Mark died.

The other thing I remember most about that summer was our

camping trip. Once a year we would take this big camping trip with these friends of my parents' the Gilmans. They had an eighteen-foot ski boat that we would take across the lake to this area on the east shore called the Green Monarchs that didn't have any houses or anything. And no roads, either. You could only get there by boat.

The best thing about this place was this old canoe tied to a tree near the shore. The canoe was just an old wooden thing that was there every year under a tarp and nobody ever stole it and my dad said it had been there since he was a boy and used to come out there with *his* dad. No one actually owned the property so no one knew how the canoe got there. It leaked pretty bad so you could only take it out for a few minutes on the lake, but that was my favorite thing to do—get Mary or my father to paddle around in it with me. The paddles used to give you slivers really bad, but I didn't care. Then the very last year we went there, there was suddenly a brand new aluminum canoe tied to the tree. Somebody had just gone out and bought it and left it there for people to use.

My father had told me this story once when we were camping there about when he was a boy and the old canoe was still in good shape and you could take it out on the water for more than a few minutes at a time. He and his younger brother Jim went around this cove to the west and found an old mine shaft. When they built the dam, the water filled up the tunnel opening and my dad and his brother would just paddle the canoe right into the opening until it bottomed out. Then they would leave it there and take a flashlight back into the cave. My dad said you went a ways in and you came to a place where the tunnel forked in two and you were far enough inside that you couldn't see the light from the entrance anymore, and that was when they would always get scared and turn around.

So with this new canoe I decided I would take Mark with me to the mine shaft. My mother didn't like the idea. She kept saying Mark was too little and I wasn't old enough or responsible enough and didn't know how to paddle a canoe well enough and the cave was around the bend where no one could see us. The Gilmans were trying to talk us out of it, too, because me and Mark were both pretty disappointed, I guess, and they were saying maybe next year. My father didn't usually get involved in these kind of arguments, and actually he was probably more protective toward Mark especially than even my mother was, but I guess what happened was everybody kept talking about "can't do this" and "can't do that" until he finally got offended that everyone would think his boys couldn't do something. So my father said, "Barbara," which is my mother's name, "let 'em go, for God's sakes. Luke can paddle that thing all right and Mark's got more sense than to fall out of a boat. Let 'em go." Then he went down and helped us into the canoe and gave us a push from shore himself. But then when we started drifting away he was watching us really close just standing there on shore, and I could see he was having second thoughts. "Be careful," he said, looking at me. "You're carrying precious cargo." He kind of kicked around at the rocks on shore. "Both of you boys," he said, but I understood he meant Mark and not me.

Besides being really smart, Mark was also what you call a musical prodigy. My grandmother taught him how to play the piano when he was only four, just like she did me and Mary, but by the time he was five he was already getting so good that she said he needed a better teacher, someone who was more a professional and wouldn't let him develop bad habits. So my dad started paying for him to take lessons from this woman who had gone to some expensive music school back East and used to play with a symphony before she got married and moved to Sandpoint, and she said Mark had unlimited potential. Even though my dad was a cop, he used to play the piano a lot when he was younger, and when he found out Mark was a prodigy he was always my dad's favorite after that.

I felt this huge sense of responsibility paddling the canoe around the bend where we'd never been before. Mark was in front of me and he was only six and couldn't help paddle much. It was hot, the middle of July, and Mark kept wanting to trail his hand through the water and I wouldn't let him. I was afraid he *would* fall out of the boat, and he barely knew how to swim. It was very quiet with just the sound of the paddle dipping into the water, and I liked how quiet it was and the little whirlpools the paddle made. The sunlight kept hitting the water like thousands of tiny flash-bulbs and the mountains were big and quiet up ahead of us.

I was paddling close to the shore but still I knew the water was over our heads. Lake Pend Oreille was carved straight down by glaciers thousands and thousands of years ago, and in some places if you walk in just a few feet you're over your head. So when you're out on the lake you have this feeling of being way above some-thing, of water going cold and dark down beneath you further than you can imagine.

I got us around the bend, and just about the time my arms and shoulders started cramping up and making me worry that I couldn't keep us going much longer, there was suddenly the tunnel entrance plain as day. I paddled in and right away everything was louder and cold. The water lapped up against the sides of the tun-nel and echoed. I let the canoe drift in until it scraped on the rocks and you could feel the scrape vibrate through your feet. Me and Mark both had on flip-flop sandals and I told him we should take them off so he did.

What I wasn't ready for was how cold the water would be. When we got out of the boat, it was up to about my ankles, and my feet immediately went numb. Lake Pend Oreille is cold as it is, because it's so deep that even in the summer the water can't get warmed up all that much. But there in the entrance to the mine shaft where the sun never reached the water, it was about twenty degrees colder at least. It actually seemed like it should have been frozen over.

Mark was out of the canoe too, into the water. "Luke, ouch!" he started saying. "Ouch, it's burning my feet."

I flipped on the flashlight and shined it up ahead of Mark, and I could see the water went on for a hundred feet or so it looked like, even if it was really shallow. You could see the shape of the tunnel, too, cut out square and straight and angling down into the ground. "It's not burning your feet, it's freezing them," I told Mark. "Sometimes things are so cold they remind you of hot." I shined the light down into the water. There were little tiny whitish minnows swimming around my feet. "We just have to go a little ways and then it's dry land," I said.

"No," Mark said. "It hurts." He was picking his feet up one after the other, lifting them out of the water. "I don't want to."

The pain in my feet was starting to get to me, too, and I guess I should have just called it quits right there. I should have seen Mark was too little for that kind of adventure. But I was thirteen, and something about how my dad had let me be responsible for the first time and the story about the fork in the tunnel, and how my dad and his brother had gone that far before they got scared and turned back kept making me want to go on.

Even to this day I wish I hadn't. Sometimes still, right while I'm in the middle of my whole other life, I mean far away from Idaho and twenty years older and with my own wife and kid, sometimes I'll be driving down the road or standing in the middle of the frozen food aisle at the grocery store or even listening to a song that makes me feel happy on the radio, and all of a sudden I'll think to myself how I shouldn't have made Mark go back into the cave. Or I'll even think of little things that had to do with the cave, like for instance years later, one night right before one of my football games when we had just gone out on the field and started doing our stretches, it occurred to me that I could have pushed Mark in the canoe up to where the water ended. It was my weight that was making the boat bottom out, not his—he hardly weighed anything—and I could have told him to get back in the boat and then pushed him. From where I was standing on the field I could see out across the black water of the lake, and I started imagining being out on the water again and paddling into that cave, and I wanted so bad to go back there and do it all over again, and when Mark said the water was too cold I'd say, You get back in and I'll push. You get back in, Mark, I'll push.

But what I did instead was I told Mark to come on, and I grabbed his hand and started walking before he could get back in the canoe.

He didn't say no or try to stop me. He was like that, a really agreeable little kid, who always wanted to please me if he could.

The rocks were slippery and what with the flashlight in one hand and holding Mark's hand with the other we both nearly fell down a lot of times. Each time one of us would slip we'd use the other one for balance. My feet were pretty much numb and I was starting to shake all over. Mark stopped and let go of my hand. I shined the flashlight on him. He had his arms wrapped around his chest and he was shaking, too. "Don't do that," he said, and put one hand over his eyes. "I'm froze to death," he said.

I should have stopped, I know, but I was desperate to at least get as far back as where the water ended, and I figured everything would be okay then. We were getting close. So what I did was I picked Mark up and carried him. I still had the flashlight in one hand, and the beam from it was bouncing all over the cave, and I just sort of staggered ahead the last twenty feet or so. I was a fairly tall kid but still I wasn't *that* much bigger than Mark, and the way I was carrying him was holding him in front of me with his head on my shoulder and his legs wrapped around my waist with one of my hands under his butt and the other around his back and still trying to hold onto the flashlight at the same time.

I started losing my balance and tipping forward, so I kind of ran the last few steps to the rocks and then fell over on my knees and elbows with Mark underneath me and the flashlight clattered on the rocks. The beam shined ahead down the tunnel.

I knew Mark had landed hard, and I heard him grunt. I put my hand under his head and rubbed my elbow with the other hand and asked him if he was all right.

He wasn't crying or anything. He just said, "I scraped my bottom." I grabbed the flashlight and shined it where he was pulling down the band of his shorts for me to see. He had a strawberry patch there that would turn into an ugly bruise.

"You okay?" I asked him.

"Yes," he said.

I stood up and shined the flashlight down the tunnel. It just seemed to go down and down, a little steeper than before, but you couldn't see the fork yet. "You ready?" I asked Mark.

He just sat there, picking up rocks and dropping them one by one. "Do we have to?" he asked. He was talking through his teeth.

I sat down again and felt how cold his feet were and started rubbing them. "Don't you want to go see some more of the cave?" I asked him, trying to make it sound exciting. I told him about how Dad and our uncle James used to go back to where there was this fork in the tunnel and then they'd get scared. I asked him didn't he want to go further than Dad did?

"*I'm* scared," he told me, just in this tiny flat voice that sounded like it didn't have any hope in it at all. I guess he knew I would keep on going no matter what. I guess when you're thirteen and out to prove something you don't think about anything or anyone else, and even though Mark was only six, he knew.

I said, "Well, we'll sit here a minute and warm up and I bet you'll feel better." I picked up a rock and threw it out in the water, and you could hear it splash and echo, and the light from the cave mouth made reflections from the water kind of ripple across the cave walls. The light at the cave mouth looked really bright and I have to admit sort of warm and inviting. The tunnel had dropped down enough that you could just barely see the tip of the canoe pointing up from the rocks, like a tooth sticking up in a huge mouth. "You don't have to be scared," I said. "You've got me with you." I shined the light on Mark for just a second. I didn't want him to get mad at me again. He was sitting there looking down at the rocks. His hair was messy and he had a sunburn from the day we'd already been at camp. He looked kind of helpless and worn out.

I talked real quiet then. "You remember Daniel in the lion's den, don't you?" I asked him.

"Yes," he said. I was pointing the light back over the water and looking that direction, but I could tell he still had his head down.

"Daniel wasn't scared, was he?"

"No."

"That's right," I said, "because he had God looking out for him."

I kind of ruffled his hair and he pulled away from me. "The same way I'm looking out for you," I told him. At the time I thought this made him feel better, but it didn't. It only made me feel good.

But he got up from the rocks. "Okay," he said. "I'll try not to be scared."

I wished right away we hadn't taken off our flip-flops. The rocks were sharper than the ones underwater, and you kept landing on them on your arches and it hurt like hell. The tunnel wasn't steep, but we were definitely going down slowly, and I was starting to get nervous that it was taking so long to get to the fork. "Do you know what they call cave explorers?" I asked Mark. He didn't answer. "Spelunkers," I told him, thinking the word would make him laugh but it didn't. He was usually a real talkative kid, and the way he was being so quiet was kind of eerie. I couldn't think of anything to say to get him talking so we just went on in the dark.

Then the flashlight shined on the fork. "We're here," I said. I hurried Mark along. "This is where Dad and Uncle James used to come," I said. I thought about what a long time ago that was, and how the cave was just the same, and it made me feel big again. I remembered what else my father said, and I shined the flashlight back from where we'd come. Just like he said, you couldn't see the cave mouth at all. It was like we were totally closed in.

"Okay," Mark said, and let out a huge breath. "Can we please go back now?"

Up until he said that I had thought just making it to the fork would be fine. But then I knew it wasn't. I shined the light down the two tunnels. The one on the right dipped down much sharper, and I could see that where it went around this bend just a little ways ahead there was more water. But the trail to the left was level and dry. I could see at the end of the flashlight's beam where this one bent around, too. I said, "Look down there," and pointed. "See that bend? Let's just go to that bend and see what's around there."

"No way!" Mark said, with as much force as you could say something when you were six years old. "I'm not going," he said.

It was the first time since we started that he really sounded like he was arguing with me, and I guess that gave me an excuse to get angry at him. "Fine," I said. "You stay here," and I started to walk ahead with the flashlight like I was going to leave him there in the pitch-dark cave. I don't think I would have, but it was pretty goddamn mean.

I was walking ahead with my back to him, and then behind me I heard this voice say, "You're going to leave me here." It wasn't like a question, and it wasn't like he was accusing me of anything. It was just this tiny voice that sounded lost and all alone. He just said it like it was something he knew.

It almost made me change my mind. It made my heart ache to hear him, but instead of dropping the whole idea completely, what I did was go back and grab his hand and pull him along kind of rough, and I said, "Come on, then," even though he hadn't asked me to take him.

It took maybe a couple minutes of stumbling along before we reached the bend, and as we rounded it, there it was, the end of the tunnel. It just ended there in a big pile of rocks. For a second I was incredibly relieved, and I felt big and powerful like I'd done something no one else had in all these years. I'd been to the end of the cave. Then I noticed a flash of metal there in the rocks and I pointed the flashlight—beer cans, Hamm's and Olympia and Budweiser, littered all over the rocks. Suddenly the cave wasn't big enough or dangerous enough and I hadn't done anything important. I just stared at the cans. It was just some place where teenagers came to drink.

Then I heard Mark and flashed the light over toward him. He was sitting down scrunched up against the cave wall with his head in his arms, and I could see his shoulders shaking. I ran over to him as fast as I could. I knelt down next to him. I said his name.

Then he let the crying out. Big sobs that jerked my guts out every time his shoulders heaved. I was thirteen years old, and I thought I was pretty big, I guess, and above any childish kind of things, and I don't know how long it had been since I hugged my brother, or how long it had been since I cried. But I did them both then. I sat there and held my arms around him with the flashlight shining from the cave floor and we both cried. "I'm sorry," I kept saying. "I'm sorry. I didn't know how much it scared you." But I had known. Maybe that's why I was crying.

After a while Mark started telling me, "It's okay, Luke, it's okay," and him saying that made us both calm down a bit. We sat there getting quieter and quieter. Then when it was totally silent, Mark said, "It's a really great cave."

I don't know what was so funny about that, but I started getting the giggles, and after I started Mark of course got started too, and then it was like the echoes of our laughing made it even funnier.

"I'm sorry I made you come all the way back here," I finally managed to tell him.

"It's okay," Mark told me. "It was fun."

He was a great kid, who would say things like that just to make me feel better. He started rubbing the spot on his rear end, and I tried to pull down the band of his shorts to see how bad it was.

"Cut that out," he said, moving my hand away. "I promise it doesn't hurt." He was pretty brave, too. I bet Jake would be the same way.

The walk out was a lot more fun than the walk in. We could see the cave mouth getting bigger and bigger, and how bright the day was out there. I told Mark how we were like Tom Sawyer and Huck Finn, which was a book my third-grade teacher Mrs. Hensley read to us. I told him how they went into a cave and found lots of treasure.

"All we found was some cans," Mark said, but neither of us cared by then.

When we got to the water we ran the whole way through, falling down over and over and soaking our shorts and T-shirts, but it didn't matter because in just a minute we were in the canoe and back into the sunlight, which just about totally blinded us at first.

I was about worn out so I paddled really slow, and the sun felt good and warm. Then right when we got around the bend, we saw Dad. He was in his swimming trunks and half-stumbling through the water along the rocks. He wasn't in the greatest shape, and he looked pretty tired. It was obvious he was heading for the cave.

Mark yelled at him, and he looked up and saw us. The sun was bright so we were all shading our eyes, but by the time I'd paddled over to within talking range, trying hard to make it look like I still had all my strength left, I could see by Dad's face he was pretty angry. I don't know if Mark saw it, but he said the right thing: "Dad," he said, sitting up tall in the canoe, "we went all the way to the back of the cave!"

My father kind of stood there huffing and puffing for a few seconds, his hair all wet and his body pale and flabby, and then a big grin spread over his face. "You're kidding me," he said.

"Nope," Mark said. "We went all the way around the curve to where the cave ends," like it was the most fun he'd ever had in his life.

The canoe drifted into shore, and my father bent over and grabbed onto the edge and turned it parallel to the shore so he was kind of in between the two of us. He stood there looking at me.

"It's true," I said. "He'll tell you the whole story," of course at the same time hoping Mark wouldn't mention several things. But even if he did, it would have been okay, I wouldn't have gotten mad at him for anything. In fact I don't think I ever got mad at him again his whole life.

But instead of right away asking Mark questions, my dad still just stood there looking at me. And we didn't say anything to each other, but for maybe the only time in both of our lives, we looked at each other right square in the eye, man to man, with a kind of respect.

He smiled at me and winked and asked Mark, "So what was it like in there?" Then he motioned for me to get up front with Mark and he climbed in the canoe and took the paddle. He explained how he had just been out for a little swim, but now that we were here he might as well go back to camp with us. I don't think even Mark believed him.

We started gliding over the water fast and smooth. My father was out of shape, but he was a big man with strong arms and shoulders, and he could sure paddle a canoe. Mark sat between my legs in front and he talked and talked like usual now, and I could hear the paddle dip, and every once in a while my father would ask a question, and the mountains and the trees all around and the hot sun made me feel like we were sailing across a cup of tea. Just us guys, the three of us, alone in our own teacup, talking and sailing along. It was a nice idea.

Mark told it all like it was the greatest thing he'd ever done, going down and down in the cave with the flashlight like plunkers, that's what he called it, back and back further and further like Tom Sawyer and Daniel in the lion's den. He didn't say a thing about getting dropped on the rocks, or being scared, or me being mean to him, or crying, or the beer cans. My dad was saying next time he'd like to go with us. By the time we got to camp, the whole thing seemed like the kind of adventure we'd expected it to be.

Me and Mark talked and talked about it all the rest of the afternoon, and that night around the campfire playing cards, and before we went to sleep in the tent while our mother shined the flashlight on us and put Noxzema on our sunburns.

Three weeks later he was killed in my father's patrol car.

Maybe it's how quiet and pretty this place is that's bringing back memories of being in Sandpoint with Mark when I was a kid. There's an oak tree here, a big one that's got plenty of room to spread, and lawn chairs. There's a tire swing hanging from a walnut tree over by the fence that I could teach Jake how to use if he was here, and one of those old seat swings that two people can sit and talk on over close to the pasture.

Jake and Jenny would love this place. It's all laid out in little cabins that are far apart from one another and private. The one I've got, G, is a small one just for one person, but there's bigger ones, too, like D. The office is in these people the Bergstroms' house who run the place. They live upstairs. Everything's painted white, with yellow window shutters. It would make you feel warm even if it wasn't summer.

Inside, my cabin has hardwood floors. There's a big old wooden dresser. The bathroom has black and white tile, and a big bathtub with one of those old circular curtains you pull all the way around for the shower and those legs that look like lion's feet. I have a little bed with an old-fashioned wooden headboard with a flower design carved into it, and a white bedspread with the little raised dots on it like you see in the homes of old people, like Jenny's Aunt Eunice. There's fresh lilies in a blue vase on a table by my bed. An old black rotary telephone that I'm not allowed to call long distance on unless I make a deposit. In my room it smells like clean fresh water in old-fashioned mop strings. I can remember this even right now while I sit outside looking out across the pond where Mrs. Bergstrom says you can hear frogs at night and past the field grown over with tansy and on up to the red barn and the silos on the hill.

On the wall in my room is a painting of this exact scene. It's done in very bright colors on a sunny day just like today. The windows on the barn shine in the sunlight, and when I asked Mrs. Bergstrom when she showed me to my cabin she said the windows of the picture were made with mother-of-pearl inlays.

If I paid the phone deposit I might try to call Jenny at her parents' house. I would say, Come up to Wisconsin. It's pretty here and quiet. If I tried to call Jenny at her parents' house and she was there, I don't know what she'd say. I don't know if she would talk to me at all. I don't know if she's angry or just disgusted or doesn't love me anymore. She would let me talk to Jake. Jake would say he loved me.

But if I tried to call Jenny at her parents' house and she wasn't there I could start all kinds of problems. Her dad might get on the phone and yell at me and tell me how he'd known I was always good for nothing, and I would tell him exactly what I'd always thought of him. That could ruin things. If Jenny wasn't there and she hadn't called her folks yet to tell them anything, then I would have to either think up a lie fast or explain the whole thing. Either way wouldn't be good, and we'd end up having to call the police to say Jenny was missing with my five-year-old son, and I would probably get in trouble some way. If Jenny wasn't there and hadn't told her folks and I had to do it myself, she'd never forgive me for it, for showing to her mom and dad just one more time what a fucked-up mess we'd made of life, which I think is her opinion.

In Great Falls, Montana, when we were living there and I was bartending in this place that was like a lodge-style joint with a big fireplace and big wooden chairs and tables and things like snowshoes and bear traps on the wall and ice stretching out like fingers on the windows during the winter and nothing but white outside, snow blowing and blowing like it always does in Great Falls, there was a guy I worked with whose wife and daughter had left him. His daughter was four, he told me. We were setting up for the day, a Sunday when I worked day shift, and he was laying the lunch menus on the tables and wiping the tables with a wet rag. He said his wife and daughter disappeared last year, he didn't know where. He didn't seem too worried about it. I said had he tried to find her and he said no, his wife was a gnarly bitch. I said didn't he care about his daughter, she was only four years old. He said at least he got to see her grow up a little ways.

What you need is some directions. They should come to you in a big cardboard box, and you should open it and there'd be all those Styrofoam peanuts and when you dug down through them there'd be a little booklet containing all the directions you'd ever need. First, they'd say, check the contents of the box—one wife, one child. Then they'd go from there and tell you how to think and feel and what to do. Insert wife A and son B into slot C. Make sure they are secure.

Tonight I'll go out to the races here at the Dells in my truck and see if I keep winning. And somehow if I do or don't it doesn't seem to matter. I've made enough money already, and if my run ends now it would be greedy to ask for more.

A father, maybe. Maybe that's what everybody needs. Even fathers need fathers, because fathers are sons, too. Anybody can be a father. God, Jesus, a doctor at a mental hospital, a professor in a class. A guy who bets on dog races. A father is anyone with answers to the questions that keep you awake at night. My grandmother was my father for a while. Maybe Jake's got another father now. Maybe Jenny is his father, or Jenny's dad, or one of those guys Jenny knew in high school who would no doubt be hanging around.

Everyone needs someone they can go to and ask. But sometimes the questions get too hard to answer. After Mark died I would wake up sometimes in the middle of the night and hear my father in the kitchen. He would be opening and shutting the cupboards. He talked to himself while he did this. I got out of bed and went quietly across the floor in the dark of my room and pulled open the partition that I had for a door. There above the stairwell I was the only one that could hear. My sister Mary's room was in the basement, and my parents' room and the room that used to be Mark's were on the other end of the house. My dad's voice floated up to my room like a ghost, and the sound of him slamming the refrigerator door. "Nothing to eat," he would say, talking loud like he wanted someone to listen. "Nothing to eat in this house," he would tell someone. I'd hear the cabinet doors open and shut. Then the drawers would open and shut, the knives and forks sliding around. Then finally the cabinet doors under the sink, and the whiskey bottle clinking against a glass. Then the banging and slamming would stop, and I'd hear him pull up a chair at the kitchen table. He told Bible stories. He'd tell the whole story from beginning to end of Jonah in the whale's mouth or Lazarus rising from the dead. I would get sleepier and sleepier crouched there, listening. Then he'd get loud again. "Why'd you have to do that?" he'd ask. "Why'd you have to make it so it was me?" He'd kind of stop and wait for an answer, waiting there a long time, with the kitchen lights shining. "Why did you *do* that?" he'd say, his voice beginning to flutter. "Why don't you *talk* to me?"

JUNE 16

So apparently it doesn't matter which track, either. Last night I won $647.50. After a while, you start to ask why. The thing is I always knew I had a good system and that it should start to pay off someday. I guess that's what always kept me going when Jenny said to quit. I felt like I should have been winning enough money to keep going and not have to go back to the same old dead routine of serving people drinks and smiling all the time and putting up with crap from owners and managers. With dog racing I could be my own boss, and I didn't understand why it always had to end.

I went out to a bar after the races last night, one of the tourist places downtown by where they do the boat tours for the Wisconsin Dells. I got the idea to go out while I was counting my money in the truck. I was out there in the parking lot going through my whole wad of dough, and I actually had this moment when I finished counting where I went, "Hmm, $647.50, a so-so night." As soon as the thought went through my head I realized how ridiculous it was. I mean, before last week, six-hundred-fifty-odd bucks would be the best night I ever had.

When I realized how I was so nonchalant about this you might say, I kind of sat back and stared out the windshield. Since I always get the hell out of the track real quick after the last race if I don't have money to collect—the last race was one of the few races I didn't win money on last night—all the other people were just getting to the parking lot. There was this one family that I sort of liked. There was a wife and this husband with the usual khaki shorts and one of those striped button-down shirts that pretty much yell out the fact that you're on vacation, and two little kids, a boy and a girl, who kept jumping around. The wife, who was kind of attractive in a maternal sort of way—like not really sexy but just nice, you could see—kept saying to her husband, "How did you *know* that, Larry? You must be *clairvoyant!*" She said it about three times. And Larry, who was like really proud of himself but trying to be modest, too, said, "I don't know, I just had a feeling," walking along with his hands in his pockets and a shit-eating grin. The little girl was doing this cheerleader thing with little jumps and leg kicks. The boy kept hollering, "I want *pizza!* I want *pizza!*"

Then this girl walked by the truck that I'd actually talked to at the track earlier. She was with her father, who apparently is an owner of some dogs that race at the track from what she told me. Her name was Sarah, I think. You get to be as old as I am, and where you've been so many places, that you get to the point where you don't pay much attention to names. I can remember the *people,* but their names just seem like unimportant attachments. Most of the time anymore I don't even *hear* people's names when they introduce themselves. I say, "Hi, I'm Luke Rivers," and they say, "Hi, I'm Mumble-mumble." That's what I hear.

Anyway, it was after I'd won another hundred bucks or so on a quinella that I struck up a conversation with her, or she struck up one with me. I'd come back from the window to collect, and her dad was standing down at the rail talking to these two old guys. So I noticed when I sat down that this girl I'm calling Sarah was all alone about ten feet down the bench from me. I don't know if she was what you'd call stunningly pretty, but she probably could be called that, at least she looked that way to me. She had straight blonde hair that was parted in the middle and tucked behind her ears like Jenny's is now, where they have to keep putting loose strands behind there all the time. She had brown eyes like Jenny, too, only smaller and much darker, almost black, and a very cute nose that was turned up just a little at the end and a nice, even mouth with kind of thin lips and straight teeth. She definitely had a great figure also, and she wasn't shy about advertising. She was wearing a black halter top with no bra and if she leaned a little bit forward you could see the white line where her breast started that can drive you crazy if you let it. But I have in the years since I've known Jenny become pretty good at not letting myself form mental pictures, you might say. Her arms were tan and soft and round, not skinny and not plump, just nice and medium. She was wearing Levi's 501s that fit her perfect and they had a hole in one knee, and even her knee looked good. The best part was she was wearing those old flip-flop sandals that cost about a dime, the kind everybody used to wear when I was a kid like me and Mark had in the cave, and her feet looked great in them, like they had invented the things thirty years or so ago with the specific idea that she would come along some day and wear them on her feet.

I was just sitting there looking at my program, although I was definitely aware that she was all alone and sitting fairly close to me, when all of a sudden I glanced over at her and she was looking at me and smiling. She had a nice smile, too. "You're really raking it in, aren't you?" she said to me.

That took me by surprise. I was shocked that she knew this about me. Right at that first moment, my heart kind of jumped in my chest because I guess the whole weirdness of what's been happening seemed like it had come to the surface somehow. It was like I thought for a second she was this messenger sent from the Greyhound God himself who had come to say this to me and then explain things.

I must have looked very shocked and confused on the outside, too, because she laughed and said, "You've gone up to collect after almost every race."

So naturally there was a logical explanation I just hadn't seen. I have to admit I was a little disappointed. I kind of smiled and turned my eyes out to the track where they'd started the dogs walking, and said, "Not a bad night." Then I looked back at her.

"How much?" she asked, meaning how much money had I won, and tucked her hair behind her ear. She was leaning forward just a little, but I made sure not to notice.

"I'm not really keeping track," I said, which would have been a total lie before but now I was telling the truth.

She laughed again and glanced toward her father at the rail. "You just win like this all the time," she said, not like a question but more where you say something straight out only mean it sarcastic, or just teasing in a nice way.

I said, "Lately," answering her the same way back.

We were flirting, basically. I suddenly became aware of that and started thinking all kinds of things that you can't have going on in your head and still hope to carry on a conversation. First I felt guilty. Then I thought about how I looked. I started recognizing what kind of guy *she* was flirting with and I wondered what the hell for—my hair getting all scraggly and how I haven't shaved since the day I first decided to leave Rapid City, and a faded blue T-shirt with a grease stain right near the left armpit where it looks like sweat, and jeans that hadn't been washed in so long that they were dirty around the pockets where I take my hands in and out.

All of this added up to really throw me off balance, and there was a definite awkward pause, and then I said something really stupid, which was, "Do you come out to the races a lot?"

She went ahead and explained to me about how she came out sometimes with her dad because he owned dogs, and how she was trying to spend time with him during the summer while she was home from the University of Wisconsin because her mother had died last winter.

I told her I was sorry about her mother, and I mentioned that my dad had died a few years ago but I didn't say anything about Mark because that doesn't seem like quite the same thing. She said she was sorry about my dad, too, and that pretty much ended the discussion. I think things worked out a little better at the bar later on. It turned out I even played pool with her boyfriend.

Somehow after I sat there watching the people in the parking lot after the race, and then the parking lot was mostly empty and Sarah and her dad had left without even noticing me, it made me kind of lonely and made me want to just be around people some more for a while. So I chose this bar to go to on the tourist strip by where they do the boat tours of the Dells. The Dells is a nice place that most people have never been to or heard about, except if you're from the Midwest, that's a really good example of how to basically ruin a good thing by running it into the ground. The whole idea behind it is that they have this really pretty river with unusual rock formations, and sometime a long way back some guy got the idea of giving boat tours and people started coming to see. But then they started putting in amusement parks and water slides and wax museums, and the next thing you know the place looks like Las Vegas, all lit up from end to end with flashing lights and neon signs. They've got about fifteen go-cart tracks and water-slide parks made up to look like Mount Everest and roller coasters with big statues of Greek guys and even a big huge Trojan horse whose job is to stand there by the side of the road and look as silly as possible. The whole place is crowded with people from Illinois or Minnesota or Michigan who come here in the summer to throw their money away. We never would have come here at all except for the fact that Jake gets a kick out of it, and they have a really good dog track.

If you take a boat tour, which we did one time with Jake after we'd won some money the night before, you go in this kind of god-awful ferry-like thing with a red, white, and blue canopy up the river. The river's very narrow and winds around a lot and the scenery is pretty and also very unusual. There's these cliffs all along the shore that are layered like some artist cut them carefully out of clay in patterns that look like leaves stacked one on top of another and balancing there, and all along the trees hang over the riverbank, and if you take the tour right about sunset, like we did, the water looks almost dark red. It was the only time we ever took Jake on a boat, and it made me pretty nervous. I kept being afraid that Jake was going to fall overboard, even though the rail came up to his shoulders. I stood there behind him holding onto his shirt. Jenny said, "He's okay, Luke. He's four years old," which he was at the time. "He knows how to stand on his feet." But Jenny doesn't know some things. I kept picturing him leaning out and falling over into the water that looked thick and the dark color of blood and disappearing underneath there.

But on the main drag in town there's lots of little bars. I chose this place that looked like the liveliest one called The Bend. As a bar, it didn't have much character—just a regular sports-type bar like you could find in any town anywhere. Of course they had Green Bay Packers pennants and University of Wisconsin stuff all over the walls, but the only thing really unusual or interesting was an old piano up close to the front entrance with a bunch of old sheet music tacked up on the wall behind it, and which nobody ever played as far as I could see. They had the Braves game on TV, and I sat and watched it and talked to some old farmer about the weather. Everything's about farming around here, especially the weather. Once you get out of downtown, it's all bright cornfields and horses and cows and white fences and more red barns than you can believe. Like their license plate says, *America's Dairyland*.

Pretty soon I got bored with the weather and said to the old guy nice talking with you, and then I went and put up quarters on one of the pool tables. There were these three guys who looked like frat boys playing cutthroat. One had a T-shirt with Greek letters on it, and another one had a Wisconsin Badgers T-shirt with a Rose Bowl insignia, and the last one was wearing a UW hat. The guy in the hat was obviously the best pool player, and when they got done with the game the other two went to a table and left him to deal with me. And he turned out to be this Sarah's boyfriend, but I didn't know that yet.

I ordered us both a beer and he looked at me sort of surprised and trying to figure out what I was up to, or what sort of guy I was or whatever, and I racked. I told him my name was Luke Rivers and he said he was Buddy, which I can actually remember now because it was an unusual name.

Next to betting on dogs, what I'm best at is playing pool. To be a good bar player like I am, the kind of guy who can beat maybe nine out of ten guys who shoot at bars and think they're pretty good, you basically just have to understand that most pool players, that aren't pros or anything, beat themselves. They do this in five ways: One, they don't really understand angles and banks. Two, they don't keep their cue perfectly straight. Three, they don't know the difference between hard shots and easy shots. Four, they forget about the leave or don't know how to give themselves good leaves. Five, they don't concentrate. Master those five things and you'll beat almost anyone at any bar across America.

But this Buddy kid played a good break and dropped a solid and then four more in a row, which had me worried. Even though I knew I was better than him, that's a pretty big hole to crawl out of. What was even worse, when he missed he got totally lucky and left the cue ball somewhat behind the 8 down on the rail, and I barely had a shot even. But I made a pretty tough bank on the 12 ball to the side, and I ran off three more pretty easy then. Two of my balls were jammed up against each other on the rail, though, and I could see I wasn't going to have a chance to bust them up so I started doing what I would normally do in a situation like that, which is start asking the guy I'm playing questions about himself. I asked him was he from around here and he said yeah, his dad owned a dairy farm close by, one of the few in the area that was still making money. I asked him did he go to the University of Wisconsin and he said he just graduated and he was taking a year off before he went to law school to help his father modernize some stuff on his farm—"get out of the nineteenth century" is what he called it. Then right when I was getting ready to make my last shot before I would have to waste a shot breaking my two balls off the rail, I asked what was his major and he said, "Philosophy."

That got my attention, of course. I wanted right away to tell him I took a philosophy class once, but I was afraid he might start asking questions about *me* then and he wouldn't pay much attention to my answers and therefore might actually concentrate totally on his own shots and make them, which I didn't want him to do. That was why I was asking him questions about himself in the first place, as well as the fact that I was pretty desperate for a little conversation. It worked out great, though, because right when I broke up my balls on the rail, leaving them real carefully down on the same end as the 8, I asked him who were his favorite philosophers.

He said, "Well, I don't know if you'd call them *favorites.*"

I asked what did he mean, and right then he took his shot, and to my surprise actually made a tough bank and left himself set up for his next one, although he was still going to have a hard time with the 8 down on the other end. He said, "Well, you don't have favorite philosophers the same way you would, say, *movie* stars," like in this vaguely condescending voice. He made his next shot and only had the 8 left, so even though he had a lot of green to work against I had to get him off track the best I could and fast.

I said, "What about Plato?," who was the guy I remembered best.

He sort of snickered, but it worked. I could see he was thinking of his answer and not the shot as much as he should have been. "I *sympathize* with Plato," he said, "but he was pretty *pathetic,* really."

He was starting to irritate me with the way he said words like that, like *symp*athize and pa*thetic*, as if he had to draw your attention to exactly the way he meant them or you might not fully understand what he was saying. I said, "Really? How's that?" and he paused and lined up his shot but his mind was only half on it and he missed. But the 8 came back to his end, which meant I still had my work cut out for me. "Shit," he said.

I lined up my first shot and laid the 9 in the corner real gentle. But I was listening to what he said, too. He said Plato's trouble was that he was essentially searching for perfection in a world where it didn't exist, and I made my other ball and then stopped to listen to him before I tried the 8, because it was going to be a hard shot and I had to totally concentrate.

I asked him did he mean that whole World of Forms idea, and he looked sort of surprised for a second, and said, "Right, *exactly,*" and then I could see he had a little higher opinion of me than before although maybe not that much. But you see, that's what a little education will do for you, like I mentioned about keeping up with current events also and that sort of thing.

I kind of nodded and then I studied my shot for a few seconds and I saw it clear and knew it could be done. I called 8 ball in the corner and pointed with my cue.

"You're cutting that?" he said.

"Gonna try," I said.

"No fucking way," he told me.

The cue ball was close to the side rail, I'd left myself long and the 8 ball was pretty close to the back rail, so what I had to do was just brush it on the side but still hit it hard enough that it would turn over two or three times to reach the corner pocket, which meant that the cue ball was going to come off the back rail pretty hard and there was a definite chance of scratching in the opposite corner on the other end. But it looked to me like it was going to hit the side rail instead, and the back, and then end up more or less in the middle of the table, although I was hoping I wouldn't have to hit it hard enough to bring the side pocket where I was shooting from into play. At any rate, going back to my five points of pool playing, it was an angle that most people don't think you can make, and after you do they always ask you what kind of English did you put on it, even though there's no English involved. It's just math, geometry like in high school. Triangles. You can see the shape right there on the table if you're looking.

I slid the cue back and forth to the ball a couple of times real careful and making sure it was absolutely straight, then I let the cue go straight on through the ball, and I could feel it was perfect whether Plato was right or not, and the cue ball kissed the 8 and came off the back rail wide enough that I didn't even have to look to know I'd been right, and the 8 ball rolled real pretty once, twice, and then plunked down into the pocket. I didn't even look for the cue ball. There wasn't any sound from it and I could feel it right there in the middle of the table. I rested the cue on the floor and grabbed the chalk.

"Jesus," he said. "Nice shot. I didn't think that had a chance in hell," which I already knew. Then—and this is something that makes me think this Buddy is an interesting guy in a lot of ways— he said something that a real good pool player would never say to another guy that just beat him, but which shows how he, Buddy, is still an all right kid even if he did grow up with money because his dad has a farm. "Where'd you learn to shoot like that?" he asked me.

What that amounts to really is admitting that the other guy is better than you are, which you never want to do. If you play a guy and after one or two games—I can usually tell after just one—you realize that the other guy is better, you shouldn't say anything at all. The other guy knows it, too, that he's better, believe me, but if you don't show any expression at all, like if you just act totally unimpressed and keep racking the balls and playing the game, you might put just the tiniest doubt in his mind. And then, I don't know if I can explain this right, but if he starts playing from inside that doubt, like he becomes aware of his own tiny doubt and starts thinking about that when he's taking his shots, then he might start making mistakes.

Back in Great Falls there was this guy named Link who hung out in this bar I worked at called The Saddle. If we ever had another kid, me and Jenny, and it was a boy, I might think about mentioning that name to her—Link. It has a nice sound and a nice idea behind it. Anyway Link was the best pool player in The Saddle when I went to work there, but when I would play him, after I got off work sometimes, even though he beat me probably nine out of ten times on average, I would never tell him how great he was or act like he was better than me. I just kept racking 'em up. Pretty soon it got to be four out of five maybe, then three out of five, and I could see him struggling with his shots, even the easy ones he could make in his sleep. After about two months or so *I* was the best pool player in The Saddle, not because I was actually better than Link, but because Link couldn't beat *me*. I got to where I beat that guy every time we played. And I was kind of proud of that actually, how I'd become the best pool player there just because I did it with my mind, like my mind was stronger than his. With a guy like me who's had the problems I've had, it's very important to feel your mind is whole and strong. And sometimes I think, when I kind of review a lot of events that happened in my life over in my head, like what happened to Mark and then my dad after Mark was dead and then my time in Orofino, that these events helped and prepared my mind for things, for situations that were bound to come. And sometimes with Jake especially I feel like I'm still preparing for these things, for dangers and opportunities.

But this Buddy won't ever beat me at pool. He had the best chance he'll ever get against me last night and he didn't win, so for him it was okay to ask that question and actually showed that he's a more modest guy than you would think, that's not hung up on being the best at everything and particularly better at stuff than guys like me who don't have money like he does. Although I guess I do have some money now, which I keep forgetting, but not a vast fortune or anything.

So anyway when he asked me that question, I said, "Places like this one, pretty much."

He shook my hand and split to go over to the table with his friends. I don't think he even paid attention when I said maybe sometime I'd give him some pointers. I gave up the table to these guys who wanted to play partners and went back to the bar for a while, and here's where it got really interesting. The Braves game was over with, and I didn't have anyone to talk to, and I was getting bored again and ready to go home, and also pretty drunk by then. I decided to order one last draft beer, and then I went to the john.

When I came back out and started up the little staircase to the bar level I saw right away this Sarah, or the one who I think is named Sarah, sitting on a barstool about three stools down from mine all alone reading a book and drinking a beer. Right away this threw me into what you'd call a very awkward position. The ending to our conversation out at the track wasn't exactly a rousing success in my mind, and what I was afraid of was that she hadn't seen my beer sitting there a couple seats away from her. If she hadn't, then if I went up and sat down she might look up from her book and all of a sudden see me sitting there and think that I came to sit by her on purpose. So this was embarrassing for me, but I couldn't see any way out of the situation other than leave my beer there on the bar and just go home. But then what if by chance she *had* actually seen me, for instance on my way to the john, and then saw me walk out. I would look like an idiot, like one of those drunks that forgets they ordered a beer and staggers out in the street without drinking it. I wasn't anywhere near the staggering stage, but still.

What I ended up doing was going over to play the jukebox. I figured that was a way to stall, and I could keep my eye on her to see if she glanced over and saw a full beer sitting there on the bar and my pack of cigarettes.

There was some pretty good stuff on the jukebox, classic rock and oldies, which is mostly what we listen to when we're on the road. Then I found a Johnny Cash CD, one with a lot of old stuff you don't run across too often, stuff my mom used to listen to, and so I chose "Big River" which I hadn't heard in forever. Then I stopped on *More of the Best of the Greatest of the Beach Boys,* or something of that type, and I started to push "Catch a Wave," but before I knew it I had hit "God Only Knows" instead, and then I turned around and headed for the bar because I guess you only get two selections for a dollar nowadays.

On my way to the bar she kind of glanced my way, and I realized right then that the reason I'd played "God Only Knows" instead of "Catch a Wave" was that it was a romantic song, and that if me and this Sarah were to strike up another conversation that song might come on in the middle of it, and she would know I'd played it, and it would be a nice, pretty, simple love song that would go good in the background while we were talking. And I have no idea what to say about that.

Then I sat down and of course she paid no attention to me whatsoever. I was sort of relieved at that. It was like I'd been dreading having to talk to her in a way. She was a very pretty girl, but I doubt at all on the same wavelength as me, what with everything I've been through.

But now that I could see this Sarah either didn't recognize me or wasn't interested in talking to me it helped me relax and put me in a position to I guess you'd say just observe what she was doing. Of course I tried not to be too obvious about it. She was drinking a Heineken and reading a book. She'd put on a blue flannel shirt over the halter top so there wasn't the distraction due to her figure like out at the track. Her hair kept getting in her eyes, and finally she did this thing that I thought was wonderful and graceful the way that women sometimes are. She reached in her purse which was on the bar without looking and pulled out this hair-band thing and kind of twisted it around the fingers on her right hand. Then she used that same hand to hold the book down flat on the bar and with her left hand she grabbed her beer mug and balanced it on the top edge of the book to keep the page open. She pulled her hair back with her left hand, gathering up all the strands with a little help from the hand that had the hair-tie thing around it, and in about two seconds twisted it all up with the hair thing in her right and made a perfect ponytail. Then she put her left hand on the book, picked up the beer mug with her right, took a drink, and set the mug back on the bar. She picked the book up in her left hand and held it out in front of her and put her other hand in between her knees, which were crossed with one leg swaying real slow back and forth in tiny circles with her sandal hanging off her foot. And the whole time she was doing this she never once stopped reading her book. It was one of the prettiest things I've ever seen a girl do, for some reason.

While I was watching her do this I was taking a cigarette out of my pack to have a smoke. I'd gotten interested in her book because it obviously must have been very fascinating to her. She was sitting on my left, so I couldn't see the front cover, but if I bent a little over the bar I could kind of see the back. I couldn't read the name, but the book cover was plain black with lots of white words, and a couple of those quote things at the bottom that they put on books to let you know how important somebody said they were. It wasn't a Harlequin romance, in other words. I was definitely interested in what this had to say about her personality, and I was staring at the book trying to figure it all out and at the same time lighting my cigarette with my lighter.

Then I heard somebody laughing, and I couldn't figure out who because there was this horrible loud music filling up the air, something that sounded like garbage can lids crashing together. But then I realized it was her. I looked up real quick at her face and she was staring right at me.

"You lit the wrong end," she said. As soon as she said it I tasted the tobacco on my tongue and smelled that chemical smell of burning filter. I looked right in front of my face, and there was a little orange-blue flame shooting up there.

"Shit," I said, and snubbed out the cigarette in my ashtray. "Sorry," I said, for no apparent reason.

"It's okay with *me*," she said, and laughed a little again and turned her eyes back to her book. But then she looked right back up at me and said, "Oh, right, you're the one from out at the races who wins lots of money all the time." She smiled at me in that teasing way again. "You can afford to smoke your cigarettes backwards."

There was something phony about the way she did it, I'm fairly sure of that—the way she looked at her book and then right back up at me like she'd just remembered something. It didn't look like she'd just remembered something, in other words, but like she was consciously trying to make it look like she'd just remembered something, only she couldn't quite pull it off naturally, the way she had with the hair band for instance. I'm fairly sure of that one thing. She already knew who I was before she said so.

The first guitar notes of "Big River" came over the speakers. I wondered if she knew Johnny Cash and what she thought of him.

I asked her. "Do you like Johnny Cash?"

"Mm-hmm," she said. "Is this him?"

She kind of blew it there, but I'll give her some credit in that it's not one of the songs you ever hear by him on the radio. But still, how can you not recognize Johnny Cash. "I mean, of course," she said, and kind of rolled her eyes and went back to smiling the same way she always seemed to.

Then I got a little stuck. "I'm Luke Rivers," I said, and held out my hand to shake. It wasn't too bad, but still a little awkward. It sounded too formal, like I was trying to sound kind of suave and sophisticated. I really wasn't, I mean considering my overall what you'd call dilapidated state it would have been impossible anyway, but I really wasn't trying to sound that way.

She held out her hand real pretty and took mine for a second and said, "Nice to meet you, Luke. I'm mumble-mumble."

I swear. That's exactly what I heard. It sounds impossible, I know, but I was surprised at how friendly she was being and the touch of her hand, and I forgot to listen, simple as that. It's only now, today, that I think I hear "Sarah," but I'm not sure.

What was also throwing me off was that I could see Buddy making his way straight toward us, not angry exactly but with something on his mind, no doubt about it. He came up and put his hands on both her shoulders from behind, and he was looking at me the whole time. She was kind of startled and leaned forward real quick, but then she turned around and saw who it was and leaned back, and he gave her a hug.

"You taking care of yourself?" he asked her, and I'm not positive but I think he shot another look my way.

"*Buddy,*" she said, like she was exasperated. "I'm reading a book."

He reached over her shoulder and looked at the cover, not because he was curious or anything but just because it was kind of the right thing to do at the time. But then it was interesting because you could see he didn't care about the book at first, but then when he saw what it was he got interested and looked at it longer than he meant to. He was just a guy who liked books, even when he didn't mean to.

"Why don't you come over to the table?" he said.

She looked over where he'd been sitting and sighed. You could tell she didn't want to go over there with his friends. "I think I might go home," she said.

He told her to come sit at the table a minute and then they could all go over to his apartment for a while. So she went. That was the end of it. They both smiled at me before they walked off, although Buddy's smile was kind of half grimace.

"God Only Knows" came on, and right at first I regretted that Sarah wasn't sitting there next to me and I could talk to her some more, but then I forgot all about her and started thinking of this one time a long time ago when Jenny and I were first engaged. She and her parents took me out to this place called Eason's Catfish House where all the First Baptist Church people got together every Sunday night for "All You Can Eat" fried catfish and black-eyed peas and hush puppies, and Jenny got up to go to the bathroom and there I was, a long-haired guy from up North sitting there with Mr. and Mrs. Beamon and the rest of the church people and everybody quiet and uncomfortable and sneaking peeks at me like I was an alien or a movie star. And then when I just about couldn't take it anymore, out came Jenny from the bathroom in her blue dress and her hair done up, and she smiled at me and everything was fine.

For just a second, sitting there all alone at the bar, I decided that maybe if I could win all this money at the track whenever I wanted to I could maybe do other things with my mind, too. So I thought to myself that I would close my eyes for the rest of the song, and when I opened them Jenny would have come out of the bathroom there in Wisconsin and she'd be sitting next to me. The song was pretty, sitting there listening to it with my eyes closed and imagining Jenny, and then it was over and I looked up and standing right there in front of me was the bartender, checking to see if I'd fallen asleep on my stool. I put a couple bucks tip on the bar and hit the road.

When I drove the truck home to the cabins there was no one else out driving and a little fog slinked along the road and the tall trees came toward me fast and smooth like they were running from the moon, that hung there like a streetlamp right in front of me.

JUNE 17

One week since Jenny left. Mississippi's on central time, just like here, so that means it's 1:00 P.M. there too, Jake's lunch time. It's hotter there I'm sure, although Wisconsin's in the middle of a heat wave. Yesterday was ninety-four, one degree off the all-time high for June 16th.

Right now Jenny's in her mom and dad's kitchen making Jake peanut butter and crackers. Kids are funny. Jake, for instance, won't eat bread. I even forced some into his mouth once to show him it wasn't so bad, but when I did he gagged and nearly threw up.

He'll eat hamburger buns, for God's sake, but not bread. So we even sometimes buy hamburger buns and make him peanut butter and jelly hamburgers, that's what he calls them. You can't call it a sandwich and you can't put it on bread. These things stay the same whether it's in Mississippi or Wisconsin or wherever. I can still know what he's up to.

I'll bet Jenny's dad is outside pushing Jake on the swing. The last time we went back down there for a visit, which was a couple of years ago, Mr. Beamon kept insisting on dragging Jake down to the schoolyard to swing every day. "Just me and my grandson," he'd say. I didn't mind that, except I wondered a lot if he was trying to tell Jake bad things about me or get Jake to tell him things that he thought were bad about me, that Mr. Beamon would think were bad I mean. But there was also something else I worried about, and that's also what worries me now, which is whether Jenny's dad is pushing Jake too high on the swing.

If you've ever been to a park and pushed your kid on a swing, then maybe you know what I mean. What these guys do—and it's always men, because women are way too reasonable for that kind of thing—is they get their kids on the swing and start pushing them, and then they get to talking to some other guy there with his own kid, and pretty soon they each start bragging about how great their kid is, and before you know it they're like involved in this competition to see whose kid can go higher. They don't *say* so, of course, but you can see it happening right in front of you. One kid's going a little higher, and the father of the other kid notices this and starts pushing his own kid a little harder, and the other father notices this and starts pushing *his* kid just a little harder, and so on and so on till the kids are whizzing through the air like cannonballs while their dads talk about how many goals they scored in their last peewee soccer game.

One time in Great Falls I had Jake down at the park swinging and there was this other dad there with his kid, on his lunch break it turned out. He looked like he was probably a construction foreman or something, or maybe a contractor—one of these guys that wears jeans and boots so that the manual laborers will still think he's a regular guy but who always makes sure everything he's wearing is new and he keeps his shirt tucked in and shaves every day and never gets dirty so that other people will know he's one of the bosses and not one of the workers. He even had a cell phone on his hip, in fact, and I suppose because of that I was a little biased against him already. Just like ties, I have what you'd call a severe dislike for cell phones.

Anyway, I'm down there with Jake just swinging along real peaceful and easy, and here comes this foreman guy and sticks his kid in the swing right next to Jake, kind of tosses him in there like a log almost and the kid looks to be about three.

Right away he starts shoving the kid so hard that it looks like he's trying to send him to Jupiter, and he's saying, "There you go, Ronnie boy, there you go," and little Ronnie's hanging onto the chains so tight you'd have had to break his fingers to get him loose.

Everything had been just great up to then, it was a nice spring day, for Great Falls at least, the wind not blowing too hard and the mud not up to your knees, but I noticed Jake right away started looking at Ronnie and wishing he could go as high as that himself.

I could tell in just a minute he was going to start saying, "Push me higher, Papa," and it made me hate this Ronnie kid's father even more.

There he is pushing his kid higher and higher like a lunatic, and I can see Jake is straining to get his swing to go higher and just about ready to ask me, and then this Ronnie kid's dad whips out his little phone and punches some numbers real quick, and then starts arguing with somebody on the phone, saying something like, "Well send *another* truck over there, for Jesus Christ's sake! They want trucks, trucks make 'em feel better, then send a whole goddamn *fleet* over there, I don't give a shit, so *what* if there's nothing for 'em to do, I'll take their fucking money, they want trucks, give 'em *trucks,* for fucking shit's sake," going on and on like that, cussing a blue streak, and the whole time pushing his kid Ronnie higher and higher the angrier he gets. Jake's starting to say, "Papa,

Papa!" and I know what he wants, to go higher like Ronnie, and finally I can't take it anymore and I shout out, "You're pushing him way too high!" and stare right over at the guy. "You're gonna kill your *kid,* you dumbass!"

He looks over at me for a second. "Excuse me," he says, "I gotta go," real polite all of a sudden into the phone.

Then he put his cell phone back on his hip with one hand and with the other hand grabbed the chain on the swing when it came back and almost sent his kid flying out into space, and got dragged along a few feet himself and fell on his ass under the swing, so that his tough guy thing didn't come off quite like he wanted it to. I knew that was going to make him even madder, so I real carefully got hold of Jake and the swing when they came back the next time, and Jake said, "What are you doing? I want to *swing.*" But he saw pretty quick what was up when old Ronnie's dad had got up and brushed himself off.

He came at me like one of those little terriers that's not afraid of anything because you're on one side of the fence and they're on the other, only there wasn't any fence and he was a lot bigger than a terrier, more like a German shepherd. "What did you say?" he said to me, his face all twisted up and his hands clenched already.

This guy was not quite my height, but a lot sturdier, and looked like he was probably in a lot better shape, like he was a jogger or a weight lifter or something, and I was scared plenty. But there are some moments in your life where you can't back down, I guess, and this was one. I had Jake standing right there next to me. In fact, he was actually trying to get right in between me and the guy, like he did sometimes when Jenny and I would argue. I held him back real gently with my hand and looked at him and said, "It's okay."

What I was hoping, I kind of hate to admit it, is that the guy would maybe recognize what sort of situation he was in, with the kids there and all, but when I looked him in the eye all I saw there was this totally violent rage.

"I said you were pushing your kid too high in the swing," I told him as plain as I could. "It's dangerous."

The guy shoved me then, and I fell back into Jake and had to keep my balance and hold Jake up at the same time.

"Hey!" this woman shouted that was over with a couple of other moms and their kids at the merry-go-round. "This is the *park*," she said. "This is a *kid's park*, for crying out loud." Everyone in the whole joint was stopped with what they were doing, watching us.

I shouted over to her that maybe this guy didn't understand that so well, but everything was going to be all right.

That only pissed him off more. He got right in my face, and said, or growled more like, "Don't you fucking try to embarrass me, you piece of shit. You've got no right telling me what to do with my own goddamn kid," etcetera, etcetera, going on that way, cussing up a storm.

I don't know what happened to me then. A lot of stuff was going through my head. Number one, I'm sure, was that I had Jake right there beside me, kind of peeking around my leg, and I couldn't stand to look bad, and I also couldn't stand to think what would happen if this guy like knocked me out cold and I had to go to the hospital or something. Would Jake know to stay put and wait for the police and not run off and get lost? Would he know how to tell the police to get him home? And then somehow I was also thinking about how I was a starter on the football team when I was a senior, even if it was just at split end where I was getting hit a lot more than I was doing the hitting, but I knew I'd been hit harder on the football field than this guy could ever hit me. And then somewhere else in my head I was also thinking this—that I didn't want anything in the world more than I wanted to knock that guy's head clean off his shoulders, and then maybe stomp on it while it was lying on the ground. I could just about picture it. I hadn't ever been so angry in my life as I was right then all of a sudden, not even when I used to punch the walls, which was more of a sad feeling than angry, and not even after Mark was dead, which wasn't like being angry suddenly but having it build up over a long stretch of time in a small way that kept growing, like molecules sticking together.

What I did was, right while this guy was in the middle of his cussing, I kind of leaned into him and got my face about an inch from his, where I practically could have kissed him, and I absolutely fucking *yelled,* "If you say one more cuss word in front of these kids I'm going to *beat . . . your . . . ass!*" I can't even begin to describe how good that felt.

And the guy backed up—just for a second, and that's all it took. When he stepped back, I stepped forward. "Do you hear me?" I shouted right into his face again, which I admit was a stupid question.

He backed up again and this time I let him. I could see him sizing me up, my long hair and scraggly flannel shirt and all which he'd obviously noticed before, but also now how I was kind of long and lanky and athletically built enough, and *really really* angry besides, and he just kept on backing away.

"I'm on my lunch break," he said finally, looking at me and then around at the moms and the kids. "You're lucky," he said, pulling Ronnie along by the arm.

"Oh, shut up!" this one woman called out to him from over at the merry-go-round.

But the guy just kept looking at me. "Go back home to your trailer," he said. "Don't forget to cash your welfare check on the way." Then he went to his truck and got his kid in and got in himself and drove off, burning rubber when he hit the road. Me and Jake were just left standing there, holding hands by the swings. It was really quiet.

Then this woman, the same one that had been doing all the talking, called out, "Good for you!" looking over at me. "Good for you."

Then Jake picked up on it, the way kids lots of times just do what adults do. "Good for you, Papa," he said. "Good for you," still holding my hand.

I started to cry. I put my hand over my eyes and my shoulders heaved, and then the tears started coming out.

Jake pulled on my sleeve and wanted to know what was wrong,

and I was having a hard time saying anything. And then right away here comes that same lady to rescue me. She sat me down on one of the swings and sat down herself in another and played and talked with Jake and at the same time told me this story about the hard times she and her husband had when they were young and he was an apprentice plumber and she was a maid and they couldn't make ends meet. I told her I had a job, I wasn't on welfare, even though it was true we did get food stamps and Jake was on Medicare or whatever it's called, which were things Jenny used to take care of getting us all the time and I never even had the guts to use the food stamps at the store. I mean I didn't tell her that last part, but just the part about working, and she said, "I know, I know. You're a good father, I can see." She was a middle-age lady wearing an ugly pink shirt, kind of fat, and I liked her about as much as anybody I ever met.

Anyway, last time we were in Mississippi, Jenny's dad said he was going to put up a swing set in the backyard, so he's probably pushing Jake in it right now. I hope Jenny knows not to let him push Jake too high in the swing.

I ended up not going to the track last night. I did some laundry and took a shower and shaved and dressed myself up in my new jeans and a new shirt, but I somehow couldn't get myself motivated to go. It was like I knew I'd win more money, and the fact that I knew it ahead of time made it not very interesting.

Instead I stayed here and counted all the money I already won, pulling it in fistfuls out of my gym bag. I've lost track of how much I won when, and where I spent what, but the amount I'm carrying around at this very moment is $3,304.15. Like I say, not exactly a vast fortune, but more than I've had at what you'd call my disposal than ever before in my life. And I made it at the races like I said I would.

After I counted the money I thought I'd watch TV. The TV's one of those old-fashioned kind with the twist knob on a stand, and I get channels 2, 4, 6, and 7 and that's it. I watched "America's Funniest Home Bloopers" or something like that for a while, and then I turned it off. TV's a waste of time, but I used to be able to watch it without paying any attention to it, like I could just kind of daydream and stare at the screen, like I said before about watching infomercials late at night and thinking about betting on dogs, but now I seem to watch closer the people on the TV and what they're actually talking about, and it depresses me. I don't mean just the news, but shows like this "Funny Home Bloopers" also, where like this little girl hits her dad in the wiener with a baseball bat on accident and everybody in the studio audience laughs and meanwhile the guy is rolling around in pain on the ground and you can see an old dirty kid's swimming pool in the background and two rusted-out old cars up on cinder blocks. It's just not that funny to me.

It made me start thinking about that Sarah and her book, and how sort of appealing and pretty that was, and I decided I wanted something to read. Needless to say I didn't have any books.

But in the nightstand I found a Bible—not one of the little New Testaments passed around by the Gideon guys, but a full-blown Bible, Old Testament and all, with the old-fashioned black cover, and a King James too, not one of these "Modern Living" versions or whatever. It was the real thing, or what I'd been raised to believe was the real thing.

It made me very nervous to find this Bible there, and for a few seconds I became very aware of things like the ticking of the big old alarm clock on the dresser and the darkness outside and the stars and the wind blowing a little bit, making a tree limb scratch across the outside wall and a shadow pass across the window.

I already admitted that winning all this money at the track had got me thinking quite a bit again about God or Jesus or the Greyhound God and what is the meaning of things, or is there any, like I'd almost quit doing with Jake and Jenny around. So when I found this Bible, kind of came across it unexpectedly like that, I was at the same time hopeful and also what I think you call apprehensive, meaning that I wasn't quite sure what was going to happen. When I first opened the book, too, it made this feeling stronger, because there on the inside cover was a family tree the same as my grandma's Bible had. The page was yellowed and tender around the edges, and on a line at the top it said a woman's name and the year 1902. Below that there were spaces for a whole bunch of names, but only two were written there, in the same handwriting as the first name. One of them was a boy's name, different from the last name of the woman at the top, and by the name were the dates 1937 and then d. 1944. Next to that name was a girl's name with the same last name as the boy, and next to her name it said 1939, and then in a different handwriting that looked like a man's, d. 1986. Below that was one name, a girl's, with a different last name and a different handwriting, too, that looked like another woman's, and the date next to it 1957.

It was a sad family tree, with lots more blank spaces than filled ones, and people that died too young and names that never got carried on. I started thinking about the boy especially, wondering how and why he died, was it because of World War II, but then he would have had to live someplace else, like in Europe. But he was only seven years old, and that made me think of Mark of course, and I started feeling sorry for him and his family and probably would have stayed on that page trying to figure out the whole family history for a long time, except that I looked up to the corner of the page and there it said "$1.00," written in faded pencil. That made me turn the page quick, because I didn't want to even think how someone had taken their old family Bible, with the names of all these people in it, and sold it at some yard sale or used bookstore. I couldn't stand the thought of that, and how that was the way the book ended up here in my room so I could read it.

I tried not to think of it, and I started thumbing through the Old Testament, reading a little here and there, but not really paying attention because my mind was still on the family that used to own the Bible. But then finally I started realizing some of the stuff I was reading, and it made me feel almost like I was going to get sick or that something really frightening was about to happen to me, and I started picturing and sort of sensing in a strange way very old things like my grandmother's shoe closet and the piano in our living room and a certain way the streetlight shined through my bed-room curtains on nights when it would snow.

Everything that I had been glancing through was about blood and death and violence, and it was almost like I could start to feel the room spin around me, or around the page that I was reading, and the night seemed to be getting blacker and blacker outside the edges of the page. There was Gideon and his trumpet and Moses and the Red Sea and the plague visited on the people of Egypt and Solomon saying to cut the baby in two.

The worst was Abraham and Isaac. God making Abraham take his only son and get ready to stab him to death just to prove that he would do it if God said so. I couldn't quit picturing that moment, the moment where Abraham was raising the knife, and his son Isaac must have been lying there thinking how strange this was, listening to his father talk with God about his life, but how he must have trusted his father, and how he was thinking maybe about how this would soon be over and what kind of game could they play when they got home, and all the time his dad standing there ready to kill him, stick a knife right in him like he was nothing. And right then I heard the words in my head that Buddy used when he was talking about my supposedly impossible pool shot, *No fucking way.*

I kept hearing it over and over, *No fucking way.* No fucking way could you have my kid—Jake, Jacob—no fucking way, not if it meant the goddamn world had to explode.

It was an awful book, and I couldn't see how my grandmother had ever made me believe in it, or why I had ever wanted to believe in it, and I started to feel sort of panicky, thinking that maybe I had made a really terrible mistake in refocusing, one that I wouldn't be able to come all the way back from even in the morning. It took me forever to get to sleep.

Today things seem better. It was a beautiful morning, and I went out and sat under the oak tree. There was a hummingbird feeder, with a hummingbird hovering at the red water inside. The world didn't seem like such a bad place.

But I think I have to do something about Jake and Jenny soon. When I woke up this morning it felt totally natural to me, to be just a guy alone in a room with a few things, and nothing planned for the day. I didn't feel like a man with a wife and son at all, and the problem of having to find out something to do about them. I felt open to anything, like back in the old days, and nothing worried me, not for a few minutes anyway, there in my room with everything so quiet and empty.

JUNE 18

Her name is Sarah. I know this because she stayed in my room last night. Nothing happened. She slept in the bed and I slept on the floor, but I'm not denying the future possibility. It was there from the start, I can see it now.

I went into town about an hour ago to this little diner a couple blocks off the strip called The Hen House. While I was sitting there having my eggs and hash browns and bacon, I was feeling very good, remembering how it was to wake up and see Sarah lying there asleep on the bed. Usually when I'm in a good mood like that I feel like talking to someone, but this morning I was happy to be quiet and listen to the knives and forks clatter on people's plates and their voices humming like bees and the waitresses pouring coffee and smiling. I felt like I filled up space in there, quiet and polite and sipping my coffee.

Last night I won $978.40. Obviously that wasn't the most interesting thing that happened, but I think I've been too careless about the money and how I'm keeping track of it. Because no matter what happens, the money that I'm winning is partly for Jake, because Jenny can't go on forever not letting me know where he is. She's not that kind of person anyway. Sometimes when you're right in the middle of things happening, you get worked up in your head and people that you know as well as you know yourself start seeming different, and usually worse, like you start imagining them doing all sorts of things that they're really not capable of. There's no way that Jenny is trying to take Jake out of my life, or not let me be his father. It's just a decision she made to leave because she thought that was best. She just didn't have enough confidence in me. Maybe I'll try to call her tomorrow. At any rate I need to keep better track of the money. I kind of feel responsible to keep going to the track and making money.

Tonight I'm supposed to be meeting Sarah at the dog track, down in the seats by the rail where we met the other times. It seems like the wrong thing to do, maybe, even if it's just to meet and talk and get to know each other better, and when I think about it I get a feeling that pulls me out over all the miles I'm away from Jenny and makes me wish I could ask her about it and make sure that this is what she wants. And I would feel better if I could run my hands across her face and through her hair and hear her tell me that she loves me but it's not working. And then I could show her all the money in my bag and say, What's not working? Here. And hold it out in my hands.

Last night was more or less like usual. It was another pretty night, T-shirt weather again, but this time I was dressed in this long-sleeve brown button-down shirt I'd bought that day in Rapid City. I could see Sarah and her dad down by the rail.

I was betting in a not very inspired way, but feeling sort of responsible and making sure I was doing things right. It was a small crowd, and I could hear the track lights buzzing up above, and the dogs barking off in the kennel before every race. There were people having conversations all around, in the little groups that they'd come with, about the topics that concerned them. I listened to some people talking about this friend of theirs Jade, a guy named Jade, which I thought was interesting, who'd up and had a hernia. That's how they said it—he just up and had one, out of the blue. Apparently, according to one of them, guys about Jade's age in their thirties just sometimes had hernias, and there was nothing you could do. Some other people, dressed all nice like they were coming from an office party maybe, were talking about politics. This one guy wearing a tie, probably the boss by the look of things, kept going on and on about the death penalty in a loud voice. The death penalty was good old frontier justice, goddammit. All these people saying it was cruel and unusual, when what we ought to be doing was like in the old days when you hung people in the public square or used the guillotine. And with the sex offenders we ought to cut their nuts off, too.

What a fun guy *he* was. He had a beer in his hand and you could tell he'd had a few already, and he was kind of soft and chubby and sweating all over so that he'd have to take off his glasses and rub the sweat off his face, and he was smoking a big, stinking cigar on top of that, so he didn't have enough hands to take care of his bodily needs and would have to set the cigar or the beer down every two seconds to wipe himself off or loosen his tie.

Listening to the guy made me tired. Not tired of what he was saying, I mean, like getting angry and wanting to tell him off necessarily, but just plain tired, like sick of people in general and really hopeless about the whole human race and the crap they spent their life doing, not just him but all the people who had to sit there and listen to him and not say anything. Which included me, I guess.

Anyway, I finally couldn't stand it anymore, so after I went up to bet on the 8th race, I didn't go back to my same spot but down by the rail just across the aisle from Sarah and her dad. It turned out Sarah's dad must have had a dog in the 8th, because when they started loading in the dogs, he said, "Well, here goes," and patted Sarah on the knee and got up and waddled down to stand by the rail. He's this short, stout guy who wears a baseball cap with a logo of some farm supply company and takes it off every minute or so to scratch his bald head.

The 8th race started, and I found myself watching Sarah's dad as much as the race, trying to figure out which dog was his. I had the 6, and a 6-1 quinella, which had great odds even though the 1 dog was kind of suspect—a little tiny dog about 54 pounds down on the rail, which you don't want usually because little dogs on the rail have a tendency to let themselves get squeezed in. And that's exactly what this one did, so I figured my quinella was gone. But the 6 was right up there, along with the 4, and it was about the backstretch when I started seeing the 4 was Sarah's dad's dog. Mr. Morgan's.

The 4 was on the outside, running neck and neck with my 6, and Sarah's dad was leaning this way and that, pushing his ass from side to side like that was going to help the dog, and pounding his hand on the rail. They stayed even all the way up the stretch until about the last hundred yards, and then his dog pulled out real steady and won by a length. He let out this big whoop and kind of did this dance where he thrust his hips forward and back and shot his fists up in the air and actually made me laugh and I almost lost my cigarette out of my mouth.

I'd almost forgot about Sarah herself for a split second, and I wasn't ready when she started talking to me. "So," she said, "did you win on that one?"

I looked over at her and she was smiling the way she does. I don't know, but it hit me again how pretty she was right then, the smile on her face and her blonde hair so natural and kind of shaping her face. It almost made me feel like not saying anything, like talking would ruin just looking.

But I talked. "No," I said.

"Too bad," she said. She pulled her hair back and swung her legs around toward me. "You'll know better next time," she said. She was wearing tan shorts that were just that—short—but a plain white T-shirt that wasn't so distracting, and the same sandals as before.

"That your dad's dog?" I asked her.

She nodded. "Has my name, too," she said. I looked down at the program in my hand, and sure enough there it was, I don't know how I hadn't noticed before, Morgan's Sarah. "He has a dog named for me and my brother, and one for my mom, too," she said. She smiled that big smile again. "Sarah's the only one that wins."

For some reason all the nervousness I'd had before around her was gone, and I felt good and in control of things, like one of those moments in your life when things stand out clear and it seems like they were made just for you, and you think to yourself, I'll remember this. The way the wind picked up right then and blew in the night's first cool moment, and the smoke from my cigarette fanned out sideways and I leaned back in my seat, and Sarah kind of curled herself up against the wind, crossing her arms in front of her and leaning over her legs toward me, just hovering there close like the hummingbird by the oak tree.

"How's the rest of the night been?" she said.

"Pretty good," I said, and I looked back down at my program and started thinking about the 9th race. I heard her laugh, just a little bit. Her dad came and sat back down and after that we never talked, not until the end of the last race.

On the last race I hit the quinella, a real solid bet that went off at ridiculously high odds, and I guess I couldn't help getting a little excited when the dogs came across the line. I got up to go cash my ticket, and I admit it, I turned into the aisle that was the direction she was sitting in, where I could have gone the other way. But right when I walked by she stood up, and her dad was busy talking to some guy next to him, and she said, "You hit that one, didn't you?" And I laughed and said I didn't think it was that obvious, and she smiled back.

Then she asked me if I was going to The Bend. I actually didn't know the answer to that until right that moment. I told her sure and she said, "See you there."

I thought about those three words the whole time I was driving back to the cabin to put my money away, wondering what it was she meant. Did she mean like the time before, like Hey, how are you, nice to see you, or did she mean more like we would sit down together and actually talk. And I thought again about why she seemed so interested in me in a way.

When I got to my room I tucked all but a hundred dollars of the money away in a corner of the gym bag with the rest, and then I went to brush my teeth and ended up staring into the mirror above the sink. I was still pretty clean-shaven because my beard doesn't grow too fast, and my new brown shirt made me look a little bit more respectable than I would have normally with my scraggly hair.

I went through a mental checklist and thought about how my jeans were new and clean and I had on my Birkenstocks. When I looked down at my feet, though, my toenails were like big long claws or daggers practically, and I didn't have any clippers. So I put on some socks and my old white Stan Smith Adidas tennis shoes. They didn't look so great, but better than my feet. Then I bit off my fingernails, sitting there on the bed.

Then I went back to the mirror, but I was about through looking at myself. I was starting to feel like Jenny or my sister Mary standing in front of the mirror for so long. Also I decided like I always do eventually that I was actually an all-right-looking guy, getting a little too thin but with a nice face, or an honest face, or whatever.

Right before I left my room, I thought of one last thing, which was to take off my wedding ring and put it by the sink. But I didn't do it. As a bartender, I've seen enough guys with white indents around their ring fingers making asses of themselves with cocktail waitresses. I always despised guys like that, and I ended up being kind of ashamed of myself for even thinking about it, and it ruined my mood a little when I was waiting for the taxi to show up and get me. I called a taxi, for the obvious reason that I didn't want to end up driving home in the same shape I was the other night.

When I got to The Bend, she wasn't there. It was about midnight. I figured I'd wait half an hour, because I wasn't too interested in just staying there and drinking by myself. I ordered a Heineken and then went and sat at a table this time, over by where Buddy and his friends were sitting the other time. Buddy wasn't there either.

At 12:30 I saw her march past me up to the bar in her shorts and her white T-shirt with the same flannel shirt I'd seen her wearing before. Buddy was right behind her, walking along real casual with his hands in his pockets. They sat at the bar and ordered beers. They kind of laughed and talked for a minute, and Buddy lit up a cigarette. After a couple of minutes this girl who'd been talking to a few guys down toward the end of the bar sort of excused herself and walked over and sat on a barstool next to Buddy. She was pretty enough, I guess, with long brown hair and a mini-skirt and legs a little on the thin side.

I'd just about finished my second beer when Sarah looked over at me. Because of where I was sitting, kind of behind her and over towards the front doors, she had to turn around to do it, and I knew by that that she'd seen me when she came in. She saw I was watching her, and right away held her index finger up in the air, like to say Just one minute, and then she put her hand on Buddy's arm and leaned over toward him and said something to him and the girl, and then she grabbed her purse and her book which she'd laid on the bar and her beer and came over and sat with me.

At that point I didn't know about the Buddy situation, so I was a little concerned we might have some trouble, and he did turn around and look over where we were and kind of shake his head, I thought, but that was about it. Anyway I was looking over at him and not at Sarah.

"Hel*lo*," she said. "I'm *here*." She was smiling again with that teasing look on her face. She was sitting kind of halfway across from me, with one leg over the other and swaying back and forth.

"Me too," I said, not really sure if it would come out sounding like a joke or not, but she laughed.

"Hey, you're drinking my beer," she said, really fast like that, like she just hopped from one subject to another. She does that a lot, I found out, so it's a little hard to keep up with the conversation at times, and for a while I was afraid she'd think I was stupid. But probably everybody that talks to her has the same trouble. She's just the opposite of Jenny, how she just says things without thinking and doesn't worry about it and expects you to keep up. Whereas Jenny always thinks about what she says. She has this way of staring you right in the eye while she kind of takes in exactly what you just told her, and what you were probably thinking when you said it, then she'll kind of bite her bottom lip for a second before she decides what to say back. She's very considerate is what I think you'd call it, Jenny, meaning she considers very carefully the words that come out of her mouth. For Sarah words are more like smoke rings, I think, just popping out and going up and disappearing.

Anyway I didn't understand her at first about the beer. I thought she meant I was drinking from her actual *beer*, like I had reached across the table accidentally and grabbed hers instead of mine and started drinking from it.

"Heineken," she said, and reached out like she was going to pat my arm real gently, but then stopped her hand in the air about two inches from my arm—like she did a pantomime of touching me.

Then I saw what she meant. "Oh, right. Heineken," I said.

"You switched," she said. "From the other night."

"I do that," I told her. "I'm dangerously unpredictable."

I'm not sure where that line came from, but I didn't stumble over it and it came out easy enough. But she dropped a bomb on me right after that, believe me. She kind of looked at me a second, sizing me up in a way, and then she smiled and leaned in toward me. "Let me just ask you one question, Luke Rivers," she said, saying my name in that half-joking way she says almost everything, "before we talk about anything else."

I told her okay.

"Where's your wife?" she said.

I looked at her there across the table, at just how attractive she was, and I thought I was a lucky bastard to even be sitting there with her, and what an easy thing it would be to say, We're getting a divorce, or We're separated. But I haven't made up my mind about a lot of things yet, so I just told her the plain and simple truth. "I don't know," I said.

"Don't know," she said back, and took a drink of beer and looked at how much was left in the bottle. "Don't know as in Don't know where she is right this minute, or don't know as in Don't know where she is at all."

"Don't know where she is at all," I said. "Since a week ago."

"Kids?" she said, looking up from her beer.

"One. A boy. Jacob." Automatically I reached for my wallet and pulled out this little family photo we had taken for real cheap at Penney's in I think The Dalles, Oregon, where we lived for a few months when Jake was two. "He's five now," I said, thinking how I didn't even have any pictures of him nowadays to help me remember him how he is. And of course they change every day, too, kids. They get a scrape on their chin or a haircut.

"What does he look like now?" she said, staring at the picture.

"About this high," I said, holding my hand out just above the table, but then raising it a little and lowering it a little again and realizing I didn't know. "He looks like me," I said. "He's like me, but littler."

She smiled, but not teasing, just very soft and nice. "Your wife's pretty," she said, and handed the picture back to me. I put it in my wallet without saying anything. "And you don't want to talk about it any more right now," she said, looking at me.

But she was wrong about that, right at that very moment. It was like she'd hit a button inside me or turned a knob, and everything was ready to pour out into her hands. The only thing I wanted to do all of a sudden *was* tell her everything, just start at Rapid City or even way before that in Mississippi and let the whole thing go. I missed Jake and Jenny really bad right then, because somebody had finally asked me, but all I could do was kind of grit my teeth and stare at the blurry neon lights above the bar. I couldn't say a thing.

"Maybe we shouldn't be talking right now," she said, and started to swing her legs around like she was going to leave. Not in an angry way, but more like she could tell she'd upset me.

"No," I said real quick then. "No, we should be talking now. It's okay. Believe me."

She looked at me close again for just one second, like she was making sure she had me in focus before she snapped a picture. "All right," she said, and started looking light and happy again, like before.

"I could use a beer," I said, and she said so too, and I went to the bar and got the beers and came back to her. Buddy didn't even look at me.

When I got back, I asked her what I really wanted to. I took a drink of beer and said, "What about you?" and she asked what did I mean. So I said, "I mean isn't this kind of strange? I don't know what your deal is with Buddy over there, but isn't it a little odd for you to be sitting here with me?"

That cracked her up. She laughed really loud, almost like a guy's laugh, but at the same time it went up and down in her throat in a really nice way that sounded like music, like specific notes in a certain order. "Well, *Buddy* might think it's strange," she said. "But it doesn't matter. Not the way you think it does. Buddy's my brother."

That certainly explained some things.

After she'd got done laughing a little more at the look on my face, we just started talking. It was like we'd been sitting there night after night in the same place talking to each other for years. Not like we were getting to know each other, but like we were right in the middle of knowing each other for a long time. We didn't talk about too many really personal things, although she did mention her mother again. Her mother's name was May. She died of breast cancer, right there in her bed because she'd insisted on going home. The whole family was there. She said she missed her mother a lot, and it was hard to be at home. She felt guilty about leaving her dad practically every night to come down to The Bend, but she couldn't stand the house at night, all alone with her dad already gone to sleep. She asked me about my father and exactly how long ago he'd died. I still didn't say anything about Mark.

But we talked mostly about less personal things. I told her a little about what Idaho was like, because she said after she found out where I was from that she'd always wanted to travel out West. Practically everybody you meet east of say Iowa says that, but I doubt most of them ever go.

Finally Buddy came over to the table, and he didn't look angry or concerned anymore, like he'd just kind of resigned himself to the fact of Sarah talking to me.

Sarah said, "How'd it go with Taylor?" and Buddy shrugged and pushed his red U W cap back on his head. "Poor Taylor," Sarah said, not really sorry for Taylor you could tell, but more pleased that her brother was a good-looking guy that girls fell for.

"Now, come on," Buddy said, "I'm taking her to a party after hours." He slid his hat down and leaned back his chair. "I'm doing the respectable thing."

"Oh, certainly," Sarah said. "Always the gentleman."

You could tell they talked a lot that way.

The three of us played a little pool, and after that Buddy went off with Taylor and some other people and left me and Sarah at our table. Then it was closing time and I was ready to call a cab. "Where are you staying?" Sarah said. "I'll give you a ride." I had kind of expected it but kind of not.

We walked to her car parked down by the river where they start the boat tours. Looking at the river going by real quiet down below and the tour boats tied at the docks made me remember that time with Jake and Jenny. "We took the boat tour once," I said. "A long time ago." It wasn't really a long time ago but it seemed that way.

"Welcome to Wisconsin Dells," she said. She bent over and

picked up a rock from off the pavement and threw it way out in the water. It wasn't what you'd expect a girl to do, and she had a pretty good arm also.

"You play softball?" I said.

"Nope," she said. "I just played sports with Buddy and his friends."

She had a great car, an old white Toyota Land Cruiser, which is like a kind of Jeep. My friend Jeff Lundy in high school who I talked about before had one. It's definitely an all-purpose vehicle, and you can take the top down too.

Instead of going straight to the cabins Sarah wanted to swing by Buddy's apartment and get some beer. It was too late to buy it at the store, and she said Buddy wouldn't mind if she got a six-pack from his fridge and he was off somewhere with Taylor anyway. Buddy had an upstairs apartment above a drugstore, which was right on the corner next to The Hen House actually, but I just waited in the car and didn't get to see the inside of it. She came out with a six-pack of Heineken.

One thing I hadn't counted on earlier that night was her coming home to my room with me. The place was a disaster. I thought about making her wait outside while I cleaned up a little, but I figured that was rude and she would know then it was a mess anyway and maybe think I was trying to hide something, too.

When I opened the door, it was worse even than I thought. First off there were clothes strewn all over everywhere, clean ones and dirty ones because I hadn't bothered hanging anything in the closet or putting anything in the drawers, including underwear just laying out in plain view, which I went after real quick to put away. My gym bag was in the middle of the floor and I practically tripped over it. Then there was a Pizza Hut box open on the bed with two crusts left in it and the Bible flopped open on the bedspread.

I got the pizza box and Bible off the bed, and Sarah just plopped right down on it, the bed I mean, and set the beer next to her and said, "Looks like you're adjusting well to bachelor life." Then she thought about it for a second and apologized. I told her it was okay, because it *was* okay then. I wasn't getting upset about the subject like at the bar.

I sat down in the little chair at the writing desk over by the door. I asked did she want to watch TV, and got up right away to go turn on the set.

She said no, not now. "Could I have a cigarette?" she asked me.

"I didn't think you smoked," I said, and she said only whenever she felt like it. She reminds me of Jenny that way, having a kind of dry sense of humor where she says funny things with a straight face, like when Jenny made the toast to all the dogs at Rapid City Greyhound Park who made us what we were today.

I told her sure, but how I'd made a habit of not smoking in the house.

"Let's not smoke in your house then," she said. "Is outside okay?"

We went outside and drank beer and smoked on the swing. You could see the moon big and almost full hanging in the sky right above us, and you could hear the frogs, and leaves rustled around in the trees and made that sound like ocean waves, like they do when it's quiet and you're listening. There were puffy little clouds that looked blue in the dark sky.

We talked about ordinary stuff, like how hot it's been, and other stuff that was more like dreaming, like what are your favorite places you've ever been and what would you do if you had the choice of anything in the world. We smoked three cigarettes apiece and finished our beers and went back to the room. After that we talked some more and never watched TV and finished the six-pack. By then it was turning daylight out, and I told Sarah I'd take her home if she didn't want to drive. She asked if she could just stay.

I told her all right and offered her the bed, and I took the bed-spread and a pillow and laid it on the floor and went to sleep with my old jean jacket over me.

When I woke up, right at about ten o'clock, she was sleeping, quietly curled up on her side with no covers. I wouldn't have known she was alive or even real except for one arm rising and falling with her breathing. At first I looked at her like she was a sculpture or a picture, but then her legs were long and tan and part of her rear end was showing from her shorts and a few little golden brown hairs, and she seemed very real and very alive then. And I was glad about that and felt strong and very much alive myself, knowing that I would have to make a decision soon. Because there wasn't any doubt at that moment how I felt. Not like I was imagining things in my head, but living right in the middle of them.

I woke her up, and she rubbed her eyes hard and said, Oh my God, she forgot to take out her contacts and would I get her purse. I asked if she wanted to go for breakfast, and she said no, go ahead, and would I meet her at the track tonight.

She was gone when I got back from breakfast.

Last night lying on the floor, or this morning really, I had that same old feeling I had at the track, one of waiting and listening. I heard Sarah settle down to sleep, and the wind outside blowing steady but still no storm, thinking about the clouds and the moon. Then it seemed like the clock on the dresser ticked louder and louder, and I started measuring my breath by its ticking, waiting there alone but not alone, staring into the moonlight at the small objects of my room.

JUNE 19

We met at the track and she was alone. Her dad didn't have any dogs racing last night. I asked her why meet at the track then, and she said she wanted to see all this money I was winning. She was definitely joking, but it turned out to be pretty frustrating because I didn't win. I mean I won, but just regular and not the way I've been winning.

She got there only about ten minutes before the first race, wearing Levi's and a gray sweatshirt this time, and her hair put up with one of those things where you stick a pin through two holes and get your hair wound in the middle of it somehow.

I'd been there about fifteen minutes eyeing the program and the tote board, so I had a pretty good idea which dogs I was interested in. I explained to Sarah how I had to go up top and get a look at the video screens that listed the daily double odds because they only show win and quinella on the tote board, and she said go ahead and she'd wait, and she tried to give me money to get her a beer but I wouldn't let her pay.

Having someone with me was a good feeling. I thought the whole time I was up looking at the screen about how I'd explain to her what I'd decided to bet on, and then how I'd win the double and probably a quinella on one of the first two also, and then I'd keep winning all night long and she'd be amazed and see what I'd been talking about all along and ask me, "How'd you do that?" Maybe she'd even say, "You must be *clairvoyant*."

I bet the 3 to win and a 3-1 daily double and a 3-4 quinella. They had the dogs loaded in when I got back to the seats, and the bell rang and the rabbit squeaked to life down on the rail and I suppose I looked kind of desperate to get my smoke lit and take my drink of beer in time but Sarah didn't say anything. I told her what I bet and she nodded. Then the dogs were coming past us, and my 3-4 were both in pretty good shape, but I felt like I just had to say to her, "I'm not too sure about the 4." She nodded again, watching, but maybe not too interested. The problem with the 4 was that it finished consistently in the top half, but almost always fourth and occasionally third, regardless of what class, like it just enjoyed running in the middle of the pack—a groupie, like I said before.

And sure enough, the 3 got up for first in the end, but the 4 finished fourth as usual. I'd seen it coming but still I was surprised and a little embarrassed.

"You won!" she said, trying to look kind of bright and impressed, but her eyes were wandering around and she was thinking of something else. "You got the first half of the double, too."

I said, "Twelve dollars and change," in a way that told her it wasn't nearly what I'd been expecting.

Then she did one of those things I was talking about before, where she starts up with something else out of the blue. "I'm thinking about switching my major," she said. "This fall. To something else."

I was thinking about how to explain my system to her since she'd seemed so interested in how I was winning all this money before, and I didn't know what to say about her major. "What *is* your major?" I said.

"Communications," she said. "When I was a kid I always wanted to be like Barbara Walters. Is that ridiculous or what?"

I shrugged. "You're prettier," I told her.

She didn't look at me or smile and just kind of stared out across the track. Right then I was actually more concerned with the fact that it was time to go cash my ticket, and obviously she didn't know this like Jenny would and was holding me up. I didn't know any graceful way to get off the subject, so I just said I'd be right back, and she said okay.

After I collected my big twelve bucks I went to the men's room. It was occurring to me that things weren't going as smooth as the night before with Sarah, but I thought about this while I stood there taking a leak, which when you think about it is actually a time when things come to you kind of clear, standing there just doing your business and staring at the wall, and I realized that if the whole thing fell through it would almost be a relief. That's what I thought while I stood there staring at the little squares of yellow tile.

When I got out of the bathroom I saw a very unusual thing. There were these two guys coming from the hot-dog stand, and one of them was a midget carrying a hot dog and the other one was this kind of big burly guy, more meat than muscle. I fell in right behind them walking, and of course I was paying attention to them because how could you help it. The midget had on a Green

Bay Packers T-shirt and tan cut-off shorts that you could tell were actually kid's jeans from like JC Penney or Wal-Mart. The big guy had a beard and a flannel shirt and work boots and what we used to call carpet-layer pants, the kind where the guy who came over to your house to lay carpet or fix the dishwasher was always bent over on his knees with his pants down to where it showed the crack of his ass.

They were laughing about something when I got behind them, and the big guy sort of ruffled the midget's hair while they just kept walking along, and he said, "And now for a couple of beers," which meant they were headed for the beer stand up ahead.

After that they walked for a few seconds, and I was catching up with them because of the midget's having to take small steps, and when I was about ten feet behind them the midget said, "I never had a friend like you before, Tucker. I never had someone like you to look after me." And they walked on for a few more seconds, and then the big guy stopped, and right when I was coming up on them so I had to sort of dodge to the side, the big guy reached down and picked the midget up and held him. He just sort of put him over his shoulder and held him there. I almost ran into them, and when I turned around to maybe say excuse me, I saw the big guy had tears in his eyes and the midget was holding on tight to his neck with both arms, making sure the hot dog didn't get in the big guy's hair.

When I sat down with Sarah again I could feel that she was still kind of distracted and possibly not in a very good mood but I kept thinking about this guy and the midget. I kept hearing the midget say, "I never had a friend like you, Tucker," and kept seeing Tucker pick him up in one motion and hold him tight right there in front of everyone at the ticket windows.

Sarah had started talking again about how she'd be a senior in the fall and she really ought to have some idea what she wanted to do with her life, but I was having a hard time listening, and then suddenly she said, "What's wrong?" like she was very worried, and she put her hand on my knee. I couldn't really say anything, didn't feel like I could explain to her about what I saw the way I could have with someone I knew better. Well, I mean Jenny of course, why not go ahead and say. Jenny who knows everything about me almost, that I was in an institution even, and how I sometimes get upset by certain things.

But I couldn't say anything to Sarah, even though the worry in her voice was making me even worse, and what came out of my mouth was a noise not quite like a sob, but almost. "What *is* it?" she said, like she was afraid something really terrible had happened. I couldn't look at her. I felt her hand tighten on my knee, then go loose, and then she took her hand away. "Maybe this is just a really bad idea," she said. "I apologize. I don't know what I'm thinking." She crossed her legs and I could feel her kind of curling up into herself. "Jesus, Sarah," she said.

Of course I knew what was going on. She thought it was Jake and Jenny again, and for a second or two I wavered, like I could see my life taking shape in one of two ways growing out of that very moment, and I could go one way if I just said, Maybe you're right. But again I didn't do that, like I also chose not to the night before. "It's not what you think," I said.

"What is it, then?" she said, and her hand was back on my leg. "Tell me." Her voice was soft and pretty.

I didn't have anything else to do but tell her then, as strange as I knew it might sound. And I was okay at first, I was getting through it just fine, until I came to the actual part where I tried to tell about how Tucker lifted the midget up, how he just leaned over right out of the blue, this big guy, and hoisted his friend up into his arms. And then it was one of those moments where the thing that's got hold of you gets even stronger in trying to tell it, and my voice broke. I could feel Sarah's hand there tight on my leg, and she was moved in very close to me on the seat, and I could smell her hair. She didn't say anything, just moved her thumb very slowly back and forth on my thigh and waited. I kept trying to say it, and the words wouldn't come every time I got near them, and my mouth would hang there open and tears would cloud my eyes and I'd have to suck in my breath real hard and try again. Finally I got it out, with my voice wobbling over all the words, about how he just picked him up and hugged him right there in front of everyone. Like they didn't care about anyone else in the whole place and didn't even know anyone else was there and it was only them in this one single second where everything seemed just right. Then I managed to get a good deep breath, but I still was having trouble and just sat there with my tongue pressed hard against the inside of my cheek.

Then I felt Sarah's other hand on the back of my neck. "I'm glad you told me," she said, and I felt her rubbing my neck with her soft fingers. I put my head down and closed my eyes and just relaxed all over, and right away I could feel the whole thing changing—how what I'd seen with Tucker and the midget was starting to slide into being a story, sort of, that I'd told to Sarah, and that whenever from now on I remembered Tucker and the midget I would also remember this moment where Sarah rubbed the back of my neck and made me feel better, and the two things would never be separate from each other in my mind. And I thought for a second about how that's a problem with most things in life, that they never stay separate from other things and are always becoming part of something else. But even as I thought it, I knew I felt better, and I knew that it was only because seeing Tucker and the midget had been such a separate, small thing in the world in the first place that it had made me feel the way I did and made this moment with Sarah. In other words everything was okay, and I lifted my head.

It wasn't until right then that I saw the dogs were already on the backstretch. I hadn't even heard them go past, or any of the people shouting. I watched them in what you'd call a vague way, just seeing them stream around the far turn and hearing the voice of the track announcer high above and feeling Sarah close to me, and then they were all the way around and just about to hit the wire when it occurred to me that I'd forgotten to bet the race and I couldn't remember my combination in the double. "Did we hit the double?" I shouted, because everybody was yelling, and Sarah said, "Hmm, let's see. That would be our dog ri-ight . . . *there*," she said, kind of loud because all the noise had just stopped, and right then our 1 dog came across the line about ten lengths behind all the rest.

"Oops," I said, and she smiled. She patted me on the leg and I looked at her eyes.

"Okay now?" she said.

"Yes," I told her.

Then she reached out and put her hands on my face and looked at me, then leaned in and kissed me for the first time, just a short kiss, but hard right on the mouth. She dropped her hands back into her lap. "Can we have fun now, then?" she said.

"Yes," I said.

After that we got more into the betting, and I explained my whole system to her, all except for the Greyhound God part, although she did pick up right away almost on the light a cigarette and take a drink of beer thing, which she thought was very amusing, and I admitted to being superstitious. She paid attention and even seemed interested in how much thought I'd put into my whole system, but then like I say it kept not working like it was supposed to. I'd have one of the dogs in the quinella but not the other, or my win dog would come in second, or whatever. I kept just missing all the time. Actually I did hit enough to make it seem like my system was working if you hadn't seen how well it was working before. I hit a quinella in I think the 6th race that paid about seventy bucks and another one that paid maybe forty after that and a win bet that was more like just a safety bet that paid close to twenty. So by the time we were through I was up about $100. Overall, I don't think she was too convinced by my system, and she probably wondered if that was really all I did to support myself these days. Like I say, though, we had a good time and drank a few beers and ate hot dogs.

Then the last race was over and we were heading for the gates. We were just getting into a crowd of people when Sarah touched my elbow and said, "Is that them?" and nodded her head. I looked over and there was Tucker and the midget by the beer stand, talking to the bartender. Tucker was leaned on the counter saying something to the bartender and then he hitched up his pants, and the midget was sitting on the counter with a beer. They looked happy and like they weren't ready to go anywhere at all.

I said, "No, it was some other big guy with a different midget," and she rolled her eyes at me and pulled me along by the arm.

She didn't want to go to The Bend afterward. Instead we took my truck and went to Buddy's apartment. You had to go up a flight of old creaky stairs with a wooden banister to where there were two apartments, one at the back and one at the front which was Buddy's. He was at the apartment this time, with this other guy named Jordan who turned out to be his neighbor. I didn't see it at first, but it definitely turned out that Sarah had known he was going to be there all along and that the get-together was all planned out.

It was a nice place with hardwood floors and a really high white ceiling and white walls with paintings hanging on them that Buddy said a friend of his did. They were mostly just colors and shapes put together in an interesting way, the kind of paintings where I wonder if the person is really a good artist or not. Like if he was there and I was in the right kind of mood I would say, "Draw a dog for me," and see if he could do it. The wall facing the street was brick with two big high windows cut in it and a plant hanging in each one. There was furniture that all looked very tasteful and clean and a brand-spanking-new kitchen and a little bedroom and bathroom tucked off to the side of the main room that looked like they had interesting things in them, old photographs of people I didn't recognize and posters of movies I didn't recognize either. And books everywhere—a huge bookcase that stretched all along one wall in the main room and was just made out of planks stacked on bricks and another one in the bedroom that was glassed in over a desk by the bed. It was very impressive and a little intimidating, just the sheer amount of knowledge in the room.

Sarah sat with me on the couch, and this Jordan guy went to the fridge and got us both a Heineken, which I was starting to wonder if it was the only beer these people drank. Then Sarah did all the usual introductions, with Jordan I mean, and then also to Buddy, a "You remember Luke" kind of deal.

Buddy said sure and he'd be with us in a minute. He was doing something at this desk with a computer which had like colored graphics and stuff on it.

This Jordan guy I could tell right away was stoned to the bejesus. As soon as he got our beers, he kind of melted into a chair and stared at this small TV Buddy had on a little stand with more books underneath by the brick wall. MTV was on, one of those awful shows they have where they give advice to kids in supposedly a hip way. This Jordan guy's brain was just sunk into it immediately, you could see. He looked a little older, too—not quite my age but probably late twenties—and he had a buzz cut with long sideburns and a T-shirt and jeans that showed he was way too thin. I had him right away figured for a speed freak, or maybe even crystal. You see them all over in America when you're a bartender. It doesn't matter if you're in Wisconsin or Montana or New Orleans.

It's funny how a stoned guy can make everyone feel uncomfortable. There we were on the couch, me and Sarah, with Buddy plunking away on the keys at the desk, and this Jordan just staring like he was in a black hole that sucked all the what you'd call potential conversation in.

"Jordan?" Sarah said. "Are you in there?"

"Sure," Jordan said, without the look on his face changing one single bit.

Fortunately Buddy was done in just a minute, and came and sat in a chair across this coffee table from me and Sarah. He asked how was I doing and if I'd been playing any pool. Sarah told him I won a hundred dollars at the races, which made me wince, and Buddy said "Wow," like he was impressed. The whole thing was kind of condescending. Buddy excused his rudeness—that's how he said it, "Please excuse my *rude*ness"—but he was working on streamlining the farm's production and maximizing yield, which seemed like a strange way to talk about milk.

Then Buddy said, "Jordan, can you turn that fucking thing off for once in your life? Can you wean yourself from it in the interest of sociability?" Sarah laughed. I imagine this Jordan guy is someone Buddy has to tell to go home on a regular basis.

Jordan grabbed the remote control from the arm of his chair and clicked off the TV. Then he stared at the blank screen for a few seconds, and then took a deep breath and turned toward me and Sarah and looked at us like he hadn't ever seen us before. "You guys okay with those beers?" he said. We'd hardly had time to finish even half of one.

Then we just chit-chatted for a few minutes, Sarah telling them about my system while I sat there and wished I'd remembered to tell her not to mention it. Buddy actually seemed interested, though, even though Sarah had already told me he hated the dog races and wouldn't go near them. Again it struck me how he was an interesting guy, someone who just couldn't help sinking his teeth into things.

But the whole time I could see Sarah had something on her mind that was making her impatient. I should have figured it out right then. She was leaned forward on the edge of the couch with her legs straight out in front of her, holding the beer on her knees and peeling off the label, which she then folded in a little pie-shaped piece and tossed on the table. "So," she said. Not like the beginning of a sentence but an entire sentence all by itself.

Right away, like this was a kind of code word he understood perfectly, this Jordan leaned his butt up off the chair and scrunched into his pocket with his hand and pulled out a baggie of dope. Buddy got up and went to the kitchen and came back with a red plastic bong that was about as tall as Jake. He held it up in the air when he sat back down and said, "Do you mind?" looking at me.

"No," I said, "go right ahead," and Buddy grinned. I definitely gave the wrong impression I realized.

I don't smoke dope. Never have, not once. Beer is enough for me, considering the trouble I've had. Drugs of any sort have always scared me. But I've been around all sorts of people who did drugs, so much so that they don't even make me uncomfortable, and after the first time or two not even the people around me. They just pass the stuff right by me and don't even ask. I've hung around with potheads and speed demons and coke freaks and acid burnouts and I was once even almost a roommate with a woman in Crescent City, California, who turned out to be a heroin addict, although I found out just before I moved in and that kept me from doing it—moving in with her, I mean. And I have absolutely nothing against drug addicts, except the fact that they usually turn out to be very needy in some way it seems to me, I mean in some way other than just the drugs, and things can get messy when it's time to leave.

Anyway it was clear to me at that point that the whole reason for going to Buddy's place was to get high, and they'd arranged it all beforehand. Later back at my room Sarah explained to me that Jordan was Buddy's friendly local dealer, that's how she put it, and I said how nice that he lives right next door, and Sarah said Buddy would agree.

They gave Sarah the bong first and it was clear she was a real pro, packing the bowl tight and knowing how to use the carb and everything. I'm familiar with the whole routine, although it's definitely been a while, and I haven't seen it often since I met Jenny. Naturally when Sarah got done she passed it to me and I had to explain how I didn't smoke dope but it was fine with me if everyone else did, and they were cool about it. Sarah was definitely more relaxed already, and leaned back into the couch close to me.

They smoked dope a while, and I wished they'd left the TV on, regardless of what kind of stupid show it was. I got me and Sarah another beer. Buddy finally got around to asking me what kind of work did I do, and I told him I bet on dogs. He raised his eyebrows and nodded. Sarah said I really did, my system worked she could tell already, and she squeezed my hand.

Jordan said, "Really? A system?" like he hadn't heard it before, and it was pretty funny even to me who wasn't stoned.

The conversation went on kind of about nothing. I disappointed myself by making a joke about how the bong was as big as my son, and Sarah thought it was funny, sort of, and said I should have had it there the night before when I couldn't remember. But I noticed how even though she was stoned, she knew there was a side of it that wasn't funny, the Jake side namely, and that it was something I shouldn't have said and probably wasn't proud about saying. And she leaned over and put her head on my shoulder for a second and I could smell her hair again instead of the pot smoke. When I looked up, Buddy was throwing a glance over at Jordan out of the corner of his eye, but Jordan was too stoned and stupid to even notice I'd said anything about a kid.

The bong went around once more, and then Buddy gave it to Jordan to go put away, but Jordan dropped it and it spilled all over the place. "Jesus," Buddy said, and went to the kitchen for some paper towels.

"It's a good thing you don't have carpet," Jordan said.

So on and so on, etcetera. The interesting part started when I had to go take a leak. When I passed by the bedroom I noticed Buddy had this really nice old-fashioned wooden chess set on his dresser, and after I was done I asked if he wanted to play, and he said sure we could.

The chess game idea had an added bonus in that we'd hardly pulled the chairs up to the kitchen table before Jordan decided to leave. When he was safely out the door, Sarah said, "Jordan," and kind of shook her head, which pretty much summed up everything.

Buddy kicked my ass. He's a good chess player. He played real smart and defensively and just picked up on little mistakes I made because I don't really understand the game the way good players do, and will get too aggressive and end up sacrificing moves here and there to get out of the trouble I caused myself. I don't think he ever doubted he would win, but I hung in there for thirty or so moves, I guess. He said "Good game" afterward and even halfway meant it.

But the thing about it now, after it's over with, is that I had a pleasant evening just sitting there with them in Buddy's apartment playing chess. The game was interesting and I admired Buddy's intelligence and Sarah looked great sitting there at the table reading her book.

When I think about it, it's the first time since Jenny left that I sat in a room with a couple of people and had a friendly conversation and just killed time. It actually reminded me a lot of days in Orofino, where me and the depressed guy who taught me how to play would play one game after another with maybe one or two other patients sitting around to watch, and there wasn't anything to worry about for that little space of time, no one to answer to and no pressure to make a better life.

And even before Jenny left we didn't have any friends. It was always just the three of us for a long time. Jenny would at times when we got to new towns strike up friendships with people at work where they would do stuff like go to lunch on their days off, or she would get friendly with one of the neighbors if they seemed respectable, dressed their kids okay and didn't let them go around looking dirty and behaving bad, but these were always just kind of casual acquaintances because we never stayed long enough to make real friends. And then we never had people over to our place because of how Jenny felt about stuff like the fact that we never had actual bed frames and just had mattresses thrown on the floor or sometimes box springs to go with them but that was it, and a couple of ratty chairs we'd got from a yard sale or used furniture store, and not very nice sets of dishes. The dishes were about all we'd keep when we moved from town to town, other than the T V and the stereo and our clothes and maybe a lamp. We'd sell what we could at a yard sale sometimes, if we didn't head out of town just on an impulse, and then just leave the rest.

So it had been a long time since I'd just sat around with people that way, over at someone's house. After we got done playing chess me and Sarah left, and it was more or less understood she was coming to my place.

When we got there it was really late, or early depending on how you look at it, and we had both basically gotten partway undressed and under the covers before we even stopped to think what we were doing. It just seemed to happen that way. We were under the covers with her just in her panties, and me just in my boxer shorts, and just the light from the half-closed bathroom door and the moon through the window.

What surprised me most wasn't the way we turned to each other automatically, without even any words, but how her body felt, how young her body was, her breasts heavy and firm and round, and her arms and legs and stomach smooth and tender but at the same time firm and strong. I understood then what Jenny meant about getting older and having a child, how it changed a woman, although I really couldn't feel the difference before when I touched her, or couldn't remember exactly what she'd felt like before. And that's not to say Jenny's out of shape now by any means, only that you can't be exactly what you were at twenty, and I know this from my own body too.

So I thought me and Sarah were headed in a definite direction, and I was ready, and she was too by what I could tell, both of us completely undressed by then and her pressed against me tight. She felt good. But then when I moved on top of her, she suddenly pushed me up with her arms and said, "Let's not get ahead of ourselves, okay?" and that was all right with me.

Then we just lay in bed together and I was thinking of some things. I thought some about Jenny, of course, and how what I was doing didn't seem right, but how she was the one who left without even getting in touch with me. And I thought about new things, like how it had been going at the races but didn't exactly go the same way last night and why. I thought about Sarah and how she'd seemed to just pick me out to be with for some odd reason. I thought about how nice it had been with her already, and how comfortable. What a good place my cabin was to be in, quiet and warm with the clock ticking softly on the table.

Sarah was almost sleeping. I could feel her relaxing in my arms, but there was one thing I wanted to ask her. It was hard because some things hadn't been going right, like how I hadn't won money at the track really with her, and how that didn't exactly fit in, but still I had the same feeling, so I asked her, "Do you ever meet people where it seems like it's part of a plan?" She didn't say anything but I could tell she was awake and listening. "Like somehow you were supposed to meet someone at a certain place and time and get to the point of things?"

I could feel her pull away, just barely, like what she was going to say she didn't want to say up close to me. "Luke," she said, "I like you. We're having fun here, right?" I didn't answer. "Fun? Nothing serious?"

She didn't get what I meant. She's not old enough to understand that when you get to a certain point, it's not like you're looking for some one certain person who equals your fate or your destiny and was meant just for you. You're just looking for someone who can help you get over some hurdle in your life, just get from one point to the next. And if you're lucky you find someone who can help you do that over and over again.

I said, "You don't see what I mean."

Then she kind of squirmed back in closer to me. "What, then?" she said. "Tell me."

I said, "I mean do you ever think you run across a person at a certain time to get answers to some things." She didn't say anything so I figured she still didn't understand me. "Like there are things you've been looking for answers to, and at one particular point in your life a person comes along who can help you get those answers, like it's been arranged for that person to be there and help you."

The room was quiet except for the clock and the wind outside. "No," Sarah said. "But I'd like to do that for you if you think I'm that person."

Then we didn't say anything, just held each other and went to sleep.

I dreamed about Tucker and the midget. I mean there were more people in the dream, but they seemed to be at the center somehow. There was Tucker and the midget and me and Sarah and Jenny and Jake and my father, all sitting around in these lawn chairs on a huge grassy lawn with fountains and flower gardens everywhere. Everyone was talking but I couldn't hear anything, or like I could hear them but couldn't understand or was too sleepy to hear what they were saying. I kept getting the feeling that someone was watching us, but nobody else seemed to feel that way. They were all happy and talking to each other, and we were drinking these bright red drinks in tall glasses which had a slight sugary taste, and I finally figured out it was the colored water from the hummingbird feeder. But the lawn and gardens and fountains weren't like here at the cabins in Wisconsin, more like the hospital in Orofino only more beautiful, like a place where everything was real without any plastic sunflowers. I started thinking it was Dr. Blumenthal watching us, maybe from a high window in the hospital which was around somewhere but not where I could see. I started thinking he would come to get me and take me to the ward if I couldn't be happy and act like everyone else did. So I started trying to talk to Tucker and the midget who were sitting right across from me and like I say seemed to be the center of everything. But they couldn't hear me or didn't want to listen. I felt invisible, like everybody else was really there but not me. Then Tucker did it again, picked the midget up from his chair and put him over his shoulder, and came walking straight to where I sat. He turned around so the midget could face me, only it was Jenny then and not the midget anymore. Jenny hung onto his neck and she was very small and she smiled at me and said, "Luke, I particularly like your new friend, Sarah."

What bothered me was that it wasn't how she would say it, Jenny, if she ever was to say such a thing. The words she used didn't match up with who I knew she was, like I had forgotten how to hear her voice and see her picture the right way in my head. And the whole time there was someone watching.

JENNY

JUNE 21

The house is yellow with a big picture window facing east to catch
the morning sun. When I wake up, I shut the door to Jake's room.
He has a little bed with Star Wars sheets and pillowcases in the corner across from the door. He sleeps sprawled sideways, his arms
thrown out wide and his legs tangling the sheets. We leave the door
to both bedrooms open at night. I was afraid he wouldn't sleep well
in his very own room. But it's me who hasn't been sleeping well,
alone in the room across the hall in the double bed.

Right now I watch him through the side window above the

table, playing in the sandbox with the boy he met from next door. The boy, Jeremy, is a year and a half younger than Jake, and Jake is very polite and patient with him. He's hardly been around children, and expects them to behave reasonably, like adults, although it's hard to imagine where he got that notion. I don't see how he could have gotten it from Luke and me.

When Jeremy throws sand and it gets in Jake's hair, or when he bangs the toys too hard on the wooden frame, Jake looks stunned. Then I can see him gather himself up in a straight line, his shoulders back and his head high, and explain to Jeremy carefully how he shouldn't act that way. How it doesn't make any sense to throw away the sand or break things.

It's been harder for Jake than for me. The house, the new sofa, the new draperies I chose but have yet to put up in the windows— they don't mean much to him. Of course, they do to me.

Jake wants to know when Luke will come. He wakes up in the morning and looks for him. He walks quietly into every room. He stares out the front window, as if Luke might magically appear out there beyond the birch trees, standing in the street. What I don't tell him is that I'm not sure I want Luke here.

Luke's mother has been wonderful. All during the long drive across Montana, I tried to think what I would say to her. Hours and hundreds of miles passed, and I was not even aware of the other cars and the bare hills. After we'd passed Butte and it was dark, Jake started to cry. Where was his papa, he wanted to know, where were we going without him? I said, "We're visiting Grandma Rivers. Don't you want to see Grandma Rivers?" He said he wanted to see Papa. He begged me to stop and call the motel in Rapid City. If I didn't call the motel, Papa would wonder where we were, and start walking to try to find us. Then no one would know where anyone was, and we'd all be lost.

I held tight to the steering wheel and pushed the accelerator. "Go to sleep," I told Jake, but he cried for a long time.

We got there at three in the morning. Crossing the lake was like a slow dream, staring ahead at the string of lights at City Beach. Luke's house was dark when we pulled up, with the streetlight glowing over the yard. A Volvo was parked in the gravel driveway. It didn't look right for Mrs. Rivers, but I had no way of knowing. I unhooked Jake's seat belt. He was sleeping, and it was all I could do to lift his dead weight.

I rang the bell for a long time, bent over halfway to help support Jake with my knees. A strange man answered the door. Jake yawned and rubbed his eyes, and I set him down on his feet, holding him to make sure he could stand while I looked at the man in the doorway. He switched on the porch light and peered out at us, and Jake buried his head into my hip, holding on to my leg. He was an attractive older man with salt-and-pepper hair, wearing a bathrobe. His hair was messed up on one side where he'd been sleeping. I looked wildly around at the other houses on the street, thinking I had come to the wrong place. But it was Luke's house. I held Jake's head in close to me.

"Are you looking for Mrs. Rivers?" the man asked me.

She had sold the house and moved across town to an apartment complex by the lake. *The Tamaracks,* the wooden sign said. The man hadn't known the apartment number, and I sat behind the wheel in the parking lot, staring at the landscape lights dotting the lawn and pathways. Beyond the apartment buildings was the lake, yellow lights floating lazily across the water through the gaps in the buildings. Jake unbuckled himself and crawled up front and sat in my lap. I told him, "Go to sleep."

When it was light enough to see, just an hour or two, I woke up Jake. I got a hairbrush from the glove box and fixed his hair a little, and wiped the corners of his mouth. I checked myself in the rearview mirror, but it was hopeless, and I was too tired to bother with how I looked anyway.

We got out and searched for the apartment. I knew Luke's mother would be the kind to make sure her name was on the mailbox. At the third building, I found it—Mrs. John Rivers, 3E. I stood staring at the name, wishing that I could turn around and walk away. *We found it, now let's leave.* But there was no way to do that. We trudged up the stairs.

She was already awake, I knew as soon as she answered the door. She was wearing a gown, loose and big and covered with flowers. She stood there motionless, her hand held at her throat. Then, without a word, she pulled us inside.

"My gosh, Jenny. My gosh," she said, and hugged me. "Jacob," she said, and went down on her knees to hug him tight, even though Jake barely responded. She was a stranger to him. She asked him a few questions and he nodded or shook his head. "You want to watch TV?" she asked him, and took him to the sofa and handed him the remote control. "I've got cable, that channel that shows all cartoons. I think of you every time I see it, how much Luke said you liked cartoons." She helped him flip through the channels until they found it.

Then she took me by the hand and led me to the kitchen. I had smelled coffee the entire time, but it wasn't until I saw the pot that I knew how glad it made me—a fresh cup of coffee, not the horrible coffee I'd been drinking on the road. She poured me a cup, and said, "You're exhausted, I can see."

I looked around, silently. It was a nice, homey apartment, split-level, with a wooden banister leading upstairs from the living room. New gray carpet in the living room and on the stairs. Mrs. Rivers had the same old, beat-up furniture, and it looked like it all belonged somewhere else. "There are two bedrooms upstairs," she said, and I nodded and smiled. She smiled at me and patted my hand. She scooted her chair a little closer. "Where's Luke, Jenny?" she asked me.

I told her South Dakota, we had left him in South Dakota.

"I always knew something like this would happen," she said, and looked over at Jake where he sat on the couch, staring at the TV. "Well, at least you came to the right place."

Then I told her what I'd been preparing to the whole way from Rapid City. I told her that I was sorry, but I couldn't live with Luke anymore, that I needed a home. I didn't know if I loved Luke anymore, but that hardly mattered. I just wanted to stay in one place. I barely had any money, just a couple hundred dollars, but I could get a job that would start earning money right away. If she, Mrs. Rivers, could just loan us a few hundred dollars. All I needed was enough to get us into a small apartment. I would pay her back the money over a few months' time. Jake needed to go to kindergarten. He needed to have friends. We needed a place to stay.

"Okay, Jenny," she said. "Slow down. Don't be so upset. We can take care of all of that, don't worry." She patted my hand again and leaned forward to hug my neck, and I leaned in to make it easier. "Right now let's just stop talking. You need some sleep. My gosh," she said, looking at Jake on the sofa where he had fallen fast asleep, the remote hanging from his opened fingers. "South Dakota."

She took me upstairs and put me to bed in the guest room, which looked like it had never been used. The lamps on the end tables were new and still had plastic around the shades. On the dresser across from the bed were three pictures in gold frames—one of Mary at graduation, one of Luke in his football uniform, and a school picture of Mark against a fake background of blue sky and clouds. I'd seen the pictures before, in the other house, hanging on the wall in the basement. Luke's mother pulled the covers up under my chin. I could feel myself falling to sleep. "I need to get the things in from the car," I said. "Jake needs to brush his teeth."

"I'll take care of Jake," she said. "You go to sleep." I closed my eyes and saw the pattern of her flowered gown floating down my sight like it was carried on a breeze.

I woke up in the afternoon. I could hear Jake laughing downstairs. I lay there for a minute, watching dust specks glide lazily through the sunlight from the small window. Then I got up and used the few things Mrs. Rivers had in the small upstairs bathroom to make myself look a little better.

They were at the kitchen table playing checkers. "He learns so fast," Mrs. Rivers said when I sat down with them. "He is just taking me for a *spin*," she said.

Jake bounced up and down in his seat. "Watch this," he said. "This is my king." He double-jumped her, and laughed through his teeth. A little white speck of saliva landed on the board, and Jake wiped it off with his finger. "Sorry," he said, and looked hesitantly at his grandmother.

She waved his apology away. "Oh, honey, it's just cardboard," she said. "Spit on it when you want to."

Jake laughed again and looked at me, delighted, as if he wondered where we'd been hiding her for so long. "Spit on it whenever you want to," he said. "That's funny."

"Jenny," Mrs. Rivers said, wiping one eye behind her glasses, "I want you to know he *just learned* this game and he is taking me to the *cleaners.*"

"He's a little competitor," I said.

"Just like Luke," Mrs. Rivers said. "Luke couldn't stand to be beaten at anything."

Jake looked at Mrs. Rivers, understanding for the first time, no doubt, that this was really his father's mother, that she knew things about him even I couldn't know. Then he looked at me. I smiled the best I could. "I beat her two times already," Jake said.

I sat and watched them play. For the first time in so long, sitting relaxed there in my chair, I felt peaceful and my heart beat easy.

When we were all ready, Mrs. Rivers drove us to the bank in her old blue Cutlass, the same car she'd had since Luke and I first met. I waited awkwardly off to the side, holding Jake's hand because it was crowded, while Mrs. Rivers wrote out a check. When she finished she hurried us into line. "Now, I want you to know I have plenty of money from selling the house," she said. She showed me the check, made out to "Cash" for five thousand dollars. I covered my mouth with my hand. "You take this," Mrs. Rivers said. "Jenny, you *take* this money," she said, in a fierce little whisper that nearly scared me.

We've been to her house for supper almost every night. She's excited for tonight because the IGA had catfish, and she found a box of fry mix. She says it will be just like home. I didn't tell her that I hate catfish, that it reminds me of being dragged to Eason's Fish

House in Mendenhall every Sunday night for as long as I could remember. But the suppers have all been pleasant, though sometimes a little sad. Last night, while I was giving her a hand with the dishes, Mrs. Rivers said that she was surprised I hadn't known about the house. She had told Luke nearly a year ago that it was up for sale. I said he must have forgotten to mention it, or maybe he had mentioned and I'd forgotten, though I knew that wasn't so. Then she paused a moment with her hands under the running water, and I saw the look in her eyes like the time when she tried to give Luke his father's ties. But she didn't cry, and I stopped my hand from reaching for her shoulder.

When I'm with her here, I wonder how Luke has been so hard on her. I've never heard him say that she did anything to hurt him. But maybe she never did enough to help him, either. When I think of Luke before he met me, from the stories that he's told, I think of a boy and then a man going through hard times all alone.

Jake is testing Jeremy on his colors. He sits in the sandbox with colored blocks behind his back and pulls them out one by one for Jeremy to see. Jeremy sits across from him, with his legs crossed the same way. I stand in the wet grass in my bare feet, holding a cup of coffee. The grass warms slowly in the sun, partly because of the cool, sharp mornings here and partly because it has grown too long. I have to buy a lawnmower today. I've never mowed a lawn, but I'll learn how.

I say, "Ten more minutes, Jake. We have to get things done if you want to go swimming." We discovered yesterday that there's a public access dock within walking distance of the house, in the opposite direction from what the neighbors call the "pole yard" at the end of our street, with its stacks of neatly cut, round lumber and the noise in the distance of saws and machinery. It seems like the lake is in every direction here, that you can't help running into it, walking or driving. Sometimes I think we've washed up on an island from a passing ship.

"What color is this?" Jake asks, pulling a block from behind his back.

"Yullow," Jeremy says.

"What color is this one?"

"Gween."

Jake nods his head in praise. "Very good, Jeremy. That is very good." He holds both blocks in front of Jeremy's face. "Yellow. Green."

When I was little I would stand like this in my Aunt Eunice's yard before church, dressed in my Sunday clothes. I would watch the families arriving for church across the street. They drove into the parking lot in their shining cars, and I could feel how hot it was there. I was glad that Aunt Eunice lived across the street so that I could come out of church and walk quietly away from the other people to our cool car beneath the carport.

I would dawdle in the lawn as long as I could before church, running back and forth like my mother always told me not to do in my dress and white Sunday shoes, or picking the flowers off of the magnolia tree. That might have landed me in trouble, too, but Aunt Eunice always pretended that she'd asked for them. *Thank you, Virginia. I'll put these in a bowl immediately.*

They all lingered in the house until eleven o'clock sharp, so that we always had to sit in the front pews. My father said, time and time again, that there was no shame in sitting front and center at the Mendenhall First Baptist Church, and he couldn't understand why a whole congregation of Christians should avoid it so. Really, he loved to make his grand entrance only moments before the service began.

My father and mother and my grandmother and Aunt Eunice. My mother's sister, Peggy Ann, and her husband Arthur and their two boys, J. P. and Arthur Jr., who were perfect in front of their parents but mean otherwise. All sitting in the house before church, drinking ice tea, Aunt Eunice making sure that lunch was properly set to simmer on the stove for our return. Sometimes, I would watch for one of my friends from school to appear across the street, and I would run to her and ask if I could sit with her through church.

At first, this way of avoiding the stares when we walked down front scared my mother and father, who thought I had run the two blocks to downtown. But soon they became used to it, and didn't mind. One Sunday when I was ten, I walked very quietly to the far end of the yard and the magnolia tree. I stood there for a few seconds, touching the hard leaves, then I pushed aside the branches and stepped underneath.

Sitting against the trunk, it was cool and lonely. Through a gap in the leaves, I watched my family cross the street to church, bending my neck this way and that way to keep them in view.

I sat there for what seemed like a long time, looking out through the leaves. Then I got up very slow and quiet and walked in the sunshine to the back door of the house. Aunt Eunice was deathly afraid of "robbers," as she always referred to them, so she locked her front door whenever she went out, even though few people in Mendenhall bothered to do so. But she always left the back door open because she had an equally strong fear of forgetting her key and getting locked out of the house. Once she had done that, and J. P. had to stand on a ladder to cut a little hole in her living room window screen to get to the latch. Then when he got the screen out and tried to crawl through the window, he lost his balance and fell into the house, knocking over and breaking one of Aunt Eunice's matching lamps. So Aunt Eunice had to buy a new window screen and two lamps, and she never quite got over it.

The back door opened into the kitchen, and I walked in to the smell of black-eyed peas and okra and cornbread and ham. I took a spoon from the cupboard and ate peas right out of the pot, which my mother would have punished me for, making me go outside and pick a switch from the pear tree. It was only after I'd taken a knife and fork to the ham in the oven that I realized I was in trouble. I could rinse off the spoon and no one would miss the peas, but there was no disguising the damaged ham.

I'm not sure what my plan had been to that point, or if I'd had one. I sat at the kitchen table for a few minutes regretting my mistake. I got up and rinsed the knife and fork and spoon and put them back in the cupboard, but that wouldn't do any good. I thought about suggesting that a robber had eaten the ham, but only Aunt Eunice would believe it, and I would only be in more trouble after she'd gone on a frantic search for stolen jewelry and lost heirlooms. So I decided to quit worrying and just enjoy the half hour I had left to myself until I would have to pay for the sin of missing church. It even seemed like a fair swap in a way.

I always loved Aunt Eunice's little bedroom at the top of the stairs. It was the tiniest room in the house, not counting the bathrooms. In her room she had nothing but an old chest-of-drawers with an oval mirror above it, a little night stand with an oriental lamp, and an old double bed with a huge wooden headboard scrolled with roses. It was the same bed Aunt Eunice was born in. My mother says it stayed in the little bedroom for years, and no one was allowed to use it. Aunt Eunice slept down the hall with her husband, Harold. The children, all of whom eventually moved away, to Jackson and Biloxi and Mobile, had bedrooms downstairs. But after Harold died suddenly of a heart attack on the same day I was born—July 5, 1974—Aunt Eunice left the bed she shared with her husband and returned to the one down the hall which she'd slept in when she first entered the world. And then no one was allowed to sleep in her marriage bed, including Aunt Eunice. She keeps the same arrangement to this day.

I sat on Aunt Eunice's bed that morning when I was not at church, and the time moved very slow, and I was glad for that. Aunt Eunice always kept her little flowered draperies drawn, and I watched the sunlight through them. Everything in the room was so old, and there was nothing to see through the drapes that told me I was in Mendenhall.

It began to seem that I was somewhere else. A scene took shape in my mind, but I didn't know from where. I saw a little street with shops, a jeweler's and a bakery. A cobblestone street with carts driving slowly past, the drivers hunching from the sun at the reins, pulling their caps down low over their eyes. People walking by, stopping at the shop windows, a father and a mother and a small child, dressed in simple clothes. Everything was simple. There were no fine carriages or lacy dresses or top hats and walking canes. There was nothing romantic, no knight in shining armor or handsome prince, no boy I knew from school that I would cast in that role.

I believed in the little town and the little street like I had believed in nothing before, nothing but the small facts of my everyday life in Mendenhall. It was not even that I liked the little town and the little street so much, that I had any real wish to be there. It was just that all the evidence pointed to it. When I looked at the window I felt sure that outside were the street and the shops and the people. I could even hear the street and its noises, and when I looked around Aunt Eunice's room everything seemed to fit. The chance that I was in Mendenhall seemed less likely, that I would have been born accidentally into that certain time and certain place and still belong there. I felt like I was in a place of my own choosing. I lay back on the bed and closed my eyes, not happy or unhappy, listening to the noises on the street.

Then my mother was in the doorway. I was in Mendenhall again, and I had not gone to church. My mother was as angry as I knew she would be. Why wasn't I in church, she wanted to know. Did I think I was old enough to make a decision not to go to church on Sunday? Was that something that would make God feel good toward me? I told her I didn't care what God thought of me, still lying on the bed, not even knowing why I chose to say it.

"What did you say, Virginia?" my mother said, her voice louder and even more stern. "Speak up."

"I don't care what God thinks of me, *ma'am*," I said, as if that were why she was angry.

She was on fire then, coming for me fast across the room, and I tried to get to my feet but wasn't quick enough. She had me turned over on the bed in an instant, spanking my bottom. I lay there till she was through. She couldn't spank hard enough to really hurt me.

"Is there anything you'd like to say?" my mother asked me, smoothing out her dress. I had rolled over onto my back again, and was lying there like I was when she came in.

"Nothing that wouldn't land me in more trouble," I said.

"What would you like to say?" she asked me.

"I'd like to say 'I hate you,'" I told her. "But then I'd get spanked again."

My mother's mouth fell open slightly, and I could see her eyes fill with tears, or maybe the expression on her face just told me so without my having to see it. She turned and left the room, and I felt sorry as soon as I heard her feet on the stairs.

Nobody ever asked if I believed in God. My parents simply assumed I did, the same way they assumed I believed in other things. I can't remember a time when I did not know that my father was the one who slipped a dollar under my pillow after I'd lost a tooth, that it was my mother who filled my Easter basket, that it was the two of them who were responsible for the heap of presents under the white-flocked tree. I didn't *want* there to be a Santa Claus. I didn't *want* a fat stranger to land on our roof and bring presents down the chimney. I was much happier knowing that my mother and father gave me things. For years I pretended to believe because I didn't want to spoil their Christmas. It was important to them, not to me. Only after Jake was born did I start believing in Santa Claus—only when I was the one buying the presents. Then it was fun to believe.

I understood very early that my life would always consist of the people and things around me, nothing else. The first time I saw Luke was at Randall's Steak House on Highway 55 where my father had taken me for lunch. He waited on our table. I thought he was attractive, but not shown to best effect in his cheap black pants and shoes and white shirt. The shirt especially made him look too thin. His hair was long and tied up in a ponytail—the only time I've ever seen Luke wear a ponytail—but he'd gotten it all wrong, tying it too low with a plain rubber band so that it puffed out on the sides and made him look like he was wearing a hair net. But his eyes had a softness that appealed to me, and there was something very natural about his gestures and the way he moved.

When Mr. Randall came to the table like he always did, my father cut up a piece of steak and looked down at his plate and said, "Cute new girl you got there, Joe."

"Which one?" Mr. Randall said. "Where?"

My father glanced up and pointed with his steak knife to Luke where he was waiting on another table. "Could use a little closer shave, but right cute nonetheless," he said. "You combing the trailer park for help these days?"

Mr. Randall stood there looking at Luke in that slow way he always had, looking at him like he'd seen him for the first time. "Figured I'd give him a chance," he said. "Nice boy. Comes from Idaho." Mr. Randall rubbed his chin. "Where is Idaho?"

"North," my father said.

Mr. Randall grabbed my father's shoulder and squeezed, in that way men do who've known each other a long time, still looking over at Luke. "Doesn't hurt to have someone a little different around here now and again," he said.

"So you say," my father said, cutting his steak. "Customers seem to like him."

Luke was walking back to the kitchen, and the old couple at the table stared after him, the wife mumbling something and leaning over the table. I knew it was the last time I'd see Luke at Randall's Steak House unless he cut his hair.

I probably would have forgotten him entirely if I hadn't seen him on the way to Eason's Fish House that Sunday. We were passing out of town on Mays Bridge Road, just at the far edge, about a mile before the bridge and Eason's, the black section of town. We were driving by a little run-down gray shack next to the park with the old wooden swings and broken seesaws.

There was Luke sitting on the porch in a metal folding chair, looking out at the road. I leaned up in the back seat and looked out the window. At first I thought he'd seen me, but after we'd passed he still stared out at the road, as if he hadn't even noticed our car go by.

My father asked me if that wasn't the boy Joe Randall had hired. I told him I thought so. Then he told my mother the story, finishing it in Eason's parking lot while I got out of the car and heard the sigh of Strong River as it flowed beneath Mays Bridge.

I started driving by there once or twice a day in my new convertible. It was just a few weeks after graduation and the car still looked like it belonged on a showroom floor. It felt strange to drive down there, and I suppose a little dangerous, like the day at Aunt Eunice's when I played hooky from church.

But Luke was never on the porch again. Once I saw him on the road, walking from town. For a second, long enough for me to touch the brakes, I thought of stopping to offer him a ride. I kept driving, though, blistering myself for the brake lights he must have seen, watching him in his shorts and T-shirt from the corner of my eye in the rearview mirror.

Finally I stopped the car at the park one day. I couldn't believe I was doing it, pulling off the road into the red dust of the rutted little parking area. I checked my hair in the mirror and adjusted a bra strap so that it didn't stick out from my blouse. It was deadly hot, the middle of the afternoon. I headed down the dirt path straight to the wooden swings in the shade of a huge oak tree. I knew I couldn't stay long. I didn't know how I would explain if anyone saw me, but it was unlikely that any of my friends would drive up that road. The only reason to go there was Eason's, which wasn't even open during the day. Still, it was risky.

I saw Luke right away behind the shack. He was sitting in the same chair, in the small shade from the back door overhang. He didn't seem to be doing anything other than smoking a cigarette. He stared off into a wild tangle of kudzu behind an old backyard hen house with the roof caved in. In the patchy grass of his yard there were two shiny hubcaps, silvery white in the sun.

I started swinging slowly, keeping my legs close together, trying to look, I suppose, both dignified and whimsical. Luke never looked over once. He seemed absorbed in the kudzu.

There were two black boys in the park, a little boy about five or six who was playing with a truck in the sandbox, and his older brother, probably ten or eleven, who was straddling the broken end of the seesaw and reading a comic book. The smaller boy had been watching me the whole time, and he finally abandoned the sandbox and came over to the swings. He sat in the one next to mine, and I smiled at him but he looked away. His feet didn't touch the ground. He started rocking back and forth vigorously, but it got him nowhere. "Terrence!" he shouted, in a husky little voice. "Gimme a shove, Terrence!" Terrence looked up from his comic book but didn't move. I dragged my feet in the red dust and brought my swing to a stop.

When I got behind the boy and started to push, I saw Luke coming down the dirt path. His hair was frizzy and all in his eyes, and he was wearing cut-offs and tennis shoes with no socks and a T-shirt from some bar in New Orleans. "Hi, Curtis," he said when he got up close, and the boy craned his neck and smiled and looked shyly away again. "I'll do that," he said, moving in behind me. "You go ahead and swing."

I didn't want to swing, but I didn't have any choice then. I was terribly embarrassed. He probably thought I was fifteen, an overgrown adolescent who hadn't given up swinging yet. The heat was miserable. No one in their right mind ever stayed outside on a Mississippi summer afternoon. My legs were sticky with sweat where I held them together on the swing. I told myself over and over again, *One more minute. One more minute and I'll leave.* We didn't even speak. Luke was pushing Curtis, and I was just there swinging. I had never felt more stupid. I told myself that I hoped I had learned my lesson. That I would quit trying to be different and just do things normally, in the way Mendenhall did things.

When I had told myself for five minutes or so that I had better get off the swing and leave—at least he would see that I had a car, that I was old enough to drive—a black woman came out from a little house across the road from the park. She stood on the porch step and shouted, "Terrence!"

Immediately Terrence closed his comic book and walked away

toward home. "I got to go," Curtis said, and Luke stopped the swing.

"See you later," Luke said.

Curtis turned and smiled and then stuffed his hands in his pockets and fell back in stride. "Hold up, Terrence!" he called out.

"Wait up, Terrence!" Luke shouted. "Wait for Curtis so you can help him cross the street."

Terrence stopped then, but didn't turn around, and I could see his mother shade her eyes and stare at Luke and me on the swings. Then she opened the door and went inside.

Luke watched Terrence and Curtis till they were in their yard. He was sitting on the swing next to me, twisting and turning so the chain wrapped up, acting like a little boy. "You like to swing?" he asked me. Then, "You were at the restaurant a week or so ago."

I wasn't sure what to respond to, or how.

"How old are you?" he said.

Did I like to swing? If so, how old did that make me? If not, why was I there? Yes, I had eaten at the restaurant, but did being there with my father, who I had already guessed cost Luke his job, incriminate me? How old *was* I, anyway, now that he asked? Should I be seventeen, or fib a little bit, say eighteen or even twenty? After all, it was only a week until my eighteenth birthday. And how old was he? He could have been thirty or sixteen.

"I realize there's a couple stumpers in there, but just go on ahead whenever you feel like giving it a try," he said to me.

I laughed. "Seventeen," I said. "Yes, I was at the restaurant. It's too hot out to swing."

"Very good," he said. "I'm Luke Rivers. Who are you?"

He offered me a glass of water and we went up to his house. I was nervous but not afraid.

The inside of his house was no better than the outside. The floor was old splintery pine boards, and you could see through the boards in places to the dirt below. One corner of the living room floor was caved in. To the left of the front door were the other three small rooms, none of which had doors on their broken hinges. The kitchen was first, just a sink and a refrigerator and an electric stove, and no counter space. Then the bathroom, an old claw-foot tub with a rubber hose attached to the faucet to wet your hair, water dripping into a small sink and leaving a brown trail to the drain. At the back was the bedroom. All I could see in there was a kind of pallet made from old quilts on the wooden floor, and a feather pillow with no pillowcase and a rumpled white sheet with a hole in the middle. In each room there was one bare light bulb.

"I haven't got all the way moved in yet," Luke said. "Have a seat."

There was a card table with a metal folding chair in the front room, and I sat down. Luke brought the other chair in from the back yard. Then he brought me some water in a plastic Mardi Gras cup.

We started talking easily then. He told me how he'd picked Mendenhall at random off the map, just because he wanted to move away from New Orleans. He said he was a bartender, but the only job he could find was at Randall's. He wasn't working there anymore, though.

"It's a dry county," I said.

"That's what I hear," he said. "I didn't know there even was such a thing."

I told him he could probably get a job in Magee. He said that's what he'd heard, but he didn't have any way to get there. I told him I could drive him. "Carry" him there, that's what we always said in Mississippi. He had a good laugh at that, and I don't think I ever said it again.

He said thanks, but he didn't see how that would help any. He'd still have to get over there every day. He said he was just thinking about taking the money he had left and buying a bus ticket back to New Orleans. He thought he could get his old job again.

I told him I'd drive him every day. He asked if I could pick him up, too. I had to say no. I knew there was no way I could get out of the house that late.

It worked out, though. He found a job that week—not bartending, but working as a clerk at The Beer Barn, the place where you could drive through and pick up beer and cigarettes and potato chips. I drove him there on the afternoons he worked, and at night he would convince some customer to come pick him up from work and give him a ride back to Mendenhall. Other nights, he would walk a mile down the highway to the store manager's house, and she would let him sleep on the sofa. She was a single woman in her thirties, not at all attractive, but still I worried about the arrangement. Luke said there was nothing going on, that she was just a nice person. On the mornings when I picked him up, though, she would rarely speak to me. Once, when Luke was in her bathroom shaving, she asked me if I knew what I was getting into.

I knew. From that first afternoon at Luke's house I knew. I knew that he would never make any money, that he had no great future ahead of him. It didn't matter to me.

I stayed at his house about an hour, just talking. Finally it was so hot in there that I had to leave. He had a window AC unit in the bedroom, but he rarely used it, never minded the heat. He walked me to the creaking screen door, and when we were on the porch stoop he held my arms and said just once, "Is this okay?" He never asked again, not like Wesley Mund, who I'd been going with for two years, with his constant pleading and his eyes like an excited dog's.

Luke kissed me, a long kiss that had a lot more to do with sex than any sort of romance, and that was exactly what I wanted. I felt sticky and hot in his arms, and there was no attempt to cover up the heat in the air, the hard June sunshine. The kiss was exactly and completely itself—nothing more, nothing less—and my body felt strong to me, and my head completely clear. It would have been difficult to leave, even that first day, if Luke hadn't wanted to let me.

Within a week we were having sex. The first time was there in his little dilapidated house on the floor, his makeshift pallet. I could feel the pine boards under me. They were hard on my back, but I pulled Luke tighter and tighter into me. I wrapped my legs around his legs, my arms around his neck, and pulled as hard as I could pull. My own voice surprised me, first louder and louder sighs, and then I could feel my vocal cords tighten and the sound coming out of them, and then I finished hard, my hips pumping and my head twisting from side to side without my having any control. Right then he pulled out of me, though I held him almost frantically, trying not to let him out, and he finished. Then he lay on top of me, his mouth in my hair, and his thin body wasn't heavy enough to suit me. I wanted his body to weigh as much as what I felt inside. I could hear thunder roll along the air, and we fell asleep to the sound of rain pelting the air conditioner.

When I woke up, I started to cry. Luke didn't ask what was wrong, just stroked my hair gently out of his sleep. I pulled him on top of me again, and it was the same, that fierce feeling of wanting him attached to me so that he couldn't let go, so that he would become part of me just like my hands or my face.

I know Luke thought it was the sex that drew me to him, that I was a young girl who had not had much experience, and that I'd discovered something new and thrilling and secret. That was true, but not the reason. I wouldn't have wanted sex with Luke if that's all there had been. But Luke had something else—he was real.

People in Mendenhall had never seemed real to me, the real person always hiding somewhere behind the outward behavior, deep inside where you couldn't see. Aunt Eunice seemed real, but in a different way than I was. Aunt Eunice didn't have much use for artificial smiles and false humility. When I rode with her to the grocery store or the gas station, she never waved at all the other cars like everyone else did. When strangers waved at her, she called it Christian foolishness, and she knew I loved to hear her say that. But even Aunt Eunice was real in a way that made her part of Mendenhall, like the First Baptist Church or the courthouse or the house she lived in. Mendenhall and Aunt Eunice had merged over so many years, so that what she did or said could only seem different and a little eccentric within the city limits. On the few occasions when Aunt Eunice traveled—to see her daughter in Biloxi, for example—she carried Mendenhall with her in the same way she carried her suitcase. The things that made Aunt Eunice real were small, and defined by her surroundings. I knew that I'd be like that if I stayed there.

But back then I was still real, a seed deep inside my own body, moving in a world where people were like faint suggestions of themselves, or shadows.

It wasn't the sex. The sex was just my way to spread and cling. A natural growth of who I was then, eighteen and still in Mendenhall.

Luke was real. All the places he carried, and I knew there were many, he shook from him like dust or rain. His realness was naked and undefended, even in those first days when his eyes and his body did most of the talking, and I wanted to cover and protect him, and at the same time make him part of what made me real. I had to attach our selves. Because he was a person, not a place.

When he told me about Mark, I knew that we wouldn't be separated. He had told me everything else then, each time like a test, and I would have to think very carefully about my words as if there were right and wrong answers. But Mark was what he held back, the part of himself that made the final test.

We were on the sofa in the living room, and my mother and father were at church. Usually when they had gone, Luke would take me by the hand and lead me back to my bed. Afterward we would rush to fix the covers, and I would have to go over Luke's side myself because he never made the bed in a way my mother would believe.

But that night he lay still with his head in my lap while I ran my fingers through his long hair. His hair was a sign of him. Not as big as a symbol, but a sign or an indication. There was no music and no television. There was nothing romantic. He was explaining to me again how God was impossible, or how if he wasn't impossible you had to find a different way to explain him. He said, "Because if there was just one person, even," and it was like he'd become lost in his idea, and he reached his fingers to his forehead and rubbed them back and forth, and I could feel the moment sharpen in the room, the objects in the room coming clearer to my mind, the sofa and the TV and the coffee table. "If there was one person, even, just one time," he said, "when God wasn't good or God wasn't aware of everything or God wasn't powerful enough to help anybody, then it all wouldn't be true." He looked at me then, looking up into my eyes for a long time while I thought about what to say. I told him, Right, it wouldn't be.

He told me how his father had taken Mark with him in the patrol car to buy some groceries. It was that kind of town, where the cops drove around in the patrol cars even if they were off duty, riding with their kids in the front seat.

When they were about a block from the Safeway, a blue Mustang pulled out in front of Mr. Rivers and started driving down the center of the road, not really on the wrong side but not on the right side either.

Luke's father knew who they were—a couple of high school boys about Mary's age who'd been getting deeper and deeper into the kind of trouble Luke said you could get into in his small town. Drunk driving, drug possession, a breaking and entering just recently at the stereo store. Mr. Rivers had dealt with them before, and said later they'd always seemed polite and genuinely sorry and even a little bit puzzled at the things they'd done. They were just kids—harmless kids.

The Mustang coasted through the stop sign across from the Safeway store, and Mr. Rivers turned on the lights. The boys pulled over into the parking lot.

Mr. Rivers could never forgive himself for pulling up to the car on Mark's side. Luke said that was the thing that always hurt him, Mr. Rivers, that drove him into himself when he was around his family and at other times drove him into his work or into needless odd jobs around the house or into drinking. Luke said you could even see it, how his father's eyes would look at nothing, at a space somewhere in front of him where there wasn't any object, and the cords in his neck would tighten and he would begin to mouth words, his lips moving silently and his face numb.

When Luke's father pulled up next to the Mustang, the boy in the passenger seat had already leveled the shotgun. It was summer and the windows were rolled down, and the air exploded, and the top of Mark's head was almost gone. Mr. Rivers was hit too, in the neck, but he didn't even know until later. He sprawled across the seat and held his son, screaming for help, screaming for anybody, until finally a checker from the Safeway was leaning in the window, screaming along with Mr. Rivers. "Call the police!" Mr. Rivers shouted at him. "Call the goddamn police."

It was in papers all across the country, Luke said. Mr. Rivers wouldn't let anyone watch the TV. The other cops were at the house constantly, behind the closed bedroom door where Mr. Rivers lay sleeping and not sleeping, sometimes talking and sometimes not, a bandage on his neck.

The boys had been on LSD and weren't really even sure that they'd done it when they were found less than an hour after the shooting, parked by the lake. Both of them cried when they were told it was true, that they'd killed John Rivers' son. They'd nearly convinced themselves it never happened. Later this would help them at sentencing, where they got thirty years for second-degree murder, tried in adult court.

Luke talked about how Mark had wanted to go to the grocery store to get a pack of baseball cards. He and Mark had been playing a game of checkers, and Mark heard Luke's father say he was going to the store, and Mark whispered to Luke that he wanted to go because he could talk his dad into buying baseball cards. Luke said how he had always thought of that, how Mark must have been thinking at the moment before he died that he hoped he got a Reggie Jackson.

He talked about Mark's piano recitals. He said that, on Sunday afternoons that spring and summer, his father had made it a kind of ceremony. The family, Luke's mother and father and Mary and Luke and his grandmother, too, would take the chairs from the dining-room table and place them in an arc around the piano. Mrs. Rivers would serve lemonade. Then Mark would sit down and play. Mr. Rivers would stand by the piano and turn the sheet music for him. Mark always ended the recital with his favorite piece, Beethoven's *Moonlight Sonata*, reaching desperately for the keys with his tiny hands, and almost always finding them. Luke said on nice days when the front door was open and sunlight filled the room, he would close his eyes, and the music would sound so sad and smooth that it felt like Mark was not reading the notes on a page, but finding them in the air around his head and turning them into a song.

Once, months after Mark was dead, Luke said he was in his room when he heard the sound of the *Moonlight Sonata*, three tiny notes, all the same. He had not heard the piano since Mark died. It was simply understood that he and Mary's lessons had come to an end, and that there was no need to practice. Luke slipped quietly down the ladder from his room and walked through the kitchen, praying hard that Mark would be there somehow, sitting on the piano bench. But in the living room was his father, standing over the piano, holding down one key. When he saw Luke there, he said nothing, and shut the piano lid. He crossed the living room and stared out the front window with his hands in the pockets of his uniform slacks. It was a gray winter day, and an icy drizzle streaked the windowpane, blown under the awning by the wind. "Back to work," Luke's father said, and put on his coat and left the house. Luke watched him pause to zip his coat before he got into the patrol car.

I sat and ran my fingers through Luke's hair and looked at the clock on the mantle to see how long it was before my parents would be home, and everything was quiet and clear. "They won't be home for twenty minutes still," Luke said.

Then I told Luke I never believed in God, because I knew I could tell him then. I knew we were past the point when his ideas or my ideas mattered. Everything was solid and definite between us.

None of it matters now. It all seems like it happened a long time ago, to different people. I don't even recognize myself in that eighteen-year-old girl anymore.

I'm not sure when I lost track of her, or why. It wasn't the years of restaurant work, the sore feet and wounded pride. It wasn't all the years so far away from home, listening patiently to the grocery store clerks while they tried to guess whether I was from Texas or Tennessee. It wasn't Jake, not in the way Luke thinks that changed me. Jake changed Luke more than me. Jake brought back Mark for Luke, and the fear that something horrible would happen. From the time Jake was born, Luke was always afraid, and always finding ways to escape that fear. He became a person who runs from fear, but who carries what he fears along with him, out of love.

I think I lost myself somewhere on Interstate 90, maybe someplace on the dry, dead stretch between Rapid City and Sioux Falls, going back and forth there for the two-dozenth time. Maybe one day when we were nearly out of money again, and heat waves rose from the road, or snow flew against the windshield, and I didn't know if we were looking for a dog track or a new home. Maybe it happened when I found out you couldn't be a person without a place.

I have a place now, and I'm keeping it. Next week I start training as a teller at the bank. Again I have Luke's mother to thank. She got me the job. She told the bank president about my position, as delicately as possible I'm sure, and he's recently divorced, and I could tell at my interview I'd have to deal with that. But I've dealt with that kind of thing plenty before. I'm glad to be out of restaurants.

Luke will be here soon. Wherever he is and whatever he's doing, I know he'll be here soon. But I don't think he knows how far away I've gotten. Sitting on this bed in this little house, listening to Jake rummage through his own closet in his own room, searching for his sandals to go to the lake, I am a long way away, beginning to hear the noises outside the window again, like the girl long ago at Aunt Eunice's.

LUKE

JUNE 23

When we'd come back to the cabins from the Sunday matinee at the track, and we'd as I think you call it consummated the relationship, we were just lying there in bed next to each other and talking, looking up at the wooden slats of the ceiling.

"That was amazing," Sarah said.

"What was?" I said. I thought maybe she was talking about the sex.

She looked over and slapped me on the belly and smiled. "Out at the track," she said.

We'd won over $3,000. It started with the first race, where I'd picked out an 8-8 daily double and an 8-1 quinella and the quinella came in and paid about $125 and then the double paid off in the 2nd at around $400.

We won at least *some* money on every single race of the matinee except for one, which was the 9th race, I think, when Sarah convinced me to bet on something totally opposite of my system just to see what would happen, and we lost. But we won pretty much everything else, and it was the most fun I've had at the races in a long time. I've got to say this about Sarah, that she has a way of enjoying herself right inside the moment that's happening that I've never quite seen before in anyone else, except maybe Jake, and that's because he's just a kid.

And it was the same with sex. She had this idea about not getting ahead of ourselves, but once she'd kind of given up on that and given in to the moment instead, both of us sunburned and tired and happy, it was like that was all there was—sex—and she just sort of devoted all her energy and her thinking to what we were doing with our two bodies there in the bed.

But it wasn't that way for me. I was inside of her and we were having sex and I was enjoying it, the feel of her legs around me and the motion of her body, but I was also somewhere else, above the whole thing and separate, seeing and thinking how she was all one piece and all right there. It was like there was one of her and two of me.

So I was kind of still thinking about that, and I didn't say anything back about the races, and we just lay there a while and almost fell asleep. Then Sarah started telling me stories. The stories were about being little and growing up with Buddy on their farm, and it sounded like a happy childhood. There was one story about how Buddy used to always talk her into cleaning the stalls for him even though that was his job, and another one about how she was fishing at their pond with her dad when she was really little and this fish she caught tugged her into the water, and other things of that sort.

But there were no stories about little brothers who got shot in the head when all they wanted to do was go to the grocery store, and no stories about alcoholic fathers with hearts broken so bad they couldn't love their families, or mothers who were lost and all alone and didn't know how to help anyone, or sisters who just wanted someone to love them no matter who it was, or anybody like me. So it was kind of hard to relate to. It seemed easier when she talked about her mother being dead.

I'd felt that same way around certain people before, like in the middle of talking they had suddenly slipped away into a place I wasn't allowed, that I couldn't get to in their eyes or their voices. And it made it hard for me to relax. Sarah decided to read for a while and got up and got her book. She propped up her pillow and sat back with me in the bed and found the page she was on and asked me to play with her hair. She likes to have you do that, start with your fingers at her neck and just run your hand slowly all the way through her hair. She says it's something her mother used to do. I did that for a while as she was reading. But the more I ran my fingers through her hair and watched her, and everything was quiet except for the clock again and the soft sound of Mr. Bergstrom on the riding lawn mower who I could see way out by the pasture, the more I started to feel like I was there with a stranger in my room. I felt like I didn't know Sarah at all, like I had never even talked to her before, and I started looking around the room, at the old TV set and the antique mirror above the dresser and the vase on the nightstand with the fresh flowers, and it was like I was in a place that I didn't belong at all, in the middle of some other life that wasn't the one I was living. And I started trying to find myself in this life, sort of figure out my place in it, and I couldn't. Sarah was still reading along like nothing was happening, and my fingers were still going through her hair, but I could feel myself getting lost and somewhat scared, and I immediately started telling myself to refocus.

I didn't have time to think, really, I just had to *do* something, and so I reached over and grabbed the Bible off the top of the nightstand where I'd left it. I opened the front cover and sat staring at the names there, the family tree I talked about before. I read the names over and over again, this time paying attention to them really carefully, and putting my finger right beneath each name as I went. Anna Cornwell, Patrick Gallagher, Marion Gallagher, Sylvia Harrington. It was like these names were part of a secret code I had to get to the bottom of, and I read them as if I was very carefully detecting it. But really nothing happened in my head, nothing was coming clear, and I just said the names in my head as a way to keep myself from falling off the edge of whatever kind of dilemma it was I'd gotten into.

Then Sarah reached over and held down the page so she could see better. "I know her," she said.

I looked at the page, still trying to decipher it sort of, like Sarah was seeing something there that I was supposed to see. "Who?" I said.

"Sylvia Harrington," she said. "She lives about a mile down the road from us." She took her hand off the page. "Weird."

"What?" I said. "What's weird?"

She looked over at me. "Nothing," she said. "Just that her Bible would be here in this room. Somebody like that that I've known my whole life."

I wanted to ask her more about Sylvia Harrington and the other people, but she went back to reading her book. I wanted to ask her if she knew how Patrick Gallagher died, and why there were hardly any children and hardly any names. But instead I stared at the names a little longer and the different handwritings, and as I looked at them things started to take shape again, like I'd thought of them before. I started to think of how I'd come here to Wisconsin and found this place and pulled off from the road like on an impulse, and how this room had sort of become mine because of it, and how I'd met Buddy on accident right after I'd first talked to Sarah, and then how we, me and Sarah, had seemed just to drift toward each other, and then finally what she'd said the other night when I asked about us being together, how she said she'd like to help me if I thought she was that person. And now how she knew this lady from the Bible. All of these things started coming together so that it *did* seem like my life, and it *did* seem like I belonged there, like it was a result of choices I'd made and chances that had worked out in a certain way. I could see how I had got there in the room.

Sarah was right next to me with her elbow resting against my belly. She didn't have a stitch of clothes on and I could see her left breast, that was closest to me, pulse just a little with her heartbeat. One leg was out straight and the other was kind of out sideways with her knee hanging over the edge of the bed, and when I looked down at her I could see pretty much everything there was to see. Jenny has always been a little shy when it comes to letting me see her in the light.

So I had set the Bible back on the nightstand and was just looking at her. Sarah closed her book and dropped it over the edge of the bed and reached over and started kissing me, and this time we were just the same there together, one of me and one of Sarah.

When we were finished, she got on the subject of the races again. The races had obviously been a big thing for her. "My God," she said, and she put her hand up to her forehead for a second, and then pulled a little strand of her hair down in front of her eyes and examined it for some reason. "You won *every . . . single . . . race.* What the hell *was* that, Luke?" She brought her hand down and slapped her thigh. "I need a cigarette," she said.

I reminded her how I didn't like to smoke in the house.

"Shit," she said, and started to get up to put on her clothes.

"Wait a second," I said. "All right." I got her the cigarettes out of my pants pocket and brought her the ashtray from the desk.

She sat there propped up in bed smoking for a minute, then she blew out a big stream of smoke and shook her head. "I don't see how you can sit there and be so calm about the whole thing." She looked over at me. I shrugged. "Luke," she said, and put the cigarette in the ashtray where it was between us and reached over and grabbed my arm with both hands. "Don't you get it? It's like you don't even know what's happening." Of course I was very interested in this because maybe she was right, but I didn't say anything. "Things just don't *happen* that way. You don't just say, 'Oh, I've got this system,'" and she started imitating my voice, the way I talk, "'and I come out here and bet six dollars on the first race and four dollars every race after that so that I can't possibly lose more than blah, blah, blah, and the key is long odds, blah, blah, and I win every race and walk out with three thousand dollars.'" Then she went back to her own voice. "You've got to be *kidding* me," she said. "You're crazy."

"We didn't just bet four dollars on *every* race," I said.

She picked up the cigarette from the ashtray and took a drag and put it back. Then she punched me on the leg. She has a lot of boyish mannerisms like that, I guess from growing up on a farm. "Well, why don't you bet more money all the time, you asshole?" She didn't really say it like I was an asshole, but just teasing. "You could be driving around in a Mercedes."

"I already told you, that's not how it works," I said. She kind of groaned, I don't know why. "Why are you getting so worked up about it now?" I asked her. "I already told you what was going on."

"Right," she said. "Well." She snubbed out her cigarette and thought for a second, holding her hair out of her eyes with one hand, then she reached over really fast and grabbed me by both my shoulders and looked me hard in the eyes. It was kind of funny, and I chuckled a little. She looked irritated for a second, but then she smiled. Not a phony smile like she was just trying to go along with me, but more that she realized how she was getting a little overexcited and could see why I found it humorous. "This system," she said, and nodded her head at me, like she was somebody's mother giving a lecture. "Don't be stupid. *Nobody's* system works that well. *Nobody* gets that lucky. It's not possible." She got out of bed and started walking back and forth across the room. "And you've just been going on like this for weeks—like, 'Ho-hum, whatever.'" She stopped in front of the mirror and folded her arms under her breasts and looked at herself. She was standing where I could see her both front and back, and even though we just finished having sex it was still hard to separate my feelings about her body from what she was talking about. I wanted her to get back in bed with me. "How much money have you won, then—total?" she said, looking at the mirror.

"I don't know," I said. "I'd have to stop and figure it up. I think about eight or nine thousand dollars."

"Eight or nine thousand dollars," she said. "Betting four dollars a race. Mostly." She held her hand out in front of her, palm up, like she was trying to sort of get a point across to her reflection. "Four fucking dollars a race." Then she turned around to me. "Luke," she said, "there is *something happening here.*"

The way she had spun around was very pretty, kind of like a ballerina, just twisting around on her toes instead of lifting and moving her feet, so now she was standing right in front of me totally naked with her legs crossed at the ankles. Something about it made me angry. I was admiring how she looked, but she wasn't thinking of that at all, like her mind had gotten absorbed with all these questions about the races and she couldn't think of anything else, sort of like Jenny when she gets started about houses with yards and two bedrooms.

So a little sliver of anger got into the back of my head somehow, and then started getting bigger very fast. I kind of scrunched into myself and clenched my hands in front of my chest and said, "*Okay* then. So give me some fucking *help!*" It felt good just to have got that far, and I loosened up and laid my hands in my lap. "That's what I meant the other night," I said. "Maybe you can help me figure out what *is* this thing."

After that she got very in control, sort of, and came over and sat with me on the bed and put her hands in my hands. She said all right, then, we should just try to be rational about the whole thing and think it all through and decide what to do next now that we at least agreed there was something not quite normal going on, and it was good because now I could stop pretending, and she only knew one thing for sure, which was that she needed to get the hell out of this room. That was fine with me, I told her, but would she come lay down again for just a minute. So we lay there very quiet for just a minute with the shadows getting long and the sound of voices outside somewhere.

That night we went and sat on a hill and looked down at the river and the town of Wisconsin Dells. But before that we were at The Bend, drinking beer and talking about the races again but not really getting anywhere, mainly because all of Sarah's ideas as you'd say revolved around stuff like magic and ESP, which I'm fairly sure is getting off on the wrong track. I mean if I truly was clairvoyant or extra-sensoried or could see into the future or make one dog's legs go faster than all the others' or anything of that sort, it seems like something I would know about. I mean I would get some sort of picture in my head beforehand, wouldn't I, like those women who the police call to find dead bodies all over the place that you see on TV. They're always seeing stuff like the bottom of a well or a pool underneath a waterfall. So it stands to reason that I would actually *see* which dogs were going to cross the line first, but I don't.

Anyway, Sarah talking about those things made me remember that family from out at the track before, with the husband who was so pleased with himself because he picked the winner in one single race and the wife who thought he was clairvoyant. It made me laugh a little right in the middle of something Sarah was saying. That family, the little girl with the pom-poms and the boy wanting pizza. I said, "Look, I really don't think it has anything to do with *me*. Other than my system, I mean."

Sarah grabbed a cigarette from my pack and lit it. "I'm going to end up owing you a whole carton," she said. Then she sat there looking around the bar. It was right at nine o'clock on a Sunday night and we were the only people in the place other than the bartender. The TVs were blaring all around with baseball games and golf results and car commercials. "It doesn't have anything to do with you," she said. "So who does it have to do with, then. Me?" She looked at me like she was just daring me to try and pull something over on her.

"What I mean is," I said, "I don't think *I'm doing* anything."

She nodded at me and crossed her legs and leaned over the table. "I see," she said. "In other words, it's not something that's happening inside, but something coming to you from somewhere outside, like a miracle."

She just said it very plain that way. Then we sat there and stared at each other. My stomach was feeling empty and a little queasy, and I thought of how we'd hardly eaten anything all day other than hot dogs and peanuts out at the track. We were pretty drunk too, I guess. "Maybe," I said.

There was one thing in particular that kept bothering me, so I brought that up then, which was how she could be so sure after seeing it happen just one time that there was something strange going on. I mean I'd been out at the track practically every night for two weeks with pretty much the same thing happening and it hadn't led me to any conclusions, so how could she be so sure? I asked her why was it that Jenny didn't think anything like that on that very first night in Rapid City? And I mentioned again about my system.

So then she brought up what I have to admit were some pretty good points, which were: One, that Jenny had only been there at the very beginning, so naturally it wouldn't seem so unbelievable to her, but that unless I was lying to her, Sarah, which she knew I wasn't, it had been happening regularly since then, which couldn't be the result of either luck or my precious system. Two, that because I'd been by myself the whole time, and had gotten used to the whole thing, and couldn't get anyone else's outside perspective, I had lost the sense of how unreal it was, how it defied any logical explanation, and that if I thought back toward the beginning I'd realize I probably had this same feeling, too, and in fact I still did, or why had I asked her that question about finding the answer to things? What other things were there? And, three, that Jenny wasn't the one who had come along at the right time to help me get the answers anyway, like I'd said. It was her, Sarah.

She'd gotten pretty worked up about the whole thing by then, and I had to keep asking her to whisper. I didn't really want her to whisper, actually, but just not practically yell. Anyway this led to a slight argument, our first one, and we sat there quiet for a minute after. The pool tables and the old piano sat there dead still and empty and only the bartender and the little laser light things on the jukebox moved at all. Then Sarah finally reached under the table and put her hand on my leg. "Let's get out of here," she said. "I know a good place."

That's how we ended up on the hill. Before we drove there in Sarah's rig we stopped at the store for beer and cigarettes.

To get to the hill, we drove down this winding gravel road out of town and then turned right onto this even windier gravel road that started going up the side of this bluff. About partway up there was a wide spot in the road where Sarah parked the Land Cruiser. It was getting almost totally dark by then, even if it was the longest day of summer, and there was just a tiny line of dark blue sky still hanging on the horizon. Sarah got out and told me to come on. I grabbed the beer and followed her. "Wait a second," I said. "Why don't we just drive up?"

"Road doesn't go to the top," she called back, and by that time I couldn't even see her already, except where the outline of these bushes was shaking and all the noise of cracking twigs. I figured I was going to lose her if I didn't hurry, so I started crashing through the bushes after her.

Right away I could see this wasn't going to be a picnic. I was wearing shorts, and the bushes were scratching holy hell out of my legs and twigs kept getting stuck in my Birkenstocks and I couldn't see where I was going at all, except up. "What the hell are we doing?" I said.

Her voice came to me from a little ways above. "Once you get through this first part, there aren't so many bushes," she said. "Just keep up."

So I did the best I could. I started using the six-pack to whack away at the underbrush in front of me and at least let me know what was there, but there were still skinny branches and stuff you couldn't see, and I fell down a couple of times and once got my hair tangled in a bush. But I shoved on through, and after a minute or so I was out into the clear.

The first thing I could make out was that the hill was pretty steep, a lot steeper than you would have guessed if you'd been standing off in the distance someplace. It looked just like a solid wall rising straight up ahead of me, although I could see sky up at about a ninety-degree angle, which told me at least there wasn't too far left to climb.

But then my eyes got adjusted a little to the moonlight coming through the trees, even though I couldn't find the moon. Everything started to take shape little by little, the trees and the rocks and the colors in the sky, like really faint picture images growing out of the dark and appearing only in the slightest shadows of blue and gray. But then there was one patch that seemed lighter than all the others, and I realized it was Sarah's white shorts, and suddenly I could see her shape pretty clearly there ahead of me.

She looked like she was hanging off the side of a cliff. There was a rock face that was practically vertical, it seemed like, and there was Sarah about halfway up, reaching around with her hands to find the best place to hang on and pull herself up. She got her hands where she wanted them, and then I could see her bring up her leg, and then decide not to and put it back down, and then back up again and she kind of rocked up and down, testing out her footing, then she put her weight on the leg and pulled up with her hands.

The rocks underneath her foot gave way, and the whole weight of her body came down so that she was just hanging by her hands, and my mouth opened wide but no sound came out, and I dropped the beer. I couldn't do anything but stand there and look. Then she found a place to catch herself with her other foot and she adjusted her handholds so she was balanced again and I could hear her laughing. "You there?" she said.

"Yeah," I told her. I looked at her white shorts up there glowing in the dark. She looked like she was in the middle of the air. "Maybe we should, like, not do this," I said. She didn't say anything, but was starting to check where to put her feet again. "Sarah," I said, but she didn't pay any attention.

The next thing I knew she was scrambling up, and it all seemed to happen in one smooth series of motions and then there she was, her dark outline and the white shorts at the top of the rocks. "Okay," she called down, kind of impatient. "Now you."

"How am I supposed to get up there with this," I said, and I held up the beer, and I could see her bring her hand up to her eyes, like she was trying to keep out the sun. "The six-pack," I said.

"It's not so hard," she said. "Come on. Be a man."

So of course what else was I going to do. It turned out not to be as hard as it looked from down below because it wasn't nearly as straight up as it seemed, and you could kind of lean your body weight over forward so you didn't have to worry about tipping back. After a few minutes I was up there with her, pretty winded but still in one piece.

Then the ground leveled out and there we were, on top of the hill. Not many stars were out yet, but a few, and the moon was low in the sky, and big like you could reach out and grab it. It was more a half moon now, but so bright you could see the other half, like a shadow of itself. "See how big the moon looks?" Sarah said, and I told her that I saw. "It's just an optical illusion. It's not any bigger now than when it's up high in the sky. I learned that in astronomy class."

It seemed kind of obvious, and not really something worth teaching in college. "Well, yeah," I said. "The moon always stays the same size."

"No," she said. "You don't see what I mean. We think it *appears* to be bigger because it's lower in the sky, but even that's an illusion. It's exactly the same size *in the sky* right now as when it's higher up, only it looks bigger because you can compare it to the horizon line." She started staring out at the moon, as if she was trying to figure this out all over again for herself.

"Hmm," I said. I watched her watch the moon. It seemed like she was made to do that, maybe, she looked so perfect sitting there. "*What?*" I said.

She laughed, still watching the moon. "I can't describe it right," she said. "Never mind. Trust me."

"I think you just make things up as you go along," I said. Then I sat there looking at the moon, too, trying to figure out what she was talking about, but I couldn't.

Down below were the lights of Wisconsin Dells and the river in the moonlight. The whole town was lit up like a carnival all the way south to Lake Delton, and you could see the line of cars crawling in and out of town and even make out the forms of little tiny people at the closest water slide. Sarah took me by the hand and we walked through the pine trees to the other side of the hill and looked out across the valley toward Lyndon Station, which was too far off to even see. There were just lights from farms and houses scattered around, and here and there through the trees a car's lights winding down a road. Sarah showed me where you could see the Bergstroms' cabins if you looked way off north of town. The wind was blowing up the hill and it felt good in your hair and on your face and the trees made that noise overhead that sounds like ocean waves.

"Where would you rather sit?" Sarah asked.

"This side," I said.

Sarah plopped down and pulled me down with her. "Hand me one of those," she said, and I gave her a beer. She popped it with the opener on her key ring, and of course it went spraying all over the place because we'd forgotten about me dropping it and banging it all over on the way up. But it wasn't like we were anywhere that you had to be too concerned about getting soaked with beer.

We drank our beers and smoked a cigarette or two. A couple cars glided by below down on the road.

"So," she finally said. "Maybe you're right. Maybe I should wait till I've seen it another time. But I just know there's something going on that's not normal."

I asked her if she'd ever had that feeling before about anything. I was starting to wonder if she was one of those people who go around talking about horoscopes and seeing the color of people's auras, and I just hadn't figured that out yet. There's lots of people like that up around north Idaho, and sometimes you don't spot them right away.

"Never," she said. "I never believed in anything supernatural or paranormal or anything." She reached across my legs and grabbed another beer.

"Why not?" I said.

She held the beer out away from her this time and opened it very carefully, and it didn't spray all over. She scrunched her keys back in the pocket of her shorts and rubbed at a scratch on her leg. "This sounds silly," she said. "Considering—I mean you're a Christian, right?"

"What makes you think that?" I said.

"Gee, I wonder," she said, and put her hand up to her forehead, like she had to think about it real hard. "You're named Luke. You read the Bible."

"Yeah," I said. "But I'm not really. Not since a long time ago."

"Well, anyway," she said. "It probably sounds hard to believe, but the truth is I never really thought about it."

"You mean about God?" I said.

"God, Jesus, angels, the devil, any of it. When I would hear people talk about it, it always seemed pointless."

Then I wanted to be careful, but couldn't really think of how to, so I just went ahead. "Even after your mother died?" I asked her.

For a second I didn't think she understood what I meant exactly, because she just sat there with her arms propped on her knees looking down at the lights scattered out toward Lyndon Station. But then she handed me her beer without saying anything and lay down on the ground and put her head in my lap and stared up at the sky.

That was interesting to me, because I'd noticed something like that about myself before—how sometimes small, personal things can make you think of much bigger impersonal things, like the stars, and also the other way around. What I mean is, I'm not sure what Sarah was thinking right at that moment, but it was like my mentioning her mother had suddenly made her want to lie down and look up into the night sky and see everything that was billions of miles away. And lots of times, if I was outside on a clear night, I would see the moon and stars and then Mark would come into my mind, or Jake since he's been born. And then other times if I would check on Jake when he was sleeping, I would watch his chest rise and fall with his breathing, and his eyelids flutter maybe, and then find myself looking out a window, up at the moon and stars.

I handed Sarah her beer back, and she rested it on her stomach and then ran her hand through her hair, which I knew was my cue to play with her hair for a while. So I did. "I wanted to believe my mom was someplace nice," she said. "That she was happy somewhere."

"Like heaven," I said.

"Yeah," she said. "Except, you know, I could never even start to picture it. I mean, what does heaven look like and how are you supposed to imagine people there?"

I wanted to help her out with that, so I started thinking back to all the times I'd thought about Mark being in heaven a long time ago, but I figured out then that I'd never really thought of heaven as a place, but more of an idea, like I'd thought of Mark being there but never actually had a picture of it in my head. "Well," I said, "back when Jenny was little and had to go to Sunday school, she says they always told you about lots of white, fluffy clouds, and God was there and kind of bathed in this white light, and everybody had wings and played the harp, I think, and they lived in golden mansions."

She laid there thinking about it for a second, and then she started laughing a little, and I knew why, I guess, and then we both had a good laugh over it. I think we were both picturing the same thing, which was like *us* being there, together, and sitting on a cloud off apart from everybody else someplace and wondering what there was to do and where to leave our cigarette butts and empties.

After a while Sarah said that it actually sounded like the kind of place her mother would enjoy. She said her dad always tried to keep her mother thinking that way, which I thought was nice. I mean I don't think my dad ever gave a damn one way or the other about how my mother thought about things.

Then Sarah said, "Okay, so let's just leave it at that for now," and she sat back up and lit another cigarette. "We'll go to the track tomorrow night and see if it happens again." She scooted up close to me because it was getting chilly. "Which it will," she said.

She was right. We went out to the track Monday night and again last night and both times it was more or less the same, not winning every race but actually a little better even with Sarah than it had been going before. Sarah's come up with lots of theories, which she just sort of throws out at random when they occur to her and almost regardless of where we are—at Buddy's or The Bend, for example—and I have to remind her to keep her voice low.

Because I think whatever's happening is quiet. I listen hardest for it at the moment the dogs win. I try to tune in to the moment when the dogs cross the line, crawl into that little space of time and hear what happens there, as if it's a moment just for me. Because maybe it's exactly that, *my* system, and maybe I discovered it for a reason. And maybe it has to do with the fact that I've looked for such a long time, been all across the country again and again in the hopes of what I might find, or what I might get away from, and my time has finally come to be rewarded. Maybe I was picked out for these reasons, like the winner of some huge contest. Maybe because I was the one who discovered the Greyhound God, talked to him in my head before every race, and now, through all the money, he's talking back to me.

Sometimes I look over at Sarah when we're in bed going over the Book of Luke in the Bible, and her fingers gently hold her hair back and her eyes tick across the page, and I wonder if other people would call us crazy. And I think it's at those moments that it's best to have her here, so that I'm not doing it alone. But I always wait for her to finish, to stop talking and asking me questions about myself and about my life that she thinks are important, wait for the beer to catch up to her and the effort of studying the page, when she'll yawn and kiss me and reach for the light switch.

Then I lie there quiet in the dark and try to open myself, get down to the bare, green stem. I open myself wide and keep my thoughts quiet as possible. What if it came to me, and I wasn't listening?

Because like that night on the hill, when Sarah and I had stopped talking and she lay down in my lap again, and I let my eyes and ears open wide and heard the trees, and saw bats flit by now and then across the stars and the stars and the lights down below bright and steady, I saw and heard what a wide space the answer had to come from, how it could be practically anywhere but at the same time all around me.

JUNE 24

While Sarah was still sleeping till around noon I got out the Bible
and looked at the names in the front again and the handwritings.
The more I've looked at this Bible, the more I've started to notice
about the family that owned it. For instance there are not only
names in the front, but underlining in various places and little
notes written in the extra space on the pages in a small handwriting that's hard to read and always the same—meaning that only
one of the people wrote in the book. And that was Anna Cornwell,
I think, who must have been the mother of Marion and Patrick

Gallagher, and the grandmother of Sylvia Harrington. Anna Cornwell married a man named Gallagher a long time ago, years after she'd already written her birth name in this Bible of hers, probably when she was a little girl, because the handwriting looks that way. She had two children, Marion and Patrick, and she wrote their names in the Bible when they were born, in her grown-up handwriting now that's the same as the notes on the pages. And one of them died when he was little, and the other one grew up and married a man named Harrington, who was the one that many years later marked down the date of her death. And they had one child, Sylvia Harrington, who lives down the road from Sarah, and sold her family Bible with the notes from her grandmother at a bookstore or a yard sale.

In II Kings, chapter 20, verse 18, Anna Cornwell underlined: "And of thy sons that shall issue from thee, which thou shalt beget, shall they take away:" To the side, very small, is written "1944," the year her son Patrick died.

In Ezekiel, chapter 28, verse 14 is underlined, very carefully with straight black lines: "Thou wast upon the holy mountain of God: thou hast walked up and down in the midst of the stones of fire." Next to this is written, "This was long ago," or "This way long ago."

In The Gospel According to Saint Luke, she has underlined: "And I say unto you, Ask, and it shall be given you; seek and ye shall find; knock, and it shall be opened unto you.

"For every one that asketh receiveth; and he that seeketh findeth; and to him that knocketh it shall be opened.

"If a son shall ask bread of any of you that is a father, will he give him a stone?"

I have of course always been interested in the Book of Luke. When I was a kid, it was the part of the Bible I used to read the most, and now I've started reading it again because Sarah was actually the one who thought of it that there might be some clue there. She bought two of these big yellow legal pads, and she uses one to write down stuff from the Book of Luke and the other to write down all the results at the dog races.

And when she's reading in the Book of Luke and we're lying in bed together and I'm just sitting there being quiet, she'll sometimes nudge me and say, "Did you see this?" and I'll look and say, "Yeah," and she'll say, "Well?"

To tell the truth I haven't found much there. I mean it's definitely more pleasant to read than the Old Testament with all the violence and killing and impersonal evil, but I don't see how it's been much help. In figuring things out for me, I mean. I can see how it would be a lot of help to people who believed in it. When I was a kid I believed in it, and I was very proud to be named after a book in the Bible, and I always felt sorry for kids at school who had names like Justin or Greg.

Only one thing ever bothered me about the Book of Luke, and I asked my grandmother about it once. It must have been the year before Mark died, when my dad started to figure out how Mark was so smart and a musical prodigy and everything, and I had started to be jealous and feel a little bit sorry for myself. I remember one day during the winter I was reading the story of the prodigal son, and by the time I got to the end of it I was kind of identifying with the brother—how he questions why the prodigal son who ran off and blew all his money should get treated like the favorite when he came home. Of course, Mark never did anything stupid like that because he only lived to be six and was a great kid besides. But it was just the idea of the father liking one kid better than the other, even though he says he doesn't.

And at the time, when I was twelve or however old, I didn't know what the word "prodigal" meant, and I assumed it was the same thing as "prodigy," more or less, because if you just look at them it stands to reason. So I kept saying the words over and over in my head, like "prodigal," "prodigy," "prodigal," "prodigy," until I almost couldn't quit. To get myself to stop doing that I flipped out of the Luke section and back into Mark, but this got me thinking about something else I hadn't ever thought of up to then, which was that Mark came before Luke in the Bible. Mark came before Luke, so why had my father, when we were born, decided to name me who came first Luke, and then my younger brother Mark, so it was like he was putting him before me? The more I thought about this I got incredibly resentful, and the more resentful I got, the more I felt guilty because, after all, when you got right down to it, I loved Mark more than I loved anyone in the world. Right at that time, up in my room above the garage, I could just barely hear Mark practicing the piano, and I was looking out the window of my room where there was nothing to see but this horrible gray sleet coming down and water dripping off the bare branches of the neighbor lady's trees across the street—one of those days you get at the tail end of February in Idaho, where everything looks like slate.

I decided to go ask my grandmother. She lived three blocks away from us on Fir Street in a kind of beat-up house covered here and there with clapboard, which was not nearly as nice as she could have lived in if she'd wanted to, because my Grandfather Rivers had been a big shot with the railroad.

Walking over there in the awful weather wasn't making me feel any better, and my grandmother's house was never exactly cheery either, so I wasn't in any kind of great mood when I knocked on her door.

My grandmother was glad to see me like always, although the ways she showed it would have never been clear to anyone who didn't know her well. Once when I was still in Orofino but getting better I had been talking to Dr. Blumenthal about my grandmother, and he had asked me to describe her in one word, just as a sort of game, and due to my what you'd call limited vocabulary I hadn't been able to come up with anything except "seriousminded," but I told him that wasn't exactly right. So what he did was give me a dictionary and tell me to take my time and find just the right word. For two or three days I sat in my bed first thing in the morning for about an hour looking at words. I kept just opening the pages at random and seeing what I found there, because at the time I was trying to deal with this problem Dr. Blumenthal said I had of wanting everything to be in order. I came up with words like "reserved" and "authoritative" and "solemn" and "dour" and "rigid," but none of them seemed just right. Then I found "ascetic." I told him my grandmother was ascetic.

So being ascetic, she didn't run to kiss your cheeks or tell you to make yourself at home or offer to make you hot chocolate. Even though it was so nasty out that day, she didn't say, "Oh, you poor thing." She just kind of sized me up with one hand on her hip and her eyes scrunched up behind her glasses. "You need to get out of those wet shoes," she said. "Can't your mother buy you a decent pair of boots?" Then she went and put away the broom she'd been sweeping with. That was kind of how she'd show she was glad to see you, by like commenting on your bodily state and then stopping what she was doing to show that your visit was more important. "But before you take those off, would you please go get me some wood?" she said.

She always asked you to get her more wood. The only heat in her house came from a big old black wood stove in the living room that my uncle Joe had finally convinced her to have hooked up to heating ducts and stuff so she at least had central heat. But it was still pretty damn cold if you left the living room. Every fall Uncle Joe would drive his logging truck over from where he lived in Kettle Falls, Washington, with about six cords of wood and dump it out back by my grandma's shed. Then he and I would spend the afternoon splitting as much of it as we could, usually with me wedging the maul and him splitting with the mallet, although sometimes he'd let me split but I couldn't do it very fast. Chopping wood was one of the few kinds of hard work I ever enjoyed—just the rhythm of it, your right hand sliding up and down the handle while the axe went up and came back down, and the solid "thock" and the cracking sound inside the log when you hit it right.

So I had to go back outside in the cold to get my grandmother wood from the shed that day. When you got the wood inside you had to dump it in the woodbin and let my grandmother put it in the stove. She always claimed nobody else knew how to do it right. She would have brought the wood inside herself, too, but she always had a bad back from working hard her whole life. While she was stoking the fire she said, "Maybe you'd do me the favor of bringing another load before you leave. I don't know when some-body else will be by to see me." She said this with her back to me, there on her bony knees, looking tall and thin and ascetic in her old faded housedress. I always felt kind of sorry for her when she said things like that, but she never meant for you to. She just said it as a matter of fact. Mostly it was just me or my father who came by to give her any help, and mostly me after Mark died. My uncle James who lived right there in town almost never came by. He was an insurance salesman, and a big disappointment to my grand-mother, who never liked handshaking and lots of fast talk.

I was sitting on the couch, and my grandmother left the stove door open a notch so the wood could catch and came over and sat in her favorite chair, which had a straight wooden back and wooden armrests and a seat cushion that was about as soft as iron. "Do you have something on your mind?" she asked me, which I usually did when I came to see her.

"I just want to know one thing," I said. "Even though maybe it's selfish and not Christian. I don't care."

You'd expect her to say, "What's that?" or something, but she never did—say anything like that, I mean. Instead she brought her fingers up and held them around the frame of her glasses, like she thought they were going to jump off her head and try to run away. This was how she always said, I'm listening.

"I'm Luke, and Mark is Mark," I said. "But if I was born first, except for Mary, and he was born after, then why is he Mark and me Luke? If he's Mark, why am I not Matthew?"

She sat there thinking for a second with her hand on her glasses frame, because I suppose the way I said it sounded like that riddle about the old man with seven cats in the bag or whatever. "Do you really think, Luke," she said then, making sure to kind of pause on my name, "that your mother and father, when you were born, left a little room in the four gospels when naming you so that years later they could have another son and put him before you in the Bible out of spite?"

It was a ridiculous theory, I could see that right away. "I don't guess so," I said.

She put her hands in her lap, and then brought one hand up to the armrest to help push her up out of the chair. She wasn't that old, but her back really did hurt her most of the time, I think, and you always felt like giving her a hand up, but she probably would have bit off your fingers.

"Let me tell you something about The Gospel According to Saint Luke," she said, and went over and closed the door to the stove and twisted shut the vent. Then she walked over to her old upright piano and took her Bible off the top where she always kept it and came and sat back down. She leafed through the pages very slow and careful till she found the spot she wanted. "Luke's Gospel is special because it tells the most complete story of the baby Jesus," she said. "Listen." Then she sat up very straight and tall and started reading: "And she brought forth her first-born son, and wrapped him in swaddling clothes, and laid him in the manger; because there was no room for them in the inn."

I had read this and heard it before, obviously, and mostly from "The Charlie Brown Christmas Special," where they all laugh at the pathetic tree Charlie Brown picked out and then Linus recites this very part from the Book of Luke to show them all the real meaning of Christmas, and after that they all go out and decorate the little tree and make it beautiful.

My grandmother couldn't recite it as good as Linus, but she did a pretty good job in her own ascetic way, and right off the bat, at the very next part, I got choked up like I always did. It always happened at, "And there were in the same country shepherds abiding in the field, keeping watch over their flock at night." It was just the sound of it somehow, the way the words fit together, and the idea, too, so peaceful and calm with everybody sleeping but the shepherds.

When she finished reading she closed the book and laid it in her lap and took off her glasses for a second and wiped her eyes. Not because she got emotional like me, but because reading made her eyes strain. I think she needed a better prescription. "Matthew tells us of the wise men," she said, "but only Luke recalls the shepherds, who were closest to God." She went and put the Bible back on the piano. "Now I have to drive to the drugstore," she said. "If you would, Luke," she said, making sure to pause on my name again, "please bring in another load of wood." She touched her glasses and looked a little closer at me and frowned. "You never did take off those shoes."

I miss my grandmother at times. I think she missed me too, probably, towards the end, even though I don't have any evidence. When she died, she left everything she owned to Uncle Joe. When I found out about it—about her falling down the basement stairs and severing her spinal column there in her house and it was lucky Uncle Joe even found her because it just happened to be the time of year when he delivered her wood—I mean, when I just happened to call Mary from wherever it was we were, she made sure to remind me that I probably could have gotten some part of the inheritance because of always being her favorite, my grandmother's, except I'd gone off and blown it with the ball of fire thing. But truthfully I don't give a shit about that sort of stuff. There probably would have been a bunch of papers to fill out and everything. I was just sad she was gone.

Anyway, what my grandmother had to say that time got me over any bad feelings I had about the Book of Luke. When I read it now, different things interest me, little things. I don't care much about how Jesus was always making the lame walk and the blind see and multiplying the loaves and fishes and rising from the dead. What I notice most about Jesus now is that he had the same kinds of problems that most regular people do, and that he had to deal with them under difficult circumstances. He would get impatient at times and have to control his anger, just like you have to do with kids, and at other times he would get scared, like the night before he was crucified when he asked God if maybe he didn't want to change his mind.

And it seems to me that overall there's a great deal of frustration in the Book of Luke. People won't ever believe that Jesus is who he says he is, for instance. Over and over, he has to keep reminding people of who he is before they'll listen to what he has to say, and the way he ends up having to do this is by performing some sort of miracle.

And so in a way I think these miracles had a bad effect. On the one hand, sure, they were very helpful. People would seek, and they would find, like in the part Anna Cornwell underlined. People would ask, and they would receive. Nobody got stones instead of bread. It was all really simple because you had Jesus right there at hand. But what about later, when he wasn't around? I think of my father, how he had no doubt read all these very same words and expected all these very same things, and he would bang the cupboards at night to see if God could hear, and he would sit in the kitchen and ask question after question to God who wasn't listening.

But don't get me wrong, I still have a lot of respect for Jesus. Like I said before, I think he and God did a pretty good job, but that they just couldn't manage to get everyone in the world to be kind and forgiving and love their neighbors, and they couldn't keep the Christians Jesus left to spread his message from screwing it up and making God and Jesus out to be better and more perfect than what they were. Which left a whole bunch of people like myself, who thought about it all a little too hard, just pushed off to the side, which is where I say the Greyhound God comes in.

Anyway, if there's supposed to be a message for me in the Book of Luke, I don't think I'm getting it too well. There's only one place that's hit me so far. Right about in the middle of Luke, while Jesus is going along performing miracles and preaching the parables, these Pharisees come to him and tell him that he better leave where he's at because Herod is coming to kill him. And Jesus basically tells them to let Herod know he can go screw himself, but then afterward he says, "Nevertheless I must walk to day, and to morrow, and the *day* following: for it cannot be that a prophet perish out of Jerusalem."

I think it was just the sound that got to me at first, the words and from where they came, but as I looked at the words more I started to feel like I was walking. I was out on a lonely road someplace in the dust and the sun, and there was a long way to go and a lot of hills. And in the corners of my sight I could start to make out trees, and barns and fences, and rolling fields of windy wheat. Then I knew I was back in Idaho. I was walking down the roads around Moscow, and I could see an old truck up ahead clouding out dust around its wheels, and the sun was falling, and I was looking for a place to sleep.

And I knew I had another metaphor. Because it seems like my life since that time has mostly been that way—walking, or riding a bus or a train, or driving down a highway to no particular place. And if I wasn't doing it I was thinking it. And when the dogs ran they were doing it for me.

Jesus knew where he was going. He was headed to Jerusalem. But where am I supposed to head to? All I know is Sandpoint, Idaho. Chuck's Slough and the Green Monarchs and City Beach, where I tried to talk to people I'd known my whole life and they laughed and told stories about me. The Long Bridge across the lake and the Priest River Highway and the Safeway store, where two other Sandpoint boys I also knew killed my brother. I know the place.

If I'm supposed to be doing something or going somewhere could someone please give me better directions. Just show me where Jerusalem is.

JUNE 25

Sarah and I were sitting in bed looking at the Bible again, or I was looking at it and she kind of was, too, but she also had out her race charts and programs all over the bed and was trying to work out some pattern that had to do with the lanes, which turned out to be a dud, and it was about ten o'clock, and we were thinking about going to The Hen House.

We were kind of both in rough shape, because the night before we'd been to the races and then afterward to a party over at Buddy's. Even though we'd won a bunch of money again I wasn't in any mood for a party. All night at the track I'd been praying hard to the Greyhound God, or not really praying but trying to let him know I was there and I was ready, I was listening. Every time the rabbit squeaked along the rail and I could almost hear the chutes open before it even happened, I lit my smoke and took my drink, but I didn't say, "Please let me win." I said, "Here I am. Luke Rivers. Now talk to me."

And every time I was disappointed. Sarah kept trying to cheer me up, and after she'd go up to collect the money we won she'd come back and show it to me before she put it in her purse, and she'd tell me nothing had changed and things were still going great, whatever was happening was still happening.

She did the best she could. But afterward when we were at Buddy's I was pretty depressed again. It wasn't anywhere I wanted to be, and the people there didn't interest me. Sarah went into Buddy's room for a while with Jordan and a couple other people to smoke some dope, and the whole time she was in there I just sat with a beer on the couch and hoped nobody would talk to me.

But no such luck. That girl that talked to Buddy before at The Bend, the one he seemed to be dating, came and sat by me. She said, "I'm Taylor," and stuck out her hand. She was sitting leaned forward on the couch with her legs crossed in her skirt and sort of looking down at me where I was sunk into the cushions. I shook her hand, which was bony and slightly oily from some kind of lotion. Overall she seemed way too skinny to me, like she had an eating disorder.

I said, "I'm Luke Rivers. Pleased to meet you."

She said, "Buddy says you and Sarah are friends."

That was about how I had her figured, someone who wanted to be nosey but knew how to go about it without being impolite. "Right," I said, and that was all. I didn't mean to make her uncomfortable, but I wasn't in much of a mood for a conversation. It seemed like Sarah had been back in the bedroom for a long time, and I was wondering how much dope you needed to smoke.

She nodded and looked around for a second, probably trying

to figure out her next line of attack. "So you're living here in the Dells," she said, smiling at me. She had a little piece of something green stuck between her teeth but I didn't tell her, because I figured she was the sort of person who'd be mortally embarrassed about it.

"I never said that," I told her.

"Oh," she said, and she looked pretty uncomfortable—too uncomfortable, in fact. I can't be mean for very long.

I said, "Just for a while, I think, actually."

Then she asked me where was I living and I told her the Bergstroms' cabins. She asked where I met Sarah.

"Out at the track," I told her. "I bet on dogs for a living."

"*Really*," she said.

I nodded.

"And are you . . . divorced, then?" she said, looking at my ring.

"No," I said. "Not yet, anyway."

She uncrossed her legs and laid her palms flat on her bony knees. "So you and Sarah are friends," she said, like she was going to get this straight once and for all.

"Friends," I said, and nodded.

At that point she pretty much ran out of ammunition, so she shook my hand and said nice to meet me again, and went off in search of Buddy, who I don't think had told her he was going in the bedroom to get high.

I had gotten up to get another beer and was just standing at the kitchen sink when Sarah came in. "Not having fun?" she said.

I told her I was all right. She came up and put her arms around me, and her eyes were red and she smelled like pot, which isn't a bad smell. She kissed me, and we just stood there looking at each other. Again it sort of struck me how short a time we'd been together but how long it seemed and how much had happened. "What do you want out of all this?" I asked her. "I mean, what do *you* want?"

"Nothing," she said. "I don't care." She grabbed my hand and started to try and lead me out of the kitchen.

"Wait a second," I said. I pulled her back real gently. "Seriously."

"Seriously," she said to me, with a very serious frown. "We're being serious now." She laughed. I didn't change the expression on my face. She dropped my hands and ran her fingers through her hair and kind of slouched her weight over onto one leg and rubbed one foot on top of the other. She had her sandals off and her feet were tan and pretty.

"Okay," she said. "Let me think. I'm not exactly in the best shape to think." She put her weight back on both legs and her breasts shifted a little under her tank top. Her eyes drifted around the room for a few seconds, and then she started to take a deep breath, but it stopped halfway and words came out instead. "I just want to be part of whatever it is that's happening," she said. "Nothing really big has ever happened to anyone I know."

I was still just standing there with the same expression on my face. She reached out real fast and grabbed my hands again and squeezed them hard. "It's *exciting*, Luke, don't you think? I'm *excited* for you." She came in real close and put her face right up to mine. Some guy was coming in behind her to grab a beer out of the fridge. Sarah glanced back at him and he lifted his hand and kind of halfway smiled. Then her eyes were right back on mine again, very close, and she whispered, "It's like somebody is letting you know you're special in some way. You're very special in some way." And she kissed me really hard, like she was desperately trying to get this point across to me.

Only two people ever told me I was special before in my whole life. One of course was Jenny because after all she is my wife, and the other one, the first one, was that poor heroin addict I mentioned before in Crescent City, which she told me after I'd found out about her problem and was getting set to leave. That was obviously a more screwed-up kind of thing and not the one I wanted to remember in connection with what Sarah was telling me, but that was the one that came to mind anyway. Not the times Jenny had told me that, but that time in Crescent City.

I suppose Sarah saying it made me happy for a minute, though, but it also got the whole situation on my mind even more, like trying to figure out *how* I was special, in *what* way. Buddy showed me where he had a bottle of Scotch stashed over behind the microwave, and I started drinking it straight, pouring it into an empty Budweiser can. I got really drunk as fast as I could, and things get pretty fuzzy from that point on. I remember I insisted that Buddy play me a game of chess, and I got annihilated.

Sarah ended up driving us back to the cabin even though she probably shouldn't have, and we both woke up in the morning pretty rough. Like I say, we were just lying in bed with me reading through the Book of Luke and her working on her charts from the races, and we'd every once in a while say we should go to The Hen House but never get up to go do it.

Finally she slapped the charts down on the bed in a pile and sat up and looked at me. "I think I figured something out. I actually think I figured part of it out."

She kind of got my hopes up there for a second and I sat up and started looking at the charts with her.

"Don't get *too* excited," she said. "It's not an answer to anything big. But maybe one more little piece to go on."

"Okay," I said. "Show me."

She started going over a bunch of calculations that she'd done and she talks so fast that I wasn't quite keeping up, but almost right away this sinking feeling came over me that it all looked pretty familiar.

After a while I was sure, and I stopped her. I said, "Eight to win, 7-8 quinella."

She stopped looking at the charts. "Right," she said. "How did you know?"

"I'm clairvoyant," I told her.

She sat there staring at me. It was hard to figure out exactly what was in her expression. It could have been shock or amazement or confusion or happiness or sadness or just about anything. But I could see that whatever it was, it was a very important thing for her, this idea she'd come up with, and what happened next would be a big deal, and I knew I shouldn't tease her.

"No," I said, "I'm not clairvoyant." I leaned back in the bed and kind of whacked my head on the headboard harder than I meant to. Sarah didn't even laugh or anything. "That's good," I told her. "That's smart of you. It took me three years to get that far." I was rubbing my head and not looking at her.

"You're saying you already knew that," she said in this flat voice.

"That's the way it always is," I said. "Every track, all the time. It has to do with the staggers."

I sat back up and explained the whole thing to her, and she asked a couple of questions, like she didn't want to give up on the idea that she'd found something just yet, but she finally had to. I patted the sheet over her leg. "Like I say, though, that's good. You did a good job," I said.

"Oh shut up," she said. She kicked around with her legs under the sheet until all her charts fell off the bed. "I've been working on that stupid thing for two days. You could have told me."

"How was I supposed to know?" I said.

She sort of growled and lay down and pulled the sheet over her head. I didn't say anything else. I figured I should just let her pout for a while. I think it's okay at times just to take a couple minutes and pout. You don't want to get stuck doing it, but I think even Dr. Blumenthal would say it's sort of an okay natural reaction.

I went back to reading the Book of Luke, or more just staring at the page. Sarah pulled back the covers and reached over and smoothed the hair on my chest with her fingers. "Luke," she said. Her voice just seemed to hang there. "I don't want you to get upset," she said. She hunched herself up higher against me and kissed my cheek.

She wasn't going to say anything else unless I said it was okay, I could tell. "What?" I said.

She kept running her fingers across my chest. "Nothing," she said. Back and forth with her fingers. "Don't you wonder about them?" she said. "Jake and Jenny. Don't you think you should try to find out where they are?"

I didn't know where she'd come up with that. It wasn't anything

I'd been expecting, and it made my heart thump hard. I wondered if she could feel it under her fingers. "They're at Jenny's parents," I said.

"You don't *know* that," she said, in this voice that was supposed to be very soothing.

I took her hand off my chest and she sat up and looked at me, and I could tell she was worried if not scared. "So what are you suggesting?" I said to her, even though I could tell at that point she wasn't about to suggest anything. "Are you saying something happened to them? Something bad?"

"No," she said. "I'm not. I didn't."

"Because I would have known, don't you think?" I said. I was talking kind of loud and mean. "Somebody would have got hold of me, don't you think?"

"Luke, just . . ." she started, and she got her legs out from under the sheet and edged to the side of the bed and held her hands out flat in the air. Then she put her hands in her lap and looked at me with a soft look in her eyes. "Well, no. I don't think anyone could know where you are."

I got up from the bed and put on a pair of jeans and went over to the sink. I could see Sarah naked standing behind me in the mirror. I plugged the drain and ran some hot water and wet my face and put on shaving cream and grabbed a razor from behind the cold water knob. I dipped the razor in the sink and started to shave, but my hands weren't all that steady and I stopped and held the razor in the air.

"I'm sorry," Sarah said. "I didn't mean to worry you. I'm sure everything's okay."

I tried to shave some more but I cut my chin, and I threw the razor in the sink and watched it drop to the white bottom. Something about it felt kind of creepy, the way it settled over the drain, floating, the blades shining silver.

Then Sarah's arms were around me and I could feel her breasts. "Everything's okay. You're so sweet," she said. She kissed my back. "You're very fragile and sweet."

I wanted to elbow her in the nose. But what I did instead was shout into the mirror, very loud, no words but just shouting, and Sarah stepped back away from me.

I washed off my face and put on a T-shirt and grabbed my truck keys. I didn't look at Sarah. I didn't know where she was in the room. I opened the door, and it was hot and bright outside like it has been every day. "I'll see you in a little while," I said.

I didn't want to call from the Bergstroms' house. That was the only thing I knew. If something had gone wrong with Jake and Jenny, I didn't want anyone to see me. I didn't want any people.

Then I was in the truck, headed down the winding road to town. I looked around the road for a pay phone, like they might have just stuck one out there in the weeds. The sun was bright as fire and the sky looked almost white but there weren't any clouds, and everything I saw all around me looked cooked and dead, the weeds dry and yellow, the corn curled and brown at the ends. I was driving fast, feeling the truck try to get out from under me. I dared it to, with its fucked-up alignment and everything, dared it to pull me off the road into a ditch or a fence.

I could see now how it had all been a trick, a set-up. All the money at the races and Sarah and the feeling that something good was finally happening to me, something big and important. Jake and Jenny were dead, smashed head-on into a semi truck that first night somewhere in Iowa, or kidnapped from a rest area the way I'd always been afraid whenever we stopped and I went to piss by myself and Jenny said, "Hurry," sitting there alone in the night with our son.

The rest of the world was in on it, the trees and the cows and the fence posts and the other cars, they'd known about it all along. I gunned straight through the first four-way stop at the edge of town, and the other car that honked at me was saying, We knew, we knew it all along, why didn't you?

I saw a pay phone up ahead at the Shell station before you hit the main strip. I bounced up over the curb and across the sidewalk and skidded to a stop behind it. I jumped out of the truck, and all the people at the gas pumps stared at me, and I could see in their faces that they knew the secret too, that there was nothing good to come.

Standing at the pay phone was even hotter than the truck if that was possible. The sun pounded on the shiny metal and I felt like a blade of grass stuck under a giant magnifying glass, like the sun was following me around and trying to light me on fire all day. Behind me were the sounds of kids at the first water park on the strip, laughing and screaming. I stood there with the phone in my hand looking around at everything, the kids at the top of the water slide getting ready to go down, the people at the gas pumps going and coming like busy ants and behind them the huge head of the Trojan horse roller coaster hanging there on the horizon.

I thought it was all these people around that was keeping me from dialing the number, but then when I finally tried I understood that wasn't it at all, why I was standing there like an idiot. It was something much more simple, which was that I didn't know the goddamn number. I slammed the phone down and reached for my wallet, and I didn't have it with me. I sat down there in the grass by the sidewalk, kind of feeling helpless. A car pulled up by the phone, a white Ford Escort, and a guy that looked like an old hippie got out and headed toward me and the phone and I stood and clenched my fists and he held his hands up and walked back toward the gas station. 601, I thought. Area code 601.

I punched out the area code and the number for information. A voice that sounded like a slow robot said to deposit fifty cents. I searched my pockets, but none of my $10,000 was in there. I slammed the phone down and went to the truck in a hurry before the guy with the Escort came back, and I scrounged a quarter out of the glove box and another from under the seat.

I called again and got past the money part and what city and the robot asked whose number I wanted. "Troy Beamon," I shouted into the phone. "Troy Beamon." I got the number and punched it in. Deposit three dollars and thirty cents. I slammed the phone down again and looked at the directions. I punched in a collect call. Say your name at the tone. I looked across the road at the water slide and the kids at the top there ready to go down. "Luke Rivers!"

The phone rang. Twice. "Hi-ya!" It was Jenny's dad.

"You have a collect call from . . . Luke Rivers!"

"Luke Rivers," he said, very slow, enjoying it.

Then I was on the phone with him, Mr. Beamon. "Let me talk to Jenny. Is Jenny there?"

"Luke Rivers," he said, enjoying it again. "Luke Rivers wants to talk to Jenny."

The guy with the Escort had come back out carrying a package of Hostess Cup Cakes. He pointed at his watch. For a hippie, he seemed to be in an awful big rush. *Fuck you,* I mouthed at him, and shook my fist. He gave me the finger and headed to his car. "Just let me talk to Jenny. I want to talk to her. I want to talk to Jake."

"I expect so," he said. "I expect you do."

It was starting to sink in that they were actually still alive, that even Mr. Beamon wouldn't have been so evil that he could tease me that way if they were dead. The guy with the Escort was standing by his car unwrapping his cupcakes and listening to me. I held my hand up, a lot calmer now, and then one finger up for just a minute. "Just let me talk to her," I said into the phone. "No bullshit now. Just let us talk." I shouldn't have been using profanity with him, but I wasn't in much of a mood.

"I have been instructed by your wife to let you do that," he said, real smooth and sarcastic. "But I have got you on the line first. First you have to talk to me. A little talk with old Troy . . ."

"Fuck you," I said, and hung up the phone. The guy with the Escort was looking at me. "Sorry, man," I said, and started back to the truck.

"Bad day, huh?" he said. I turned around and looked at him again. I couldn't tell if he was trying to be funny or what. He had long black hair that was wavy and had some gray in it and he was wearing a tie-dyed T-shirt and basically appeared to have been under a rock since about 1973. He was a very strange sort of guy to have to run into at a moment like that and I didn't want to think about him at all.

"Yeah, whatever," I said, and kept walking. But then that struck me as kind of rude. He was evidently trying to be nice to me. I stopped and stared at the truck where it was parked with three wheels on the asphalt and one rear wheel on the grass. "Looking better, I guess," I said. "Better than I thought it was a minute ago." I was kind of halfway talking to myself.

"Hang tough, Brother," the guy said to me. I looked back at him standing next to the phone. He flashed me a peace sign, I swear to God. "Keep the faith."

I was on the winding road back out to the cabins when my whole body felt like it was loosening, like I was water, like someone had jiggled me and I was spreading out in waves. I pulled the truck off the road halfway down into the ditch and sat there behind the steering wheel while a car and then a tractor went by. I was parked next to a cornfield that stretched across the way to an old beat-up barn where some cows were wandering around slow inside a fence. I watched how they moved so slow except for their tails, which swished back and forth and looked like they should belong to whole different animals. In the rearview mirror I saw a line of dried blood running down my chin. I looked around for a pack of cigarettes and found one scrunched up in the crease of the seat and took out a cigarette and fished a matchbook out of my pants. My hands were so sweaty I almost ruined the matches, and I finally figured out to get the hell out of the truck where it wasn't a thousand degrees.

Sitting on the little slope down toward the cornfield, I could think a lot clearer. I watched the corn wave in the breeze, very quiet and peaceful. The only noise was an airplane humming somewhere overhead.

Okay, I said to myself—refocusing. First off, I thought, Jake and Jenny were still alive and well. That was the main thing, and I could feel a lot easier and not have to keep pushing back awful thoughts all the time. That was good, and I said a silent thank you to whoever without wasting a lot of time worrying about who. I had almost got to talk to them even, if it hadn't been for Mr. Beamon, who was obviously more interested in giving me shit than in letting his daughter and her own husband talk things over for themselves.

It was kind of surprising that I had actually been that close to really talking to Jake and Jenny. The whole time I was thinking something horrible had happened, it never crossed my mind how possible it was that Jenny could have answered the phone. Or even Jake, as far as that goes. He loves to answer the phone. We always got a kick out of it because he picks up the phone and says, "What do you want?" He's not being impolite, he just figures somebody always wants something.

But that very easily could have happened, and it made me see how totally unprepared I would have been because it had seemed just about impossible for some reason. It seemed like maybe there was a lot more to it than you could take care of just by tapping into a phone line.

But then it occurred to me how what *had* happened—my conversation with Mr. Beamon if you could call it that—had probably screwed things up pretty bad in terms of talking to Jenny and Jake. There must have been a very interesting scene going on at the Beamons' while I sat there watching the cows. Jenny's dad would be saying something like, "Over my dead body will we take a collect call from him again. 'Blank you,' he said to me. 'Blank you.'" And Jenny would be yelling at her dad about why didn't he just hand over the phone, or maybe she would be agreeing with him, I don't know. Either way Jake would be there—listening, quiet, his eyes open wide.

Really I felt like I'd screwed up practically everything. I lit another cigarette and told myself I might as well get it over with, go ahead and consider the worst. I might as well seriously sit there by the side of the road in the weeds smoking a cigarette and ask myself if I'd gone crazy, because the question was bound to come sometime. Because the scary thing about it, about having lost touch with reality once before, is that you remember all the time how when you'd lost it it didn't feel like anything was wrong.

So I sat there by the side of the road in the hot sun and told myself to think this all through very carefully, and I wouldn't leave till I was done. On the down side, there was the whole idea of the Greyhound God and how he and God and Jesus were sending a message to me. That definitely seemed like something a crazy person would dream up. But I had been going around with the idea of the Greyhound God in my head for years, and it hadn't done me any serious harm that I could tell. And it was a fact that I'd been winning all this money. There was no denying that.

And on the other hand also there was Sarah. If I was crazy, she had to be crazy too, and that would be too much of a coincidence. And this seemed like a good way for the Greyhound God to be looking out for me, because if I was supposed to reach some new level of understanding then I had to know I was okay, and Sarah was a way of doing that, giving me that kind of help.

The most important part, though, was that I was still watching myself and waiting. Even at the very worst part, when I was driving down the road thinking that Jake and Jenny were dead and I'd kind of lost it as a result, I was still somewhere in my mind observing my own behavior and not making any firm conclusions. And like I've said before, I wasn't able to do that when I was crazy.

So that was that. Everything made sense, and I even started thinking how maybe that weird hippie was sent to me for a reason. He was sent there to give me that one message—keep the faith—so that I wouldn't get lost in other worries and wander away from what was really happening. I just had to stay strong and keep refocusing and let myself have faith, not be so fragile like Sarah said. I started feeling better and I wasn't shaky anymore, and I got in the truck and went on home.

When I got there, Sarah was sitting on the bed dressed in one of my T-shirts with a bunch of her papers scattered all over. She didn't look up when I walked in.

I told her hello.

"Are they all right?" she said.

I said yes.

"At her parents'?"

I told her yes again.

"Good," she said. "Now you know." She didn't ask anything else.

I went and washed the blood off my chin and finished shaving, and when I came back I noticed the stuff she had spread out in front of her. There was a bunch of papers crumpled up, and then one sheet on the top of the legal pad that said, BEGIN AGAIN! Then she had these four little slips of paper, one with a star drawn on it, one with a circle, one with a plus sign, and one with a check mark.

I asked her what they were.

"Huh?" she said. "These?"

I told her yeah, and she said it was just a silly idea she'd had and shuffled the slips of paper together and crumpled them.

I said, "Don't do that. What is it? What's the idea?" I sat down on the bed and uncrumpled them and looked at the little drawings.

She explained how it was this test she'd wanted to try on me, and I told her go ahead, and then I sort of had to keep encouraging her that it wasn't silly. I felt sorry for her was mostly the reason. She was trying so hard to help me.

So she got the slips of paper smoothed out and crossed her legs Indian-style on the bed and put the little paper pieces down between her crossed legs. "Jake and Jenny were okay?" she said. She was giving me sort of a severe look. I think she wanted me to tell her about it, but I didn't feel like it. So I just told her yes again. "You talked to them, then?" she said.

"Not exactly," I said. "They were out."

"Oh," she said. Then she had one of those really quick mood shifts, where you could see suddenly the idea of doing this test had taken all her attention. "Okay," she said, and smiled real big, and explained to me how it worked. She was going to hold one of the slips in her hand, and I had to guess what it was. It was some kind of ESP test she'd learned about in Abnormal Psychology class. She looked down at the slips for a second and put one in her hand. "Guess," she said.

That kind of made me stop, putting me on the spot like that. I tried to really think of it for a few seconds, but then I realized that wasn't the point, because I knew I didn't have ESP anyway. The point was to make Sarah feel good. So I started doing something else, which was to make a wish, like I'd tossed a penny into a fountain or caught one of what we used to call "fairies" in the air, those seeds that used to float around in summertime in Idaho and we'd catch them and make a wish and let them go, Mary and Mark and me.

"*Guess*, Luke," Sarah said. "You have to do it a hundred times."

So I thought of my wish as fast as I could, which turned out to be this—that no matter what happened with me and Sarah, whether we stayed together or I tried to go back to Jenny and Jake or even if I just went back to how I was before, mostly alone and moving around, the whole thing between us would never turn ugly and become something that would give us bad memories. "Star," I said.

Sarah smiled. She held up the slip of paper and it was a star. I said my silent thank you. "One for one," she said, and put the slip back and shuffled them around and looked down and picked out another one.

"Star," I said again.

I ended up getting only twenty-one out of a hundred. It was a fun game, though, and we laughed at how bad I was, and I was sorry when it had to end. It was much better than all the sort of terrifying stuff that had happened earlier. One minute you're sick to your stomach because you think your wife and kid are dead, and the next you're in a whole different life with a whole different person on a sunny day in Wisconsin. And of course there's the track, where we went again last night and won more money but still didn't understand things. I told Sarah how I thought that was all right, though, how we just had to believe in what was happening and have faith and the answers would come. And she said she thought that, too.

JUNE 26

Yesterday was Sarah's twenty-second birthday and she was pretty excited about that and I did my best to be excited, too. I woke up pretty late, and she was already in the shower. After she got out she started telling me about her friends, different ones that I would meet who were coming in from Madison especially for her birthday. She seemed anxious to introduce me to these people, like to take two separate parts of her life and put them together, the way I've noticed people sometimes are if they've had a good life and are happy about what's happened in it.

Sarah had a pretty full day planned for us and she didn't know if we'd be back to the room, so we scouted around for loose money that wasn't in my gym bag until we'd rounded up a hundred dollars or so to take with us. Sarah's probably about three-quarters of the way moved in, and she's got wads of money everywhere just like I do. It's not even worth mentioning anymore when you put on a pair of shorts that's been lying around and you find a couple hundred dollars in the pockets. The bathroom counter is so covered with junk—hair brushes and contact solution and birth control pills and mascara and earrings—that I can't even use it to set down a beer. And I won't even talk about the closet.

Sarah said we needed to stop at Wal-Mart, and then we were going to her house. Every year on her birthday it was kind of a ritual between her and her dad that she would get him a present, and then he was supposed to see if he could get her a better present than she gave him. The idea was that Sarah could get him something sort of plain and ordinary and then he always got something really special for her. She said going to Wal-Mart would ensure that she didn't get him anything too nice.

So we drove over by Lake Delton where the Wal-Mart was, and Sarah waltzed right in like she owned the joint, and in about two seconds she'd already found the aisle she wanted and picked out a pair of boots and taken them to the check-out and bought them with a credit card. She seemed a lot different than most of the other people there, who mostly went around real slow and staring around in a confused way at all the stuff.

Then we had to drive back to the Dells and right through the strip, which because it was Saturday was jam-packed with cars and people weaving their way through them to cross the street. All of the different attractions along the street, the go-cart tracks and water slides and roller coasters and sno-cone stands and boat rides, seemed like they were practically yelling at you with their music and bright-painted signs. The air felt humid, and on the radio they were finally predicting rain.

We drove on out of town, and the scenery changed to barns and silos and fences and cornfields, and then we turned off on a county road that wound down a hill right away and over a little creek with a wooden bridge and lots of cottonwoods and birch trees with the sunlight sliding through the leaves. We turned off on a little gravel driveway that ran up to a big old two-story house and back behind it was a huge red barn that looked very sharp and kept up well with new paint and the roof not practically caving in like lots of the other places I've seen. There were two low red buildings leading out from the barn and four big tall blue silos behind, and some cows out in a fenced-in area and some more cows out in a pasture, and then behind them fields and fields of corn with one of those big huge metal sprinkler monsters on giant wheels stretching off to the horizon and glaring in the sun.

Sarah parked in the shade of a maple tree and left the rig running. She turned to me on the seat. "You ready?" she said.

"Sure," I told her.

Then she kept looking at me for a second, the way she does when you know she's calculating something fast. "Can I ask you just one favor?" she said.

I was pretty sure I knew what that was. "It depends," I said.

"It *depends*?" she said, and reached over and kind of slapped my leg like she was playing around. I stayed pretty serious, though.

"Yeah," I said. "It depends on what."

Then she kind of narrowed her eyes and tightened her lips for a second, looking at me close. "Never mind," she said, and shut off the engine and opened the door and jumped out with me still sitting there. "Come on," she said.

I was of course not exactly eager to meet her dad. Not that I thought he was a bad guy, I mean in fact just the opposite, but he hadn't been going to the track ever since those first couple of times when I met Sarah, and I had a pretty good idea why. It seemed like there were a lot of unsaid things hanging around in the air between us, and now to add to it there was this unasked favor, which like I say I'm pretty sure was for me to take off my ring. It all added up to a kind of uncomfortable atmosphere.

At the front door Sarah said to wipe my feet, and then we went on in. There was a big front living room with high white ceilings and a staircase over to the side. The room was filled with all sorts of old, homey furniture and knick-knacks that I'm sure would have made you feel very pleasant under usual circumstances. There were pictures of the family all over the walls, and I got a quick look at Sarah's mom, who was pretty like Sarah only a little bit chubby and small. There was a brick fireplace with a mantle and more pictures and clocks and lots of sunlight in the room and flowered curtains pulled back and potted ferns in the windows. The whole place was very clean and tidy, and it gave me a pretty good idea what Sarah did during the few hours a day she left me to visit her dad. I mean I guess her visits involved a good bit of cleaning.

But the main thing I noticed, of course, was that her dad wasn't in the room. You could hear him from the back of the house actually, whistling, and in a few seconds I recognized the tune, which was "Cold, Cold Heart," one of my mother's songs.

Sarah took my hand, and then there we were, standing side by side in the doorway to the kitchen. Her dad had stopped whistling and was right in the middle of taking the first bite out of a huge sandwich, and next to him was a bag of potato chips and a glass of milk. It was interesting to think that the glass of milk had probably come from right there on that very farm. I mean you don't usually think anything about the subject, milk.

He looked up with his mouth full and chewed and swallowed and said, "Birthday girl," and gave Sarah a wink.

"Hi, Dad," she said, and walked on in with me behind her. She sat down at the table across from her dad and didn't say anything to me, so I figured I should just pull up a chair. "I don't think you've actually met Luke," she said.

"Nope," he said. "Haven't." And he put down his sandwich and wiped his hand on his pants and reached across the corner of the table. He had big rough hands, and mine felt small and bony between his fingers so I made sure to grip extra hard.

"Luke Rivers," I told him. We looked each other in the eye the way you're supposed to.

"Pleased to meet you," he said. He dug his hand into the bag of potato chips. "Sarah says you're fond of greyhounds."

I started to say something, but then it was like right when he'd said it I suddenly became aware of this old couch behind him at the back of the kitchen, and right there on one end of it, just curled up there on the cushion like a ceramic kitchen statue, was a greyhound. The dog didn't move and neither did I. We just stared at each other. I managed to kind of laugh, and Sarah laughed at me. "You never told me," I said.

"She thought it would be a nice surprise," her father said.

I got up and started moving across the kitchen, behind Sarah's dad there in the chair, and he twisted around to watch me. I was standing there in front of this dog, and the dog started squirming a little bit and his tail thump-thumped against the couch, and he licked his lips with his long red tongue and yawned. He was a big greyhound, and a brindle color I think they call it, sort of blondish-tan, and he seemed kind of old and tired.

"Go ahead and pet him," Sarah's dad said. "He don't bite or break in half or disappear."

I reached down and rubbed his head real smooth and gentle and he licked my hand. "Good boy," I told him. "Good boy." Even though he was curled up to where you couldn't see underneath, I knew he was a male just because of how big he was. "What's his name?" I said.

I could hear Sarah's dad trying to finish up chewing, and I thought Sarah would say but she didn't. Sarah's dad cleared his throat and his chair scraped on the floor, like he was scooting himself around to have a better look at me. "Poke Chop," he said.

My hand stopped for a second on his head, and I was looking right into his old gray eyes then and it wasn't like he was a dog at all, but more like a person I knew. I turned around and looked at both of them. Sarah's dad was pretending to be occupied with his sandwich but I could tell was actually feeling very proud and getting a kick out of how I was acting, and Sarah was sitting there across from him very quiet with her hands flat on the table and a big smile on her face, like it was my birthday instead of hers and I'd just opened a great present she'd given me and she was waiting to see what I'd say.

"You're shitting me," I said, kind of looking at both of them. "I mean you're pulling my leg."

"Nope," her dad said, crunching into a potato chip.

"This is Poke Chop?" I said. Right then the dog sat up on the couch and nudged my hand with his head, and I looked at him again and patted him.

"You know Poke Chop?" her dad asked me.

"Do I know Poke Chop," I said, like in a way that showed how of course I knew Poke Chop. "I probably lost a hundred bucks betting against him."

Her dad chuckled a bit. "And Sarah said you were smart," he said.

I was getting ready to tell him about my system, about betting on long shots, etcetera, but then I didn't. I was just quiet for a second, petting Poke Chop and feeling how smooth his head was, almost like he didn't have any coat at all but just smooth skin.

"I told you he would know Poke Chop," Sarah said.

"Yep," her dad said, real satisfied. "You did say that."

I sat down on the couch and started rubbing his ears. He had a dark patch that came up on his right side, and I remembered then seeing that patch go past on his way toward the finish line, and it was like I could feel myself back at the track with Jake and Jenny, watching, especially the time Poke Chop got knocked down in the first turn and we were all happy as hell, even Jake, because even Jake knew Poke Chop. But Poke Chop got up and came back and caught our dogs at the wire anyway and won. The only time I ever saw a dog get knocked down and win. I was sitting right next to that very same dog, scratching him behind the ears. "Poke Chop," I said, and he wagged his tail.

He was maybe the best greyhound that ever ran in the Midwest.

He raced till he was about eight years old, which is practically ancient for a greyhound, at all the tracks by the time he was through—Kenosha and Delevan and Dubuque and Council Bluffs and Rapid City and the Dells—and he won everywhere he went. The last time I'd seen him run was at the Dells last fall, and even that time I bet against him thinking he was too damn old to do it to me again, and of course he won and I lost my money. It was crazy to bet against him. He was a huge dog, about eighty-four pounds, where the average male even is between sixty-five and seventy, and he ran like a fire truck, this big old hulking mass that broke out clean and shoved to the front like there was some drastic emergency.

"He don't get around much anymore, old Poke Chop," Sarah's dad said. "They used to be cave dogs, you know. Greyhounds."

I nodded my head and raised my eyebrows, but I was still looking at Poke Chop, who'd settled back down and was kind of just leaning his head over the couch edge and looking all around while I patted his belly.

"Sure," Sarah's dad said. "You go way back when, they used to live in caves or dig holes in the ground and do nothing but sit there until something came along for lunch. Then they'd chase it down and take it right back to their hole. They're not real energetic like a setter the way people think."

"Really," I said.

Sarah stood up from the table. "I've got something in the car," she said. Then she walked out and left us there.

"How'd you get him?" I asked her dad.

"Named the right price," he said. "I'm sure the owner thought he was making a killing off him just before he got washed up, but I didn't buy him to race. I just didn't want to see him old and slow and running in the D races." He got up then and grabbed a can of dog food off the shelf and opened it. "You can't tell with these owners, either. Some of them would euthanize Michael Jordan when he got old."

I'd heard the door slam, and Sarah walked back into the kitchen with the Wal-Mart bag behind her back. "Can't wait to see what I got this time," her dad said. He put the dog food on a plate and bent over real slow and put it on the floor and Poke Chop hopped off the couch and stretched and started eating. The little metal tag on his collar clinked against the plate. They seemed like a good pair, Poke Chop and Sarah's dad.

"Well, hang on a minute and we'll make this official," he said, and walked out of the room. He came back in carrying Sarah's present, wrapped in blue paper with a white bow, and set it on the table.

"You first," Sarah said, so her dad opened the shoe box and took out his boots and made a big to-do over them and put them back in the box and told Sarah to open hers.

It was a music box. Sarah opened the lid and I recognized the song right off, "Dream a Little Dream of Me," and it sounded very sweet and pretty there in the quiet kitchen. Sarah listened to it, and she sat looking at the box and kind of holding her hands lightly along the edges, and then a little smile came on her face and just as quick went away, and she closed the lid and said, "Thank you, Daddy." Then they stood there in the kitchen and hugged each other, and their eyes were closed and Sarah patted her dad's shoulder, and I knew then that it had to do with her mother, the song, that it must have been a song her mother sang. I sat there real quiet at the table.

"Well," her dad said then. He pulled back and sort of adjusted his pants around his waist, not looking at Sarah but more over toward me. "I got to get back to work. Happy birthday," he said, and leaned in and kissed Sarah's cheek. "You're getting pretty long in the tooth," he said. Sarah slapped him on the arm. "I don't know if you're at all interested in dairy farming," he said to me, "but if you're still around about four o'clock, you can come out and watch us milk."

I told him I'd like that, and he picked up the leftover food Poke Chop didn't eat and wrapped it up in Saran Wrap and stuck it in the fridge and went on out the back door.

For the next hour or so I took a nap there next to Poke Chop on the couch and he passed gas a couple of times the way I guess old dogs will do, and the whole time Sarah talked on the phone to this friend and that friend of hers up in Madison, and as I was sort of drifting in and out of sleep the dog races went through my mind, but more like the old days when I was what you'd call very anxious about whether or not I would win, like we were nearly broke and needed a quinella in a bad way, and I was trying to stay cheerful and optimistic, and I might have even said something in my sleep—"Looks good, looks *good*," maybe, seeing the dogs turning into the stretch. And at times it was like I recognized the voice in the room, that it was Sarah, and at other times it sounded more like the track announcer, like it was part of the dream I was having.

Then Sarah was beside me and I was awake. Poke Chop was sitting like a statue again, looking over at me. I felt hot, and for a second I thought I was sick and had a fever and I put my hand to my head.

"Hello," Sarah said. "You with me?"

"Yeah," I said. I was just sort of woozy was all, and worn out. I watched a fly buzz across the room and land on the stove.

"I've got one more call to Madison and then we can go," Sarah said.

I told her okay.

"Why don't you go out and visit with my dad?" she said. "They probably just started milking."

At first I thought it was because she just wanted me to visit with her dad, that that was important to her, but then later at The Bend I would remember about that last phone call and realize it was something else. But anyway I said okay, and Sarah showed me where to go, and I went out and it seemed pretty hot again like every other day and I wondered about the rain. It didn't seem to be in any hurry. I walked along kind of sleepy and slow to the long building with the tin roof where Sarah told me to.

Going in, you definitely ran into the cow smell, and there were these two ramps loaded with cows, and a kind of open area in the middle with Sarah's dad and another guy, and pipes running along the ramp rails and these control panels with buttons and hoses hanging from the ceiling all over the place. Sarah's dad and the other guy had on rubber boots and aprons, and I noticed another guy along what looked like an exit ramp since the cows were headed on it in the opposite direction. He had a hose and was bent over, and it looked like cleaning shit off a cow's leg. It wasn't exactly what you'd call an appetizing kind of scene but not too bad either for some reason.

"You decided to come on out," Sarah's dad said. "Good. We can put you to milking." The other guy laughed. He was right then taking this long hose-like deal with four clamps on it and hooking it to this cow's tits. The cows were behind the rail and the ramp came up to about waist level so I guess you could get hold of the part you had to deal with easier. "Why don't you start with that one right there?" Sarah's dad said, and pointed to this one cow that was kind of in the middle of the line with the others.

Of course at that point I couldn't tell whether he was serious, so I figured I might just as well be ready to pitch in and lend a hand, and I stepped over that way and kind of sized up the cow and then realized it was a bull because of basic anatomy. They both had a good laugh, Sarah's dad and the guy.

"Won't get much from that one," Sarah's dad said. He was standing next to this cow and the clamp things were dropping off its tits one by one, like petals falling off a dead flower. He picked up the clamps and said "Shoo! Get!" and the cow moved along. The next cow moved up and he grabbed this cup thing and held it up over each of the cow's tits. "Iodine," he said.

"What's that bull doing in here?" I said.

"Oh," he said, "just checking up on things. Wants to make sure we're treating mama right."

There was an interesting rhythm to it—sanitizing the tits and clamping on the machine and then pushing a button and the milk would pump out and go into this tube that led to a holding tank and then the clamps would fall off one by one automatically and the cow would move off most times by itself and the next cow would step in line. It made you feel kind of bad about eating them and all, when you saw how smart they were. They definitely knew the whole routine. I mean of course these ones didn't get eaten because they were dairy cows, but still.

"See, they'll go right through because once they get milked and cleaned up, they head to the feeding troughs," Sarah's dad said. He put the clamps on another cow but stood there and held them this time after he hit the button on the machine. "This one's a slow milker," he said. "The pumps drop off before she's through so you got to hold 'em."

Of course the cows all looked the same to me, but I didn't ask how he knew this one from the others. I figured he just knew. "How many cows you got?" I asked him. They were backed up further than I could see, like they were waiting for a rock concert.

"We're milking upwards of a hundred and fifty," he said. He was holding the clamps on and looking over at the guy behind me. "Keep 'em moving, Dave," he said.

"Come on up," Dave said, and quit doing whatever he'd been doing, which looked like trying to clean some shit off his T-shirt. Every once in a while one of the cows took a dump and it splattered off the cement, so I was careful to stay in the middle of the ramps.

"That's about twice what most of the farms are doing around here now. Family farms anyways." He was done with the slow milker and he patted her leg to get her moving and he did the iodine thing with the next cow and hooked her up and pressed the button on the machine and you could see milk start to pass through the long tube to the other room. "Dairy farming's gone to hell," he said. "The only way I stay ahead is this is a third-generation farm and all paid off. Most farmers are in debt up to their assholes." He said how if he wanted to, he could be buying up farms like some guys were, but the way he saw it these were his neighbors. "The whole idea turns my stomach," he said, "though Buddy says I should."

I was finding the farming stuff pretty interesting, actually, like in a way that I don't find most kinds of work, and I also didn't want to edge into a family discussion, but Buddy is a bit of a mystery to me. "I thought Buddy was going to law school," I said.

"Damn right," he said. He was turned around facing me, and behind him one of the clamps dropped off a tit and drooped there in the air. They were sort of sad-looking the way they did that, like they were getting old and dying right in front of you. "No future in dairy farming. Though I wonder sometimes if that's not what he really wants to do."

"Run the farm?" I said. I nodded at the cow, where the last clamp was hanging there and ready to drop.

He turned around and picked it up off the cement when it fell. "Keep 'em moving, Dave," he said.

"They're going as fast as they'll go," Dave said.

"How you doing over there, Slate?"

"Fine," Slate said. I guess the other guy's name was Slate. It makes you wonder why people got away from regular names, all these guys running around named Slate and Jade. "The udder on that one with the star patch don't look any better if at all."

"Let's give it till Monday," Sarah's dad said. "No," he said, "I don't want my kids going into dairy farming. I knew that a long time ago, and I never raised them that way." He kind of stopped there with the iodine thing in his hand and his eyes looked like they were floating away somewhere else. He had really pale blue eyes, I noticed, like water. "It wasn't ever a problem with Sarah. I think she liked growing up on a farm—hope so anyway since it's all said and done—but I knew she wasn't ever going to marry a farmer. Buddy, though," he said. He thought about it for a second, and then reached out and stuck the iodine on one of the cow's udders. "Keep 'em moving, Dave," he said. Dave didn't bother to answer this time.

"He likes all this? The milking and stuff?" I said. I was having a hard time seeing Buddy that way.

"Oh, yeah," he said. "I think he likes it okay. But especially the business end of things." He sort of drifted off again, standing there with the clamp thing in his hand. I looked back at all the cows herded up at the back of the building and how they seemed to be getting through faster on Dave's end. It was like a sea of cows, shifting and rolling real slow, with their heads bobbing up and down like little waves. "This whole milking parlor was his idea. He learns about all the new stuff like that before I do. Used to milk them at the troughs years ago." He started hooking on the clamps, looking the cow up and down. "Lot easier this way. What bothers me, though, is you used to get a chance to see if they were eating okay. Now sometimes you can't see they're sick until pretty late." He pushed the button to start the hoses sucking. "Buddy'll go to law school, though, and that's good because he'll be somewhere where his intelligence can get closer to its limits. But maybe he'd rather be a dairy farmer, I don't know." He kind of very noticeably glanced over my way. "Life's all about trade-offs in some ways."

You could definitely tell where Sarah got her habit of jumping around from subject to subject, and I was starting to have a hard time sorting things through. In other words I didn't know why he'd looked at me that way, but I guessed we were getting close to something about me and Sarah.

"It seems to me you're probably at a point where you need to make some decisions," he said to me.

I knew that. He didn't have to tell me. But it was hard to stand there with him like that, with him not knowing the extent of things. I liked Sarah's dad a lot, about as much as I'd liked anybody since Sarah herself and Tucker and the midget. And at the same time I didn't know if I'd ever talk to him again, and I was sure that this one conversation would never be enough chance to explain anything. I wanted to let him know how strongly I felt about his daughter, but how I was at a point where it was hard to be sure about a lot of things. I wanted to say something that could let him understand a little bit of what we'd been going through, how it seemed like there was a possibility of something like a window opening up to us, some place where light and air got through and reached you in the middle of life and everything came more clear. But I couldn't come up with any words.

Sarah's dad said "Get!" and the cow moved along, and he, Sarah's dad, looked over at Dave, trying to figure out I could tell if he wanted to have this particular conversation here in this particular place. "I don't want to give you a lecture," he said. "You're a grown man, same as me."

"I don't think a lecture would help things," I said, and then immediately wondered what I meant. I guess I was remembering Professor Wykowski and Dr. Blumenthal, and how even refocusing and finding a way to kind of reach a truce with the Problem of Evil hadn't made much real difference for me.

"No," he said, "no," like he agreed completely. He was standing there with the iodine bucket again and this time just finally put it down and didn't bother. He just left it to Dave to keep 'em moving. "I can't claim to know Sarah's thoughts on the subject," he said, pretty clearly meaning me and her. "She's had a rough time, I think, ever since her mother first got sick." When he said that, you could see he was getting into an area he didn't really want to, and his hands sort of fumbled around like they were looking for something to do but never found the iodine. "It doesn't seem like I know her that well anymore." He held his hands out in front of him, back side up, his big scuffed-up hands that still had the gold wedding band on the ring finger, and looked at them like he'd never seen them before. Then he put them inside his apron. "But I trust her. If she likes you, then there must be a good reason." He stood there looking me over for a second, like he was real quick trying to figure out what the reason might be. "All I ask is that you be good enough to consider Sarah in all this and not make a mess of things. Only weak men are selfish." He took his arms out of the apron and looked at me again like he was trying to see if I was what he'd call a weak man.

I felt pretty weak, too, right at the moment. It was like he had the advantage of being a man that everything in life was plain for, growing up and working hard and getting married and loving your family and getting older and eventually dying and rejoining your loved ones, which I could tell he believed without even asking. And there I was, believing nothing for sure from how I was raised, having no real work to show that was mine, and no family now. For just a minute I hated the Greyhound God or whoever was responsible for what was happening to me, my own little private miracle, my unending lucky streak. Because it's all one-sided is the thing, all me and no God, not like with Jesus and the others who were allowed a little friendly conversation with the power that made them or chose to help them along their way.

So it was hard to stand there with him. But then I remembered what I'd told myself by the side of the road about staying positive and keeping faith, and I thought about the wish I'd made when I picked the star in Sarah's hand. "I think I've been doing that," I said. "I've never forgot her the whole time."

We stood there and looked at each other, me a good bit taller than him and him a good bit stouter, and I wanted to reach out and hug him for some reason. He nodded at me, just one firm nod. "Okay," he said. He grabbed the iodine container and turned around to his cow.

After that we just talked, and pretty soon Sarah came in and said she was ready. Her dad said why didn't she show me the barn, so we went there and it was dark and warm and sleepy. There's something about dairy farming, I have to admit. I can see how it would make you grow up to be like Sarah's dad, like there was something in the place itself that formed you a certain way, very solid and straight. And I couldn't quite see why Sarah's dad hadn't wanted his own kids to be exactly like that.

We were just about to the Land Cruiser after Sarah had told her dad good-bye when she stopped and asked if I wanted to say good-bye to Poke Chop. I told her sure, of course I did.

We went inside and there was Poke Chop on the couch just like before. I said, "Well, good-bye Poke Chop, see you later," because I mean what else was there to say. Sarah's dad had talked to me a little about the dogs he'd bought, and how he was too attached to them and was always visiting them at the track kennels and taking them treats, and how when they were done racing and couldn't stay there anymore he'd bring them all home. I started picturing greyhounds lying all along the couch and stretched out all over the kitchen.

"You want to take him out?" Sarah asked. She had a little mischievous-type grin on her face, like she knew some secret.

"You mean like out for a walk?" I said.

She said right, and she got a leash out of the drawer and hooked it up to his collar, and Poke Chop jumped down with his tail wagging like mad. He didn't seem so old then.

We went outside, and out on the edge of the sky from the pasture she took us to I could see for the first time in weeks big clouds building. But it was still hot as fire there in the sun. Sarah handed me the leash and told me to watch where I stepped, and Poke Chop walked along just fine, light in my hand and not straining at the leash. The pasture rolled out in a little slope to a barbwire fence butting up against the cornfield. Sarah stopped. "You want to see him run?" she said. She started looking around over toward the barn and the milking parlor and the silos and then around toward the house.

"You serious?" I said. "He can still run like that?"

"Sure," she said. "I mean, I guess so. He's not crippled or anything. He could still be racing for all I know."

Which was true, actually. It had only been six months or so since the last time he'd cost me four dollars. "Are we not supposed to?" I asked. Sarah was still looking around to see if her dad or anyone was watching.

"Well, technically, no," she said. "According to my dad." A breeze had picked up and a few strands of hair went across her face and she blew at them and pulled them behind her ear. I was facing into the breeze, and it felt good. "The problem is that you can't be sure what he'll do, Dad says."

"Like he might run away or something?" I said.

She looked around. "There's the fence, right? I mean how could he?"

"Yeah," I said. "But do you think he might get hurt?"

"How?" she said.

"I don't know. Maybe where the ground's not level."

She shook her head. She looked around real quick one last time and then reached down and unhooked the chain. I felt my knees jerk, like in football at the end of the snap count, before your legs start moving.

But Poke Chop stood there as still as a post, looking from one to the other of us, like what did we expect. At the same time Sarah and I started laughing, like we'd just had the hell scared out of us by something dumb.

"Well Jesus Christ, Poke Chop," she said. "Run!" But he just stood there.

"Maybe he forgot how," I said. But I knew that didn't make any sense. "Maybe he needs something to run *for*," I said.

"Look, Poke Chop," Sarah said. "Look out *there*." And then she waved her hand toward the far side of the pasture and the fence.

What happened next is another thing that's very complicated to explain, like I said before about the petals and the stem. On the one hand it was nothing, just a dog running fast like I'd seen a thousand times before. But on the other hand I suppose it was being there, out at Sarah's farm with just a rolling pasture and no mechanical rabbit and no other dogs—just Poke Chop out there in the sun with the clouds getting big.

Sarah just waved her hand, brought her arm out to her side in one golden sweep, and it was like with that one single gesture Poke Chop understood, and for the tiniest second it was like he was trailing her arm, like she was still pulling him by the leash, and then he'd broken free. He was like a beam of light moving through empty space, passing over the field like he didn't even feel it.

My breath was gone, like I'd had the wind knocked out of me, and Sarah said, "Oh my gosh," and I saw her hands go up to her face.

The first thing I felt was fear, like it was me myself doing the running and getting ready for the disaster at the end, because you could see there was no way he had time to use up all that speed before the fence. My body tightened right up my legs and arms and neck, and Sarah started forward, running, but so slow it seemed, like the air she went through was made of glue, and the leash dangled from her hand.

But for me, behind the fear there was something else, something to recognize, like that first time out at the track when I felt myself running with the dogs and then sensed a pattern to everything. Because it was just pure running, just pure motion across the grass and the hillside. It was like Poke Chop had answered Sarah's gesture with a gesture of his own, the only one he really knew, one that said, "This is what I am, a greyhound."

There was something important in that, but I didn't have time to think of it much, standing there locked up as stiff as the barbwire fence Poke Chop ran toward, seeing him and Sarah ahead of me. When it looked like the distance between dog and fence had become impossibly small, I could see Poke Chop's legs folding in suddenly, just folding up like one of those old plastic cups that you can collapse down inside itself, and his rear end was rotating in perfect circles with his tail spinning around like a propeller. It was familiar then, the same thing I'd seen at the track when the rabbit squeaked and died on the rail but never paid enough attention to before, the motion ending so suddenly. In just a few yards before the fence his body came together under him, like it was reshaping itself, and the next thing you knew there he was, standing at the fence and wagging his tail.

By the time I caught up to Sarah, she already had his leash back on, and Poke Chop was standing with his paws up on her leg. "Shit!" she said to me, and put her hand to her heart. "I didn't think he was going to stop."

I shook my head and said I didn't either.

She held Poke Chop's head between her hands and shook it back and forth. "You scared me to death, Poke Chop," she said. He plopped down off her legs and pranced around on the leash. Sarah turned to me. "Well, you sure did *look* calm," she said.

I thought about it for a second. "Yeah," I said. "I guess I always look that way."

We put Poke Chop back inside after I stopped at the door to wipe cow shit off my sandal and had to use the hose to get it all, and then we got in the Land Cruiser and took off up the road. We were going back to the cabin to have a little nap, and I was sleepy enough, but I still kept thinking about Poke Chop running across the pasture and the way Sarah had raised her hand, and I felt like something had changed somehow, though I couldn't say what. I just knew that it had got me thinking in a new way about the whole thing we were involved in, something to do with gestures.

But it wasn't a bad thought, and didn't put me in a bad mood or anything. The top was down, and the wind whipped by and nearly drowned out the radio, and the sun was shining and the clouds were behind us. I was watching all the farms in a way I hadn't before, thinking of the farmers and their families inside getting ready to make dinner, and the cows out in the shade of the barns.

Sarah talked about our plans for the night, shouting over the wind and her hair blowing around so that she looked so natural again, the way she does so many times, like she was in the right spot doing what she should be. Her legs were stretched out long and tan and she was driving in her bare feet. "Crimson and Clover" came on the radio, and I said to myself what the hell, and cranked it and started singing. And I didn't think of anything, except that riding along on a country road with the top down reminded me of one time when Jake and I rode in the back of a pick-up truck, and I had no idea what town it was where we'd done that or who we could have been riding with. When we went through town I tried to get Sarah to stop and let me buy her a present, but she wouldn't. Then it seemed like the next thing I knew Sarah was waking me up at the cabin again, and the shadows were stretched out long across the lawn out the window, and it was time to go to The Bend.

Right from the start there was a weird feeling to the whole thing, the whole night, like everything was imaginary. The people I met didn't seem real to me, like they weren't really there or I wasn't really there being introduced to them, or that they weren't real people with feelings.

Buddy was there, wearing a suit of all things, which I was glad to see—not the suit, I mean, but just that Buddy was there, since I had been kind of afraid he had forgotten Sarah's birthday and it would hurt her feelings. People had brought balloons and birthday hats like at a kid's party. To me, it reminded me of the fact that we'd never had an actual birthday party for Jake, but only me and him and Jenny and candles and whatever presents we could afford and a birthday cake. And then thinking of Jake's birthday reminded me of Jenny's birthday which is coming up soon, July 5th, and in fact I thought of how it would have been practically nine years ago to this very day that me and Jenny first met. I couldn't get my mind on the party very well.

Buddy started things off with a toast, where he made some jokes about Sarah that I didn't get but everybody else did, and then he said nice things about how pretty she was and what a good person. Then there was a lot of drinking and talk. There were all kinds of different shots going around, and no matter who ordered them it seemed like I was buying, and a whole bunch of kids I didn't know at all were thanking me over and over and saying I was a good man. I almost never talked, but Sarah hung right by me, holding my hand and sometimes putting her arm around my shoulder, and at times I thought I caught people nodding at us and whispering.

And all the time they were talking to each other, Sarah too, and I was listening to what they said, but they seemed like actors in a movie. Really I knew they were just regular college kids, and they talked about college kid things, like classes and football games and who was breaking up with who, but then they also talked about their future careers, and lots of them were talking about jobs I'd never even heard of, and then there were these two guys off to my right who had a conversation about the bond market. I looked around the table, and they were all perfect, like they were all dressed perfect for who they were and what time it was in their lives and they talked about all the perfect things that they should be talking about at their age and even drank the perfect way, like even all the crazy things they did now would be the perfect things to talk about later on in life when they remembered their wild youth, and they weren't like real people at all in any way that I could figure out, but more like paper cut-outs of perfect people you could paste in a magazine.

All except Sarah, who was next to me and holding my hand. Sarah was different, like she half fit with these people but half didn't, and the half that wouldn't fit was the one attached to me. But it was also like only half of me fit back to her somehow, so that me and her put together made one whole thing that was only half of what each of us were, and I thought of how at the Wal-Mart we had moved so fast through all the people there, like we were cutting a slice fast through them, and all of their eyes looked empty and their bodies were like sand, just sifting out to the edges as we passed them. Really the half of me that wasn't part of Sarah was more like the people there than here, and it was only this small part of me that fought against that, that feeling of being poor and lost and empty and shuffling along the aisles, that made me at all the same as Sarah. Those were the people I was more familiar with, at the Wal-Mart, the losers with the empty eyes and falling away like sand, the ones the Greyhound God I thought took care of, someone with sympathy. But now it didn't seem that way, that there was anybody taking care of anything.

I wanted very bad to be at the track. I wanted to be there putting my money down, sitting at the finish line and watching the race unravel, my dogs moving up and up, rolling by like water, cutting across the finish line in the moment where I was waiting, listening for something. I wanted to get away from the table, I needed to refocus on my feet. Because I could tell that sitting there I was getting into a way of thinking that could lead me into trouble.

So I stood up and headed to the bathroom, and my legs were wobbly beneath me, and I felt like an old man. I thought I needed to pee, but when I got to the urinal nothing came out, and I saw that what I really needed to do was just stand there. I stared at the wall and tried to look at the white space between the graffiti.

When I finally came out, it was like being in a whole different place. The party over at Sarah's table didn't matter to me one bit, like it didn't have anything to do with me and I didn't even know anybody there, not even Sarah, and it was like I'd never been inside the place at all, like I'd been flung down in Wisconsin out of the clouds in the middle of all the Brewers posters and Packers pennants. The only thing that interested me suddenly was right up at the front of the bar, the piano.

I walked down the little aisle between the pool tables and the chairs, excusing myself to people as I made my way, and then I went behind Sarah, and I saw her head turn. I sat down on the piano bench, which was rickety and swayed back and forth, and plunked a couple of keys. It was an old upright that had been pretty banged up and all the stain faded off and the keys yellow, and I guessed it was probably a long time since they'd had it tuned, if ever. But it still had a nice sound, big and hollow.

I wanted to play a song, any song, but I didn't know what and I didn't know how. The jukebox was playing the Rolling Stones, which was good, but it was screwing up the possibility of getting a different tune in my head. Then Sarah sat down on the bench next to me and I thought the thing was going to collapse so I scooted over a bit to balance the weight.

"I won't bite," she said.

I started to explain about the bench but then I didn't. I just plunked the keys, seeing if there were any weak ones in an octave I'd need.

"Do you know how to play?" Sarah said.

"No," I told her. "I'm just fooling around." I wanted to tell her how Mark could play, how great it would be if he was here and playing the "Moonlight Sonata" or pretty much anything. But it seemed too late to tell Sarah now, that I'd had a little brother. It's like with people's names, how if you go too long without asking what they are it pretty soon gets impossible. "Do you think it's okay for me to mess with this?" I said.

"I don't know," she said. "No one ever plays it." She put her hand on my neck. "But sure," she said. "Everyone knows me here. Bang around on it all you want to." She sat there and I ran my fingers up a scale. "If that's what you want to do," she said.

I could tell what she meant. "No," I said. "I don't have to."

"Are you bored?" she said.

I told her no, it was just that I didn't know anyone, and we turned around and looked at all her friends, and she said how she knew what I meant, it was kind of a silly party, and she just had to hang out a little while. Sure, I said, no problem.

We went back to the table and I finished my beer. I barely noticed when Sarah got up and left the table, but then I saw her standing at the bar and talking to Buddy, and in a minute Buddy came over with a couple of beers and took off his coat and tie and asked if I wanted to play pool. So it was obvious they were being nice to me, taking care of me.

The pool table was a huge relief. We had to beat a couple of guys at doubles to get on, but then they left so we had the table to ourselves. I shot like a fiend, just rolling them in one after another, everything lines and corners and angles, the colors bright and sharp as little flags, and I didn't see anything past the green felt. I listened to the balls click and fall and roll through the table, and I could see the triangles in my head as clear as if they'd been drawn with chalk, just the logic of it, Angle A, Angle B, Angle C.

Some of the other guys came and sat around and played a game or two, but none of them were real, not even Buddy, and once I turned my head to call a shot and there was nobody there and it was just the wall I was talking to. They all had a good laugh, but I just went on beating their brains out.

Sarah was standing there, too, talking to me between turns, and I talked back, but not in a way where I was really doing it. In a far-off corner of my mind I was aware that she was getting pretty drunk, and I told her she should probably slow down, but I couldn't work up a voice that sounded like it had any real concern, and she didn't take it too well.

And all the time there was this other guy hanging around, a new guy, one who I hadn't met at the table. He and Sarah didn't talk much, but it was like he was tied to her, like Poke Chop on a long, invisible leash.

Finally everybody quit, they'd got bored or had enough, and I realized I had to piss really bad, so bad I could hardly stand straight. I put up my cue and turned around to head to the bathroom, but Sarah grabbed my arm and stopped me. She had a little grin on her face, and she kind of stumbled up against me. "I've got a surprise for us," she said, right up close to my ear. I looked around the bar, and it was pretty crowded, but Sarah's party seemed like it had broken up, the empty table scattered with empty pitchers and mugs and cigarette packs and party hats. I could recognize a few of the people I'd met around the bar, and Buddy was right then kind of storming out the door with his girlfriend what's-her-name, Taylor, right behind him, who'd magically appeared from someplace because she wasn't there before. She had her arms crossed in front of her with her purse slung over her shoulder and her head down, walking fast to keep up. I figured that was the last we'd see of them.

And right there was this new guy with long, stringy hair, standing about ten feet away, just casually watching me and Sarah. I looked at him and he looked at me. "I've got to go take a piss," I said.

"Just a second," Sarah said, pulling on my arm. She just stood there, swaying a little bit, smiling at me.

"What?" I said. "Hurry." I was about ready to pop.

She leaned in to me again. "Have you ever tried coke?" she said.

"No," I said.

"Do you want to?" she said.

"No," I said, and pulled my arm away, but she held on.

The whole thing was totally clear to me already, but I didn't even care. There stood this guy, and I immediately placed him with that last phone call Sarah made at her house, and I could see he hoped I wouldn't come with them, and I could see why. "Let me go to the bathroom," I said.

"Luke," she said, still holding tight. "Just this once do it with me. It'll be fun."

"No," I said. I shook my arm free and started heading toward the bathroom, toward the guy where he was standing. "You go ahead," I said.

"Go *ahead*?" she said from behind me, like she couldn't understand what she was hearing.

"Yeah," I said. "See you later." I was just a few feet from the guy, and I stopped. He shrugged his shoulders at me, just a very tiny shrug you almost couldn't tell. What hit me right then was that he looked an awful lot like me. He was about the same height, had the same long brown hair, the same kind of regular face, and he was thin like me. He was younger, of course, but he could have *been* me, really, and I could have been him. He looked bright enough, not smart, but bright enough—bright enough to go to college and slide by and sell drugs to college girls and maybe get lucky once in a while. I could have been him, he could have been me. I went on to the bathroom.

I was practically frantic to get my pants unbuttoned, and then it was one of those pisses that seems to go on for hours and feels like you're dumping out a bucket. I felt good, but very lightheaded and weak.

When I came back out, Sarah and the guy were gone. The place had thinned out a little, and there were two empty stools down toward the other end of the bar. I took one and ordered a draft beer and lit a cigarette. I watched the bartenders go back and forth behind the bar and the people come and go and listened to the jukebox off and on. For some reason, I thought about that heroin addict in Crescent City, the first one who ever told me I was special. She told me one of the saddest stories I ever heard, and sitting there at the bar it was like I could see her telling it, from years earlier in my life, there on this ratty old couch at her apartment right about dawn, with the sun starting to come through the thin curtain. Crescent City was a pretty town on the ocean where a lot of rich people lived, and I remember most of the streets didn't have regular names but just letters, like A Street, G Street, W Street. It was kind of depressing, like no one cared enough to take the time and name the streets after real people or things that would make it seem like a friendly town. And this woman wasn't one of the rich people, and I wasn't one of the rich people, and we didn't live in the nice part of town, and the people weren't very friendly. She'd been up all night, still wearing the black tank top she'd had on at the bar where I worked and she hung out and black underwear. She wore black everything, all the time, black tank tops and T-shirts and jeans and skirts and leather jackets. She had long black hair. She was older than me, about the same age I am now I guess, but still kind of good-looking even after all she'd been through.

I was sleeping on her couch, which probably would have changed if I'd actually moved in like we planned, like she was counting on, I think. But that was the first night I'd stayed there. I was going to move my stuff in the next day, and she'd had some people over, and I eventually got tired and went to the couch to sleep. I woke up late in the night and heard two people, her and a guy, talking real low at a table behind the couch. I sat up and looked over, and she was sitting there with a hose wrapped around her arm and a needle in her hand. She looked over at me, and I lay down and went back to sleep.

She woke me up a couple of hours later, a while after I'd heard the guy leave. She was there in her tank top and underwear on the couch, trying to crawl under the sheet with me. I sat up with her instead. She looked shaky and like she'd been sick. She told me she knew she had a problem, and she didn't want to make excuses. She said I was young, but maybe I hadn't had such a hot life either and I could understand things. She said she used to live in this apartment building, someplace else in California I think, and her neighbor was a middle-aged guy who was paraplegic from a car wreck and had to push himself around in a wheelchair. She and this man were good friends, they used to drink beer together in the afternoons at her apartment and watch soap operas on TV. One day they were talking about the show, and the topic turned to sex. She was the type of woman who talked about sex quite a bit with practically anybody, I remember, not in a teasing way but that's just what interested her to talk about. So she and this guy in the wheelchair were talking about sex, and then she realized that the conversation was making him nervous and maybe a little bit excited. She was ashamed of herself right away, she said, because of his condition and everything. But she thought it wouldn't be right to apologize, that that would be even worse, so she tried to just be honest about it and she asked him if he could still have sex. He told her yes, but nobody had ever wanted to, and she could see that he was hoping, and so she did what she thought was the right thing at the time, a sort of gesture of friendship and sympathy. She went over to him and got down on her knees and opened his pants and gave him a blow job. And the whole time he ran his fingers very gently through the hair on her neck. She remembered that clearly, she said. She was telling me this smoking a cigarette there in her black underwear, and I admit it was making me uncomfortable.

Whenever he came over after that, she said, the man in the wheelchair, he wanted to do the same thing. If she wouldn't, he'd never mention it, but he would get frustrated and depressed and once threw a beer bottle on the floor and broke it and cried while she was cleaning up the mess. So a few more times she gave into this sort of unspoken pressure and did the same thing again. But each time she did it, things got worse. She was young then, she said, and a stripper at a club at night because that was the only way she knew to make money, and he would try to stop her from going to work, and whenever she had guys or even girlfriends over he would hear her from next door and come knocking to see what she was up to, and he would try to get her to let him spend the night. She tried to stay friends with him, but he got very jealous and a lot of times said mean things. She was a whore, she was worthless, etcetera.

She finally started planning to move away, but she didn't know how to tell him and she was afraid to hurt his feelings. One night before work an old boyfriend of hers called on the phone, and she was having fun talking to him and kind of forgot to be quiet, she was laughing and everything, and then she heard him wheeling out into the hall and there was the knock on the door. He knew she was in there, but she pretended not to be anyway. She hung up the phone without saying another word, and sat there in her bed as still as could be, listening to the knocking from her front room. Soon he was pounding on the door and yelling her name, and telling her what he was going to do to her if she didn't let him in, and for the first time she was really scared. She lay in bed and pulled up the covers and tried to think of other things, things that made her feel happier and safe. After a while she heard voices in the hall, and an argument, and then a door slamming and him in his apartment smashing things.

Late that night when she came home from work, an ambulance and police cars were there. The ambulance was ready to leave, and she could see a blood-stained sheet over a body in the back. She said she knew who it was right away. A neighbor pointed her out to the police, and they asked her questions and told her what happened. He had slashed his wrists in the bathtub.

She lit another cigarette and looked at the floor and told me again that she shouldn't make excuses, but that event had happened in her life and it was the worst thing, but there was a lot more. She said maybe I could understand. She said she just needed to have someone and needed to feel safe.

I told her I understood. And I did, of course. I could understand about as well as anybody. But at the same time I knew I couldn't stay there with her like we'd planned. It made me sad, and for a minute I wanted to do what she wanted me to, I think, undress with her and be with her there on the couch, but I couldn't do that for her. I told her again how I understood, but how I had actually made up my mind the night before to move to New Orleans. It just rolled right off my tongue and that's actually how I ended up there. It was a dumb thing to say, I know, and a bad way of handling things, but what was I, twenty-one? Twenty-two?

She laughed some at that, what I'd said about New Orleans, and looked at the window. I thought she was going to cry or get pissed off, but she didn't. She got herself together, and she said to me, "I'm sure you'll do great there, Luke Rivers." She patted my leg under the sheet. "There's something special about you. Good things will come your way."

It made me angry there at the bar, thinking of it all again. It made me angry for the man in the wheelchair, and angry for her, and angry for myself, that we would all have to as you'd say participate in the whole shitty order of events, that each of us would have to feel bad and make decisions we didn't want to make because they were the only ones we had. It made me angry at Jesus, and all the other ones, the ones who got all the messages and just had to follow along, because how easy is that, anyway? It's a fucking piece of cake.

And so I didn't want to be angry, but I had to be. Me sitting there at a bar in Wisconsin with my little two-bit miracle that no one even knew about but me and Sarah, who'd left me stranded to go get high. Me there by myself, just trying not to let my life slip off into a bad place again because of what had seemed like, finally, for once, a good thing. I couldn't help but get angry.

So I sat there at the bar feeling angry and I guess full of spite would be the word, until finally I remembered what I'd promised myself—that I wouldn't give in to that way of thinking. I went through my whole refocusing routine, reminding myself of how I had to stay tuned in to what was happening, how the answer could come at any time and any place and I had to be ready and waiting.

That helped a little bit, and I started feeling stronger and more in control of what I was thinking. I tried to look back at what the woman in Crescent City had told me in a positive way because, after all, it was a nice thing in my life that someone had said to me. So I tried to ask myself again in a hopeful way what was it that made me special, what good things were coming my way, but I knew also that I couldn't sit there forever at the bar drinking more beer and smoking more cigarettes and still keep thinking like that. Fortunate for me, these two guys at Sarah's party I'd met stopped at the bar to talk to me on their way out, and it helped me out a bit, just in terms of getting me out of a rut, I mean. They definitely weren't *trying* to help or anything.

"Hey, man, we're taking off," one of them said. "Nice to meet you."

"Nice to meet *you*," I said, and swung around on my stool and shook his hand and then shook hands with the other guy.

They stood and looked at me. "You doing okay?" the guy said.

"Sure," I told him. "You?"

He nodded. "Where's Sarah?" The guy next to him tried not to smile.

"She stepped out," I said.

The guy nodded again and jingled some change in his pocket or keys. "Well, tell her I said 'Happy Birthday,'" he said.

"Definitely. I will," I said.

They were still looking at me. "Do you know my name?" he asked me.

"Sure," I said. "I'm a real whiz when it comes to names."

The guy next to him was trying not to smile again. I could see the guy who was talking trying to decide how far he could go, how far should he push me.

"Something else?" I said.

"No," he said. "That's it. 'Happy Birthday.'"

"You got it," I said. "'Happy Birthday.'"

He said nice to meet me again and they left. The one guy was laughing before they got through the doorway.

I had that kind of burning angry feeling in my head again, but this time they'd got my adrenalin going and I felt ready to get up and move. For a while I realized I'd been hearing a noise. It was kind of a swishing noise, like a fan. I stood up and started following it, and it led me to the doorway. Someone had propped open the door to let some air in with all the smoke, and outside I saw the rain. It was coming down in swirls, whipping around the streetlights, and the sky flashed and thunder boomed. The wind blew the rain in a mist through the doorway and I stood there smelling it and feeling it on my face. And my eyes filled up with tears. So fragile, I could hear Sarah say. But I thought to myself, who the hell is she? I closed my eyes and listened to the rain.

It made me dizzy to close my eyes, though, and I had to stop, and I decided I should probably be dealing with like my current situation anyway, which wasn't looking too good. I was in a strange town, kind of drunk and pretty hungry, and without a ride suddenly and no way to get home because I'd spent practically all the money I'd brought and couldn't even call a cab. I wondered if there was a place down by the river maybe where the cops wouldn't find you and you could keep out of the rain.

I took a look around the bar, and it was getting empty. Right then one of the bartenders shouted out last call, and he turned up the lights and cut the jukebox and all the TVs. I didn't have any better idea of what to do with myself, so I went up and ordered an Old Style and a bag of pretzels. That was all the money I had. "Hey," I asked the bartender, "is it okay if I play the piano?" I figured I might as well.

He looked at the clock on the wall, more to remind me than himself. As a bartender I'd done the same thing lots of times. "Yeah, whatever," he said. "Long as you can drink up while you play."

I grabbed my stuff and walked over and sat on the bench. I choked down a couple of pretzels and took a drink of beer, enough to where it wouldn't spill. Then I hit my thumb on middle C.

But I didn't have anything to play. There was just the sound of that one note, and I pushed the sustain pedal to let it go on breathing. It hung there in the air while I tried to think of a song.

I looked around at the sheet music plastered on the walls, hoping that might give me an idea, but it all looked way too complicated. Classical stuff, and lots harder than the "Moonlight Sonata," which would have been too hard also. But I had a picture in my head. It was a picture with very bright, happy colors—yellows and reds and greens—and two sort of cartoon figures with bright clothes holding hands, stick figures, their fingers just straight lines put together. I didn't know what the picture was, but it made me feel good, like it was taking me back a long time ago to being a kid in Sandpoint, and it seemed like fall in our living room, the sunlight bright through the front window and the leaves turned yellow on the maple trees. I kept pushing middle C.

Then three notes came into my head—E, G, next octave D; E, G, next octave D. I started playing them. Then it seemed like I was at the music store, me and Mary and my mother pushing Mark in the stroller, down on Cedar Street in Sandpoint where she used to take us to buy sheet music, and I knew the picture then. Mary used her allowance money to buy the sheet music to "Close to You" by The Carpenters, the picture on the front was red and green and yellow with the stick figures holding hands. Mary bought it with her allowance, and she learned to play it first, and when she was done with it she made me pay her a dollar to use the music.

I remembered all this while I sat there pushing E, G, D, and the tune started filling my head and the fingers on my right hand started moving to pick out more of the melody. I couldn't remember it at all, the written-out notes on the page, but I could hear the song, how happy it was and simple, and my fingers stumbled to find the right keys—D, C, D, E, B. Why do birds suddenly appear / Every time you are near.

I took a drink of beer and settled in. In just a minute I'd got the tune worked out with my right hand, and I played over it a couple times to make sure I had it down. The last time through, I could hear one of the bartenders singing real loud in this fake opera voice—Just like me / They long to be / Close to you—but I didn't care. The sense of being there in our old house in the fall was strong, and I could remember the summer too, when Mark would play for us all, and I could almost imagine that Mark was listening to me.

I started working on the hard part, coming up with the chords for my left hand. It didn't take me long just to sound out a few, enough to go along with the melody, but I had to play it really slow. After such a long time it seemed like my hands didn't want to work together.

But pretty soon I'd started getting it, the old feeling for the keys started coming back, and I even worked in a little pedal. It was right about when they were getting ready to kick me out that Sarah came back in. I didn't turn around on the piano bench to see, but I heard her talking to the bartender while he wiped tables. I could recognize her voice pretty easy, even though it sounded sort of unsteady. She said we'd be on our way and he said take your time.

She was there standing next to me then, kind of hovering, and I leaned up and scooted the bench over so she could sit and I'd still be there at middle C. Neither of us said anything. I took a drink of beer and held up one finger without looking at her, to show her just a minute.

Then I started from the beginning—E, G, D—and I struck the first chord with my left hand, and I was singing . . . Why do birds suddenly appear . . . I knew it wasn't a song she would like, and I even knew it was a little silly, but I wanted to maybe do it justice somehow, just the nice, simple tune, and so I sang it in a plain voice without trying to make fun of it or sound like some lounge singer. I just used my own voice, the only one I had.

I got to the second verse, and I peeked over at her for a second . . . Why do stars fall down from the sky / Every time you walk by . . . She smiled at me and brought her arm up in a jerky motion, like she'd been waiting for me to look at her, and started running her fingers through my hair. I hit the chorus and the bridge, where I missed a couple of keys and had to back up because I hadn't figured that part out as well. Then I was back on the last verse, and I felt comfortable and my voice sounded fine to me. I looked over at her again and she was crying. It was the first time I'd seen her cry.

I played the chorus again and one last verse with no words. I couldn't remember how the song ended, whether there were certain notes or if it just faded away, but I had found a little key progression that sounded okay with just my right hand, and I let it finish slow.

I dropped my hands into my lap. Sarah took her hand from my hair and put her hands on her knees. "That was pretty," she said, looking down. She brought her right hand up and wiped off both her cheeks. She took a deep breath that kind of jerked in the middle. "Thank you," she said. I looked around the bar and we were the only ones there, just us and the two bartenders mopping the floor and putting the chairs up on the tables. Sarah put her arms around me and I closed my eyes and we hugged each other tight, and I tried to imagine I was in our living room in Idaho and I was younger, and that this was the first time I'd ever held a girl that way.

Driving to the cabin we still didn't say much. The top was up on the Land Cruiser and the rain beat against the plastic and fogged up the windshield. We were at a red light just after you leave the strip, stopped there all by ourselves with the noise of the windshield wipers and the thunder. I was driving because Sarah wasn't in much shape. "You probably don't care," she said, and then she had to stop and wipe her eyes again. I didn't know what she was feeling, really, how much of it had to do with us in any way or how much of it was the cocaine and the beer and the booze. But she was different than I had seen her. "You probably don't care," she said again, "but I just want you to know that nothing happened with him."

The light changed and I took off, fighting with the gear shift to get into second. "I know," I said. "I knew that when you left." It was just the drugs, in other words. I realized I had known that all along. I almost felt bad for the guy in a way.

At the cabin we dried off and got undressed and went to bed. We lay under the sheet barely touching. Sarah's back was to me, and I thought she was asleep, and I looked around the dark room at the shapes there, the picture of the barn and the clock and the old TV.

Sarah reached back and pulled my arm around her waist. Her stomach was soft and warm and I ran my thumb back and forth across her belly button. "I don't know why I ever do that stuff," she said. "I'll never get to sleep." We lay there a while and she half-turned so she was on her back and I could feel her looking over at me. "You almost never talk about your wife," she said.

"Right," I said. "I guess not." I didn't open my eyes.

"Tell me about her," Sarah said.

It was true that I hadn't talked about Jenny much, other than "One time we did this" or "One time we did that." I hadn't wanted to talk about her, maybe because she wasn't there and I didn't want to miss her, or maybe because she'd left me and deep down that hurt more than I wanted to admit, or maybe because even though she'd left me I still felt like it was wrong to be with Sarah, or maybe because I thought it would hurt Sarah's feelings, or maybe because I'd just been distracted by too much happening too fast. But the whole night had gone by deadly slow, like what I used to think of in New Orleans when I would walk down by the river and watch the boats go by, so slow that it looked like they'd never get anywhere at all. Back then it was a peaceful feeling, calm, but now I felt impatient, like I was ready to get there to whatever it was.

"What do you want to know?" I said. I was ready to tell her anything.

"Well, *you* know," she said, and kind of squeezed my hand. "Just what she's like. What sort of person she is."

I let out all my breath. I could feel Sarah's pulse under my fingers. It was hard to do, and I lay there for a minute. I knew what Jenny was like, but not how to explain it. Maybe she was too many different things to explain all at once. I said, "I guess there's some bad things I could say. I don't think she has much faith in me." But at the same time I said it I could come up with logical reasons she would feel that way. "I don't think she thinks enough about big things," I said. "She always thinks about 'right here, right now.'" What I meant was that Jenny is always focused. She's a person who never has to go through refocusing. It was the first time I'd thought of that idea.

"Maybe she feels like she has to be that way," Sarah said. "Considering how you are, I mean."

"Maybe so," I said. I was thinking of something else. I'd got a clear picture of Jenny finally, in this campground we'd stayed at in Minnesota, clapping and singing with Jake at the picnic table near the campfire, listening to the car radio.

It was right when we were moving to Heron Lake, and we'd had a rough time. We still had a couple weeks left on our rent back in Great Falls even though we'd moved everything we could fit into the Honda out of the place, but we didn't have the money to get back there. I'd had three straight bad nights at the track at Council Bluffs and lost most of our money, and earlier that afternoon I'd had to fork out enough dough for the campground space because we got caught using the shower, and we didn't even have anything left for gas and food. For the first time we were so flat broke that I thought I would have to call my mother and have her rescue me, and I was very depressed thinking about this. And I had gone out to find some sticks to throw on the fire because I didn't have the money to spend on one of the little bundles of wood they sold at the office, and when I came back there were Jenny and Jake laughing and singing.

We'd left Council Bluffs and gone to Heron Lake because Jenny picked it off the map, someplace that sounded nice and like all her choices was far away from any dog track. Usually Jenny was really good at finding a job right away. She'd get dressed up and look really pretty and go down and see a restaurant manager and fill out an application and lie about whatever she had to and say she had to know real soon because she had another offer. Lots of times they'd hire her on the spot. We'd work out a weekly rate at a cheap motel, and then I'd get a job and we'd save out money till we could move into an apartment.

But Heron Lake was really small. There was only one restaurant that needed anybody for day shift, and they said it would be two weeks before she could start. I tried to get a job at this country & western bar, but the manager didn't seem to like me right off, and the only thing left to do was have Jenny try to get a job there at first as a cocktail waitress. She'd been working on the guy real hard for a couple of days. He wanted to hire her but he said he didn't need anyone right then. We were so low on cash that we couldn't afford a motel, and we were sleeping in the car in parking lots at night and spending the days at the lake. On the other shore we noticed the campground, and what we did was drive into it really slow, looking around like we were trying to decide whether to stay, making sure to ignore the old guy watching us from the office so it wouldn't seem like we were doing anything wrong. Then we'd park at a campsite behind some trees and Jenny would get out her things, her make-up bag and hairbrush and towel and her nice clothes folded careful on the back seat, and she'd walk down to the showers and get herself fixed up as fast as she could. Jake and I had just been rinsing off every day in the lake.

The third day the guy caught us. Jenny was coming right out of the showers folding her towel. I told the guy which campsite we were at, and said I was just on my way to the office to pay.

"Sure you were," he said. "You owe me for three days." He held out his hand and rubbed his fingers together. He was an old guy wearing a blue checkered shirt and his gray hair was combed real neat and he wore black glasses.

I said, "Oh, we're just planning on staying tonight," like I didn't understand.

Jake and Jenny were standing there watching us. The guy looked at them. "I saw you the other times," he said. "Three days."

"It must have been somebody else," I said. I was looking straight at him, right in the eye like I was telling the truth, but at the same time I was trying to say with my eyes, "Please, buddy. Come on, please."

He looked at Jake and Jenny again, and without turning around I had a pretty good idea what he saw, what they must have looked like there. "You look like you could use a break," he said.

I paid him for one day, which was about all the money we had.

And so then that night I went to find more wood and came back and found Jake and Jenny clapping and singing to a song on the radio. They were laughing and clapping and singing there in the firelight, and they had a deck of cards in front of them for "Go Fish." I stood there with these sticks, and they turned to me and smiled and kept singing.

The next day Jenny got dressed up and went to the cowboy bar again and talked the guy into letting her work that same night. It was a Friday night, and Jake and I slept out in the parking lot with the drunk cowboys fighting and pissing all around the car. Jenny came out at 2:30 and she had a welt on her butt where one of the cowboys had pinched her, and she had ninety-five dollars in her purse. A week later she was working at the restaurant and she'd managed to talk them into giving me a job at the bar.

I told Sarah that was what Jenny was like, I told her that whole story.

Sarah never interrupted the whole time, and when I was through she rolled over and turned her back to me, but she curled into my body tight and kept hold of my hand. In a little while she was sleeping.

But I didn't sleep, like I knew I wouldn't. Maybe I drifted off sometimes, but my dreams and my thoughts weren't different enough to tell. Sometimes I was trying to put it all together, all the money at the track and meeting Sarah and Anna Cornwell's Bible in my room and the guy who told me to keep the faith, the Greyhound God and what it was that made me special, but other times it broke down and none of it meant anything or amounted to anything and the room was empty and hollow and I didn't belong there or anywhere, Sarah like this strange body breathing next to me. And other times it was like visions, pictures of Jake and Jenny by the campfire and me and Sarah at the piano, Poke Chop flying across the grass and Tucker lifting the midget up over his shoulder again. And I was at the track, over and over I was at the track, sometimes Jake and Jenny were there and sometimes Sarah and sometimes I was all alone, but there were always the dogs, speeding past in a bright blur, colors and numbers, combinations whirling in my head, 2-3, 8-4, 7-8. The dogs ran fast, harder and harder till the track tilted, my stomach turning like on a roller coaster, and the track tilted down and down and I knew that I was hanging on hard while the world was spinning.

Four or five times during the night I just sat up in bed and put my feet down on the floor. The last time it was morning. The rain had stopped but the light outside was thin and gray and water dripped from the trees. I was wide awake. My arms and legs and chest were cool in the air, and I looked out the window and I knew. I knew that I had to get to the end somehow, that we couldn't keep going like this. I had to have some answers, and there had to be a road to get to them, to lead them through to happening. And I even had an idea about how to make it that way.

JUNE 27

"I know what we're going to do," I said. We were sitting outside on the swing. I'd told Sarah I wanted to talk to her in the fresh air for some reason.

"What?" she said, and pulled her hair behind her ear. She was still feeling pretty banged up, I could tell, but she was also right away interested. She had on a big baggy sweatshirt, and she pulled up her knees to her chest and brought the sweatshirt down over them. She looked cute that way.

"Bet all the money," I said. "One race. All of it."

She wasn't looking at me. She was staring down at the ground in front of her. "Can you do that?" she said.

I told her I thought so. I'd heard stories about that kind of thing.

She looked at a squirrel out in the grass and she was thinking. "How much money is it? We're talking about betting around twelve thousand dollars, right? On one race."

"Somewhere around there," I said.

"Okay," she told me.

That took me by surprise. I had a little speech planned and everything. I wanted to tell her that I'd been thinking about gestures. I wanted to say that there was something in that moment when she raised her arm and Poke Chop took off across the field. How it looked like both things had happened together, that they'd planned it that way. How it seemed like *doing* something, not just watching and waiting, and how if you *did* something there'd have to be an answer back. Like with Tucker at the track, how he'd just picked his friend up there and held him, and it had made everything perfect right in that moment, something pure. And if I had to *do* something to get the answers I wanted, then the only thing there was to do was bet all the money. All this time I had asked the Greyhound God for winning tickets, and he had given them to me. There was the plain fact of it, the money, the piles and piles of it, proof enough for anyone to see. And now the Greyhound God wanted some response from me. It didn't require too much, like with Moses or Abraham. No one had asked me to part the Red Sea or sacrifice my only son. It was the Greyhound God I was dealing with, the god of misfits and losers, of people who you couldn't ask for all that much. All I had was money. So I would make my gesture, my offering—"Here I am, Luke Rivers. Here's my money. Come and take it from me." And then there would be the moment at the finish line, and I would know something.

"Risk it all, right?" Sarah said. She was staring at the grass where the squirrel had been but there was nothing there. "If you lose, you lose. You're right back where you started. If you win, you win. But either way you get some sort of answer," she said. "Somehow." She ran her hands through her hair and tilted her head back to see the sky, which was still all cold and gray. "It makes as much sense as anything else." She pulled her sweatshirt off her knees and turned halfway toward me on the swing and her eyes were shining. "Do you know what dog we're betting on?" she asked me.

"Morgan's Sarah," I said.

She laughed and grabbed my arm with both hands. It was that laugh I'd heard the first night we were together at The Bend, loud and not caring about anything. She was happy. "I *knew* it," she said, and leaned over and kissed me hard on the cheek. Then she straightened around on the swing and pulled her sweatshirt real fast over her knees again. "That's great," she said. "That's a *great* idea." She was smiling and looking out at the pasture, but it seemed like a sad smile just the same. "You'll win," she said. "And then it'll all be over."

We drove to town and bought a newspaper and went back to the cabin and looked at the race charts. Morgan's Sarah was number 8 in the 10th race, what they call a Super A, meaning the best dogs out at the track. She might actually be the favorite, based on how much she'd been winning, but it didn't really matter since whatever dog I bet that much money on was going to drop all the way to 1:10, which is as low as the odds go.

Sarah said she needed to go out to the farm for a little while, and I asked if on her way she could drop me off to visit Buddy. I told her I didn't want to have to spend too much time by myself due to being nervous, though that actually wasn't the reason. There were some other things I wanted answers to also. No more two dollars here and two dollars there. I wanted to wrap it all up, the whole thing, in one day.

We stopped at the Hen House for a late breakfast because we figured we'd be too worked up to eat anything later, but my stomach was in knots and shrunk down to practically nothing, and I could barely eat. Then Sarah took me to Buddy's and came inside to make sure he was there. It was noon and he was just up out of bed. I'd kind of been afraid Taylor might be there, too, but there was no sign of her anywhere, unless she was still asleep in the bedroom. Buddy ground up some beans for a pot of coffee and Sarah said she'd be back in a while. When the coffee was done Buddy brought us both a cup to the kitchen table. "I suppose you want to play chess," he said.

I didn't, actually. Or I hadn't thought about it. All I wanted was to tell him good-bye and ask him a couple of questions. Because whatever happened that night, I had already decided it would be my last night in the Dells. I'd either be leaving with about thirteen thousand dollars and the answer to a question I'd had practically my whole life, or I'd be leaving with a full tank of gas. Either way, I was gone.

But chess wasn't a bad idea because it would be at least an hour till Sarah got back and my questions wouldn't take up all the time. We'd been playing twenty minutes when the phone rang. It was Taylor. They launched into an argument right away, apparently having to do with her blaming Buddy for being an asshole and him blaming her for showing up at Sarah's party when she wasn't invited.

While they were arguing, he was losing track of the chess game. Before long, I'd gained a strong position and I was trying to press my advantage, but I screwed up on one move and left a big hole right in the center of the board where he could move in his queen.

He was still arguing with Taylor, though, and I hoped he wouldn't see it. He started to move his knight, but sure enough, his hand stopped. I knew what that meant. He leaned back in his chair and he told Taylor, "Look, let's just forget this." I could hear her voice, kind of pleading and angry at the same time, through the receiver. "This argument I mean," he said. "I'll talk to you later." And he pushed the button to cut her off and laid the phone down in a chair. He looked at the board very quiet, and he folded his hands in his lap. I watched his face. It was like you could see behind his eyes, like actually observe his brain behind there. I knew he saw the move, and then in just a matter of seconds he'd gone way beyond it, way past where I could get, and was seeing all sorts of possible outcomes and responses I might have, which of course was giving me way too much credit because they were things that *he* would think of if he was on my side of the board, not me. He moved his queen where I knew he would.

The whole time afterward while I was losing, though, I felt more and more relaxed, and surprisingly better and better. Buddy was locked in on the game, and never let me off the hook. There was nothing I could do, or nothing I was smart enough to do, and I basically sat there and admired how he did everything so crystal clear and logical to bring the game to an end. He was just a lot smarter than me, and he deserved to win. And that was comforting to me. Because it wasn't luck, it wasn't chance, it was just the rightful order of things. The world was working how it was supposed to, which was exactly what I expected to happen later on at the track. The logical outcome of winning all that money was that I would find out why I'd been winning it. Otherwise there was no reason for winning it in the first place. It was what I counted on and wanted to believe in.

By the time the match was over I was in a better mood than Buddy. "Sorry," he said.

"That's okay," I told him. "No problem."

He got up to get more coffee. "You know, you almost had me there," he said. "You made just one bad move."

"Right," I said. "That's the difference between you and me."

He laughed. "I made a whole variety of bad moves that game." He poured the last of the pot down the sink. "Fucking Taylor." He set the pot down and stood there with his back to me.

For a second I thought maybe he wanted to talk to me, like personally. "Tough decisions?" I said.

He right away pulled his shoulders up straight and came back to the table. "No, no tough decisions," he said. "Just which way to get rid of her."

I thought he was overall a likable guy, Buddy, but he had a definite chip on his shoulder.

The phone rang, and it was Sarah, wondering why the line had been tied up and telling me she was at The Bend waiting for me. I got ready to leave, and I was trying to figure out how to ask Buddy what I wanted to ask him, but then he said he'd walk me out, and he grabbed his baseball cap and car keys off the kitchen counter. I guess he was going to see Taylor.

We went downstairs and out the door and stood there on the sidewalk. I looked over his shoulder for a second at the crowds of people passing along the main drag a block away. I could see the people standing in line for the wax museum, holding up their umbrellas. It was only then I noticed the rain. That was how soft it fell.

"Well, you guys have a good time," Buddy said, jingling his keys. He'd gotten real nonchalant about me and Sarah, it seemed to me.

"Listen," I said.

So he did. He stood there listening, looking at me. I was having a hard time thinking of what to say. I stuck out my hand to him, and he looked down kind of puzzled and shook it. "I probably won't be seeing you again," I said.

He raised his eyebrows a little.

"I mean I think I'm leaving," I said.

He kind of pouted his lips and nodded. "Well, good luck to you then," he said. "Keep working on that chess game."

"Yeah," I said. I looked over his shoulder again down at the crowds on the strip, all the colorful umbrellas. "Listen," I said again. I looked him in the eye. "If I was to tell you something that was hard for you to believe . . ." I kind of held one hand out in front of me, palm up, fingers spread.

"Yeah?" he said. "Like?"

I brought my hand up slow and ran it back from my forehead through my hair, and it felt just slightly wet with mist. "Like if I was to say I'd been winning all this money out at the track, say," I said. He kind of nodded his head up and down and his mouth was slightly open. "If I said every night I was going to the track and I was winning like a thousand dollars," I said. "What would you say?" His eyes were working me over, sort of, like he'd just come across some new way to calculate a problem.

"Congratulations," he said.

I kind of shrugged and shifted my feet. "Yeah," I said. "But what would you *say*?"

He looked at me for a second, all his features under the brim of the baseball cap making straight, regular lines. "You mean what kind of *explanation* would I have for it?" He smiled. "If you told me that?"

"Right," I said.

"I'd say you must be good at betting on dog races," he said.

"That's it?" I said. An old guy smoking a cigar walked past me holding a newspaper in front of his face. He was reading the comics.

"That's it," Buddy said. He turned his head for a second and looked at the old guy. "What are you asking?" he said, and turned back to me. "If you want, I could try to quote some determinist bullshit to offer you a logical explanation."

"No," I said. "That's all right." I held out my hand and he shook it again. I wanted to ask him something about Sarah but he was seeming a little peeved all of a sudden. "Tell Jordan I said good-bye," I said. I was walking on past him. "And hey," I said. "Thanks."

"For what?" he said. He was turned around looking at me.

I shrugged my shoulders.

Then he got this nasty look on his face. I could see behind his eyes again, and I could see right then he wasn't such a likable guy after all, and that he'd never liked me, and that he'd been saving something up the whole time for just this very moment. "Just let me tell you one thing," he said. I didn't answer him. "Don't run off thinking you're anything special."

"What do you mean?" I said. "Sarah?"

"Sarah," he said, and nodded his head real firm, just once. "Two years ago it was a high school kid who worked for the summer on the farm. Last year it was some guy from Michigan who worked at The Bend." He had a crooked kind of smile on his face. We were turned around now, and it was his turn to stare off at the crowds of people. "You're no different," he said.

That kind of answered what I wanted to know, actually—not the part about her and these other guys, I could care less about that kind of thing, but just the part about where I fit in—and I almost turned around to walk away, but then I didn't. "Why me, though?" I said. "Why do you think this summer it was me?" He was looking pretty pissed off. "I mean I'm just asking you as a point of fact," I said. "Seriously."

He took a deep breath and scrunched his hands in the pockets of his jeans and stretched. He was a pretty big guy. He looked like a sleepy lion or something. "I don't know what's on her mind any-more," he said. "Why she does things." His focus seemed to come back on me, and I nodded to show I was listening. "Why you?" he said. "I don't know. I've wondered that." He straightened himself up, like he was trying to look down at me, but we were about the same height if not build. "I suppose you've managed not to grow up in a rather charming way."

Behind him was a dead-end street and some trees and then the river, which I couldn't see. "Hmm," I said.

He laughed. "You want to go play pool and beat the hell out of me?" he said.

I looked at him there in his rumpled clothes and baseball hat and his hands in his pockets. What he'd said sounded true in a way, like something I could recognize, and I even appreciated him say-ing it in a sense, even if he was an asshole. But at the same time I felt like there was something he was missing. "I don't need to," I said, and I turned around and started walking down the street. He didn't say anything, and I heard a car start up when I was down about to the corner.

While I was walking I thought over what he'd said, and on the one hand it seemed true, if growing up meant things like being practical and making money and taking care of your family in the regular way that Americans are supposed to, and you have to act responsible all the time and not get too excited about things or too sensitive either. If that was growing up, then I hadn't been very good at it. But on the other hand, to me all of that didn't seem to be right necessarily, like it was just what people agreed on to keep them from having to come up with some other definition, though I couldn't give a better one either.

At The Bend Sarah had two glasses and a half-full pitcher of dark beer. She was pretty excited about the races, and her being like that made me not think as much about what Buddy said—about how winning the money was nothing out of the ordinary, or about me not growing up, or about me not being any different. Because at least as far as Sarah went, I figured even though Buddy was awfully smart, there were a lot of things he didn't know about people.

At five o'clock we went back to the cabin to plan out what we were doing, although we ended up not doing much. We spread out Sarah's charts on the bed and got out the Book of Luke. She said she wished we had a program to check out the other dogs, but I said I didn't see what difference it would make since we were going to bet on Morgan's Sarah regardless, and Sarah kind of jumbled her charts together and said what's the use. "But tell me," she said. She had her hair in a ponytail and she was sitting there on the bed in her jeans and sweatshirt. I noticed how dark her eyes were again and how nice her lips were without any lipstick. "What exactly are we hoping for?" she said.

We were sitting across from each other, with her up towards the head of the bed and me near the foot, and she leaned in towards me. It had started to rain again, and you could hear it just prickling against the window. "I mean I know," she said. "It's some kind of understanding of things." She took out a cigarette from the pack lying on the bed and lit it and took a drag and exhaled hard. "But I mean, what really?" She leaned in again and kissed me real lightly on the lips.

I knew the answer to the question, of course, but it was hard to say. I had a hard time putting my finger on it. What occurred to me right away was that I wanted to say something about Mark. My mind went back for some reason straight to the cave, and me and Mark in the cold and the dark there together when the day outside was hot and the sun shining, and it was like I knew he would be dead in just a few weeks. "It's just that you want to know what certain moments in your life mean," I said. "You just don't want them not to mean anything."

"Why?" she said. Her voice came out kind of hard and level, and her eyes looked a way I hadn't seen before. "What difference does it make?" she said. "Would that make anything be different?" I started to answer but she cut me off. "So you get some sense of how things work, why things happen. How does that change things?"

The questions were coming pretty fast, and I was starting to be afraid of sounding stupid. I reached my hand out and touched her foot, right on the top where there were a couple of little tiny golden hairs. Her toes scrunched up. It made me think of how Jake would tighten up into a little ball when you tickled him. I said, "It answers the question what are we doing things for. You know?" I sort of motioned around the room to all the shit thrown all over the place. "Like why do we get up in the morning and do this."

She shook her head, just barely. "That's not good enough," she said. She looked down at her foot where my hand had hold of her. "It's just easier to do it than not to do it," she said. "I'd be scared not to do it. That's why."

I sat there looking at her, trying to take in what she meant, and a strange thing started happening in my head. I could suddenly see her getting up every morning of her life, and as I did I could see her getting older and older, until she was an old woman with thin white hair and a shriveled-up body and big glasses covering her dark brown eyes and wrinkles all around her perfect lips. I could see her getting up on a morning when the sun was shining, and there were birds singing in the trees and the grass was covered with dew, and she was eighty years old and her blood was waking up slow and she was putting on her glasses from a nightstand and her feet had blue veins and were scooting around on a wooden floor searching for a pair of slippers. "Don't you just want it to be *about* something?" I said. "That the things you remember most out of your whole life and stay in your head forever have something to do with something important?" She was looking down, and one corner of her mouth turned up. She looked like she felt sorry about something. "*Everything* can't be *nothing*," I said. "It doesn't make sense. There's a reason why bad things happen in the world."

She kept looking down at her foot, and I could see the smooth skin above her ankle and she didn't seem old at all. She nodded her head a little and took a drag on her cigarette. "And the dog races have something to do with that?" she said.

"Of *course* they do," I said. "Of course they do." I fished out a cigarette from the pack and picked up the lighter off the bed and lit it. I was trying to sort it out in my head, what the last three weeks of my life and the last two of hers had been all about. It seemed like what you'd call an absurdly short amount of time. "Or am I just fucking crazy?" I said. They weren't the words I wanted to come out of my mouth, but they were the ones that did.

She looked like she had to think it over for a second. "No," she said. "Unless I'm crazy, too." Which of course was pretty much the same conclusion I'd come to earlier. "*Something's* been happening," she said. "I don't guess there's any way to deny that."

"Right," I said. "I agree."

She nodded real slow, and she snubbed out her cigarette in the ashtray, and I snubbed out mine too, even though I'd only smoked it partway. "I guess that's why I was so fucked up last night," she said. "I just wanted to get away from it for one day." She got up off the bed and went over and sat at the writing desk in the little chair and looked out the window where it was gray and rainy. "I've been happy the whole time, but maybe it's started to bother me some, too," she said. She came over and grabbed another cigarette and went back over to the desk. "Because I don't like to think about all that," she said, kind of angry. "I'm not like you. I don't want to spend all my time thinking about reasons for why things happen. It doesn't make my life any easier." She looked over at me, kind of squinting at me like she was trying to see me better, and I wondered if she had her contacts in. "It seems hard being you."

It was sort of like what Jenny had always told me, but not quite.

Jenny had always said I took things too hard. But then there were other times when she wondered how I could let things not get to me. It was confusing sometimes, but I think it depended on what kind of things.

I went over to Sarah and kind of squatted down in front of her and held her hand in my hands. She set her unlit cigarette down and put her hand on top of mine. "But we're not crazy, right?" I said. "It makes sense to go bet all this money."

"Yes," she said. "I want to."

But she still had kind of a confused look on her face. I could see why it was harder for her, because she didn't know anything about the Greyhound God. It hadn't been part of anything to her like it had been to me for years. To her, it was just like the finish of the last two weeks, whereas to me it was much bigger and more complicated. "Let me just tell you this," I said. "This didn't just start with the money. It goes back a long time before I met you, and even before I met Jenny." I was thinking of Mark saying he wanted to go to the grocery store and my father at night in the kitchen and that philosophy class, and the ball of fire and the guy who felt like he was falling and the night I first went to the dog track. "It probably sounds dumb, but it's like something personal between me and God or whoever, and it goes way back. Even my father had it, really. You could even say it's practically inherited."

I was thinking I probably shouldn't have said that, because it would probably open up a whole bunch of new questions, but it didn't. Instead Sarah yawned and slumped her shoulders, and she said she just wanted to lie down and rest for fifteen minutes, would I please wake her up in fifteen minutes.

I used the time to go around and get all the money together. I searched through the pockets of all our pants and shorts and threw the clothes in a pile in the corner. Then I took the wads of money out of the gym bag and from my wallet and sat down with it all at the desk and stacked it all together and counted. We had twelve thousand, two hundred eighty-four dollars and seventy-five cents.

I cleared out some stuff from Sarah's purse and stuffed all the money in, then I went and took a shower, since in the back of my mind somewhere I was telling myself that if I did somehow lose it might be a while till I had enough money or opportunity to take a shower again. I decided when I was drying off that I'd keep out the two hundred eighty-four dollars and bet only the twelve thousand just in case.

Sarah was asleep, and I didn't want to wake her up yet. It was 6:23, so we still had plenty of time, especially considering we didn't really have to be there till the 10th race.

I picked the Bible up off the nightstand and sat at the desk again. I leafed through it kind of slow, looking at the places Anna Cornwell underlined, and feeling that sad, awful feeling like I had before. I turned one last time to the Book of Luke, and I read the story of the shepherds. Finally I closed the book, but then I opened the front cover and ran my finger down the faded family tree. And I thought Sylvia Harrington was wrong. Even if you couldn't believe it anymore, even if you gave it up when you looked around the world and saw so much trouble, it was still a nice story about Jesus, how he thought we could all be better to each other and have hope for what would come, and especially when it was a Bible that had been passed down to you and you were the last one left on that poor family tree, you should have tried harder than to just throw it away.

"What time is it?" Sarah said from behind me, in that panicky voice like when you wake up and think it's maybe a different day.

"Quarter to seven," I said.

I could hear her rustling under the covers. "Come here," she said. "Lie down next to me."

I did, and she wrapped herself around me. "I want to take the Bible back," I said. "I want to take it back now."

Sarah asked what I meant, and I said I wanted to give the Bible back to Sylvia Harrington, that that seemed like the right thing to do. She said maybe that wasn't such a great idea, Sylvia Harrington was a little bit odd, but I said to think of it as a necessary gesture.

She said okay finally, and went to fix herself up real quick. When she was ready we drove out the road toward her house, and the rain started coming down harder. When we went past her place the cows were all in the barn and there was one light on in an upstairs window. Sarah glanced at the house and looked away. The windshield wipers swung back and forth and Sarah flipped on the headlights. "Sylvia Harrington's place is another mile up the road," she said.

We drove up a little rise and there was a small white house up on a hill. We parked in the driveway below, and when we got out a little black dog came yapping down the slope. There was an old barn out behind the house, but it was leaning to one side and the roof was mostly caved in and there weren't any silos or cornfields, just an open area out back full of weeds. Off to the side of the house was a goat tied to a tree, chewing something slow and staring our way. The dog ran around us while we hurried up the slope in the rain, sniffing our pant legs and wagging its tail and jumping away.

"Okay," Sarah said when we got to the porch, "I hope you know what you want to say." She hadn't told me anything else about Sylvia Harrington being odd, but I figured I could handle it all right. I was holding the Bible tight against my T-shirt underneath my flannel shirt. Sarah rang the doorbell.

For a long time nobody answered, and we would have left except all the lights were on inside and there was a truck parked in the driveway. As soon as she opened the door, the dog scooted in fast between her legs and started shaking itself on the carpet. "Dimples!" she shouted. "Dimples!" The dog started turning circles. We were still standing there on the steps, just barely out of the rain.

"Can I help you?" she said, finally looking at us. She was wearing a yellow dress that looked like it was the wrong size someway. She had some kind of white thing holding up her hair that almost looked like a crown. "You're the Morgan girl," she said. "Good God! You grew up when I wasn't looking." Then she stared at me kind of suspicious.

"I have something that belongs to you," I said.

She hustled us on inside, and sat us at opposite ends of this old smelly orange couch in front of the TV set. There was some show about Hollywood people blaring loud. "Hope you don't mind," she said, and sat down in this green easy chair where she had a TV tray stood up in front of it and started eating mashed potatoes, which was the only thing on her plate. I had the Bible on my lap and she kept glancing at it and then up at me. "I hope you didn't come to give me an earful," she said to me.

"No," I said, petting the dog and trying to keep it from getting its muddy paws all over me.

"Dimples!" she said, but the dog wasn't about to give up, so I finally let him up on the couch, where he put his head in my lap and started slobbering on the Bible. I pulled it out from under him and wiped it on my T-shirt.

"I brought you this," I said, and held it out in front of me with both hands.

She reached over on this end table and grabbed a pair of horn-rim glasses with little fake jewels or glitter or something on the frame. They made her look about ten years older and twice as silly.

Sarah grabbed the Bible from me and leaned out and handed it to her. She sat there holding it above her mashed potatoes. "Well?" she said.

"Open it," I told her.

She did, and sat there taking it in for a second. "Well, I'll be damned," she said. "Where'd you run across this? I got rid of this thing at a yard sale must have been ten years ago."

"Like you say, just came across it," I said. I leaned forward and the dog got off my lap and went over to bother Sarah. Sylvia Harrington was still just sitting there looking at me through her weird glasses. "I thought you might want it back," I said.

She closed the cover and set it on her armrest. "What in hell for?" she said. "If I'd have wanted it, I wouldn't have got rid of it in the first place."

"I just thought maybe you'd changed your mind," I said.

"Never change my mind about anything," she said, and started watching the TV. It was some Hollywood premiere or something with lots of celebrities outside a theater that you practically had to yell over the top of. She forked up another mouthful of mashed potatoes.

I looked at Sarah and she shrugged. "That Bible goes a long way back," I said.

"It sure does," she said, but she was still interested in the TV. "You know these people aren't real, don't you?" she said. "Oh, they're real people, all right," she said, like one of us had questioned her on it. "But just not the way they really look. They airbrush out all the blemishes." She turned and gave us both a sharp look. "Even on TV."

"I didn't know they could do that," Sarah said.

"You better believe it," she said. "They can do pretty near anything. If you see them in person, they don't look anything like that. I saw Brooke Shields one time at the airport. She was tall, but that didn't impress me. There's lots of tall people. I'm five-foot-seven myself."

I'd definitely met stranger people, but I was having to admit Sylvia Harrington was a little hard to deal with. She reached around behind her ass where she had a little purse stuffed into the seat and took out a long cigarette and lit it.

"We'll get out of your hair in a minute," I said. "I just wanted to give your family Bible back because I thought it was something you should keep."

"Oh, God no," she said. "I can't have old things like that cluttering up the place." Maybe she was some kind of unusual neatness freak in a way. The house was a wreck, everything stale and dirty and stained, but it was true that she didn't have much stuff around. There were only two pictures on the wall that were hanging crooked, and one with a cracked frame and both looked like just pictures of flowers cut out of a magazine. Behind her there was a built-in bookcase with no books whatsoever, just some bills and envelopes scattered on it and a couple of little porcelain statues that were knocked on their sides.

"But couldn't you make room for *that*?" I asked her. "Look inside there. That's your *family.*" I could picture the sad family tree on the inside cover, and read all the names there in my mind.

"Not anymore," she said. She tapped her ash out into her mashed potatoes. Then she got sort of snippy. "You just take that back where you got it," she said. "Someone paid good money for that. What are you, a thief?"

"I don't think he thought of it that way, Mrs. Harrington," Sarah said.

"Anyhow, just the same," she said. "And listen. Let me say one more thing." She dragged on her cigarette and her fingers sort of fidgeted around with it and she tapped it into the potatoes again. "I don't like your hair. I know most people have got around to accepting it, but not me. You look like a girl with five o'clock shadow to me," she said.

I couldn't think of what else to say. I wanted to make her feel something, maybe something sad, about this Bible and the names in it. But I couldn't make her feel anything. It was like her life on the page there, really, but I didn't know what to say to make her think that was important in any way. We got up, and she handed Sarah the Bible and said to say hello to her father and it was a rotten thing about her mother but life goes on and she hoped Sarah had common sense, kind of throwing a glance at me. I was glad she hadn't seemed to notice my wedding ring.

After she ran us back outside, Sarah handed the Bible to me. "Do you want to leave it on the porch?" she said.

"No, she'd just throw it away." It was like an orphan suddenly, this Bible, and I figured I better just keep it myself because there was no one else who cared. It was making me very tired for some reason.

Sarah started laughing when we got back in the Land Cruiser. "I warned you," she said.

"Yeah," I said.

"That was a nice dress, huh?" she said, and laughed again, and I had to smile a little bit, too. But I held the Bible tight under my flannel shirt.

It had stopped raining when we got to the track, and there were little yellow-colored puddles under the streetlights in the parking lot. I'd expected the track to be completely dead, what with it being Sunday night and raining off and on, too, but there were buses in the parking lot and quite a few cars, a pretty good Sunday night crowd. When we started walking to the gate, it was right near the end of the first race it turned out, and not exactly a roar came from inside but at least a pretty good round of cheers and shouts, and the track lights lit up the night and made it pretty. I could feel my steps getting longer and lighter. It felt like the old days when just showing up at the track could get my heart pumping.

We bought a program out of habit and went outside to our usual seats. It wasn't raining but the air felt warm and muggy and I took off my flannel shirt. The atmosphere was what I guess you'd call almost festive. Most of the people seemed like tourists, probably, and not the regulars who were mostly inside since they don't get too excited about being up close and watching the races. If the weather's bad, they stay in.

There were groups of people all huddled around talking loud and making jokes. They were all dressed nice and looked to be part of one big group, the way they kind of drifted back and forth between each other, and I noticed they were all wearing little name tags stuck on to their shirts. I asked Sarah and she said she remembered now they were having a cardboard manufacturer's convention out at the Holiday Inn. That explained it, the big crowd on a Sunday night. They were all standing around because the metal bleachers were still wet, and there was a guy wiping down the bleachers with a towel so they could sit, which nobody would have ever done if it hadn't been a bunch of big shots the track was hoping to impress. I didn't bother to wait for him to get to our seats, just wiped off a spot with my hand. We'd already gotten wet anyway.

When the dogs came onto the track with the lead-outs before

the 2nd race I picked up the program from off the Bible which I was still holding in my lap and I realized then I didn't have anything to do. We'd only come out to bet on one race. Sarah asked if I wanted to bet on the others, and I told her no, that didn't seem like the right thing to do.

So Sarah and I just used the time for talking. The idea of betting all the money was sinking into my head further and further, and how that would be in the moment when it happened, and how everyone would know because of the numbers flashing on the screen, although I doubted many of the convention people would even recognize how unusual it was.

"Did I help you much?" Sarah said.

"Yes," I told her.

She came in closer to me. "I don't see how," she said. She was smiling. The dogs were on the backstretch in the 5th race. "Tell me."

"You were the one that showed me the whole thing," I said. "If you hadn't said something was going on, I probably would have just kept on forever."

"No, you wouldn't have," she said. "You already knew. Tell me."

I wanted to make my wish come true when I chose the star and also what her dad said. And at the same time I wanted to make sure I *said* something that was true. I looked at her really hard, how pretty she was and what an unusual person, and I thought again how Buddy had to be wrong about us somehow, or maybe I just wanted him to be. "You made it all okay," I said. "You made it so it was okay to happen."

She put her hand behind my head then and brought me in close to her face and she closed her eyes and smiled. And I almost said I love you, but I didn't. And maybe she almost said the same thing.

The cardboard people were shouting and the dogs flashed at the edge of my sight and the race was done.

"I'm dying of thirst," Sarah said. "Is this a part of the whole ritual, or can we go up and get a beer?"

So we went up and got a beer, and when we were ready to head back down I looked for a second at the little information booth they have up by the front entrance, and it occurred to me that we should probably ask some questions.

There was a little black-haired guy in a red vest sitting behind the booth. He was clipping out some columns of statistics from different tracks with scissors. "Just a second," he said, not looking up.

"Are you the odds maker?" I said. I figured maybe he was clipping the things for a reason.

"No," he said, still not looking up. "I'm information. I used to make book at Vegas, though. How can I help you?" He looked up finally. "Oh, hello," he said to Sarah, and flashed her a weird smile where he sort of pulled his upper lip back from his teeth. "Her father bought Poke Chop," he said to me. I suppose I had looked a little curious. "How is he?" he asked Sarah.

"My father or Poke Chop?" Sarah said.

"Both. Either."

"Fine," Sarah said.

"What's your question?" the guy said. He scrunched up his eyes at me.

"I want to make a big bet," I said.

"How big?" he answered.

"Twelve thousand dollars," I said.

"I wouldn't advise it," he told me.

"Why not?"

"You'll lose," he said.

Sarah and I kind of looked at each other. It was sort of strange and made me hesitate. "Well," I said. "What if we don't think so?"

"Doesn't matter what you think," he said. "You lose either way. You lose, you lose. You win, you lose, too."

He explained to me once and for all about how the taxes worked then. The odds would go to 1:10, like I already knew, and I'd be taxed 16 percent.

"Okay," I said. "So I only win about a thousand dollars. It doesn't matter."

He snickered and his lip went up again. He said 16 percent on the entire amount.

That took a second to sink in, and my stomach felt a little funny. "You mean you get taxed on the *bet*?" I said.

"Yep, if you want to think of it that way," he said. He took a little calculator out of a drawer and punched out the math real quick. "Twelve thousand dollars plus twelve hundred dollars at 1:10 odds makes thirteen and two minus the six hundred take out 16 percent add the six hundred back in means you get . . ." he tapped his finger on the calculator " . . . eleven thousand one hundred and twenty-four dollars and no cents. You lose almost a thousand bucks," he said. "If you win."

I admit, it kind of dumbstruck me for a second. "You mean I *lose money*?" I said.

"You get taxed on any money paid out over six hundred dollars," he said. "Regardless of the amount of the bet." He was clipping out his little papers again.

"That's not fair," I said. I admit I was having second thoughts.

"That's the rules," he said. He looked up at me. "Change your mind?"

"No," I said, but I don't think I sounded too convincing.

"Why not?" he said. "You nuts?"

"He's betting on principle," Sarah said.

The guy kind of pouted up his lower lip this time and raised his eyebrows. "Never heard that one before," he said. "Good luck to you." He reached over the booth and shook my hand. "Next," he said, and an older man and his wife stepped up, smiling.

Sarah laughed practically the whole way down to our seats. She said she never knew hanging around with me would be so much fun. It was a surprise a minute.

I figured that was true. If it wasn't one thing it was another. The 7th race was about to start, but I didn't care. I looked at the green grass of the infield all shining and wet with rain and the blazing track lights up above with the bugs flying in and out of the lighted place and on up past to the sky where the clouds hung low like a ceiling and if you'd never seen it before you wouldn't know there was such a thing as a star. I tried to step back from myself and decide if I was doing the right thing. Time seemed to be moving by too fast for its natural pace. I felt caught up in time and going ahead too fast to the edge of something I wasn't sure I should be taken to. Everything was too fast, the dogs flashing by now and the cardboard people moving around like bees between flowers and Sarah's voice saying words I wasn't listening to.

I let out a long breath, tried to make it last as long as I could. The dogs were on the backstretch in the 7th race, and Sarah was taking the last drink from her beer cup, and even though I'd barely touched mine I offered to go up and get her another one because I wanted a minute to myself. She looked kind of worried and she didn't suggest she should come with me.

All the way up to the beer stand I made myself not think about the 10th race. I made myself think about the twelve thousand dollars instead, what twelve thousand dollars actually meant, not so much to me but to Jake and Jenny. Twelve thousand dollars was two years' rent. It was a brand new car before the Honda broke down. It was a start to Jake's college education. It was one year of bartending or waiting tables. It was one year of time for me or Jenny to get a better job.

The guy behind the booth handed me Sarah's beer and had to stop me before I walked away without my change. I started back down the steps and watched the lead-outs walk the dogs past the grandstand. Right when I got ready to push the door open to go outside, the lead-outs stopped the dogs, and they stood there in a row while the track announcer called their names and weights and kennels. It was like he was telling their life story, everything that had ever mattered about them in the world to anyone like me. I'd seen this very same thing a thousand times but never thought of it that way. It wasn't until Poke Chop that I'd ever seen a greyhound do anything but run around a track.

I listened to all the names and waited till they were through and walking toward the starting gate and then I went and sat down and handed Sarah her beer. "Thanks," she said. I could feel her looking at me, but I was staring ahead at the empty space of the track. "What's wrong?" she asked me.

Nothing, I told her, not looking at her. I wanted to say I'm not sure I can do this, but I couldn't say it. For five years I'd been coming to the track in order to get to one moment. That's what it had been about all along—five years of trying to use my brain the best I knew how to have something I could win at that made a difference. And now that the Greyhound God seemed to have got me there I wasn't sure what to do.

When my father died and we were living in Spokane and Jake was just a baby, when my father's heart stopped in a patrol car just like the one Mark died in for no reason any doctor could figure, we left the apartment at night to go home. Driving down the road I felt like there were things to be afraid of. It was like we were trapped in a rushing cage that had come unconnected from everything, going down this strip of road that depended on me keeping my hands tight on the wheel. I looked in the mirror at Jake's thin hair in the dim light where he was sleeping in the car seat. I wanted to pull off the road and get in the back seat and me and Jenny hold our baby tight and pray, but there was no God I believed in there to protect us who I could pray to. My body was tight and my throat was choked and I thought I was going to get sick. So I started looking out the window to try and refocus. We were nearing the state line, and something familiar came slowly into view. Off to our right, with its metal roof gleaming and the lights poking up into the sky, was Spokane Greyhound Park, where I had sat on a cold, wet night and felt there had to be a pattern to everything. And as we passed the lights seemed to grow and grow, like the whole place was widening to reach me, and I felt suddenly warm like when I was a kid swimming in Lake Pend Oreille and I would pass through a spot in the water that was warmer for no reason, and I watched the track for as long as I could keep it in my eyes, and for that short time it felt like heaven. That's how the track always felt to me.

Sarah's hand got tight around my arm. "Luke," she said, "something's really wrong, isn't it?" She sounded a little bit scared. I was feeling pretty upset, and I couldn't trust my voice to tell her everything was all right or my hands to hold hers between them without shaking.

I gripped my hands on the edge of the wet metal seat. "If we're gonna do it, we better go do it," I said, not looking at Sarah. We'd agreed that we should make the bet early since it might take them a while. I looked over at her and she had a serious expression on her face, staring out at the track. "What do you think?"

She looked at me kind of surprised. "You mean you're thinking about not betting it?"

"I don't know," I said. "It's a lot of money."

She crossed her arms in her lap and looked out across the track again and narrowed her eyes. "It seems like it's happening awfully fast, doesn't it?" she said. I knew what she meant—the 10th race getting so close already, me and her, everything. It was like summer was ending in June. "But what if this is exactly what you were supposed to do all the time and you didn't do it?" She opened her purse and looked at all the money we'd stuffed in there, and she laughed just a little and shook her head. "It *is* a pretty impressive stash," she said.

But she was right. It was definitely what you'd call an ironic twist, when you consider how many times Jenny had practically begged me to quit betting at the track and I'd gone right ahead like a regular gambling addict, even though I always knew that wasn't what I really was, and now here at the very end of the line along came temptation in the form of this quiet voice in my head telling me not to bet.

"So I've been winning money hand over fist every night for almost the last three weeks," I said to Sarah. "I bet long odds, four dollars a race. Every race there's a one out of eight chance my dog will win, but my dog wins every time," I said. "Or almost."

Sarah scooted in close to me and took my hand. "I'd call that an accurate summary," she said.

I squeezed my eyes shut for a second and nodded. "You're

smarter than me," I said. She started to say something but I shook my head. "So do me a favor. Take one minute and see if you can come up with a logical explanation."

"Tell me when to start," she said.

"Now."

I counted the seconds in my head, and I looked at her close for one last time, her pretty hair and her pretty dark eyes and her lips slightly open while she was thinking. "Time," I said.

She reached out and pulled a strand of hair behind my ear. "Sorry," she said. "Fresh out of explanations."

"Okay then," I said.

She grabbed her purse and I put the Bible and the program and flannel shirt in my left hand and we went inside. We walked up to one of the special betting windows to a woman wearing glasses with kind of poofed-up brown hair that would have been popular back when she was in high school. She looked about the same age as me. "Just set your purse up here," I said to Sarah, and I pulled my wallet out, too. The woman kind of waited on us, ticking her fingernails slightly on the countertop like she had a song in her head. "This is a bet for the 10th race," I said. And right when I said it I understood. Of course I had to lose money. That was the whole point. I had to lay out everything I had, and I had to do it with no hope of anything more in return. That's what the Greyhound God was asking for. I pulled two hundred bucks out, which left me about enough for a couple more beers and a pack of cigarettes and a tank of gas. "Twelve thousand two hundred dollars on number 8 to win."

She laid her hand out on my two hundred dollars and stopped it there. Sarah pulled out the twelve thousand, which was rubber-banded in three huge rolls. "Wait, wait, wait," the lady said. She was holding her hand up to Sarah. "You need to understand the taxes," she said. "You don't want to bet that."

"But we *can* bet it, right?" I said.

She looked my face up and down, probably wondering where I got the money from. "You *can*, but you'll lose money. Let me go get a supervisor here to explain to you what—"

"Then we want to," I said.

She looked at me like she was blaming me for something, like I'd ruined her night somehow. "I still need a supervisor," she said.

She went and got this cocky little guy with a crew cut who looked like he worked out and he wasn't about to take any shit from anyone like me. The lady told him about the bet, and he checked out me and Sarah.

"You know you'll lose money," he said.

"Yeah," I said. "We've been told about a thousand times."

"What are you up to?" he said, folding his arms in front of him.

"Nothing," I said. It was starting to look harder than I thought, and I wondered if they were going to try to stall me till it was too late, although I couldn't see why. It wasn't them that stood to lose anything.

"We just happen to like that particular dog a lot," Sarah said. She smiled at the guy. "She has such a pretty name."

The guy just barely glanced at her, and then he frowned and looked back at me. "You working with a bookie?" he said, tilting his head up like he knew it all.

"No," I said. "I don't know any bookies." I wasn't sure what he was driving at.

"Right," he said, rocking back on his heels and nodding his head up and down. "You like to tell that to the police?"

"Well, no," I said. "I want to bet on the 10th race. How long would it take them to question me?"

"Look," Sarah said. "You can't just accuse us of something. We don't even know what you're talking about. We just want to make a bet."

The guy stared at her this time. "Drive down the odds, bet on another dog with a bookie where you won't have to pay taxes if you win?" he said. "Doesn't ring a bell?"

"Would we have to bet twelve thousand dollars to drive down the odds?" Sarah said, which was a very smart answer that I wouldn't have thought of and it didn't look like the guy had thought of it either.

He gave us both one last sarcastic look. "Go ahead," he said, nodding at the woman. "You'll have to fill out paperwork if you win," he said. Then he walked off toward his little office where he'd come from.

The money didn't take any time to count. She just stacked some of it up neat and whirred it through this little machine and then stuck some more in and whirred it through again and so on. Then she punched it out on her keyboard and up popped one ticket, 10th race, number 8, $12,200 to win.

I gave the ticket to Sarah and she put it in her purse. She smiled at me. "Good luck," she said.

When we started down the steps you could see right away it was pouring down rain, and there was lightning in the sky. There wasn't a single person left out on the bleachers, except for one cardboard salesman who was doing a little dance outside with a beer held up in one hand and all of his buddies who'd come inside were laughing at him through the window like he was maybe the funniest guy in the world.

"Shit," I said.

We stood there watching it rain. "What do you want to do?" Sarah said.

"Let's go stand down at the bottom," I said. "Maybe it'll be over quick." I didn't actually see any point in getting soaking wet, but on the other hand if I wanted to get my message from the Greyhound God, I wasn't sure I should have the roof of the building in the way.

The 9th race was over, but they hadn't brought out Morgan's Sarah and the other dogs yet. We watched the guy dance outside the window until he finally gave up and came inside. Right then the odds disappeared from the 9th race and started flashing on for number 10. In about two seconds there it was, number 8, 1:9, which actually meant 1:10 except they couldn't show it, because they don't put room for a 10 on that side, which should tell you about how often it happens. Every other dog was 99:1.

A buzz went up behind us, and I heard one group of the cardboard people huddled near us laughing. Someone had made a joke about it obviously. From a little ways behind us I heard a guy say, "Holy shit, Andy, there you go. Take your pick," and Andy said, "It won't stay that way."

But of course it did. Some of the other dogs came down a little bit, but none under 20:1, and three of them were still at 99:1. A lot of people were staring at their programs and then looking up at the screen and then staring into their programs again.

Then the dogs came out onto the track, the lead-outs in their yellow raincoats with the hoods over their heads. I watched Morgan's Sarah until the tote board flashed three minutes to post, and she looked good—alert and ready to race and not hanging her head like the other dogs in the rain.

"One more thing," I said.

We walked back up the steps and went and bought two fresh beers and a new pack of smokes and I stood there and unwrapped the cellophane. Sarah lifted her cup and I stopped her and said not yet.

"I'm scared half to death," she said. "I need a drink."

I looked at the tote board lights. "You've got to wait one minute," I said.

The lead-outs were heading the dogs toward the chutes, and you could see Morgan's Sarah prancing along with her tail wagging and tossing her head. The rain didn't seem to bother her one bit for some reason. It was still coming down hard, and lightning lit up the sky to the south. We were standing down at the windows again. The odds were still 1:9 on number 8, and the stands were buzzing and people were running up the aisles to place last-minute bets. The odds were so high on the other dogs that nobody could resist. Under normal circumstances, I'd have had a $2 win bet on the longest shot in the field.

"So we're staying in?" Sarah said.

I handed her my flannel shirt. "Nope," I told her. "Hold this over your head."

We stepped outside and Sarah pulled the shirt up and started to head down to the bleachers. "Wait a second," I said. "Stand here under the awning." Way down to the left I could see the dogs getting ready to go into the chutes. My hands weren't shaking and my heart wasn't pounding hard and time seemed to move along just right. Maybe I was feeling a little like Poke Chop, like I was doing what it was I was made to do. This is me, the guy who bets on dog races, who believes in the Greyhound God.

"Wait till the rabbit starts up," I said. I set my beer down and tapped out two cigarettes from the pack and handed one to Sarah. "You got your lighter?" I said.

She handed me her beer and fished it out of her purse. "Here," she said.

I handed her beer back. "Set that down on the ground," I said. "When the rabbit starts up, light your cigarette and then take a drink of beer."

She set her beer down on the concrete, then stood back up and laughed at me. "Just like Luke Rivers?" she said.

"Just like Luke Rivers." But not exactly. I didn't say anything about praying. I'd be the only one doing that, though Sarah I'm sure would be hoping in her own way.

The first couple of dogs were in the chute, and I could hear them barking through the rain. It was coming down even harder if that was possible, the drops practically ricocheting off the pavement the way they used to do in Mississippi and New Orleans. The lightning seemed closer now, lighting up the trees.

I made sure I had all my stuff situated right—cigarette and matches in my hands, beer and Bible and program at my feet where I could grab them easy. Sarah had her cigarette ready to light. She smiled at me and kind of bounced up on her toes but didn't say anything.

The bell rang and startled me right above our heads and left a ringing in the air it seemed. The rabbit squeaked and my heart started pounding then. "Okay," I said, and I struck the match with my hand cupped and saw the end of my cigarette glow. I breathed in, let the smoke out, picked up my beer cup and drank. I prayed without thinking any words, because I was afraid for them to be the wrong things. From the corner of my eye I could see the dogs escaping the chute.

"Now let's sit," I shouted, and we burst into the rain, me with the Bible and program in one hand and my beer in the other and Sarah losing the shirt when she tried to run with it over her head but running on ahead with me anyway. We hurried into the seats already soaking wet and my cigarette was soggy and broke when I flicked the ash and I tossed it away and the dogs rushed by. The mud was flinging up behind them, and I thought how mud was bad for small dogs like Morgan's Sarah, how it made it hard for them to keep on their feet. She had a good start though, and was going just wide of the 6 dog into the turn when she slipped, sliding wide and almost falling like I had been afraid, and the 4 dog behind her went down completely and nearly slid into her legs. Sarah let out a little shriek and put her hand to her forehead.

That was the last thing I saw besides the race. Morgan's Sarah didn't come off the turn dead last, but she was sixth and separated from the pack in front by a few lengths, and if she wasn't exactly as good as Poke Chop she was going to have to be close at least.

When they hit the backstretch I had shut everything else out. I saw the dogs clear, but there weren't any edges, like I was seeing through a telescope. Very slowly I lost the noise and the feel of the rain, and the track announcer's voice faded away like the end of a song, and there wasn't any crowd behind me warm and safe inside, and there wasn't any Sarah, but just the dog with her name. And still I heard that ringing from the bell, like it had gone way above the thunder, high into the sky where it was calling someone there.

Morgan's Sarah gained ground on the backstretch, but then she made a mistake. She came up on the 3 dog, and instead of going around tried to jump over, the way they'll do sometimes, and it cost her a couple of strides. It didn't look like there was any way. But she started picking up ground outside again. I knew there wasn't room for any more mistakes, and at the far turn I thought for one instant it was all over, because the 2 dog slipped out into the 5 right in front of her. But they fell just wide enough for her to run by inside, and there on the turn she was in third place.

It was like I could see it happening then, like I knew how it would end, watching them hit the stretch. The lead dog was fading and Morgan's Sarah drove on the rail, her legs turning like wheels and the mud flinging from her feet into the rain, and I could see her eyes, and then I could feel myself there with her on the track, pounding the stretch toward home, and I tried to think of rising, and think of hearing a voice from the sky, of making that perfect moment where everything would come together at the finish line. But I was only out there in the mud running fast and low.

Deep inside me I felt Morgan's Sarah pulling up the track, gathering the other dogs in until I could feel her pull even, and she pulled ahead and part of me pulled with her, out there in the rain and the mud connected to that thread, that rope that pulled me along down low to the ground and always kept me so, and I knew it wouldn't change. Nothing was happening but a dog race. But my heart and mind raced along out there with this dog, and I could still hear the ringing high in the air but knew I wouldn't get there and it wouldn't get to me, and the track lights splintered into gold before my eyes.

She flashed past, three lengths clear and almost flying, and I was glad for her, the dog, because she'd had to try so hard, make such a brave effort. And all that was left was that tiny ringing, like a pretty finger faintly circling a rim of crystal.

And then there was just the rain, pounding hard and hissing in the air and on the concrete. The noises of the track came back to me slowly, the last shouts of the people inside who had hoped Morgan's Sarah would lose, and Sarah's voice above me where she'd been jumping up and down and shaking the bench next to me. For one brief instant I felt like Sarah was me, up above and listening, and I was my father, down below at night in the kitchen. There was never an answer for him, and now there was none for me. I felt silly for having expected it.

Then I couldn't say I felt anything. I grabbed the Bible and stood up and started walking. I held myself steady with my hand on the back of the wet bench. "Let's get out of the rain," I said.

Sarah tugged at my arm gently when we got inside, and I turned to her. She was smiling, but just a little smile, like it was left over from winning the race. The rest of her face looked like one big question I guess you could say, and questions need answers, and I didn't have any. "I have to pee," I said.

She looked at me for a few seconds just the same, and her mouth fell open a little, and she ran her tongue slowly across her upper lip where a raindrop had made its way. Then she took her hand from my arm and ran it back through her wet hair and looked out at the racetrack.

"I have to pee real bad," I said. "I'll be back in a minute."

And I left her there not looking at me. I walked up past the betting windows and on out the turnstiles to the exit. Outside it had nearly stopped raining, the way it will do so quick with summer storms. The wind was blowing, and there were just scattered raindrops here and there. The raindrops on all the cars showed up golden under the streetlamps. I walked between the rows of cars toward the highway at the far end, holding the Bible tight in my hand, my wet hair plastered to my face. Up ahead I could see a man standing by a car, and a little flame flashed in front of him, and I could see the red glow of a cigarette. It was Tucker.

I walked straight over to him. He was leaned up against the side of a Chevy Malibu, smoking and looking at me. I stopped in front of him. "Where's your friend?" I said.

He took a long drag on his cigarette and looked behind him in both directions, like he thought I might be trying to distract him while someone snuck up behind him to hit him over the head. "What friend?" he said. "Who the fuck are you?" He was wearing a tight black T-shirt that barely stretched over his big shoulders and arms, and the cigarette and the streetlights made his eyes glow in a way I didn't like.

I held my hand out at about my waist. "*You* know," I said.

"Oh, *him*," he said. He flipped his cigarette away and quit leaning back against the car. "*That* little shit," he said. "You *know* that little shit? You wouldn't happen to know where that little shit *is*, would you?"

"You picked him up," I said. "I was right there behind you. You ..." But I quit talking, because I didn't like the look in his eyes again.

I backed away real slow, backing into the parking lot a long way, like I couldn't get my body to turn around, and he leaned against the car and reached in his back pocket for another cigarette.

I headed toward the highway again and my steps got quicker, and soon I was running and my wet clothes were like a suit of armor, but it felt like my feet never touched the ground. I ran all the way to the little access road and then along it to the highway and the bridge from Lake Delton to the Dells. I stopped on the bridge. The water below was black and calm and peaceful. I stood next to a little puddle that glistened on the pavement. Its surface was smooth where it had quit raining. I still had the Bible in my hand, and it seemed to be getting in my way somehow, and I thought about tossing it into the water, but I didn't. I was breathing hard, and I felt like I might have a heart attack. I didn't think anything standing there, except that I had no idea what time it was. I had lost track somewhere. Then I realized if the Land Cruiser came along I wouldn't have anyplace to hide there on the bridge, so I started walking on toward the Dells.

Soon I was in the middle of all the attractions, the colored lights and signs. Off to my right was some music playing, something that sounded like a calliope, like the riverboats played passing by the wharves in New Orleans, where you could hear them over the roofs in the French Quarter and they always sounded like ghosts.

I walked further up the street, getting into the main part of the strip. The closer I got, the more people there were. I kept feeling like I was breathing hard, like having trouble with my breathing and my heart racing too fast, and to make this better I started raising my arms up together and holding the Bible over my head in both hands. Then I would lower my arms and walk along as relaxed as I could again for a little ways and then raise my arms over my head again. People on the sidewalk moved out of my way. They passed back and forth, headed to the different attractions. They all had the same looks on their faces. They all seemed to be anticipating that something important was bound to happen now that the rain had stopped.

I walked past the Trojan horse standing there with floodlights blazing over it. I hit the main intersection where the road forked right into town or left out into the country and I had to decide which way. There on the corner was the Sho-Boat Bar, with a big paddle wheel stuck on the side of the building, and people walking in and out laughing. I started walking off to the north, away from town.

Soon it was much quieter. There were no people where I was walking, only the yellow lights of farmhouses and a few cars going wide around me to miss me on the road. I watched one car's headlights, and I saw from them that I wasn't on the road to the cabins, but I didn't stop to think of it. Gravel crunched under my feet. The night was black except for the scattered lights and the layer of whitish clouds overhead.

I walked and walked in the dark, and every once in a while I would go past a farm and a streetlight burned in the yard or by the barn or the house, and a dog would bark at me. Finally I stopped in a place where there were no lights, no farms or houses or buildings of any kind. The road was going up the side of a hill through pine trees on either side. My shirt and pants weighed a ton, and I could feel the rain in them working its way into my skin. I took my shirt off and the air made me feel better.

I stood there a while looking at the dark trees and the ribbon of road and I had a sense of having been there before. Not the actual place, but the feeling of it somehow, the gravel road and the water dripping softly from the trees. "You have walked up and down in the midst of the stones of fire," I said. "Walked. Up and down." I was saying the words out loud, testing the shape they took in the air. "In the midst of the stones of fire." I felt thirsty. Walking up and down, stones, fire. They were words that dried you out and made you thirsty.

And then I realized that I *had* been to this actual place before. I looked at the road curving up ahead and turning around the side of the hill, and I thought of how I'd ridden up it with Sarah, parking in the little turn-out and fighting through the bushes up the hill.

I started walking up faster then, the Bible in my left hand and the shirt in my right. It wasn't long before I was breathing hard and my heart felt like it was going too fast again. I kept my eyes peeled for the turn-out, I don't know why. I could have walked up the hill from anyplace.

The road came around a little bend, and a ways ahead I could see where it widened into the turn-out. I walked on up there, and looked up the side of the hill at the tangle of bushes and trees. I adjusted the Bible and shirt, got them both in my left hand, and I started on through. It was a hard time with all the bushes and no one to lead me. No matter how careful I was to part the branches and twigs, they kept scratching my chest and arms, and before I'd gotten through the first thick part I had to stop and put on my shirt. I was getting pretty cold, and the feel of the wet shirt as I struggled to get it over my head and pull it down didn't help any. I had to search around on the ground to find the Bible where I'd dropped it.

I walked on up, falling every once in a while or getting tangled up in the bushes. It seemed like a long time before I got through and was standing looking up at the rocks. This time there was no moon, but I could still see the outline of the top of the hill and all the trees. I got a good grip on my Bible and found a place for my feet and started edging along the rocks kind of sideways going up slow. I was feeling pretty tired, and I wished I had some water, just a glass of water, somebody to stand there and hand it to me and I could say "Thanks." My wet shirt clung to me and made it hard to move my arms, and I kept thinking of myself falling, tumbling down and down.

But I didn't think to go back down or find a way around the rocks. Soon I'd made it to the top of the hill. I flopped down on the ground and put the Bible in my lap and looked down at the town of Wisconsin Dells, breathing hard and wiping my muddy hands on my wet shirt. There weren't as many lights this time—the streetlights, sure, but not as many of the flashing bulbs and neon of the roller coasters and water slides. It didn't look like much was happening. The cardboard manufacturers had all gone to sleep. Only here and there through the trees you could see a car pass, its headlights shining on the wet pavement.

I got to my feet, and had a little trouble setting my weight on my left knee, like I'd twisted it somewhere on the way up. I hobbled on across the little clearing to the other side where I could sit and look down toward Lyndon Station and the lights where Sarah said the cabins were. It was dark and there were no cars and only the wind blowing steady from the west up there across the little clearing.

I wanted to lie down, and I thought about taking off my shirt again first, but decided the wet grass and ground would be even colder on my bare back. I set the Bible at my side and eased down onto my elbows and then settled down my head where there weren't any sticks poking me.

For a long time I lay there and looked up at the sky. I didn't want to do anything but sleep. I just wanted to drift off into nothing and I didn't even care about coming back, about when I would ever get up and leave. But I was shivering, and when I would close my eyes I seemed to feel it more, and my knee throbbed, and so I kept opening my eyes until finally I agreed with myself to just lie there and look at the clouds.

They seemed to be thinning, like turning into ghosts of themselves, and to one side I could start to see a lighter place where I knew there was a thin moon. The clouds moved toward it through the air, thinning out and getting whiter by the second, and I imagined them getting sucked into the light of the moon and swallowed there.

Then sometime there were gaps between the clouds, and a scattering of stars. Straight above my head there was one star, very bright, and it pulsed with just a little red. My eyes stuck to the spot, and when a cloud moved in between me and the star my eyes stayed right there, and the wispy cloud would pass and the star would shine down till it almost hurt me. Soon there was nothing in the sky, no clouds, no moon, no other stars, only that one shining bright and pulsing and stretching out in points like a red diamond.

It seemed to hang right there above me and never move at all. When the clouds moved across, it would seem to rush toward them, but then they would pass and it would be there right above my head. I turned my head from side to side, but it seemed to go with me. I closed my eyes for a long time, and when I opened them it was right there in the very same place, like it wouldn't ever leave me.

And I thought of how far away it was, that star. It would take lifetimes and lifetimes to get there. But it seemed very easy somehow, too, very easy just to separate from your body and float away, rising up and up until you reached that hot center, that ball of fire. Maybe that really was where we all came from, and where everything returned to.

And I started to feel like I was going there, beginning my long journey, quietly separating from myself and rising into the night air. It was like what I'd wanted to happen at Mark's funeral, how I kept hoping the coffin lid would open up and Mark would float away.

I drifted there beneath the star. And soon the star was bigger, so big that it had swallowed me, or filled me up. There was nothing in the world but the inside of that star, or the star inside of me. And this would have been all right. I didn't want anything else, I didn't want anything at all, I had floated free from everything. But while I knew I was inside the star or the star had gotten inside me, the star itself didn't know anything. There was nothing in the world except me and the star, but the star didn't know it, only me, and it seemed then that if I was going to be anything, if I could actually hope to *be* anything in the world at all, I would have to be the star. Being myself was nothing, because the star didn't know me, and my knowing the star made it the only real thing. But I didn't know how to become the star.

And so I was nothing, I decided, and the star filled up everything and made it all go white, and it may have been then that I was sleeping.

Or maybe not. The next thing that I knew of, other than the whiteness, was something like a memory. I was in my grandmother's living room, and there was a ray of winter sun through the windowpane, and she was in her chair reading about Moses to me. But it was me who was in the story, too, and that part was more like dreaming. I was sitting somewhere in a patch of tall green grass, and there was a little stream. It was a slow little stream, running flat through the grass, just burbling along in the sunlight. The stream barely made any noise, and it was drowned out whenever the cold wind picked up and blew through the grass around me. It was like a little stream you might find in Idaho in the early spring.

Next to me on the ground, halfway hidden in the grass, was a basket. It was an old straw basket, the bleached color of straw. In the basket was a baby, moving its tiny hands in the air with its eyes closed. The baby wasn't crying, but he looked like he might cry.

I picked the basket up by its thin handle and moved to the edge of the stream. Very carefully I set the basket in the water, and the water tried to tug it away from me. I held on, making sure the basket felt like it was floating, and I took one last look at the baby and let my hand go and watched the basket float away. It turned in a circle, slightly, slowly, and the baby's hands waved in the air. I watched the baby's hands go out of sight, and I was alone in the windy grass beside the stream.

And at the same time then I was on the hill in Wisconsin, my arms folded across me, shivering, the wet ground under me and the trees pointing up into the sky. I couldn't find my star anymore in all the other stars, which took up every inch of the whole wide space. I was glad I couldn't find it. I lay there on my back a while looking out toward every corner of the night at what I guess you'd call the multitude of stars.

It was a lonely walk back to the cabins, and cold, and my knee hurt although it loosened up some, and it took a very long time. I thought a lot about my flannel shirt I left at the track. I thought a lot about the warm bed waiting for me, though now I'm here I won't sleep. I looked around a lot at the stars fading in the sky, and the night getting lighter and turning purple on the edges to the east. I watched the moon.

I thought most about how I would have done things differently. The last three weeks seemed washed away, and it was like I could almost start them over, and everything seemed very plain. When Jenny and Jake were gone that morning in Rapid City, I would have taken my money from the track and marched out of the motel and got on the phone and called Jenny's parents to tell them I was on my way. Then I would have bought that truck, but I would have pointed it straight toward Mendenhall, Mississippi. There wouldn't have been any Sarah, or any dog track, or any miracle. Just me and my truck going down the road. I could almost think I'd done it like that, it felt so clear and real to me.

When I got to the cabin all of Sarah's things were gone. All my clothes were folded neatly on the bed, and my gym bag was next to them, and the bed was made. My shaving cream and razors and deodorant were in a little row by the sink. My sandals were set out neatly on the floor at the foot of the bed.

On the writing desk was a yellow sheet of paper with a woman's handwriting. I knew what it was. I laid the Bible on the bed and got undressed and cleaned myself up and put on dry clothes and drank some water straight from the faucet. Then I sat down at the writing desk and read Sarah's letter.

It was very pretty, the kind of letter from someone who knows how to say what they want the right way. It told me again how I was special. It said how maybe I didn't believe that because she thought Buddy had probably told me some things. I don't know how she could have seen that, but she did. It said how knowing me had changed her, how she would go through her life for a long time thinking of the sort of person I was and how I would want her to be if I was with her. And it said even after that she wouldn't forget me. And she asked me if I would please not forget her, even if that was selfish of her and might sometimes make things uncomfortable in my life with Jake and Jenny. And the letter apologized for that. And then Sarah thanked me, and then she wrote her name.

At the very bottom it said this: Look under your pillow. You might have had a visit from the tooth fairy.

I pulled back the spread and picked up the pillow, but it was the wrong one, Sarah's pillow, and there was nothing there. I picked up the other pillow, and underneath it were stacks of hundreds and fifties and twenties in rubber bands and some loose bills too. Every single bit of my eleven thousand dollars and change.

So I'll have my money when I go to meet Jenny. I'll put it in my bag beneath my clothes and my bathroom things and my shoes, and I'll put the Bible on top and zip the bag closed. I'll pull the bedspread back up and make it look neat again. I'll take one last look at the writing desk and the clock and the picture of the barn with the shining windows. I'll fold up Sarah's letter and put it in my pocket, and then I'll turn out the lights.

I'll get on I-90 toward Madison. I'll stop at the first truck stop I see and get one of those huge plastic mugs and fill it with coffee and get a package of chocolate doughnuts or whatever. Then I won't stop again until I have to. I'll go get Jake and Jenny in Mississippi and take them to Idaho or wherever Jenny wants, even if she wants to stay in Mendenhall. I'll try to make it so we won't ever be separated again.

Because there was one other thing I thought while I was walking here, something about the story of Moses and how they put him in the basket in the stream. I thought of how that was what me and Jenny had done, sort of, with Jake. We'd started him off in his little basket, and now it was my job and hers to keep him moving along downstream. When he washed up against the bank we'd have to step down to the water and help him get moving again.

And when the water got faster we'd have to run alongside. And we'd have to let him know we were there the whole time, even if we didn't know the place he was going to or we were going to either.

And I thought about how that wasn't so small. It was as big in its own way as all the other big things I'd felt like I had to know and couldn't find. Because you have to be very brave. It's all you have, really—that connection with the people you're close to—and there aren't any guarantees. You have to be brave to keep going. That's no small thing.

Maybe the Bible got it all wrong from the start. All that time wasted looking for a savior, someone to give you something more than what you already have. Like how even when I couldn't believe in the Bible anymore I made up the Greyhound God, something childish, because I wanted someone to make my life have meaning.

Maybe they even told all the wrong stories about Jesus in the Bible. They started off right, telling the story about him being born under that one special star which was a kind of metaphor I think, but not one that showed how special Jesus was but showed instead how alone he was in the world, like everybody. Just him and his own ball of fire. And I think they did a good job by putting in the shepherds. But then it skips to all the obvious big things, like the miracles and offering to save everyone and take them all to heaven and getting crucified and rising from the dead, and doesn't talk about the other big things that were maybe more important when it came to Jesus. Like all those years when he was just a man, a carpenter, learning how to hammer nails and saw boards and fit them together well. And all that time while he worked he was thinking and practicing. He would think about what were the best things people could do, how was the best way to spend every second of the day to try to be as perfect as a person could be, what God should be like if there was one. Like he knew all along it wasn't just doing, but what it was you did. Not just gestures, but the right ones. And very slowly he learned and got better, and it was hard work all the way, he wasn't a rich man in a big house, but very ordinary and plain. And finally he tried so hard and reached so high that he rose up through the air, and he didn't know where the air was taking him, it might have been to a star, but he wasn't afraid and kept rising until he found himself suddenly at God's feet, if there was one. And only then God saw him, and he was surprised, and he thought how it must be his true son to have come all that long way. God didn't set out to make Jesus in his image. Jesus made himself in God's image. He didn't ask God to show him anything. He didn't ask God to explain to him what his life was all about or save him. He saved himself, and then went back as God's son to try to save other people. So after all this time I think I understand. God didn't make Jesus his son; Jesus made God his father. The Greyhound God is me.

JULY 3

I started feeling a little downhearted from the minute I didn't see any sign of the Honda. I'd come a long way, after all, across Wisconsin and Illinois in the hot sun, and the truck breaking down on the other side of St. Louis so I had to sleep by the highway and spend a whole day getting the alternator fixed, and then on down through Memphis and Mississippi in the heat. I didn't like pulling in at the Beamons' and not seeing the Honda there, only Mr. Beamon's Cadillac, and a swing set in the backyard sure enough, but no one in the swing. It wasn't what I'd pictured.

But I went on up the walkway and rang the doorbell. Then there was Mr. Beamon. He stood there behind the screen door, looking at me. Neither of us said anything. The sun was hot and I could feel sweat trickling down all over me. Then Mr. Beamon shook his head. "You're two thousand miles in the wrong direction," he said.

And right then it came to me, I don't know why or from where. I shook my head back at him. "Idaho," I said.

He nodded. "Idaho."

I must have looked like I was going to keel over right there, because he opened the screen door and came out like he was ready to catch me. I backed up to the edge of the porch. "If you'd just listened to me on the phone the other day instead of cussing me," he said, and probably could have gone on about that for an hour except I turned around to leave. "Hey, now," he called out when I was halfway back to the truck. "Luke," he said. "Son." Not "son" like I was his son or anything though, but just how they say that to anybody in Mississippi. "Son, come on back here." But I kept walking. "Luke!" he said, and I turned around. He held open the door and we were looking at each other. I noticed for the first time he looked about ten years older than the last time I'd seen him, his hair gone mostly gray and his shoulders sunk and his hands looking kind of big and veiny. "You get your narrow ass in here," he said. "If you go on without Joanne feeding you I never will hear the end of it."

I stuck there on the sidewalk, thinking of Mrs. Beamon's ham and biscuits, feeling a little like a skittish stray dog. "You look awful," Mr. Beamon said. I went back up the walkway and he led me in the door.

And it was fine, I have to admit. They made me go take a shower and Mrs. Beamon had lunch on the table when I got out—hot cornbread and a ham sandwich and what they call butter beans— and they even made kind of a fuss over me. They tried to get me to spend the night even, but I said no. I said I wanted to get where I was going.

"You should clean yourself up a little bit, get a haircut," Mr. Beamon said. The usual. "You don't want to show up looking that way."

"Yeah," I said, but not like I really meant it. I was sitting at the kitchen table looking out the window at the swing set in the backyard. It was under a big oak tree in the shade.

"Be nice if we could get a little use out of that," Mr. Beamon said. He was sitting across from me turning a toothpick around in his fingers and tapping it on the table. "Hard thing not to see your little girl and your grandson for so long," he said, and his voice broke a little at the end. Mrs. Beamon was behind me in the kitchen washing dishes, and I could hear the dishes stop clattering for a second.

"Yes, sir," I said. "I know," still looking out at the swings.

I finished as much as I could of my lunch and drank the rest of my ice tea and then I said well, I'd better go. Mrs. Beamon gave me the address and the phone number in Idaho, pressing the slip of paper into my hand. When I looked at it later, I thought I could almost picture the exact house, and Jake and Jenny there, only a few blocks from where I used to live.

Then we were out on the porch. "Good-bye," I said. "Thanks."

They were standing there looking at me, Mr. Beamon in his nice clothes from the store and Mrs. Beamon in shorts and a little flowery shirt. "I think you can work things out with Jenny if you try," Mr. Beamon said. We were standing there looking at each other in the eye and it felt like there were about a thousand things floating in the air. "If you'll just be a little reasonable," he said. "If you'll just do a little better."

I felt a little tingle of anger, and my chest got tight like it was filling with words, but I tried to slow down, and there was something in his face that made me see all of a sudden that he might actually be hoping things would work out somehow, which was needless to say quite a shock to me. But you could see it in his expression. "I know," I said. "You're right. I plan to do better. You'll see next time we come for a visit."

There was a weird moment where Mrs. Beamon kind of lurched ahead and hugged me like someone had pushed her from behind, and Mr. Beamon shook my hand a long time while he didn't say anything and I didn't either.

Then I was on the road. Back up I-55 and then I-70 and I-80 heading west across the plains, the windows rolled down and the radio keeping me from falling asleep. The corn and the cows and the little hills off in the distance, and at night just the lights of the road, and then a few hours sleeping at a rest area with voices of other people in the night passing on their way to the restrooms, like it always is, like dream people who talk to you in your sleep.

I thought of Jake and Jenny most all the way, and living again in my hometown. I thought of Sarah, too, and I thought of what her father said, and I hoped I hadn't made a mess of things.

But I think when Sarah wrote that note it meant good-bye, that she knew what was happening and it was okay. I still picture her sitting on a bench at the races, or there in my little room, and I don't know how long I'll go on picturing those things. But as I got further west I thought more of Jenny and less of Sarah. And I thought a lot about gestures, too. I still believe in them, even though the others didn't turn out so hot. I thought of how it was a matter of making the right one, of standing there with Jenny and doing and saying the right things, real things that would make it better. And I thought about what Mr. Beamon said, too, about how it would be when I got there, and I finally stopped in a town in Wyoming and took care of my hair and my clothes and some things for Jake and Jenny.

And then I was just east of the state line, driving a back road that would take me through the little towns in southeastern Idaho like Soda Springs, and then to I-84, and then highway 95, and then home. It was late in the day and I was passing through the dry mountains with the sagebrush and the small pines and the sun was low and red in the sky. I was taking it slow because the truck had had a hard time, and I knew by then I was going to make it before Jenny's birthday. I was passing through the towns and by the big ranches and trying to take it in, that I was back in Idaho.

I came into a valley and there were no cars on the road ahead, and I passed by a little town off to my right that had an old railroad depot and most of the houses and stores looked dark and deserted, like a ghost town, and in the middle of one of the dusty streets I could see a man and a woman and a young girl walking along and holding hands. They were walking away from me, and the little girl leaned her head against her father's side, and the father put his hand on her hair, and they looked to me like people who'd been alive for hundreds of years somehow and never gone through any changes.

And so as I came up out of the valley and into another stretch where I could see cars again and there was a tractor and a truck out behind a barbwire fence, everything getting darker in the setting sun, I felt like I still had a little piece of some old time in me, when God was still real to people, and there weren't any questions.

The sun was dipping big and red down into the horizon, and I came up a hill through the sagebrush, and the sun seemed to rise back up like it had decided the day couldn't end just yet, and then ahead of me in the road was an old wooden church. When I got near it the sun lit up all the windows and behind the church was a little graveyard under some poplar trees and closed in by a picket fence.

It was at the top of a hill, and you could see off from the church in every direction, the sun going down and the mountains up ahead, and miles on up the road the next town with only a few tiny streets, and I thought it looked like maybe the prettiest place in the world if you didn't count Sandpoint, which had the lake and lots of trees and Jake and Jenny.

I slowed down and pulled off the road in front of the church and shut off the engine and got out and stretched. The air felt good, not as hot as it had been for so many weeks. I looked at the sun and the shining church windows and the shadows stretching across the graves from the tombstones, and I checked around once and then went and jumped the wooden fence.

Everything was quiet. The wind wasn't blowing very hard, and the dead people had nothing to say. I wandered through the headstones, and stopped before a plain white one that said Joshua Jones, Beloved, 1911–1919. Another little boy. One more reminder.

But I told myself it was all right. I looked at the headstones around him, and there was Bertrand Jones and Lucille Jones and a lot of other Joneses. Joshua Jones at least had company.

The sun was halfway gone, like it was being dipped into the dark earth on a string, and a long black shadow lay across the green grass of Joshua Jones' grave from the poplars, and I was thinking of gestures again.

I went back and hopped the fence, and I went to the truck and unzipped my bag and took out Anna Cornwell's old Bible. My Bible, I had come to think of it. I tossed it over the fence and looked at it there in the weeds for a second while I got my breath back, and jumped back over and eyed a car going along the road, and then picked it up and went over and stood at Joshua Jones' grave.

I wanted to say something, but I didn't know what to say. So I just thought instead. I thought of all the people I'd known who were gone now, one by one, starting with my grandmother, picturing her kind, ascetic face, and I told her good-bye. Then Mark, his round face and his sandy blond hair and his smile that was so much like Jake's. And I said good-bye to Mark, too. And then my father last, I'm not sure why. Maybe because it was hard to find the right picture.

But I finally remembered him in a way that I thought was right. He was sitting very straight, his hands in his lap, not a smile but a half-smile on his face, looking at Mark while he played the "Moonlight Sonata" on a summer afternoon with a breeze coming from the doorway. Next to him on the end table was a glass of lemonade. I said, Dad, good-bye. I'm leaving now. Then I put him with the others, each of their faces, in little straw baskets and floated them off downstream, and I pictured their faces lit by a red sun, not a fiery red, but a peaceful sleepy red, like the sun going down there in Idaho.

And I felt the Bible in my hand, the rough black leather, and I opened it up to the first page of The Gospel According to Saint Luke, where I could read the big black words, and I set the Bible down on Joshua Jones' grave.

Then I climbed the fence again and got in and started the truck, but I thought of another thing. I scrounged in the side pocket of my bag until I found a pen, and then I got out and picked up two pebbles from the edge of the road. I hopped the fence again, and I walked back to Joshua Jones' grave, wondering what kind of little boy he might have been, and deciding he must have been a good boy, beloved, and the sun was almost gone and the shadows were thick like deep water.

I got down on my knees on the raised ground, and I found the right page again from where the wind had blown it, and I un-capped the pen, and I wrote in big thick letters right after the last word, making lines and filling them carefully in—RIVERS. I looked at the page there in the shadows, the words in bold I'd looked at so many times and this new one crowded in. THE GOSPEL ACCORDING TO SAINT LUKE RIVERS, it said. I thought for a second about what it would look like to whoever found it there, how they might think it was wrong to write in a Bible that way, or how they might think I was saying I had written the things in the book, or that I thought I had found some special kind of enlightenment that made me better than everyone else, or I thought the things in the book were about me. But it was really a message just to Joshua Jones, and all the people like him who had died and gone on and what that had meant in my life. And where you put your name is at the end.

I put one pebble at the edge of each page. And then I left the little church and the tombstone.

And I think that's all I have to say—only one more thing. I drove the truck into the next little town with its quiet main street, and the houses were lit up with people inside, and the sun was a tiny red line over the hills, and wispy pink clouds stretched out across the sky like cotton candy at a carnival. The breeze came in the open window and ruffled my shirt, nice and cool, and I turned the radio knob trying to find a station and it was suddenly playing country music, something old and simple and sad, and I remem-bered it was one of my mother's songs. And I started singing the words, and I looked around, and I let myself wonder one more time about God, and I told myself it would be the last time for a long while. There was the town passing by with the houses and the shops, and the sun had disappeared but strung a pink light through the clouds, and I was singing an old song, and I was going home. The whole world felt fine to me. And I thought this one last thing about God, which was how if there wasn't one it was too damn bad for him.

JENNY

JULY 4

I was in the yard pinning clothes to the line to dry in the sun. The sun has been out every day here; you catch yourself thinking it will never go away. Jake was in the sandbox, shoveling sand into his little blue pail. He shovels sand at the beach, he shovels sand at home. You'd think someone was paying him.

The red and white truck pulled up right behind the Honda where it was parked on the street, but I barely looked up. I thought it was a friend of the two boys who rent the house across the street.

Then he was standing in the yard, looking at me and Jake, a

man with close-cropped brown hair wearing a gray suit in the warm summertime, his shoes buried in the high grass and yellow dandelions. I've mowed the yard twice, but it's hard to keep up.

Even though my father had called to tell me Luke was coming, even though he'd said Luke was driving a red truck, I didn't know him when he came. Or I couldn't make myself believe it. The man standing there looked nothing like Luke.

I held a clothespin in my hand, a white blouse hanging from one pin before me and curling in the breeze. Jake had his back turned, shoveling sand. The man in the yard pulled a bouquet of daisies from behind his back. He looked like an ad in a magazine.

"Jake," I said. Jake looked up at me, and I nodded my head for him to turn around. In a second, he was out of the sandbox and running through the grass. Luke leaned down and opened his arms wide, and Jake was suddenly smothered in his father's new suit, half-concealed by the flowers.

Every day Jake had talked about him, but I hadn't really known. It's hard to know with children, even your own, how much they really feel things or how much they simply say what they think they ought to. But there he was, clinging to his father, his little hands squeezing Luke's collar. Luke knelt in the grass and hugged him closer.

I took a deep breath and finished pinning the blouse to the line. I walked slowly across the lawn in my bare feet, my arms folded in front of me, watching the ground for nettles and bumblebees.

Then I was facing him, and he didn't seem real to me. "Just one second, little man," he told Jake. "Let me say hello to Mama." He straightened up with one arm still around Jake and held the flowers out to me.

"I call her Mom now," Jake said. "I'm going to call you Dad. I've been practicing."

Luke patted Jake's shoulder, looking at me. I smiled, because I noticed for the first time that Luke had nice ears.

"Thank you," I said, taking the flowers. "They're pretty."

Then he had gotten around Jake somehow, or *through* Jake almost, it seemed, and he had me tight in his arms, and I couldn't help it. The flowers dropped at my feet. I got my arms inside his suit, and pulled him in hard with my hands against the damp shirt on his back, and I felt my body next to his. Jake was watching, and I closed my eyes, saying to myself, *There wasn't supposed to be any touching.*

He had looked big in the suit, but he was thin as a bird pressed to me, all ribs and shoulder blades. It was like that first time on the pallet in his little room, how his body hadn't been big enough, hadn't been suitable for containing inside all he meant to me.

I waited for him to let go first. I thought he had to let go of me. I wanted him to know I couldn't, and to know that he had to do it for me. But his hands stayed tight around my waist and in my hair. So I shut my eyes harder and loosened my own hands and stepped away. I was still close to him, looking into his face. He was clean as a whistle, other than a little skin peeling from a sunburn on the left side of his face, and he smelled like cologne.

I stepped back, got some distance between us. I looked Luke up and down, taking him in, the suit and tie and haircut, and it was getting more difficult and surprising by the second. Jake was feeling it, too, looking up at his father's short hair with his mouth hanging open a little.

"I stopped at a motel in Coeur d'Alene," Luke said. "Just long enough to shower and shave and change." He knew what I was thinking, which was how long had he managed to keep himself that way.

"The new you," I said, folding my arms again. "New truck. New clothes. New hair."

"The new me," he said. He smiled. I bent down and picked up the flowers. They were hand-picked, dusty from the road. We were quiet for a few seconds, and then Luke hoisted Jake up into his arms. I looked at the daisies and pulled out dead petals and evened up the stems. "So are you going to show me around?" he said to me. He looked around the yard and over at the front porch. "I think I was here once when I was a kid. Someone I knew in grade school lived here."

"No," I said, and my whole body seemed to vibrate.

He set Jake down and slouched a little in his suit. He looked up over my head and squinted into the sunshine. "I understand," he said. "I don't blame you."

I finally agreed to let him sit on the porch steps with me. The steps were cool in the shade, and I curled my dress around my legs.

We didn't know what to say to each other. Jake ran inside to get something he wanted to show Luke. I knew what it was—the chessboard I'd bought him downtown because he insisted his father was going to teach him how to play. We listened through the screen door to his feet pounding across the floor.

"He's got his own room?" Luke said.

I nodded.

"Good," he said. He stuck his fingers inside his collar and fiddled with his tie. "I bought the tie first," he said. "I got the suit to match the tie." Then he smiled a little to himself.

A dog trotted down the sidewalk on the other side of the street, its tags jingling. It made me think of how Luke had paid for the suit and the truck with the money we'd won at the track, and it all seemed less interesting then. At least he had the truck to show for it, which was more than I expected.

"And my mom loaned you the money?" he asked, looking across the street at the dog where it stood sniffing at a tree.

"Your mother *gave* me the money, Luke," I said. "She would have given it to us anytime you wanted."

He turned his head and looked back down the street, in the direction of his old house several blocks away. "I didn't want her to give me any money," he said.

"I think that's bullshit," I said. It felt good to say something fast and angry. "That wasn't ever the reason." I turned and looked at my house. "*I* wanted this," I said. "Not you."

He tilted his head down for a second and then looked around. "It's a nice neighborhood," he said.

Jake's feet were pounding across the floor again. I could hear the chessmen sliding in the cardboard box. The screen door creaked open and swung wide and banged shut against the door frame. Jake held the game out to Luke.

"Wow!" Luke said. "Hey!"

They set the board up right on the front walkway, sitting in the grass on either side. It was getting late in the afternoon, and the shade from the house caught them at a slant. I wondered how Luke must look to the neighbors, sitting on the grass cross-legged in a gray suit, playing chess. He went through all the rules very carefully and slowly, and his mind didn't seem to be anywhere else.

I went inside and made orange Kool-Aid. I took it out to them in the new glasses.

"Thanks," Luke said.

"Would you like something to eat?" I asked him.

"That's okay," he said. He reached out like he was trying to take my hand. "Cutting down. Gotta lose some weight." He patted his stomach, which sounded like a leather drum.

I could feel again how thin he was when I'd held him. "How did you let yourself get that way?" I said.

"You don't like it?" he asked. He raised his arms and looked down, pretending that I was talking about the suit. I didn't like the way he was acting. He wasn't like Luke, but some boy from Mendenhall. Or like Nick Travers, the bank president, all smooth and charming in his suit. I tried to think of Nick Travers, how he'd kept asking me for a dinner date, as if this thought might put something between me and Luke. But it wasn't any use. I couldn't even picture his face. I turned around and walked back into the house.

I fixed Luke a sandwich in the kitchen, and put some potato chips on a plate. I thought about calling Mrs. Rivers, but I didn't want to get her hopes up for anything. She knew Luke was coming, but I didn't even know if he would go see her. I half expected, if I told him he couldn't stay here, that he would get in his truck and drive away.

They had quit playing chess by the time I got back outside. Luke huddled over the box, putting the pieces back in. He was talking to Jake about something, and Jake was looking down the road.

I went down the walkway and gave Luke the plate. "Thanks," he said, looking me in the eye, as if there were something solemn and astounding about this particular ham sandwich.

He got his glass of Kool-Aid and sat down on the porch steps again, and I stood in the yard, waving one foot back and forth through the grass. Jake sat down next to Luke, his arms hugging his knees. I watched Luke try to eat, but he could barely swallow a mouthful. He might as well have tried to eat the plate. I said, "You're a grown man, Luke. There won't always be someone around to tell you you have to eat."

He let out a sigh, a bite of sandwich still stuffed in his cheek. He set the plate on the porch. "I've just drank too much coffee," he said. "I drove about 5,000 miles." His eyes got that look in them then, like he was seeing something far away. Then he looked at me. "Listen," he said. "I was wondering if I could take Jake around a little."

I looked down at my foot going back and forth in the grass. "Where?" I said.

"You could come, too," he said.

"No, thanks," I said. "Where?"

He swept his hand out, as if to indicate the whole world in general. "I don't know. My old house, maybe."

It made me think of how he hadn't even told me his mother moved.

"A place I used to take Mark fishing when we were kids," he said. "That sort of thing."

He meant Chuck's Slough. I wondered if he thought I'd forgotten all his stories. I stopped waving my foot in the grass. "You're not getting him into that truck," I said.

I almost wished I hadn't said it. The look on his face was very sad. Certain things that are said between people will always be remembered, and it would be so nice if they could always be good things. But it doesn't work out that way.

And maybe my mind was painting too dark a picture. But maybe not. I could see the two of them roaring down the highway somewhere in South Dakota or Iowa, Luke handing Jake a program and telling him to check out the odds for the first race.

"Hmm," he said, shaking his head and staring at my knees. It made me aware again of my body under the dress. That feeling was still underneath everything. Luke rubbed his hands over his face, covering his eyes and staying like that for a moment.

"What's wrong, Dad?" Jake said.

"Nothing," Luke said. He pulled his hands away and tugged impatiently at his tie.

"Here," I said, and stepped toward him. It felt dangerous, moving closer, a strong tug like going underwater. I jerked roughly on his tie, fixing the knot so it was tight and even.

"Thanks," he said, for what seemed like the dozenth time. "I haven't quite got the hang of it yet."

I stood back and put my weight on my heels. "Yet," I said. "Are you planning on wearing a tie every day?" He just looked at me. "Did you want me to ask if they'd make you a manager down at the bank?"

Nothing I said could make him argue with me. He simply wouldn't do it, and that was new to me. I expected some yelling. I expected some visible frustration. I did not expect this flat refusal to argue his case, and I wasn't sure what to make of it. But I was beginning to get my point across; he could see it wouldn't be easy. I think because so much of Luke's life has been hard, I always wanted my part to be easy. Maybe I've been afraid he wouldn't love me if I made things hard.

"No, I don't think I'd make much of a banker," he said, and then he tried to smile for me, just a little one that didn't match the sad look in his eyes. I held my hands tight around my arms and put my feet together and shut my eyes for one second. I bit my bottom lip and stared at the porch steps.

Then I looked at my house and thought of the rooms inside, Jake's little room and his toy box and his closet with his little jackets and shoes. All the furniture I'd bought, the new dishes, all the time I'd spent cleaning. I looked at the birch trees and the sun in the sky. "Maybe you and your father could take a little walk," I said. They looked at each other, and Jake nodded and grinned. "But you have to be back in thirty minutes for supper." Jake hopped up and started out across the lawn. "And put on your sandals," I said.

When they had gone, I paced around the house, the picture of them walking up the road still in my head. Luke in that impossible suit, his hand in Jake's hair. Jake trying hard to keep stride. I walked through all the rooms, not really knowing what I was up to, flushing the toilet because Jake had forgotten again, taking a cup back to the kitchen. I ignored the stacks of folded laundry on the sofa waiting to be put away, the rugs that needed vacuuming. When I finally remembered Jake's supper, I only had time to fix a can of Spaghetti-Os and boil some frozen peas. I didn't feel like eating.

They came back on time, and I met them on the porch. Jake was talking a mile a minute and marched right past me. Luke stood in the walkway, and in a few seconds Jake was beside me again, quiet. "Your supper's on the table," I said. "Wash your hands and eat."

Luke and I stood there looking at each other, not saying anything. There was something odd about how quiet he was. No long stories about the dog races, nothing about all the things he'd done and all the things he'd seen. It made me wonder about what he'd been doing the whole time. And there was something about the hair and the clothes. Because his short hair wasn't cut in a way he would have chosen before. It was the way younger men's hair is cut in movies or on TV—a trendy cut, in fashion, something Luke wouldn't know to tell a hairdresser. And his suit was too sharp, too tasteful. And his shoes were the same. Even the cologne, which I felt like I could almost smell again from being close to him before, was something light and fresh that Luke wouldn't have known to choose. He looked *truly handsome* for the first time in his life, I thought, not just *nice* or *approachable* or *interesting,* but he hadn't learned to look that way from me. It was as if he were younger somehow, or had been with younger people. Someone younger than me.

"What are you doing here?" I said. "What made you come here—really?"

"You're my family," he said with no hesitation.

I looked down at the porch steps again. "We'll be eating and getting ready for the fireworks show," I said. "We're meeting your mother at 8:30."

"Okay," he said. He held his hands out, palms toward me, as if to say what do you mean. "Can I come, too?" he asked.

It sounded just like him, just like a little boy. "I'd rather you didn't," I said. "Why don't you come by the bank tomorrow at noon, if you can stay in town that long. We'll go to lunch and make some arrangements."

He stared at me as if he weren't sure who I was, whether he had come to the right house and was speaking to the right person, but he didn't look stricken. He didn't look like a lightning bolt had hit him from the sky. I had imagined him looking that way. But it was hard to say how he looked.

He held his index finger in the air. He shook his head, not to say no, but like he used to do to get the hair out of his eyes. But he didn't have any hair. I think we registered this at the same time, and there he stood with his index finger in the air like some ambitious junior executive, and everything was quiet for a moment while we tried very hard not to laugh. Certainly the whole scene, had we been able to imagine it nine years ago, would have made us laugh. It would have been quite a hoot, back then when being broke and irresponsible seemed almost a point of honor.

But now it was only funny for a moment, and everything turned serious again. "I'll be back in a little while," he said. He turned halfway, but he was still looking at me there on the steps. "I'm not going anywhere."

I went back in, and standing at the kitchen sink I heard the truck start up, a loud grumble. I knew then that no matter what he'd done, no matter who he'd been with the past three weeks, it was only that *I'm not going anywhere* that kept my stomach from dropping at the sound of him pulling away from the curb.

I sat down across from Jake at the table and rested my head in my hands. With Luke around, we somehow ended up eating things like Spaghetti-Os. Jake ate them as fast as he could, spoonful after spoonful, never taking his eyes from his plate.

"Have a bite?" I said, and leaned toward him. He scooped up a bite and held the spoon across to me and put it in my mouth. It was so awful I had to spit it out in the sink. When I got back to the table, he was done with the Spaghetti-Os and working on the peas. "We aren't buying those anymore," I said. "We need to eat healthy."

He didn't answer.

"Are you okay?" I asked.

"Yes," he said, looking up from his plate. He didn't know why I'd asked.

"Seeing your dad didn't upset you?" I said.

"Why would it upset me?" he said, looking at me with those dark eyes, so much like Luke's.

"Well—" I said, but then he burst into tears.

I knocked my chair back and ran around the table and put my arms around him. He jumped up before I could say anything, but I caught his arm, and he tried to pull it free. "Did he go *away*?" he shouted.

I grabbed him and held him close to me. "No, honey," I said. "*No.* He'll be back in a few minutes." He was still crying, and his arms shook. My heart thumped in my throat. "*Goodness,*" I said, staring out the side window at the sun starting to go down behind the lilac hedge. I thought, *My God, I've got trouble here.*

The phone rang. "Can I get that?" I said. "Are you okay?" Jake nodded.

It was Mrs. Rivers. "Jenny!" she said. "Luke's here!" I didn't say anything. "He's *here,* I mean, at my place," she said. She said they'd called Mary, and Mary was coming right over, and they were having a regular reunion. Considering the fact that Luke had finally gotten here, she thought she would cancel our plans for the fireworks show at City Beach. She was sure that the three of us would want some time alone.

I told her Jake had really been looking forward to the fireworks show. He started arguing with me, telling me no, he didn't care, and I motioned for him to hush. "Jenny," Mrs. Rivers said. We were quiet on the line. "I know what you're thinking." Her voice lowered to a whisper. "He's different now," she said. "I'm his mother and I can tell."

She wished me an early "Happy Birthday" and said she'd see me tomorrow. I washed the dishes and looked outside at the basket with the clothes I'd forgotten to hang. I'd have to bring Jake's things in and throw them in the dryer so that he'd have something to wear to Luke's mother's in the morning. But I didn't go get them. I sat and looked out the dining-room window. In a while I saw Luke coming up the road in the truck. The truck suited him. It was his style. "Jake," I called out, "he's here." I heard his feet thumping in the hallway.

I put up the pots and glasses and plates, then I went outside to sit on the porch. Luke was still wearing his suit, bending down to pick clothes out of the basket and hang them on the line, and Jake was helping. "They won't dry," I said. "It's too late."

"Just trying to help," Luke said.

"I don't want to go to the fireworks," Jake said. He was barefoot again, his sandals tossed out on the lawn.

"Isn't the grass wet by now?" I said. "You'll track grass all over the floor."

"I don't want to go to the fireworks," he said.

"I know. I heard." I wanted to go to the fireworks. It was one thing we'd managed to do with Jake every year, regardless of where we were. "You can change clothes any time you'd like," I said to Luke. He was taking the wet clothes off the line and putting them back in the basket. "You've made your impression," I said.

"I have?" he said, not looking up.

Jake threw a shirt on the ground. "I don't want to go to the fireworks!" he shouted. "Pay attention to what I say!" He stood firm in the grass, bending his knees with each word, slapping his hands on his legs. "I am *not going* to your damn fireworks!"

It was quite an outburst, really—at least for Jake. The kind Luke doesn't often get to witness. It's always been the case that he saves the worst for me.

"You shouldn't talk that way to your mother, Jake," Luke said.

It was getting late, and the sun had dropped all the way behind the hedge, though the sky was still light. There wasn't a cloud anywhere, just a layer of milky blue. I started to tell Luke that I didn't need his help, that I could handle Jake on my own, but then I didn't. I felt something inside me go soft, the air feeling cooler on my arms and a little breeze touching my hair. I looked at Luke there by the clothes basket, standing in my yard, Jake just off to the side, and I started to feel Luke as a part of things. I felt like we were all winding around each other, like a braid. The breeze swirled at my dress, and I closed my eyes and pulled it around my knees. I ran one hand slowly from my knee to my ankle and back, a chill passing over me. When I opened my eyes, Luke was looking at the curve of my calf, and then he looked away and pulled a clothespin from the line. I didn't care anymore about Jake cussing or talking back to me or whether we went to the fireworks.

Luke said we could see them from the alley, where nothing was in our way. The alley stretched toward City Beach. He said people watched from the streets and alleys all over town. That way you didn't have to fight the crowd.

I didn't tell him no. If he wanted to stay and watch the fireworks in the alley, that was fine. When he said we would start a fire and roast marshmallows, that was fine too. I only asked that he not get us arrested, and he reminded me that his father had been a cop.

I went back to the house to put on shoes and I told Jake to wear his sandals. Luke was taking him to the store to buy marshmallows and graham crackers and Hershey bars. I watched them drive off in the truck, and when they got to the corner Luke turned on the headlights, like he always does even before it has really turned dark.

I sat back down at the table and rested my chin on my hands. I rubbed the spot where I'd worn my wedding ring. I'd taken it off only after my father said Luke was on his way. Luke was still wearing his, but that didn't mean anything.

The hedge was dark outside the window, the sky still blue behind it, but darker, almost turquoise. The window was open to let in the breeze. From somewhere in the neighborhood I heard the whistle and pop of fireworks. They'd been going off all weekend. I looked at the thin branches of the lilacs poking into the sky, and thought of how much I missed fireflies. Here bats swooped over the yard at dusk, no fireflies.

If Luke had been with someone else, I knew it was something I wouldn't be able to let alone. It would gnaw at me, and at some point, during an argument or lying awake in the middle of the night, listening to the wind in the maple tree, I would ask him. And I knew he would tell me. But I didn't know what difference that would make. I didn't know whether I would want him to leave. And so even though I wanted to be angry, wanted my face to flush or a cold prickle to run up my scalp, I couldn't make it happen. It didn't help me with the decision I had to make.

It just felt good to sit quietly in the dining room and watch the sky darken—sit there and forget about the laundry and the lawn and how I was going to pay rent when the money Mrs. Rivers gave me ran out. I wasn't worried anymore that Luke would leave, and knowing he had Jake with him felt comfortable and safe. I understood for the first time that I was never quite comfortable with Luke's mother watching him. She was wonderful, and she doted on Jake, but I was never quite sure that she wouldn't let him wander off from the yard. I was never sure, when he spent the day at her apartment, that she wouldn't decide it was okay to leave him out wading in the water while she went inside to get a cup of coffee or a magazine. With Luke I knew. His overprotectiveness seemed like a blessing, and I could just relax. By the time I heard the truck pull up outside, I think I had nearly fallen asleep.

I walked out to the porch. Jake carried a grocery sack in one hand and twirled a new Atlanta Braves cap around in the other, and this time Luke had a box of sparklers placed on top of a big package with silver wrapping paper and red ribbon. Presents. He'd remembered presents.

"Happy birthday," Luke said, there in the gray light.

"Sparklers?" I said. "For me?"

I took the package inside and left it on the sofa, saving it for the morning. When I reached the alley, Jake was gathering sticks and Luke was wadding up newspaper. In the neighbor's shed, there were the remnants of last year's woodpile, and Luke sneaked over the fence and grabbed a few pieces of wood and some kindling. "Never miss it," he said. He started the fire right behind the shed. He said he knew the old couple who lived there, the Andersons, and he was afraid Mr. Anderson wouldn't like it much if he looked out the window and saw a fire burning in the alley. The shed would be our shield.

We roasted marshmallows and ate them off the end of the sticks, never bothering to get out the graham crackers and Hershey bars. I think we were all more tired than we wanted to mention. The fire-light flickered on the shed. It was already past Jake's bedtime.

Jake was burning his third marshmallow in a row, and I suspected he was setting them on fire deliberately. Luke's turned out a perfect golden brown, and they would trade each time, Luke eating the burned ones. By then I was marshmallowed out.

"That's enough, Luke," I said. "I don't want to make him sick."

"Sick," Luke said. "You can't get sick on the Fourth of July, can you?"

"Nope," Jake said. He had dried marshmallow all over his chin.

They were standing across the fire from me, and the smoke was blowing my way. I liked the smell, even though my eyes stung. Their shadows stretched and twisted on the shed.

"You know, we're not really talking here," I said. "We're not saying anything."

"Okay," Luke said.

The air was cooling fast, and I had chill bumps on my bare arms and I shivered in my thin dress. Luke saw, and he came over to me. I thought he would rub my arms, try to hold me. But instead he took off his coat and put it around my shoulders. Cologne mixed with the smell of the smoke.

"What do you want to know?" he asked me.

I nodded toward Jake. He was staring into the fire, his eyes getting heavy.

"There's nothing I want to say that I can't say in front of Jake," Luke said.

Jake looked up at his name, then his eyes went back to the fire again. My heart hurt for him, my poor little boy, so sleepy. But I knew he didn't want to go to bed, and this might be a night he would always remember. I thought he would like to remember us standing there in the dark together, and how he'd been dazed by the firelight.

"Are you still trying to solve the riddle of the universe?" I said.

"No," he said. He answered right away, like he had been expecting it. "Not for a while, anyway."

"What does that mean?" I said. "A while."

"Well," he said. He looked thin in his white shirt, and almost as bright as the fire. "I don't know exactly," he said. "I guess I mean not until I earn it."

I wasn't quite sure what that meant, but it suited me. "And you're content to stay right here?"

"Yes," he said.

"I mean it, Luke," I told him. "I'm not going anywhere with you ever again. Not for a long time, at least." He had his hands in his pockets and was looking at the fire. I could see his Adam's apple move slightly above his tie. "You have to be happy right here."

He nodded slowly, almost as if he were dazed by the fire the same as Jake. Then he looked over at me. "I can be," he said.

"No more dog races?" I said.

"No more," he said. He shifted his hands in his pockets. "I'll tell you what I *would* like, though. I'd like to adopt a greyhound someday. Someday when we could maybe buy a place out in the country. Someplace where we'd have room." He swept his hand out from his pocket, and Jake looked up at him. He was getting ready to say something, tell me one of his stories, but then he stopped and let his hand fall.

I didn't ask him what he'd intended to say. Instead I thought of my house here, being inside it, all the work I'd had to do. I'd forgotten I would ever have to leave. "How will we get a house out in the country?" I said. "Tell me."

"I'll work hard," he said. "You'll be working too. And it'll be easier once Jake's in school."

Then there was a long, rambling speech, a real Luke Rivers production of the kind with which I'm familiar, and it set me strangely at ease. He didn't want to be a bartender anymore, he said. It was too late to be a dairy farmer, but he wouldn't mind delivering milk. Delivering milk would be preferable to working with his Uncle James or his brother-in-law Roger, in an office where he would have to be an asshole. He would call his friend Jeff Lundy. Jeff Lundy delivered milk. Delivering milk was a job that you could break down into five parts, as near as he could figure, and all of which matched his capabilities. One, you had to load up a truck tight and fast, which he'd learned from packing all our things in the trunk of the Honda to move quick out of town. Two, you had to drive long hours, for which he was obviously qualified. Three, you had to unload stock, which involved heavy lifting, something that would be pleasant hard work and keep him in better shape. Four, you had to keep track of inventory by writing things down on a list, and keep track of who needed how much of what, and the system he'd thought up at the dog races and his years of bar stocking made him what you'd call uniquely qualified for this. And five, you had to be friendly. He was always friendly.

By the time he was finished, he'd nearly convinced me. "If these fireworks don't start in two minutes, I'm going to bed," I said.

"The sky's almost dark enough," he said.

Jake wobbled back and forth in front of the fire, like he was ready to tip in.

"Jake," Luke said softly, carefully. "Why don't you come over here?"

Jake dragged himself over, and Luke put his arms around him.

Then there was a movement by the fence, and it scared me half to death.

"Hello, Mr. Anderson," Luke said, as if he'd been waiting for this all along. There was Mr. Anderson standing by the fence, dressed in a ribbed tank top, cowboy boots, and long, flowered boxer shorts.

Jake looked up at me. "That man forgot his *pants*," he whispered.

I wasn't sure what to say. It certainly wasn't anything you would ever see in Mendenhall.

"I saw sparks," Mr. Anderson said. "I thought the shed caught fire." He stared at all of us, his eyes blinking, as if *we* were the sight to see.

"We're just waiting for the fireworks," Luke said. "Thought we'd roast some marshmallows."

Mr. Anderson looked at the fire, and I thought he was going to say something about the wood. His big stomach moved in and out, filling his tank top and going slack. His boxer shorts hung down to his knees. I turned my head away so he wouldn't see me smile. "I think they've got a rule against burning things," he said, looking over to his shed at the woodpile.

"Yeah," Luke said. "They've got rules for just about everything." He was standing with his arms around Jake, wearing a tie, back there in the alley talking to a man in boxer shorts and cowboy boots. "I think they try to make it so you can't go out of the house without your pants on, too."

I had my mouth shut tight, but it was hard not to let them hear me laugh, and I had to walk away a few steps, putting my hand to my mouth and pretending to cough.

"That may be," I heard Mr. Anderson say. "That may very well be." I turned my head and saw him staring at the fire, leaning on the fence and rubbing his chin. I kept walking, holding my hand over my mouth.

"Mr. Anderson, you might not remember me," I heard Luke say.

There was a long silence, and I felt my cheeks relax and the smile fade from my face. "No," Mr. Anderson said. "Can't say I do."

There was another pause, and I turned and started walking back. Luke was stepping toward the fence, holding Jake's hand. "I'm Luke Rivers," he said. Mr. Anderson cocked his head. "John Rivers' son?" Luke said.

"That a fact?" Mr. Anderson said. He rubbed his chin again, looking at Luke and Jake. "I thought you got killed."

There was nothing funny anymore. I found myself moving toward Luke, my hand held out slightly before me.

"That was my brother Mark," Luke said. "A long time ago. He was a little boy."

"Right. I remember," Mr. Anderson said. But he still looked confused.

"I'm the older son," Luke said. I reached out and put my hand lightly on his sleeve, and he glanced at me.

"Oh, sure," Mr. Anderson said. "Sure." He held his hand out, pointing with a curled index finger. He moved his finger up and down slowly and I could see an idea pass across his features. "You must be the one . . ." he said. Then he was completely still. He looked like a statue of a circus clown, his face red in the firelight and nothing moving.

Luke shifted his feet, like he wanted to get the ground under him better. "Yeah," he said. "That's me."

Mr. Anderson nodded slowly.

"This is my wife Jenny and my son Jake," Luke said.

Mr. Anderson was still nodding. He pulled at the band of his boxer shorts. Then his eyes shifted slightly, and he seemed to see me and Jake for the first time, and he looked us up and down for a moment. He looked back at Luke. "Well," he said. "How you been?" Then he reached over the fence and shook Luke's hand.

After that he told us to enjoy ourselves, and he shook Jake's hand and called him pardner, and then he waved and walked away, his cowboy boots slipping on his feet. "Make sure that's put out good," he called over his shoulder.

"I will," Luke said. He stood there with his feet spread apart a little wide, as if he were ready to lift something. His face was set firmly and his eyes looked sharp, staring up the alley where he expected the fireworks to explode any second in the sky. And I knew his mother was right. He had changed somehow. I didn't know what the change was, but a month ago he couldn't have stood there that way, with that steady look on his face. He couldn't have had that simple conversation with Mr. Anderson. He would never have told Mr. Anderson who he was. Anywhere else, but not in this town.

"There are still things you're not telling me," I said.

"Right," he said, still looking down the alley. "A lot, actually. What do you want to know?"

I couldn't make myself ask him. I didn't ask anything.

"There's still plenty of money," he said. "I thought maybe you were wondering."

"No," I said.

He nodded, not looking at me.

"How, though?" I said. He glanced over at me. "How is there still money. Since you mention it."

"Well," he said, as if it were fairly obvious. "Of course the races."

"The races," I said. "Things went well for you at the races."

His eyes narrowed, and I could see that faraway expression on his face. His body looked tight for a moment in the thin white shirt, then his shoulders shrugged. "I just kept winning," he said. He raised his eyebrows for a second, then puffed his cheeks out and exhaled. "It's nothing I can explain."

He was still looking up the alley, and Jake was bent down picking up gravel from the road and building it into a little pile in the dark. I pulled Luke's coat closer around me and looked up the alley, too.

"It's kind of quite a bit of money," Luke said. "A what would you call it—a nest egg."

Of course I was curious, but I wouldn't ask how much. It would have felt too much like giving in. I had to be content with guessing how much money constituted a "nest egg" to Luke. "You were in Rapid City?" I asked.

"At first," he said. "Then the Dells."

I thought of Luke there in the Dells, walking around in the midst of the tourists and roller coasters and boat rides. "And you were a perfect angel," I said.

He didn't answer right away. He was still looking down the alley, and I imagined he was hoping the fireworks might save him. He turned toward me, and the fire lit up one side of his face. But his eyes weren't on me. They were peering through the hedge behind me, and I turned for a second to see my house with the bright windows and the yellow light stretching over the lawn. I looked back at his face. He was still looking at the house, as if it were some place he might never get to.

He said, "I was with someone. Someone I met."

I was glad, I really was. I was glad he had said it to me. I was watching Jake, and I could see by the way he held a pebble up in his hand, poised in the air, that he was listening. I was crying before I knew, but hardly any, really. I wiped the tears away with my hand.

"I don't want to make excuses," Luke said. "I really don't."

Jake looked at me, and I smiled at him and wiped my cheek again. "The fireworks will be in just a minute," I said. He rolled his eyes and pretended he was falling over. "I know," I said.

"I waited in Rapid City for you to call," Luke said. His voice was quiet. I thought of how many times I'd been close to calling the Black Hills Motel. Things would prompt me—driving by the Safeway store, seeing a Braves game on T V. But I wouldn't. Maybe I made a mistake, but I don't think so. I think I did what I had to. "I don't know," he said. "I don't know what I want to say. Things got pretty rough," he said. "That's all. I got pretty far away." And I thought of how far away I had gotten, too.

"It's like your life is this little basket, you know, this little basket floating down a stream," I heard him say, but I wasn't really hearing him. I was seeing Jake scoop up gravel in his hands, making a V shape in the road. And then I realized Luke wasn't talking anymore, that he'd quit what he was saying.

"But that's just a metaphor," he said. "That's all it is." He kicked one foot just slightly in the gravel. He was impatient with himself, I could see. I turned toward him, and the muscles in his jaw moved. He was trying hard to find the right thing to say, to do, whatever would make it okay. I wanted him to be able to. "The *real* thing," he said, but he didn't have it yet. He was still trying. Then his eyes moved away from the alley and the sky, and they met mine, and I could see that he'd found what he wanted. One side of his face was lit by the fire, and his eye gleamed gold and black. "Shit, Jenny," he said. "I love you. I love Jake. I loved you both a long time." He turned away, looking up the alley again, and I thought I could see a long, slow breath leave him. He held his hands at his side, and straightened up to his full height, and he tilted his chin to the sky. He looked bigger than he really was somehow, as if he took up more space in the world than someone his size should take. Maybe because his body didn't seem big enough for who he was again, at least to me.

And I thought as I had so many times before that it was probably harder to be Luke than it was to be me. Harder to be someone whose mind keeps going out and out, asking why all the time, what things are real. What's real to me is what I choose each day to *make* real. Jake and I at City Beach on Saturday. Jake and I in this house.

But there might come a day when it won't be like that at all. Maybe someday the world around me will seem as strange as the town of Mendenhall seemed that time when I lay all alone on Aunt Eunice's bed, imagining a different place outside the window. Maybe the face that stares at me, old and sagging, from the mirror in the morning won't be the one I expected. And when I think it's time to fix Jake's breakfast he won't be there, won't have been there for years. And people and places from the past will crowd the hallways of the house, and the rooms will be spare like Aunt Eunice's, designed for keeping only memories. And then it will be so good to have Luke there, someone who knows what these things mean.

There was a thud in the distance, and I turned in time to see the streak of yellow in the sky before it burst into blue. It was just as Luke said—the alley stretched toward the lighted sky, and the lilac bushes and the shed made a perfect frame. Luke moved Jake over to me and went to get the sparklers by the grocery sack. Jake leaned his weight back against my legs, his head inclined to see the fireworks showering far away. The soft pops came to us when the sparks were nearly gone.

Luke handed us each a sparkler and lit them all, and we stood quietly, the fire popping and shifting at our backs. The fireworks in the distance looked like colored umbrellas. The sparklers fizzed and crackled in our hands, shooting golden sparks into the halo of light from the flames.

We stood in a row—Luke, then Jake, then me. Luke switched hands with his sparkler, and then I felt a light touch on the hand I held at Jake's neck, and I closed my hand around Luke's fingers.

For a little town in Idaho, it was an impressive show. With each pause in the display, I expected it to end. Several times I thought we'd seen the finale. But then another flame would shoot into the sky and break apart in orange or red or green. Sometimes little wings of different color shot out to the side, spinning crazily. Luke's hand was warm, and Jake was happy. We lit more sparklers and then settled back the same way.

I thought of my parents in Mendenhall, of the Fourth of July when I was a little girl. I wondered if they were doing what we were, if they were sitting on a quilt at Simpson County Park the way we used to, or lying on their backs staring into the sky above the oak trees. Then I realized it would have been hours ago.

And so I pictured the sun moving slowly from east to west and slipping over each little town's horizon, and all the families who had gathered just like ours. And some of them had better lives than we did, but some had worse. I pictured the sun moving over them all, sliding farther and farther west until it left the land and dipped into the sea. I moved in closer to Jake and Luke, and as I did I could almost feel the people near me in this little town, coming close together in the streets and alleyways, tilting their heads to catch the last colored blossoms in the wide dark sky.